HERMANN BROCH

THE DEATH OF VIRGIL

Hermann Broch (1886–1951) was born in Vienna, where he
trained as an engineer and studied philosophy and mathematics. He gradually increased his involvement in the intellectual life of Vienna, becoming acquainted with Ludwig
Wittgenstein, Sigmund Freud, and Robert Musil, among
others. *The Sleepwalkers* was his first major work. In 1938,
he was imprisoned as a subversive by the Nazis, but was
freed and fled to the United States. In the years before his
death, he was researching mass psychology at Yale University. *The Death of Virgil* originally appeared in 1945; his last
major novel, *The Guiltless,* was published in 1950.

INTERNATIONAL

HERMANN BROCH

THE
DEATH
OF
VIRGIL

Translated by
JEAN STARR UNTERMEYER

VINTAGE INTERNATIONAL
VINTAGE BOOKS
A DIVISION OF RANDOM HOUSE, INC.
NEW YORK

First Vintage International Edition, January 1995

Copyright © 1945 by Pantheon Books Inc.
Copyright renewed 1972 by Random House, Inc.

Library of Congress Cataloging-in-Publication Data
Broch, Hermann, 1886–1951.
(Tod des Vergil, English)
The death of Virgil / Hermann Broch ; translated by Jean Starr
Untermeyer. — 1st Vintage International ed.
p.   cm.
ISBN 0-679-75548-9
1. Virgil — Fiction. 2. Rome — History — Augustus, 30 B.C.–14 A.D. —
Fiction.   I. Untermeyer, Jean Starr, 1886–1970.   II. Title.
PT2603.R657T613   1995
883′.912 — dc20   94-34712
CIP

Manufactured in the United States of America
10 9 8 7 6 5 4 3

IN MEMORIAM
STEPHEN HUDSON

CONTENTS

WATER—THE ARRIVAL

STEEL-BLUE AND LIGHT, RUFFLED BY A SOFT, SCARCELY perceptible cross-wind, the waves of the Adriatic streamed against the imperial squadron as it steered toward the harbor of Brundisium, the flat hills of the Calabrian coast coming gradually nearer on the left. And here, as the sunny yet deathly loneliness of the sea changed with the peaceful stir of friendly human activity where the channel, softly enhanced by the proximity of human life and human living, was populated by all sorts of craft—by some that were also approaching the harbor, by others heading out to sea and by the ubiquitous brown-sailed fishing boats already setting out for the evening catch from the little breakwaters which protected the many villages and settlements along the white-sprayed coast—here the water had become mirror-smooth; mother-of-pearl spread over the open shell of heaven, evening came on, and the pungence of wood fires was carried from the hearths whenever a sound of life, a hammering or a summons, was blown over from the shore.

Of the seven high-built vessels that followed one another, keels in line, only the first and last, both slender rams-prowed pentaremes, belonged to the war-fleet; the remaining five, heavier and more imposing, deccareme and duodeccareme, were of an ornate structure in keeping with the Augustan imperial rank, and the middle one, the most sumptuous, its bronze-mounted bow gilded, gilded the ring-bearing lion's head under the railing, the rigging wound with colors, bore under purple sails, festive and grand, the tent of the Caesar. Yet on the ship

11

that immediately followed was the poet of the Aeneid and death's signet was graved upon his brow.

A prey to seasickness, held taut by the constant threat of its outbreak, he had not dared move the whole day long. Now, however, although bound to the cot which had been set up for him amidships, he became conscious of himself, or rather of his body and the life of his body, which for many years past he had scarcely been able to call his own, as an after-tasting, after-touching memory of the relief which had flowed through him suddenly when the calmer region of the coast had been reached; and this floating, quieted-quieting fatigue might have become an almost perfect boon had not the plaguing cough, unaffected by the strong healing sea air, begun again, accompanied by the usual evening fever and the usual evening anxiety. So he lay there, he the poet of the Aeneid, he Publius Vergilius Maro, he lay there with ebbing consciousness, almost ashamed of his helplessness, at odds with such a fate, and he stared into the pearly roundness of the heavenly bowl: why then had he yielded to the importunity of Augustus? why then had he forsaken Athens? Fled now the hope that the hallowed and serene sky of Homer would favor the completion of the Aeneid, fled every single hope for the boundless new life which was to have begun, the hope for a life free alike of art and poetry, a life dedicated to meditation and study in the city of Plato, fled the hope ever to be allowed to enter the Ionian land, oh, fled the hope for the miracle of knowledge and the healing through knowledge. Why had he renounced it? Willingly? No! It had been like a command of the irrefutable life-forces, those irrefutable forces of fate which never vanished completely, which though they might dive at times into the subterranean, the invisible, the inaudible, were nonetheless omnipresent as the inscrutable threat of powers which man could never avoid, to which he must always submit; it was fate. He had allowed himself to be driven by fate and now fate drove on to the end. Had this not always been the form of his life, had he ever lived otherwise? had the pearly bowl, had the halcyon sea, had the song

12

of the mountains and that which sang painfully in his own breast, had the flute-tone of the god ever meant anything else to him than a circumstance which, like a receptacle of the spheres, was soon to draw him into itself, to bear him into immensity? He had been a peasant from birth, a man who loved the peace of earthly life, one whom a simple secure life in a village community would have fitted, one for whom because of his birth it would have been seemly to be allowed, even to be forced to abide there, but who in conformity with a higher destiny was not allowed to be free from nor free to stay at home; this destiny had pushed him out from the community into the nakedest, direst, most savage loneliness of the human crowd, it had hunted him from the simplicity of his origins, hunted him abroad into the open, to ever-increasing multiplicity, and if thereby something had become greater and broader, it was only the distance from real life, verily it was this distance alone which had grown. Only at the edge of his fields had he walked, only at the edge of his life had he lived. He had become a rover, fleeing death, seeking death, seeking work, fleeing work, a lover and yet at the same time a harassed one, an errant through the passions of the inner life and the passions of the world, a lodger in his own life. And now, almost at the end of his strength, at the end of his search, self-purged and ready to leave, purged to readiness and ready to take upon himself the last loneliness, ready to start on the inner journey back to loneliness, now destiny with all its forces had seized him again, had forbidden him all the simplicity of his beginnings and of the inner life, had deflected his backward journey once more, had turned him back to the evil which had overshadowed all his days, as if it had reserved for him just this sole simplicity—, the simplicity of dying. Above him the yards cracked in the ropes and betweenwhiles there was a soft booming in the sailcloth, he heard the slithering foam of the wake and the silver pour that sprayed out each time the oars were lifted, their heavy creak in the oar-locks, and the clapping cut of the water when they dipped in again, he felt the soft even thrust of the ship keeping time to the hundredfold stroke of the oarsmen, he saw the white-surfed coastline slip by and he thought of the chained dumb slave-bodies in the damp-draughty, noisome, roaring hull of the ship. The same dull rumbling silver-sprayed down-beat resounded from the two neighboring ships, from the next in line and the one following, like an echo which repeated itself over all the seas and was answered from all the seas, for so they plied everywhere, laden with people, laden with arms, laden with corn and wheat, laden with marble, with oil, with wines, with spices, with silks, laden with slaves, everywhere this navigation for bartering and bargaining, one of the worst among the many depravities of the world. In these ships, however, the cargo was not so much goods as gluttons, the members of the court: the rear half of the ship up to the stern's end was given over to feeding them, from early morning it reverberated with the sounds of eating and there was always a crowd of guzzlers in the dining-hall, impatient for a triclinium to be vacated, waiting, after a tussle with rivals, to tumble themselves onto it, finally to lie down and do their part by beginning a meal or maybe by starting one all over again. The waiters, light-footed, smart, flashy fellows, not a few pleasure-boys among them, but now sweaty and harried, scarcely had time to catch their breaths, and their forever-smiling head-steward, with the cold look in the corner of his eyes and the politely tip-opened hand, drove them hither and thither, himself rushing up-deck and down-deck because, apart from the progress of the meal, it was necessary at the same time to take care of those who—wonderful to relate—seemed to be already sated and now were taking their pleasure in other ways, some promenading with hands clasped upon their bellies or over their behinds, some, on the contrary, discoursing with expansive gestures, some dozing on their cots or snoring, their faces covered with their togas, some sitting at the gaming boards, all of whom had to be served and appeased incessantly with tidbits which were passed around the decks on large silver platters and offered to them, keeping in mind a hunger which might assert itself at any moment, keeping in mind a gluttony which was limned in the expression of all of them, ineradicably and unmistakably, as much in the faces of the well-nourished as in those of the haggard, in those of the slack as well as the swift, of the restless and the indolent, in the faces of the sleepers and wakers, sometimes chiselled in, sometimes kneaded in, clearly or cloudily, cruelly or kindly, wolfish, foxish, cattish, parrottish, horsish, sharkish, but always dedicated to a horrible, somehow self-imprisoned lust, insatiably desirous of having, desirous of bargaining for goods, money, place and honors, desirous of the bustling idleness of possession. Everywhere there was someone putting something into his mouth, everywhere smouldered avarice and lust, rootless but ready to devour, all-devouring, their fumes wavered over the deck, carried along on the beat of the oars, inescapable, unavoidable; the whole ship was lapped in a wave of greed. Oh, they deserved to be shown up once for what they were! A song of avarice should be dedicated to them! But what would that accomplish? Nothing availed the poet, he could right no wrongs; he is heeded only if he extols the world, never if he portrays it as it is. Only falsehood wins renown, not understanding! And could one assume that the Aeneid would be vouchsafed another or better influence? Oh yes, people would praise it because as yet everything he had written had been praised, because only the agreeable things would be abstracted from it, and because there was neither danger nor hope that the exhortations would be heeded; ah, he was forbidden either to delude himself or to permit himself to be deluded, only too well he knew the public to which the grave, the knowledge-burdening and actual work of the poet was as negligible as that of the bitterly oppressed and bitterness-filled slave rowers, the public which held the value of one to be equal with that of the other, as tribute due to the usufructuary, to be received and enjoyed as a right! However those who lolled about and gorged themselves were by no means all parasites, even though Augustus was obliged to tolerate so many of this sort in his following, no, quite a few of them had already achieved much

15

that was worthy and useful, but during the idleness of the voyage they had stripped off, with almost luxuriating self-exposure, most of what they customarily were, and the only thing which they had kept intact was their blind arrogance and their unceasing and befogged greed. Below, magnificent, savage, brutal, sub-human, but not less befogged, the tamed rowing-mass worked together, stroke after stroke. Down there they did not understand him and paid no attention to him, these up here maintained that they revered him, yes, they even believed it; but, be that as it may, whether they presumed to cherish his work by falsely pretending to be connoisseurs, or whether, no less falsely, they paid homage to him as Caesar's friend, it was of no moment, he Publius Vergilius Maro had nothing in common with them although fate had driven him into their midst, they nauseated him and if the land-breeze, in an advance-salute to the sunset, had not started to blow the stench of the meal and the kitchen away from the ship, seasickness would have befallen him again. He assured himself that the chest with the manuscript of the Aeneid stood undisturbed near him, and, blinking into the deeply-sinking western day-star, he pulled his robe up to his chin; he was cold.

From time to time there arose in him a desire to turn round to the noisy gang at his back, almost curious to see what they were up to now; but he did not do it and it was better not to, since more and more he was convinced that such looking back was in some way forbidden him.

So he lay quietly. The first twilight spread lucidly over the heavens, gently over the world, as they arrived at the narrow river-like approach to Brundisium; it had become cooler yet milder, the salt breath merging with the heavier air of the land into whose entrance the ships now intruded, one after the other slowing down its speed. Iron-gray, leaden-hued became Poseidon's element, no longer rippled by a wave. On the ramparts of the fortifications to the left and right of the canal, troops of the garrison were on parade in honor of Caesar, perhaps also as a first birthday greeting to him, for it was to his cradle-feast that Octavianus Augustus had come home; in two days, in fact the day after tomorrow, it was to be celebrated in Rome, and Octavian, who rode there in the preceding ship, would be forty-three years old. The cheering of the soldiers arose hoarsely from the banks, the flag-bearers at both flanks of the manipels, precise and practised, thrust the red vexillum aloft, timed to the cheers, afterwards lowering it aslant before the emperor, its tip pointed to the ground; in short what took place was the hearty unimpassioned performance of the salute as stipulated by the army manual, regimentally right in its military ruggedness, and in spite of that it was curiously mild, curiously soothing; it could almost be described as dreamy, so very, so exceedingly puny the cheering that floated off into the grandeur of the sunset, so very, so exceedingly autumnal the fading of the red flag overshone by the firmament glimmering into gray. Greater than the earth is light, greater than man is the earth, and man's existence avails him nothing until he breathes his native air, returning to the earth, through earth returning to the light, an earthly being receiving the light on earth, received in turn by the light only through earth, earth changing to light. And never was the earth nearer the heart of light, nor light closer to the earth than in the approaching dusk at the two boundaries of night. Night still slumbered in the depths of the waters, but with tiny dark noiseless waves it began to filter upward, everywhere in the mirror of heaven, in the mirror of the sea, above indistinguishable from below, the velvet-muffled waves dove up from the wake of night, the waves of a second immensity, of the fecund outspreading utter-immensity, and downily they began to overcast the radiance with the breath of silence. The light came no longer from above, it hung in itself and, hanging so, it was luminous but it no longer illumined anything, so that even the landscape over which it hung seemed confined in its own light. The chirping of crickets, myriadfold yet issuing as one continuous monotone, piercing yet lulling in its evenness, neither rising nor falling, vibrated throughout the twilit land; endless. Under the fortifications the slopes were overgrown

17

with sparse grass down to the stony beach, and, meagre though it was, that growth was peace, was nocturnal quiet, was rudimental darkness, the darkness of earth spread out under the departing light. Then the patches became more connected, richer in plant life, deeper in color, and very soon were interspersed with shrubbery, while on the hill-tops between the stone-fenced quadrangles of the peasants, the first olive trees revealed themselves, gray as the breath-thin fog-spray of the deepening twilight. Oh, unbridled became the desire to stretch the hand toward those still so distant shores, to reach into the darkness of the shrubbery, to feel the earth-born leaf between his fingers, to hold it tightly there forevermore—, the wish quivered in his hands, quivered in his fingers with uncontrollable desire toward the leafy branches, toward the flexible leaf-stems, toward the sharp-soft leaf edges, toward the firm living leaf-flesh, yearningly he felt it when he closed his eyes, and it was almost a sensual desire, sensually simple and grasping like his masculine, raw-boned peasant's fist, sensually savoring and sensitive like the slender-wristed nervousness of this same hand: Oh grass, oh leaf, bark-smoothness, bark-roughness, vitality of burgeoning, in this branching out and embodiment ye are earth's darkness made manifest! oh hand, tingling, touching, fondling, embracing, oh finger and finger-tip, rough and gentle and soft, living flesh, the outermost surface of the soul's darkness opened up in the lifted hands! He had always been aware of this strange almost volcanic pulsation in his hands, always the intimation of the strange separate life of his hands had accompanied him, an intimation that once and for all had been forbidden to overstep the threshold into actual knowledge, as if an obscure danger lurked in such knowledge, and when now, as was his habit, he turned the seal ring, the one finely-wrought and even a little unmasculine in its delicate workmanship, which he wore on a finger of his right hand, it was as if by so doing he could avert that obscure danger, as if he could appease the hands' longing, as if by this act he could bring them to a certain self-control, abating their fear, the longing fear of peasant hands

that never again might grasp the plough or scatter the seed and
therefore had learned to grasp the intangible, the foreboding
fear of hands to whose will-to-form, robbed of the earth, nothing
remained but a life of their own in the incomprehensible universe, threatened and threatening, reaching so deeply into nothingness and so gripped by its perils that the dread foreboding,
lifted to a certain extent above itself, was transmuted into a
mighty endeavor, an endeavor to hold fast to the unity of
human existence, to preserve the integrity of human desire in
a way that would protect it from disintegrating into manifold
existences, full of small desires and small in desire; for insufficient was the desire of hands, insufficient the desire of eyes,
insufficient the desire of hearing, sufficient alone was the desire
of heart and mind communing together, the yearning completion of the infinity within and without, beholding, hearkening,
comprehending, breathing in the unity of the doubled breath,
the unity of the universe; for by unity alone might one overcome the lowering hopeless blindness of fearful isolation, in
unity alone occurred the twofold development from the roots
of understanding, and this he divined, this he had always divined—, oh the yearning of one who was and always must be
only a lodger, oh yearning of man—, this had been his prescient-
listening, his prescient-breathing, his prescient-thinking, drawn
by reciprocal listening, breathing, thinking, into the flowing light
of the universe, into the never-ending approach to the endlessness of the universe, unattainable the pearly shimmer of its
abysmal depths, unattainable even its outermost edge, so that
the longing desirous hand dares not even touch it. Still there
was an approach and there was his thought, breathing and
waiting, listening into the twofold abysses where Poseidon and
Vulcan reigned, both realms united by the heavenly arch of
Jove. Opened and flowing now the light, the breath too was
flowing, as flowing as the current into which the keels plunged,
flood-bath of the innermost and outermost, flood-bath of the
soul, the breath flowing from this life into the beyond, from the
beyond back into this life, the unveiled portal of knowledge,

never knowledge itself, but still a presentiment of knowledge, a presentiment of the entrance, a presentiment of the path, a dim presentiment of the twilight journey. Forward on the bow a young slave, one of the musicians, was singing; possibly those assembled there, whose hubbub had been hushed in the quiet of the evening, had summoned the boy, even they aware of home-coming, and after a short interval for tuning the lyre followed by a suitable pause, there rang out, wafted back to him, the nameless song of a nameless boy; mildly flowing the song, float-ing insubstantially, like rainbow tints in the nocturnal heavens, mildly flowing the strings, soft-hued as ivory, human accom-plishments, both the song and the strings, but removed beyond their human source, delivered from mankind, delivered from suffering; this was the music of the spheres singing itself. It became darker, faces became dimmer, the shores faded out, the boat seemed to vanish, only the voice remained, becoming clearer and more dominant as if it wished to direct the ship and the timing of the oars, forgotten the source of the voice, the nonetheless-guiding voice of a slave boy; guidance the song, secure in itself and for that reason guidance, just for that reason exposed to eternity, for only the serene may guide, only the singular, wrested, nay rescued, from the flow of things, lays itself open to immensity, only that which is held fast—ah, had he ever succeeded in getting such an actual, guiding grasp?—only the truly comprehended, even though it be only for a moment in the ocean of millenniums, only the firmly-retained becomes timeless, becomes permanent, becomes a guid-ing song, becomes guidance; oh, for a single life-moment en-larged to eternity, enlarged to the limits of understanding, sus-ceptible of immensity: high above the shining song, high above the shining sunset breathed the heaven, whose sharp-clear autumnal sweetness had repeated itself unchanged for millen-niums past and would repeat itself unchanged for millenniums to come, nevertheless unique in its manifestation here and now as the silky bright shimmer of its dome was overcast by the silent breath of the oncoming night.

The song led them, though not for long; the journey between the banks of the incoming canal was almost at an end, and the song expired in the general restlessness which developed on board as the inner bay of the harbor, its leaden mirror already gleaming darkly, opened out, revealing the city built around it in the form of a half-circle with its myriad lights shimmering in the twilight like a starry heaven. It was suddenly warm. The flotilla halted to let Caesar's boat proceed to the head of the line, and now—and even this which happened under the soft immutability of the autumn sky should have been retained as an infinite unique occurrence—there began a careful maneuvering to pilot a way in safety between the boats, sailing-vessels, fishing-smacks, tartanes and merchantmen, anchored on every side; the farther one went the narrower became the channel, the more jammed the mass of ship-hulls, the denser the tangle of masts and rigging and furled sails, dead in their rigidity, living in their repose, a strange, dusky, knotted and confused network that lifted itself darkly from the shiny oily-dark surface of the water toward the unmoved evening brightness of the heavens, a black spiderweb of wood and hemp reflected spectrally in the waters beneath, flashing spectrally above from the wild flickering of the torches swung all about the decks with shouts of welcome, spectrally lit from the splendor of lights on the landing-place: in the rows of houses surrounding the harbor, window after window was illuminated even up to the attics, illuminated the osterias ranged one after the other under the colonnades; directly across the square there formed a double line of soldiers bearing torches, man after man in gleaming helmets, obviously there to keep an unobstructed thoroughfare from the landing-place into the city, the customs-stalls and custom-offices on the piers were lit by torches, the whole was a sparkling, gigantic space packed with human bodies, a sparkling gigantic reservoir of a waiting at once vast and vehement, filled with the rustling of a hundred thousand feet, slipping, sliding, treading, shuffling on the stone pavement, a seething giant arena, throbbing with the rise and fall of a black buzzing, with a roar of impatience that was suddenly hushed and held in abeyance as the imperial ship, propelled now by only a dozen oars, reached the quay with an easy turn at the designated place— awaited there by the city officials in the center of the torchlit, military quadrangles—and landed with scarcely a sound; in fact the moment had arrived which the brooding mass-beast had awaited to release its howl of joy, and now it broke loose, without pause, without end, victorious, violent, unbridled, fear-inspiring, magnificent, fawning, the mass worshiping itself in the person of the One.

These were the masses for whom Caesar had lived, for whom the empire had been established, for whom Gaul was conquered, for whom the Parthians were besieged and Germany brought into battle, these were the masses for whom the great peace of Augustus had been made, who, to maintain this peace had to be brought again to civic discipline and order, to belief in the gods and to a humanly-divine morality. And these were the masses without whom no policy could be carried out and on whose support Augustus must rely if he wished to maintain himself, and naturally Augustus had no other wish. Yes and this was the people, the Roman people, whose spirit and honor he, Publius Vergilius Maro, he a real farmer's son from Andes near Mantua, had not so much described as tried to glorify! To glorify and not describe, that had been the mistake, oh, and this represented the Italy of the Aeneid! Evil, a tide of evil, an immense wave of unspeakable, inexpressible, incomprehensible evil seethed in the reservoir of the plaza; fifty thousand, a hundred thousand mouths yelled the evil out of themselves, yelled it to one another without hearing it, without knowing it was evil, nevertheless willing to stifle it and outshout it in the infernal bellowing. What a birthday greeting! Was he the only one to realize it? Stone-weighted the earth, leaden-weighted the waters, a demonic crater of evil, ripped open by Vulcan himself, a howling crater on the border of Poseidon's realm. Did not Augustus see that this was no birthday greeting, that it had quite other implications? A feeling of harassed sympathy arose in him, a compassion that pertained as much to Augustus as to the mass of humanity, to the ruler as well as to the ruled, and it was accompanied by a responsibility no less importunate, a truly unbearable one which he himself could not account for beyond knowing that it bore small resemblance to the burden which Caesar had taken upon himself, rather that it was a responsibility of quite another kind; for this seething, befuddled, unrecognized evil was beyond the reach of every governmental enterprise, beyond reach of every earthly force however great, beyond reach, perhaps, of the gods themselves, and no human outcry sufficed to overwhelm it except, it may be, that small voice of the soul, called song, which while it makes known the evil, announces also the awakening of salvation, knowledge-aware, knowledge-fraught, knowledge-persuading, the provenance of every true song. The responsibility of the singer to arouse, the responsibility which even yet he was powerless to bear and to fulfill—, oh, why had he not been allowed to proceed beyond intimation to actual knowledge from which alone healing could be awaited?! Why had fate forced him to return here?! Here there was nothing but death, death and more death! With terrified opened eyes he had raised himself up, now he fell back on his pallet, overcome by horror, by compassion, by helplessness, by weakness; it was not hate which he felt for the masses, neither disdain, nor repulsion, he wished as little as ever before to separate himself from the people or even to lift himself above them, but something new arose in him, something of which, despite all his concern with the people, he had never wanted to take cognizance, and irrespective of where he had been, whether in Naples, Rome, or even Athens, ample opportunity to do so had been given, something that here in Brundisium had unexpectedly obtruded itself, namely the awareness of the people's profound capacity for evil in all its ramifications, their possibilities for human degradation in becoming a mob, and their reversion therewith to the anti-human, brought to pass by the hollowing out of existence, by turning existence toward a mere thirst for superficialities, its deep roots lost and cut away, so that nothing remained but the dangerous isolated life of self, a sad, sheer exteriority, pregnant with evil, pregnant with death, pregnant with a mysterious, infernal ending. Was this what fate had wished him to learn, so that he was forced back into the heterogeneous, into the cauldron of bitterly boiling worldly life? Was this a revenge for his former blindness? Never had he perceived the savagery of the masses with such immediacy; now he was forced to see it, to hear it, to experience it in the last fibres of his own being, blindness being a part of evil. Again and again sounded the joyless-jubilant shouts of self-suffocation, torches were swinging, commands resounded throughout the ship, a rope thrown from the shore flopped dully on the deck planks, and evil clamored, grief clamored, evil-bearing mystery clamored, enigmatic, yet exposed and present everywhere; amid the tramp of many hurrying feet he lay still, his hand clamped tightly to one of the handles of the leather manuscript-chest lest this be wrenched from him; yet, tired of the fever as from the coughing, tired of the journey, tired of the future, he conceived that the hour of arrival could easily become the hour of death, and it almost became a wish although, or because, he felt definitely that the time for it had not come, it almost became a wish, although, or because, it would have been a strangely wild, strangely noisy death, it did not appear unacceptable to him, in fact almost desirable; for forced to gaze into the fiery inferno, forced to hear it, his heart was compelled to the knowledge of that infernal smouldering of the subhuman.

Now, tempting though it would have been to let himself be carried off on an ebbing consciousness, to escape in this way the noise, to shut himself off from the yelling mob, the volcanic, infernal yelling which flowed incessantly and heavily over the plaza as though it would never come to an end, such an escape was forbidden him, all the more as it might lead to death; for overstrong was the command to hold fast to each smallest particle of time, to the smallest particle of every circumstance, and to embody all of them in memory as if they could be preserved in memory through all deaths for all time; he clung to consciousness, he clung to it with the strength of a man who feels the most significant thing of his life approaching and is full of anxiety lest he miss it, and consciousness kept awake by the awakened fear obeyed his will: nothing escaped his observation, neither the careful gestures and the careless comfort of the smooth-faced, young, and foppish assistant-surgeon, who at Augustus' order was now at his side, nor the stolid, estranged faces of the porters who had brought a litter aboard to fetch him, the sick and strengthless man, as if he were some fragile and precious commodity; he took notice of all, he must retain all, he noticed the barred glances, the sullen growls by which the four men came to an understanding as they lifted the burden upon their shoulders, he noticed the terribly offensive, malign odor of their body-sweat, yet it did not escape his notice that his cloak which had been left behind was now carried after him by a rather childish-looking, dark-curled boy who in a swift pounce had snatched it up. To be sure the cloak was less important than the manuscript-chest, whose porters he bade keep close beside the litter, yet a small part of the vigilance, to which he felt constrained and despite all the nap-seducing attacks of fatigue constrained himself, might be devoted to the cloak; and now he wondered whence the boy, who seemed curiously known and familiar, might have emerged, since he had not come to his notice during the whole of the voyage: he was a somewhat homely, somewhat rustically awkward boy, certainly not one of the slaves, certainly not one of the waiters, and as he stood there at the railing, very boyish, the eyes bright in his brownish face, waiting, because of constant delays caused by the press of the crowd, he cast a furtive glance up to the litter from time to time, looking softly, roguishly and bashfully away when he felt himself observed. Play of eyes? Play of love? Should he, a sick man, be drawn again into the painful play of foolishly-lovely life, he a prostrate man be again drawn into the play of the erect? Oh, for all that they were erect, they did not know how deeply death was interwoven with their eyes and faces, they refused to know it, they desired only to continue the play of their seductions and entanglements, the fore-play of their kisses, foolish-lovely eye sunk in eye, and they did not know that all lying down for love was also by some token a lying down to death; but he who was unavoidably prostrate knew it, and he was almost ashamed that once he had been one of the erect, that once he himself—when was it? unreckoned ages past or just a few months back?—had participated in the lovely, blind and drowsy play of life; and the near-contempt which those enmeshed in play felt for him, since he was barred from it and lay there helpless, this contempt seemed to him almost like a commendation. For the truth of the eye was not in sweet blandishments, no, only through its own tears it came to seeing, only by sorrow it came to perception, only when filled with its own tears to the tears of the world, truth-filled by the obliterating moisture of all existence! Oh, only when awakening in tears did the earthly-death, in which the play-entangled discovered themselves and to which they clung, become changed to death-perceiving, all-perceiving life. And for this very reason it were better for the boy— whose features did he actually bear? those of a long bygone or a more recent past?—ah just for this reason it were better for him to turn away his eyes, for him not to wish to continue a play the diversions of which were inappropriate to the time; all too unseemly that glance which could smile over its own death-entanglement, all too unseemly that it was sent upward to the prostrated one who was unable, oh, who was unwilling to respond, all too unseemly the foolishness, the loveliness, the painfulness amid a hell of noise and fire, bristling with blind activity, helter-skelter with people, yet drained of humanity. Three gang-planks were swung from the ship to the pier, the one nearest the stern reserved for the passengers though by no means adequate for the crowd of people who had become suddenly impatient, the other two assigned to the debarkation of wares and luggage; while the slaves ordered for this task ran in a long snakeline, often joined together like dogs by neck-

26

rings and connecting chains, persons of every color with an humiliated look in their eyes, human beings who were scarcely human any longer, mere creatures set in motion and hounded, bodies in remnants of shirts or half-naked, shining with sweat in the raw glare of the torches, oh, terrible, oh, gruesome, while in this wise they ran aboard on the middle gang-plank and left again by the one nearest the bow, their bodies under the burden of chests, bags, and trunks bent almost to a rectangle, while all this happened, the stewards on duty, one of each stationed at the pier end of both gang-planks, swung their whips haphazardly over the passing bodies, beating automatically again and again in that senseless, no-longer-cruel cruelty of unlimited power, devoid of every real purpose, since without being goaded the men hurried as fast as their lungs permitted, scarcely knowing more how they were treated, no, no longer even ducking when the thong slashed down, but even grimacing at it; a little black Syrian whom the stroke caught just as he reached the deck, heedless of the stripes on his back, quite imperturbably adjusted the rags he had put under his neck-ring to protect his collarbones as much as possible, he merely grinned, grinned up to the lifted litter: "Come off your perch, King, come on down and see how it tastes to the likes of us!"—, a second lifting of the lash was the answer, but now the little man, this time on the alert, had jumped to one side, the connecting chain stretched suddenly and the stroke fell upon the shoulder of his chain-fellow who had been dragged forward by this jerk, a sturdy, red-haired Parthian with matted beard who, somewhat surprised, turned his head disclosing on the visible side of his face, amidst a discolored tangle of scars, (most likely he was a prisoner of war) a shot-out, torn-out or stabbed-out eye, red, bloody and staring, staring in spite of its blindness, actually surprised, for even before he was drawn forward by the advancing chain-rattling line, a lash, apparently because it came in one stroke, whistled again around his head and split his ear in a bleeding cut. All this lasted just the length of a short heart-beat, yet long enough to stop that heart-beat for a moment: it was outrageous to witness it and not make the slightest effort at interference, unable, perhaps even unwilling to interfere, it was outrageous still to want to retain this happening, and outrageous the memory into which even it must be inscribed for all time! The blind eye had gazed without remembrance, without remembrance the Syrian had grinned as if there were nothing but a desolated, desecrated present, as if, lacking a future, a past had never existed, no afterwards, therefore no aforetime, as if those two chained together had never been boys at play in the fields of youth, as if in their homeland there were no mountains or meadows, no flowers, not even a brook babbling on and on in the distant valley at eventide—, oh, it was painful to hang on his own memories, to nurse them, to cherish them! Oh, memories unforgettable, memories full of wheat-fields, full of forests, full of the crackling, rustling, cool-walled forests, full of the groves of youth, eye-intoxicated at morning, heart-intoxicated at evening, green quivering up and gray quivering down, oh knowledge of coming hither and going hence, pageant of memory! But the conquered, beaten, the conqueror, jubilant, the stony space where all this happens, the burning eye, the burning blindness—, for what undiscoverable existence was still worth while to keep oneself awake? what future was worth this unspeakable effort to remember? what was the hereafter toward which remembrance must go? was there in reality any such hereafter?

THE gang-planks wagged stiffly as the litter was carried over them in the measured even tread of the bearers; below the dark water splashed sluggishly, constrained between the heavy black ship-hulls and the heavy black side-walls of the dock, the heavy-flowing smooth element breathing itself out, exhaling refuse, garbage, vegetable-leaves and putrid melons, everything that stewed around down below, slack waves of a heavy sweetish death-exhalation, waves of putrifying life, the only one that can endure between these stones, living merely in the hope of a rebirth from its decay. So it appeared down there; here above, on the contrary, the flawlessly wrought, gilded and decorated litter-poles lay on the shoulders of beasts-of-burden in human form, humanly fed, humanly sleeping, humanly speaking, humanly thinking beasts-of-burden, and in the flawlessly wrought and carved litter-seat, the back and sides of which were spangled with stars of goldleaf, rested a flaw-infected invalid in whom decay was already lurking. This all made for extreme incongruity; in all of this the hidden evil sheltered itself, the obduracy of a circumstance that is more complete than the human being, although he himself is the one who builds the walls, who carves and hammers, who braids the lash and forges the chains. Impossible to shut oneself off from it, yes it was impossible to forget. And whatsoever man wished to forget came back in a fresh form of reality, there it was again, always returning as new eyes, new uproar, new stripes, new obduracy, new evil, each claiming place for itself, each cramping and forcing the other in fearful contact, yet most curiously and incongruously interwoven. As incongruous as the contact of things with each other was the passing of time also; the separate divisions of time no longer coordinated: never yet had the now been so definitely divorced from the then, a deeply-cut cleft bridgeable by no span had made of this now something independent, had unhesitatingly separated it from the time gone by, from the sea-journey and everything that had previously occurred, had removed him from the whole preceding life and yet, gently rocking in the litter, he could scarcely distinguish whether the voyage was still in progress or whether he was actually already on the land. He gazed over a sea of heads, he glided over a sea of heads, surrounded by a human surf, for the present, however, only at its edge, the first attempts to overcome this surging opposition having until now utterly failed. Here at the landing for the escort-ships the police regulations were of course less strict than yonder where Augustus was being

29

received, and even should a few of the travelers have been
lucky enough to break through with a hasty onslaught, in order
to join the festival procession which was forming within the
reservation to bring Caesar into the city and to the palace, for
the litter-squad such a thing would have been simply impossible;
the imperial servant who had been assigned to accompany the
small escort as guide and so-to-speak guard was too aged, too
portly, too effeminate, and also too easy-going to rouse himself
for a vigorous pass, he was powerless and because he was
powerless he had to content himself by complaining about the
police who permitted this mob-crowding and who at least should
have set aside a decent guard for him, and so finally one was
pushed and pulled quite aimlessly about the square, temporarily
motionless, wedged in a halted zig-zag, now here, now there,
shoved on this side, jostled on that. The fact that the boy had
come along proved to be an unhoped-for alleviation; he (and
this was most curious), as though apprized from somewhere
of the importance of the manuscript-chest, saw to it that its
bearers always kept close to the litter, and while he, constantly
near, the cloak thrown over his shoulders, allowed no separation to occur, he often winked up roguishly and reverentially
with his clear light eyes.   A brooding mugginess streamed
against them from the house-fronts and through the streets, it
came flooding in broad transverse tides, sundered again and
again by the endless yelling and calling, by the humming and
roaring of the mass-beast, and for all that stagnant; breath
of the water, breath of the plants, breath of the city, a heavy
reek from the stone-fenced, wedged-in life and its decaying
specious vitality, humus of existence at the point of decay,
ascending to the stone-cool stars with which the innermost shell
of heaven, darkening to a deep and mellow black, began to
be studded.   From unrevealable depths life sprouts upward,
insinuating itself through stone, already dying on this journey,
dying and decaying and cooling in its ascent, evaporating itself even as it rises, but from unrevealable heights the immutable
sinks downward, a sinking dark-luminating breath, conquering

with its stone-cool touch, congealing to the stoniness of the
depths, stoniness above and below as if stone were earth's final
reality—, and between such a stream and counterstream, between night and counternight, red-gleaming below, clear-flicker-
ing above, in this doubled nocturnality he swayed on his litter
as if it were a bark, dipping into the wave-tips of the vegetal-
animal, lifted up in the breath of the immutable coolness,
borne forward to seas so enigmatic and unknown that it was
like a homecoming, for wave upon wave of the great planes
through which his keel had already furrowed, wave-planes of
memory, wave-planes of seas, they had not become transparent,
nothing in them had divulged itself to him, only the enigma
remained, and filled with the enigma the past overflowed its
shores and reached into the present, so that in the midst of the
resinous torch-smoke, in the midst of the brooding city fumes,
in the midst of the beastly, dark-breathed body-exudations, in
the midst of the square and its strangeness, ineffaceably, unmistakably, he detected the breath of the seas and their immortal vastness; behind him lay the ships, those strange birds of
the unknown, words of command still resounding here from
over there are followed by the jerky grate-grit of a wooden
reel, then a deep-toned singing cymbal-stroke that reverberates
like a last echo of the day-star sinking into the sea, and beyond
that is the wide-planed wind of the sea, is its million-folded,
white-crowned restlessness, the smile of Poseidon in constant
readiness to break into boisterous laughter should the god urge
on his steeds; and beyond the sea, but at the same time surrounding it, are the sea-surfed lands, all of them that he had
traversed, passing over their stones, over their humus, sharing
in their vegetation, their humanity, their animal life, interwoven with them all, rendered powerless by so much that was
unknown, unable to surmount it, interwoven and losing himself
into happenings and objects, interwoven and losing himself into
countries and their cities, how buried all this and yet how
immediate, objects, countries, cities, how they all lay behind
him, about him, within him, how entirely they were his own,

sunnied over and deeply-shadowed, rustling and nocturnal, known and enigmatic, Athens and Mantua and Naples and Cremona and Milan and Brundisium, ah, and yes Andes—, everything came to him, everything was here, washed in the chaotic light from the landing-place, breathed on by the unbreathable, bawled at by the incomprehensible, assembled to a single unity in which the far-off easily became the near-at-hand, the near-at-hand became remote, permitting him who was balanced above it all and surrounded by savagery to come to an untroubled balanced-swaying awareness; the infernal a-stir before his very eyes and he knowing it, he knew simultaneously his own life, knew it to be carried by the stream and counterstream of night in which past and future cross each other, he knew it here at this point of crossing in the fire-bathed, fire-ringed immediacy of the landing-place, between past and future, between sea and land, he himself in the center of the plaza as if someone had wanted to bring him to the center of his own being, to the cross-roads of his worlds, to the center of his world, compliant to fate. For all that it was only the harbor of Brundisium.

But even had it been the center of the world there was no remaining here; more and more people streamed through the streets, their entrances into the square overarched by transparencies of fervent welcome, and the porters were crowded farther and farther from the center of the square, so that from this point there was really no other possibility of reaching the lane of soldiers and the procession of Augustus which had already been set in motion by a fanfare of trumpets, nor did the tumult become less now that the music had to be outscreamed, outyelled, outwhistled, and with the increasing tumult there was a simultaneous increase in the violence and heedlessness of the shoving and crowding that almost came to be a purpose and a diversion in itself, yet despite this violence it seemed as if the tranquility and ease of the balanced vigilance in which he was held had imparted itself to the whole plaza, as if a second illumination had joined itself to the first visible one without altering anything of its shadow-outdazzling glare, indeed rather intensifying it, revealing, however, a second inter-relationship within the visible objective present, the dream-waking relationship of the far-off which is inherent in every nearness, even in the most tangible and obvious. And as if this easy-because-remote assurance of the second relationship had still to be demonstrated, the boy was suddenly found to be at the head of the escort without anyone being aware of how this had happened; swinging, as if in play, a torch which he must have snatched from the nearest at hand, he used it as a weapon to force a way through the crowd. "Make way for Virgil," he cried exuberantly into the very faces of the people. "Make way for your poet!" And though the people may have stepped aside only because someone belonging to Caesar was being carried past, or because the fever-bright eyes in the yellow-dark face of the invalid looked ghastly to them, it was thanks to the small leader that their attention had been aroused, thus making an advance somehow or other possible. Certainly con-gestions occurred against which neither the mischievous non-chalance of the young cloak-bearer nor his torch-brandishing were effective, and against this deadlock the ghastly appearance of the sick man was of no avail; on the contrary it intensified what was at first only an indifferent avoidance of the uncanny sight into an outspoken repugnance, into a half-shy, half-offensive whisper that grew to have an almost threatening temper, for which a wag, as jolly as he was spiteful, found the right expression in the cry: "Caesar, his Enchanter!" "You're right, you blockhead," cried the youth in answer, "such an enchanter you surely have never seen in your whole stupid life; our greatest and the greatest of all enchanters, that he is!" Several hands flew up, with fingers spread to ward off the evil eye and a white-powdered whore, her blond wig askew, screamed toward the litter: "Give me a love-charm!"—"Yes, between the legs and potently" added in an aping falsetto a ganderish, sunburnt lout with tattooed arms, apparently a sailor, seizing the amorously-thrilled squealer from behind with both hands, "Dat kinda charm you'll get from me, good and gladly delivered, you shall have it!"—"Make way for the Enchanter, make way there!" commanded the youth, pushing the gander sharply aside with his elbows, and with quick decision making a rather unexpected right turn toward the outskirts of the square; the porters with the manuscript-chest followed willingly, somewhat less willingly the guardian servant, the litter and the remaining slaves followed on as if they were all towed by invisible chains behind the boy. Whither was the youth leading them? from what remoteness, from what depth of memory had he emerged? from what past, from which future, by what mysterious necessity was he impelled? and from which past to which future secret was he himself being borne? was there only a permanent balancing in an immeasurable present? All about him were the gulp-muzzles, the shout-muzzles, the sing-muzzles, the gape-muzzles, the opened muzzles in the closed faces, all of them were opened, torn apart, beset with teeth behind red, brown, or pallid lips, armed with tongues; and looking down on the mossy-woolly round heads of the slave-porters, looking sidewise at their jaws and the pimpled skin of their cheeks, he had knowledge of the blood that pulsed in them, of the spittle they had to swallow, he knew of the thoughts in these preposterous, clumsy, intractable foddered-and-muscled machines, knowing the thoughts that were almost lost, yet eternally unlosable, which frail and apathetic, transparent and dark, trickling drop by drop, were falling and evaporating, the drops of the soul; he knew of the yearning that is not silenced even in the pang of the most bestial heat and carnality, innate in all of them, in the gander and in his whore as well, the inexterminable longing of mankind that never allows itself to be destroyed, that at most lets itself be altered to malice and enmity, continuing to be longing. Removed, yet unspeakably near, balanced by awareness, still involved with all sluggishness, he could perceive the stolidity of the sperm-spraying, sperm-imbibing, faceless bodies, their swelling and hardening members, he saw and heard the

34

secretiveness, the chance lustfulness of their approaches, the wild besotted grappling jubilation of their union and the fatuously-wise droop of their senility, and it was almost as if all of this, this complete knowledge, were conveyed to him through his nose, breathed in with the narcotic fumes in which the audible and visible were imbedded, inhaled with the mani-fold exudations of the human-beast and its daily scraped-together, daily masticated fodder; but meanwhile they had finally battled a way between the bodies, and the crowd, like the thinning lights on the border of the square, became sparse at last, losing itself in the darkness and disappearing, and the odor of it, although it still smouldered on, was replaced by the slimy, foully-glistening stench of the fish-market stalls that hedged the harbor here, quietly deserted at this evening hour. Sweetish but none the less foul, the smell of the fruit-market annexed itself, full of fermentation, the odor of rosy grapes, wax-yellow plums, earth-dark figs, golden apples being indis-tinguishable, indistinguishable through their common decay, and the stone squares of the pavement gleamed damply from being trodden on and besmeared with slime; very far behind now lay the center of the plaza, very far the ships at the dock, very far the sea, very far, though not entirely lost: the human howling there was only a distant murmur, and of the music of the fanfare there was nothing more to be heard.

With great assurance, as if accurately acquainted with the neighborhood, the boy had steered his followers through the confusion of stalls and finally entered the district of the storage houses and dockyards which with dim, unlit buildings adjoined the market-place, in the darkness more to be surmised than seen, and extended along for a considerable distance. Again the odors changed; one could smell the whole produce of the country, one could smell the huge masses of comestibles that were stored here, stored for barter within the empire but des-tined, either here or there after much buying and selling, to be slagged through these human bodies and their serpentine intestines, one could smell the dry sweetness of the grain, stacks of which reared up in front of the darkened silos waiting to be shoveled within, one could smell the dusty dryness of the corn-sacks, the wheat-sacks, the barley-sacks, the spelt-sacks, one could smell the sourish mellowness of the oil-tuns, the oil-jugs, the oil-casks and also the biting acridity of the wine stores that stretched along the docks, one could smell the carpenter shops, the mass of oak timber, the wood of which never dies, piled somewhere in the darkness, one could smell its bark no less than the pliant resistance of its marrow, one could smell the hewn blocks in which the axe still clove, as it was left behind by the workman at the end of his labor, and besides the smell of the new well-planed deck-boards, the shavings and sawdust one could smell the weariness of the battered, greenish-white slimy mouldering barnacled old ship lumber that waited in great heaps to be burned. The orbit of productivity. Unending peace breathed from the scent-laden close of labor, the peace of a producing country, the peace of fields, of vineyards, of forests, of olive groves, the bucolic peace from which he himself a peasant's son had emerged, the peace of his constant nostalgia and of his earth-bound, earth-bent, always earthly longing, the peace to which his song had been dedicated since days of yore, oh the peace of his longing, unattainable; and as if this lack of attainment reflected itself here, as if everywhere it must come to be the image of his very selfhood, this peace was constrained here between stones, subserviated and misused for ambition, for gain, for bribery, for headlong greed, for worldliness, for servitude, for discord. Within and without are identical, are image and counter-image, but still not the integration which is knowledge. It was himself he found everywhere, and if he had to retain everything and was enabled to retain all, if he succeeded in laying hold on the world-multiplicity to which he was pledged, to which he was driven, given over to it in a day-dream, belonging to it without effort, effortlessly possessing it, this was so because the multiplicity had been his from the very beginning; indeed before all espial, before all hearkening, before all sensibility, it had been his own because recollection and retention are never other than the innate self, self-remembered, and the self-remembered time when he must have drunk the wine, fingered the wood, tasted the oil, even before oil, wine or wood existed, when he must have recognized the unknown, because the profusion of faces or non-faces, together with their ardor, their greed, their carnality, their covetous coldness, with their animal-physical being, but also with their immense nocturnal yearning, because taken all together, whether he had ever seen them or not, whether they had ever lived or not, were all embodied in him from his primordial origins as the chaotic primal humus of his very existence, as his own carnality, his own ardor, his own greed, his own facelessness, but also as his own yearning: and even had this yearning changed in the course of his earthly wanderings, turned to knowledge, so much so that having become more and more painful it could scarcely now be called yearning, or even a yearning for yearning, and if all this transformation had been predestined by fate from the beginning in the form of expulsion or seclusion, the first bearing evil, the second bringing salvation, but both scarcely endurable for a human creature, the yearning still remained, inborn, imperishable, imperishably the primal humus of being, the groundwork of cognition and recognition which nourishes memory and to which memory returns, a refuge from fortune and misfortune, a refuge from the unbearable; almost physical this last yearning, which always and forever vibrated in every effort to attain the deeps of memory, however ripe with knowledge that memory might be. Verily it was a physical yearning and unquenchable. He kept his fingers tightly interlocked, he was conscious of the ring pressing into his skin and his tendons, he was conscious of the rocky bones of his hands, he was conscious of his blood and the memory-deeps of his body, the shadowy deeps of the far-off past united to the immediate present, to the illumination of the present immediacy and the present clarity, and he called to mind his boyhood in Andes, he called to mind the house, the stables, the granaries, the trees, he called to mind the clear eyes in that sunburnt face always on the point of laughter, the face of his mother, she of the dark curls,—oh, she was called Maja, and no name was more summerlike, none existed which could have suited her better—, he called to mind how she busied herself in the house and warmed it with her joyous labor, serene in her tireless activity even when, being constantly called for some little service by grandfather who sat in the atrium, she had to keep on hushing him and his furious blood-curdling outcries, the appeasement-craving outcries that never failed to start up at any opportunity, but especially when prices of live-stock and grain were in question and he, the white-haired Magus Polla, half-generous, half-niggardly, believed himself cheated by the tradesmen, whether buying or selling; oh how intense the memory of those outcries, how soothing the memory of the quietude that his mother restored to the house with an almost mischievous joy; and he recalled his father, enabled to become a proper farmer only through his marriage, whose former profession of potter the son had deemed inferior, although it had been most pleasant to hear the nightly tales of the work on the bellied wine-jars and nobly turned oil jugs which his father had formed from clay, tales of the shaping thumb, of the spatula and the buzzing potter's disk, of the glazer's art, charming tales interrupted by many a potter's song. Oh, faces of a time remaining throughout time, oh face of the mother, remembered as a youthful face, then becoming more indistinct and significant, so that in death and already beyond physiognomy, it had almost come to resemble an unchanging landscape; oh face of the father, at first unremembered, then growing further toward a living humanity, a nearer likeness, until in death it had come to be the human face divine, modeled of hard, stiff brown clay, kind and firm in its farewell smile, unforgettable. Oh, nothing ripens to reality that is not rooted in memory, nothing can be grasped in the human being that has not been bestowed on him from the very beginning, overshadowed by the faces of his youth. For the soul stands forever at her source, stands true to the grandeur of her awakening, and to her the end itself possesses the dignity of the beginning; no song becomes lost that has ever plucked the strings of her lyre, and exposed in ever-renewed readiness, she preserves herself through every single tone in which she ever resounded. Imperishable the song, ever returning, here too it was again at hand; and he drew in the air to catch the cool scent of the earthen jars and piled-up tuns, which occasionally streamed, sombre and volatile, from the opened shed-doors, in order to breathe it into his sore lungs. Afterwards, of course, he had to cough as though he had done something insalubrious or illicit. The hob-nailed boots of the porters trotted along, clattering on the stone walks, grating on the gravel; the torch of the young guide, who swung round now and then to smile up at the litter, glimmered and glowed ahead; now they were thoroughly on the march and progressed quickly, too quickly for the aged servitor, grown gray and corpulent in the lenient service of the court, who waddled behind, sighing audibly; the mass of storage and silo roofs of various forms, some pointed, some flat, some slightly sloping, towered toward the star-dense but not entirely darkened heavens, cranes and poles cast threatening shadows under the passing of lights, one came upon carts both empty and laden, a couple of rats crossed the path, a moth lost itself on the back of the litter and remained clinging there, again lassitude and sleepiness made themselves known, the moth had six legs and many if not innumerable ones the porters to whom the litter, to whom he himself, together with the moth, had been entrusted as fine and fragile cargo; he was seized with the desire to turn round—ah, perhaps it was still possible to take count of the slave-porters and their legs—, but before he could put this into action, they had reached a narrow passage between two sheds and immediately afterwards and most unexpectedly they were again in front of the city houses, pausing at the entrance to a rather steep, very narrow, very weather-beaten, very wash-behung, ascending lane of lodging houses; as a matter of fact, they had come to a standstill because the boy had halted the porters,—yes, there were really four of them now as there

had been before——, who otherwise, it seems, would have trotted
on, and the very suddenness of this interruption together with
the unexpected outlook produced the effect of a joyful recognition, produced so surprising and startling an effect that all of
them together, master and servant and slave, laughed aloud,
all the more when the boy, fired by their laughter, bowed low
and pointing the way with a proud gesture, invited them to
enter the alley-gorge.

THERE was, however, little cause for merriment; least of
which came to be offered by this alley-gorge. Dark lay the
shallow-stepped stairways peopled by sundry shades, especially
by droves of children who despite the lateness of the hour
chased upstairs and downstairs, shadowy bipeds who on closer
inspection were mingled with quadrupeds, since goats were
tethered more or less closely all along the walls; the windows
without panes and mostly without shutters looked blackly into
the gorge, black were the cellar-like, dark recesses of the base-
ment-shops from which came bickerings for better bargains,
bargains for the needs of the next few hours but scarcely for
the next day, while nearby the tapping, rattling, tinkling, paltry
and pitiable handicrafts, produced by shadows for shadows,
sent out their meagre sounds, evidently requiring no light for
their production, for just where the glimmer of an oil-wick or
candle-stump dared to show itself, even there people crouched
in the shadows. Daily life in its most wretched round of misery
consummated itself here, independent of any outward circumstances, consummated itself almost timelessly as though the
emperor's celebration were miles away from this alley, as
though its inhabitants knew nothing of what took place in other
parts of the city, and therefore the advent of the litter-squad
created no astonishment but rather an unwelcome and even
hostile disturbance. This began gnome-fashion, that is to say

with the children, yes with the goats too, neither stepping aside and so becoming entangled between the legs of the porters, the quadrupeds bleating, the little bipeds screaming, breaking out of the shadowy corners and running back to hide in them; it began when they attempted, unsuccessfully of course because of his fierce resistance, to snatch the torch from the hand of the youthful guide, but all this would not have been the worst, and even though slowly, they still went forward—step by step they climbed the street of misery—, no, these vexations were not so bad, but the women, they were the worst, leaning out of the windows, their bosoms crushed against the sills, dangling snake-like their naked arms ending in lapping fingers, and though the abuse into which their gossip toppled as soon as the litter-squad was sighted was nothing but senseless carping, it was at the same time the carping of insanity, imposing as every insanity, lifted to the pitch of indictment, to the pitch of truth, being yet abuse. Here at this very spot where house after house discharged a beastly excremental stench from the opened door-mouths, here in this dilapidated dwelling-canal through which he was being borne in the high-held litter so that he could look into the squalid rooms, must look into them, here, met by the furious and senseless maledictions flung into his face by the women, met by the ailing whine of the inevitable sucklings bedded on rags and tatters, met by the smoke of pine-brands fastened to the fissured walls, met by the steamy aftermath of the stoves and their greasy, long-incrusted frying-pans, met by the horrid spectacle of half-clad mumbling gray-beards squatting about there in the black cave-dwellings, here despair began to overcome him, here among these verminous hovels, here amid utmost depravity and most wretched decay, confronting the lowest earthly imprisonment, here in this precinct, malign with the racking of birth and the ravages of death, life's entrance and exit woven into closest kinship, one as grim with foreboding as the other, one as nameless as the other in the shadowy dream of timeless woe, here in the utter namelessness of darkness and lasciviousness, here for the first time he was compelled to shield

41

his face, compelled to it by the carping jubilation of the women, compelled to deliberate blindness while he was being carried step by step over the stairs of Misery Street.—

—: "You loafer, you litter-loafer!" "Thinks himself better than us, does he?" "Money-bags on the throne!" "If he had no money he'd soon walk!" "Lets himself be carried to work, faugh!" scolded the women—

—: senseless the hail of insults that pattered upon him, senseless, senseless, senseless, nevertheless justified, nevertheless warning, nevertheless truth, insanity heightened to truth, and every aspersion tore a bit of presumptuousness from his soul until it became naked, as naked as the sucklings, as naked as the gray-beards on their rubbish, naked with darkness, naked with loss of memory, naked with guilt, immersed in the flooding nakedness of the indiscriminate—

—: step after step they went through Misery Street, halting at every landing—

—: flood of naked creaturekind extending over the breathing earth, extending forth under the breathing heaven with its constant changing from day to night, enclosed by the immutable shores of the millenniums, the naked herd-stream of life broadly advancing, filtering up from the humus of existence, constantly filtering back into it, the inevitable togetherness of all that has been created—

—: "When you've croaked you'll stink like any other!" "Pall-bearers, let him fall, let the corpse fall!"—

—: time-crests and time-hollows, oh, myriad creatures, having been carried over them by the aeons, still being carried over them constantly in the endless twilit stream of their totality, and not one of them but intended, but would continue to intend, to float forever as an eternal soul in infinity, floating freely in timeless freedom, sundered from the stream, released from the crowd, indisplaceable, no longer a creature, only a transparent flower, growing up, trailing up alone unto the stars, released and secluded, its heart trembling like a transparent blossom on the tendril no longer to be seen—

—: borne through the vilifications of Misery Street, step by step—

—: oh, everything tended toward this phantasmagoria of timelessness, and his life also, shot up from the chaotic humus of the nocturnal unnamed, grown aloft from the underbrush of mere creaturekind, trailed aloft in innumerable windings, attached here and there to what was pure and what was impure, to the perishable and the imperishable, to objects and possessions, to people, again and again to people, to words, to landscapes, this life which he continued to despise and continued to live, he had put it to ill use, he had misused it to exalt himself, to promote himself above himself, beyond all bounds, beyond all limits, as if there could be no downfall for him, as if he did not have to return into time, into earthly imprisonment, into creatureliness, as if no abyss gaped for him—

—: "Suckling!" "Diaper-pisser!" "Cacker!" "You've been naughty and have to be carried home!" "You'll get a clyster and be put on the potty!" the derision rained down from the windows on every side—

—: the street shrieked with the gibes of the women but there was no escape from them; progress was made but slowly, very slowly, step by step—

—: yet was it really the voices of the women that shamed him with justified scorn and disclosed his fruitless delusion? was that which cried out here not stronger than the voices of earthly women, than the voices of the insane creatures of earth? oh, it was time itself that called down scorn upon him, the unalterable flood of time with its manifold voices, with the sucking strength inherent in time and time alone, time had embodied itself in the voices of the women so that his name should be expunged in their insults, and he, stripped of his name, stripped of his soul, stripped of his least song, stripped of the singing timelessness of his heart, would fall back into unutterable darkness and the humus of being, degraded to that bitterest shame which is the last remnant of an extinguished memory—

43

—: knowing voices of time, knowing how impossible the escape from the clutches of fate! oh they knew that he also had been unable to escape the immutable, that there was a ship on which despite all delusion he had had to embark, and which had carried him back, oh, they knew of the stream of creature-kind which, nakedly between naked shores of primal clay, wearily follows its course, bearing no ship, bordered by no plant-life, transparent illusions both, nevertheless reality as fate, the invisible reality of illusion, and they knew that everyone, foreordained by fate, must plunge again into the stream and that he would not be able to distinguish the spot of his re-immersion from that where he had once fancied to emerge, because the return must bring to a close the cycle of fate—

—: "We'll be fetching you soon, you tail, you hang-tail!" they shrieked—

—: and still the voices of women deriding as if he had been a disobedient child who, after seeking a sham-freedom, now wanted to steal back home, nay more, who had to be brought back on devious and dangerous paths and therefore must be scolded for such evil ways; it was carping, but still the grave voices of mothers, imbued with the darkness of time, knowing that the cycle of fate encircled the abyss of nothingness, knowing of all the despairing, all the misled, all the exhausted ones who stumble unresistingly into the abyss of the middle as soon as they are prematurely forced to interrupt the journey—oh, was not each one so forced? had anyone ever really been permitted to pace out the cycle completely?—, and most anxiously the eternal mother-wish vibrated unspeakable within the angry chiding, the wish that each child might remain forever as naked as it had been born, nakedly imprisoned in its first enfoldment, embedded in the onflowing time of earth, embedded in the stream of creation, gently lifted out and as gently lost in it again, as it were without a fate—

—: "naked, that's what you are, just naked!"—

—: unescapable the mother—, what had moved the young leader to choose this way? would he not fail? spell-bound under the maternal incantations as if it would never move again, the line stood still, halted in a terrible suspense, but soon released it went on again, climbing through Misery Street, step by step—

—: was the maternal might of the voices still not ample enough to bind forever? were they so lacking, so deficient in knowledge that they had to set the spell-bound free again? oh, lack of the mother who, birth in herself, has no knowledge of re-birth, wants no knowledge, unable to grasp that birth to be valid implies rebirth, that birth like rebirth could never occur did not the nothing come into being along with both, did not the nothing remain eternally and irrevocably at their back for final procreation, aye, unable to grasp that only from this indissoluble connection of being and non-being, this runic bond heavy with silence, timelessness begins to ray forth in its essential greatness as the freedom of the human soul, the veritable song of its eternity, no phantasmagoria, no presumption, but rather as the irrecusable fate of the human being, the fearful glory of the human lot—

—: oh, it was the divine destiny of man, it was that which was humanly perceptible in the destiny of the gods, it was their common unalterable fate again and again to be guided to the path of re-birth, it was their common ineradicable fated hope to be allowed to tread out the cycle once more in order that the future might become the past, and that every station on the path might encompass in itself the entire future and the entire past, arrested in the song of the unique present, bearing the moment of complete freedom, the moment of god-becoming, this time-free moment from which, nevertheless, the whole would be embraced as a single timeless memory—

—: frenetic street of evil that would not end and perhaps that might not end until it should have given over its last insult and sin and curse, and more and more slowly, step by step, they paced it through—

—: oh, unalterable human fate of the gods, forced to descend into the earthly prison, into wickedness, into sin, so that the cycle might complete itself first in mortality and close itself ever more narrowly about the inscrutability of the nothing, about the inscrutable main-spring of birth that would change some day to the motive of rebirth for all creation, as soon as gods and men should have completed their tasks—

—: oh, unalterable fate-imposed duty of man, willingly to level the path for the god, the irreproachable path, the path of timeless rebirth, for the attainment of which men and gods are joined, set free of the mother—

—: but here was Misery Street to be ascended step by step, and here was the frightfulness of malediction, the frightfulness of justifiable scorn, and he, spat upon from out the misery, blinded by misery, blinded by malediction, blinded by scorn, oh he, even with veiled head, must nevertheless hear it. Why had he been led here? did he have to be shown that he had not been permitted to close the cycle? that he had stretched the bow of his life further and further, beyond all measure, enlarging the nothingness of the middle instead of diminishing it? that he had removed himself with such sham-infinity, sham-timelessness, sham-seclusion, further and further from the goal of rebirth, that he had become increasingly in danger of crashing? was this, here and now, a warning? or even more, a threat? or was it in reality already the ultimate downfall? Mere sham-divinity, that had been the peak of his overstrained course, madly overstrained to exultation and intoxication, to the great experience of power and fame, overstrained by what he had dared to call his poetry and his knowledge, feigning that he needed only to retain all in order to capture the recollective power of a never-ending present, the never-ending constancy of holy childhood, which even now disclosed itself as a childish sham-holiness, an unchaste assumption of holiness, exposed to every sort of laughter, to the naked laughter of the womenfolk, to the laughter of the betrayed and unbetrayable mothers whose custody he had been too weak to escape, weakest in his childish play at being a god. Oh, nothing could be set against the nakedness of laughter, no counter-laughter

46

could withstand derision, and nothing remained but to cover one's own nakedness, the nakedness of one's countenance, and with covered countenance he lay back in the litter, still veiled when despite all hindrances, shuffling along step by step, as it were against all expectation, they were finally discharged from the hellish alley-gorge, from the savage derision, and a quieter rocking of the litter betrayed the fact that they were again proceeding on an evener course.

To be sure, their progress was not therefore appreciably accelerated; once again they jerked forward only step by step, perhaps even more slowly than before, but not as was easily seen because of ill-meant obstacles but because just here, noticeable by the human murmur, by the human odor, by the growing dampness and closeness of the human warmth, the crowd had again increased and no doubt was continuing to increase. Although they had passed beyond hearing distance of Misery Street he still believed he could feel the carping, shrieking insults in his ears as before, indeed it almost seemed to him as if they had followed him like the Erinys, intent on harassing and torturing him as their natural prey, but not less intent, however, on uniting themselves with the rapidly-mounting mass-uproar springing up on all sides, which indicated a return to the vicinity of the imperial festival, so that the torture of the chase, paired with all this jubilation, with all this tumult of power and intoxication, should persist unabated; and while he was taking in all of this, unable to repel the massed voices within and without, so unable to repel them that their raw torment almost caused him to faint, the light became similarly insistent, became so unbearably noisy, so unbearably crude, pressing so sharply through eyelids closed until now, that it forced them to blink open, their first unwilling hesitation growing quickly into wide-eyed terror: the

infernal glare blazed toward him, blazing from the entrance
of the fairly broad street through which, head to head, the
human crowd surged forward, it gleamed out with terrifying
crudity into his eyes, gleamed like some magic luminary which
converted all that moved about there into a compulsorily automatic stream, one could almost think that even the litter swam
with it, floated with it automatically, scarcely that it was being
carried, and with every step, with every forward glide, the
power of that mysterious, calamitous, senselessly-magnificent
lure became more definitely felt, became more terrifying, more
urgent, more intrusive, near and nearer the heart, growing,
growing, growing, till at one stroke it revealed itself in that
instant when the litter, shoved, pulled, carried high and swim-
mingly afloat, suddenly came to the entrance of the street; for
here, quite abruptly, wreathed by fire, surrounded by tumult,
stripped of every shield for light, of every shield for noise,
in an unshielded dazzle of light and noise, gleaming and
glittering, the imperial palace came to view, partly residence,
partly fortress, arising vulcanically, infernally, glaringly, from
the center of a shield-shaped, hunched, almost circular plaza,
and this plaza was comprised of a single conglomerate flood
of creaturekind, a massed, formed, forming, boiling human-
humus, a flood of glossy eyes and glossy glances, all of them
rigid in their ardor as though dispossessed of every other
purport, directed toward the one and only goal, shining without a shadow, a human stream of fire avid to lick this fiery
coast. Thus towered the citadel, irresistible and seductive,
amid a surf of torches, the sole significant goal of the irresistibly attracted, crowding, snorting herd-mass, the longed-for
goal of their excessive craving for direction, but for this very
reason it was also the embodiment of a terrifying, gloom-
showering, undiscoverably enigmatic power, incomprehensible
for the individual animal, incomprehensible for the individual
man, oh so incomprehensible that the question as to the meaning
and source of the overpowering attraction imprisoned in the
fiery house and shining out from it, throbbed in almost every

one of them, in dread of an answer, in hope of an answer, and although no one was able to offer the true one, yet the most modest and inadequate gave such promise of being able to confirm their hope of salvaging consciousness, of salvaging humanity and the soul that it seemed worthy of proud utterance—; "Wine," the call went up, "Free wine," and the call "The Praetorians," and "The Caesar is to speak," and suddenly someone announced in a gasping voice: "They have started to distribute the money!" Thus the citadel cast its seductions upon them, thus they spurred on themselves and each other lest the great seduction should become dubious to them, and the fear of certain disappointment in wait for them at the long-desired, mysterious walls would not allow for the abatement of the wild lust, the great yearning for participation: cheap answers for so great a hope, cheap appeals, cheap prods, yet with each cry an impulse went through the mass, through the bodies, through the souls, a bullish obscene, irresistible impulse heading stolidly toward the common goal, a massed uproar and stampede heading, thrust after thrust, into a blazing nothing. And thickly massed the herd-smell smouldered above the heads, overhung by the smoke from the torches, the smoke a-glow, unbreathable, cough-provoking, stifling, thick brown swathes that piled up lazily tier on tier, left hanging in the motionless air; oh the heavy, indivisible, impenetrable layers of the infernal fog, a very ceiling of fog! Was there no longer a way out? was there no escape? oh, back! back to the ship, just to be allowed to die there! Where was the boy?! he should, he must lead the way back! With whom lay the decision?! Ah, wedged in the crowd and in the framework of its movement, there was nothing more to decide, and the voice that wanted to lift itself to decision could not get free of the breath; the voice remained blind! however the boy, as if he had heard the silent call, sent a smile upward, a smile from the eyes, full of serene apology, full of serene confidence, full of serene comfort in the knowledge that one was already released from every decision, yes, that the one made would be the right one, and this brought cheer notwithstanding all the frightfulness to come. On every side were the faces, one after another, usual faces with their usual though greatly exaggerated greed for food and drink, and this exaggeration, surmounting itself, had grown to an almost sinister ardor, to a brutal other-worldly possession that had left everything usual worlds behind and was conscious of nothing but the instant immediacy of the overpowering, gleaming goal, ardently longed for, ardently needed, ardently claimed, so that this very present might overshadow the cycle of their whole lives and lead on to participation, to participation in the power, the divinity, the expansive freedom and the eternity of the one who sat over there in the palace. Jerking, swaying, quivering, straining, exploding in gasps and groans, the frame-work moved forward, pushing to a certain extent against an elastic resistance that was undoubtedly there since it manifested itself in equally jerking counter-waves; and, in this forced-forcing to and fro, the cries of the stumbling, the down-trodden, the injured and perhaps even those of the dying became audible on every side, unnoticed or uncompassionately disdained, but again and again out-shouted by the jubilant hails, stifled by the furious uproar, shredded by the crackling of the flames. A momentous present was at stake, an endlessly amplified herd-present thrown up from the roaring of the herd, a present flung into uproar and at the same time flung out of the uproar itself, thrown up by the wit-lost, the soul-lost, the sense-lost, by those senseless because soul-lost, their senses so overemphasized in the mass that all things past and to come were engulfed by it, absorbing in itself as it did the uproar of all memory-depths, sheltering the remotest past and the remotest future in its tumult! Oh, greatness of human diversity, amplitude of human yearning! And floating in his awareness, floatingly borne aloft over the shouting heads, floatingly borne aloft over the festival fires of uproarious Brundisium, floating, held high in the undulant movement of the present, he experienced the boundless contraction of time's onrush in the cycle of immutability: everything was his, all was embodied in him, in an ever-present coexistence, just as it had always been from the beginning, and it was Troy that was blazing about him and it was the unquenchable conflagration of the universe, but he who was balanced above the burning, he was Anchises, blind and seeing at once, child and gray-beard at the same time by virtue of an unutterable recollection, borne on the shoulders of the son, identified with the universal present, borne on the shoulders of Atlas, on the shoulders of the Titan. And thus, step by step, he neared the palace.

The immediate confines of the palace were barricaded by a police cordon; man after man armed with horizontally held lances bore the brunt of the surging crowd and offered it just that elastic resistance which had made itself felt, time after time, in the wavelike ebb which he had already noticed on the outskirts of the plaza. Behind the cordon, however, the Praetorian cohort, whose arrival from Rome seemed to be considered an unusual event, had taken over the guard of honor and its presence there was nothing more than a bumptious, over-sized idleness in a warlike setting, with patrols and bivouac fires and far-flung canteen-tents from which emanated the hope and scent of free wine, deluding perhaps, yet nevertheless gladly given credence. The by-standers were able to get so far; but no farther. And here was the very spot where hope and disappointment counterbalanced one another, causing apprehensions and suspense like every choice between life and death, like each moment of life, since each moment contains both; and when the warm breath of the flames brushed over the crowd, ruffling the tall plumes on the helmets and throwing the gilded armor into high relief, when the hoarsely-overbearing "Get back!" of the police warded off the noisy onslaught, then the madness, darting up like a flame, became breathless, and the faces with parched lips and dangling tongues stared stolidly and covetously into that momentary flash of immortality; for time was balanced on a knife-edge.

Naturally things were at their worst at the entrance to the palace because since Caesar's entrance the double line through which he had passed had disbanded and now there remained nothing to check the frenzied mob; completely devoid of order as if seized by a tornado, it whirled viscously toward this gateway which, outlined on both sides by a dense line of torches, resembled a fiery gullet, and into this they whirled, to be jammed and ejected again, yelling, dogged, brutal, trampling, frantic with desire; one could easier imagine oneself before the entrance to a circus than before an imperial mansion, so mad the bustle and brawling that ensued in contentions with the gatekeepers, so manifold the craftiness of impostors who tried to outwit and override the officials, so furious the shouts of those with permits whose rights were questioned, and of those who were kept waiting unduly; and when, at a word from the aged palace-servant whose usefulness only thus became apparent, the escort was admitted at once, the anger of those who, regardless of their standing, had been forced to comply to the entrance formalities rose intensely, yes even to the boiling point! they felt themselves made contemptible by this preference, they felt the contemptibleness of all human traits and all human institutions, they suddenly became conscious of all this because an exception had been made, could be made, for an individual, and it made no difference that it was only the exception due to one sick unto death, and to death itself. There was no one who might not come to despise his fellow man, and in the nameless and unutterable accumulation of contemptibleness, always disclosing and concealing itself anew, there dwelt man's knowledge of his own incapacity for humanity, his anxiety for a dignity with which he had been endowed but which he would never truly possess. Contempt warred with contempt within the narrow, hot funnel of the entrance. Small wonder then that having come within the courtyard, having escaped the greedy struggle, having escaped the infernal raw glare of the lights, he fancied himself free of the insult which had pursued

him into the streets and on the plaza, and felt a relief similar
to that which had been granted him by the passing of the
seasickness, the same ease of mind despite the fact that this
place which he now entered did not reveal itself as quietude;
on the contrary the courtyard seemed fairly bursting with
disorder; but after all it was only a seeming disorder; the
imperial servants well used to such contingencies preserved
strict discipline, and soon a major-domo provided with a guest
list approached the litter to receive the newcomer, perfunctorily
turning to the servant to let him whisper the name of the guest,
perfunctorily taking in the name and checking it off the list,
so without diffidence or regard for a famous poet that it seemed
almost offensive, so offensive that he found it necessary to
confirm and emphasize the servant's statement: "Yes, Publius
Vergilius Maro, that is my name," he said, and became bitterly
angry when this brought him only a curtly-polite but no less
indifferent bow, and even the youth from whom he had expected support made no sound but instead obediently joined
the procession, which at a nod from the major-domo now
moved on toward the second peristyle. However, his anger
did not last long, it vanished with the quietude that now
actually embraced them as soon as the litter was borne into
the almost complete silence of the garden-court with its drizzling fountains and deposited there in front of the megaron
which Caesar had set aside as living quarters for his guests;
the slaves were lined up at the entrance to receive them and
the hired porters were dismissed. For the youth also the procedure was the same; the cloak was taken from him and when
smiling he made no motion to depart, the major-domo hec-
tored him: "Why do you still hang around here? Make haste
and be off!" The boy remained standing, affable and mischievous, and he smiled, perchance, at the rude way in which
his leadership was acknowledged or, perchance, also because
of the futility of an effort that could not remove him, either
now or at any time. Nevertheless, was there any sense in the
boy's remaining? Was his remaining here desirable? What

could he, a tired invalid longing for solitude, do with the youth?! And yet, now this strange fear of being alone! this strange fear of ever having to lose the young guide! —: "My scribe," he said, and it was said almost against his will, as if something alien within himself had spoken out of him, alien and yet obscurely familiar, a will greater than one's own, a will-less will yet still compelling and overpowering: the night. A gentle forceful willing unfolded from the night. The garden-court was gentle, gentle the flowery breath, gentle the splashing of the two fountains, a dim, delicate, gently moist fragrance as of a spring night in autumn floated cool and fine-spun above the flower-beds, and music woven into it drifted back from the forefront of the palace like transparent strips of veiling, nearing at times, receding at others, veil after veil dotted with cymbal points, folded into the gray mist of voices on which the feasting yonder filtered beyond itself, over there a resounding, blaring light-clamor, here only a tone-mist drizzling into the immense spaces of night; the square patch of heaven stretched over the court now permitted the stars to be seen again, their breathing light once more visible though occasionally dimmed by the smoke-clouds trailing beneath them, but even these were permeated by the soft, drizzling tone-mist, sharing in the wandering-weaving misty murmur which impregnated the courtyard and shrouded each single thing, objects, odors and tones blended, mounting toward heaven in the stillness of the night; and yonder at the wall, its hard-fibered trunk faintly illumined, rearing up to the height of the roof, stiff and crabbed, black-fanned and repelling, stood a palm, even she pregnant with night.

Oh stars, oh night! Oh, this was night, night at last! And it was the breath of sounding night, damp and deep and dark, that with aching chest he sucked deep within him. But he had tarried too long already, he must prepare himself to arise from the litter and he was rather vexed that the consideration of Caesar who had sent the irksome physician to him on the boat had not extended this far, and that evidently nobody realized how very frail he was; moreover they had already taken the chest with the Aeneid into the house and it behooved him to follow quickly. "Come," he called the boy to him as he sat up, "help me," and then leaning on the boy's shoulder he tried to mount the first steps of the staircase only to realize at once that his heart, his lungs and his knees were failing him and that he had overestimated himself: he had to be carried upstairs by two slaves. They went up three flights, the indifferent major-domo in front holding the guest scroll against his hip like a baton, to the rear the tramp, tramp, tramp of the slaves with the luggage; and when on reaching the top they entered the airy guest room which had been prepared, it was easy to see that it lay in the towerlike, southwest wing of the palace. Through the open arched windows well above the city's roofs a cool breeze was blowing, a cool remembrance of forgotten land and sea, seafast, landfast, swept through the chamber, the candles, blown down obliquely, burned on the many-branched, flower-wreathed candelabrum in the center of the room, the wall-fountain let a fragile, fan-shaped veil of water purl coolly over its marble steps, the bed under the mosquito-netting was made up, and on the table beside it food and drink had been set out. Nothing was lacking, an armchair for contemplation stood near the bay-window and the commode stood in the corner of the room; the luggage was piled up in a way easy to handle, the manuscript-chest was pushed by special order near the bed, everything fitted in so neatly, so noiselessly, exactly as an invalid could have desired it, but still this was no longer the beneficence of Augustus, this was just the smooth planning of an irreproachable, fully equipped, royal household, there was no friendship in it. One must suffer it, one must accept it, sickness obliged one to do it, it was a compulsion of illness, a burdensome, bitterness-breeding compulsion, and withal this bitterness was not directed so much against the infirmity as against Augustus, apparently because he had the trick of always frustrating all gratitude. This bitterness toward Augustus—, had it not always been there from the beginning? In truth he had Augustus to thank for everything, peace and order and his own security, no one else could have brought it to pass, and if in his stead Antonius had attained sovereignty, Rome would never have found the way back to peace, verily —and even so! yes, even so! still always mistrust for this man who had already passed into his forties without actually becoming older, unchanged these twenty-five years, with the same precocious sleekness and cunning now as then, this man who held the thread of politics in his well-skilled hands—, the bitter distrust for this over-aged youth to whom one owed everything, was it not thoroughly justified? he was distinguished only by his sleekness, sleek his beauty, sleek his intelligence, sleek his friendliness which one longed to accept as friendship but which was no true friendship since it always served selfish ends, and everyone was caught in his web, into his sleek, his shining web! And now again it had come to this, once more this hypocrisy of friendship—, why indeed had the hypocrite insisted on dragging an invalid in his train back to Italy? Ah, it had been better to die on the ship, better than here in the midst of this sleek imperial household, better than having to lie here where everything was all too perfect while yonder at the imperial feast with a blare of light and sound the imperial no-youth gave himself to the noisy celebration. As a roaring, far and strange, lewdly swelling and drooping, came the clamor thence, fouling the breath of night.

Yet in the night's breath all was mingled, the brawling of the feast and the stillness of the mountains and the glittering of the sea as well, the once and the now and again the once, one merging into the other, merged into one another—, would he be allowed to return to Andes once again? — Here lay Brundisium rich in roofs and lighted streets spread out under the bay-window to which he had let himself be brought and before which he now sat in the armchair, this was only Brundisium and he listened out into the night, listened into the far-off once, there where it would have been good to die; no, he should not have come here, least of all to this well-furnished guest room bare of friendship. On the obliquely burning candelabrum candles, at one side of each, a notched ridge of wax was forming, drop upon drop quickly growing in thickness.

"Sir . . ." The major-domo stood before him.

"I desire nothing more."

The major-domo pointed toward the boy: "Have we to accommodate your slave? It was not foreseen . . ."

Certainly, the nuisance was right; it had not been foreseen.

"Still if you wish him placed near you, oh Sir, it shall be our care to please you."

"It is not necessary . . . he will go into town."

"Besides, this one here"—the major-domo indicated one of the group of slaves, "will stay over night in the next room at your bidding."

"Good . . . I hope not to need him."

"Then may I retire . . ."

"Do so."

There was already too much preparation; impatiently with folded hands, impatiently turning the seal-ring, he waited until the cool zealot should have left the room with his staff, but when this happened, contrary to expectation, the slave designated by the major-domo, a man with an orientally thick nose in his stern lackey's face, instead of having gone with the others remained at the door as if he had been ordered to do so.

"Send him away," the boy requested.

The slave asked: "Do you wish to be waked at sunrise?"

"At sunrise? why?" For a second it was as if the sun, in spite of the nightly hour, had not vanished from heaven, as if it were hidden in the westerly regions and for all that present, Helios outlasting the night, conquering the night, as powerful as the mother from whose womb he had issued.

Nevertheless he must give an answer to the slave who awaited his decision: "You need not wake me; I will surely be awake . . ."

One would have thought the man had not heard him, he stood there without moving. What could this mean? What did he want to suggest? was it as if for him who would not be called no new day would break? Here was night, motherly, peaceful night, soothing her breath, and soothing it was to imagine that she could endure forever; no, the slave was unwanted, just as unwanted as the prospect of being waked by him:

"You may go to your rest . . ."

"At last!" observed the boy when the slave had closed the door behind him.

"At last, yes but . . . but you, little Leader . . . what are you still doing here? Have you a request to make of me? I will gladly grant it . . ."

The little leader stood there with outspread legs, his round, lusty and, alas, it must be admitted, somewhat homely young peasant's face drooping a little, certainly a bit offended, awkward, with pouting underlip: "You want to send me away too . . ."

"I have sent the others away, not you . . . I am only asking you . . ."

"You should not send me away . . ." The hoarse-soft young voice had a familiar sound, its peculiar peasant undertone almost like that of the homeland. The voice was like a reminder of a scarcely-remembrable bond, something compatible in an undiscoverably remote motherly once, a knowledge of which shone also in the boy's clear eyes.

"I have no intention of getting rid of you, but I take it that you, like many others, hanker to go to Caesar's festival . . ."

"The festival means nothing to me."

"All boys like to go to the festival; you need not be ashamed of it, nor will my gratitude for your guidance be less on that account . . ."

The boy, his hands behind him, twisted himself about: "I do not want to go to the festival."

"At your age I certainly would have gone, and even today I would do so were I stronger, but if you go in my stead it will seem to me almost as if I were participating myself . . . drolly smuggled in in another form . . . look, here are flowers, make a wreath for yourself, perhaps you will find favor with Augustus."

"I don't want to."

"Too bad . . . what do you want then?"

"To stay here with you."

The picture of the festival hall into which the boy was to have been smuggled in order to appear before Augustus faded out: "You wish to stay with me . . ."

"Forever."

Everlasting night, domain in which the mother rules, the child fast asleep in immutability, lulled by darkness, from dark to dark, oh sweet permanence of the "forever."

"Who is it that you are seeking?"

"You."

The boy was mistaken. What we seek is submerged and we should not seek it as it mocks us by its very undiscoverability.

"No, my little Leader, you have guided me but not sought me."

"Your way is my way."

"From where do you come?"

"You embarked at Epirus."

"And you came along with me?"

A smile came as confirmation.

"From Epirus, from Greece . . . yet yours is the speech of Mantua."

Again the boy smiled: "It is your speech."

"The speech of my mother."

"Speech turns to song in your mouth."

Song—, the song of the spheres singing itself, reaching out over every human realm: "Was it you who were singing on the boat?"

"I was listening."

Oh, motherly song of night, resounding through all nights, echoing from of yore, sought for again with the break of each new day: "I was about your age, yes, even a bit younger when I wrote my first strophes, nondescript, hotch-potch . . . yes, that's how it was then; I had to find myself . . . my mother was dead by that time, only the sound of her voice remained . . . once more, whom do you seek?"

"I need not seek since you have done so."

"So then, I still stand in your place although you would not go to the feast instead of me? And perhaps you write verses also, just as I have done?"

Disavowing, protesting mirth appeared in the boy's familiar countenance; the freckles at the base of the nose were also a completely familiar sight.

"Then you do not write verses . . . I had already suspected that you were one of those who have it in mind to read their poems and dramas to me."

The boy seemed not to have grasped this or perhaps he disregarded it: "Your path is poetry, your goal is beyond that of poetry."

The goal lay beyond the darkness, lay beyond the domain of that maternally protected once; even though the boy talked of a goal, he knew nothing of it, he was too young to know, he had led the way but not for the goal's sake: "Be that as it may, you came to me because I am a poet . . . or did you not?"

"You are Virgil."

"I know that . . . besides which you screamed it clearly enough in the ears of the people down there at the harbor."

"It didn't help much." The mirth in the youthful face became a twinkle, became a wrinkling of the nose, so that the freckles at the base drew into many tiny lines exposing white, regular, very strong teeth which shimmered in the candle light; it was the same mirth by which he had tried to clear a path down there on the plaza for the poet Virgil, and it was the same mirth that stemmed from a very remote past.

Something or other constrained him to speak; constrained

him to it even at the risk of the boy's failure to understand: "The name is like a garment which does not belong to us; we are naked beneath our name, nakeder than the child that the father has lifted from the ground in order to give him a name. And the more we imbue the name with being, the stranger it becomes to us, the more detached it becomes from us, the more forsaken we ourselves. The name we bear is borrowed, borrowed the bread we eat, borrowed we ourselves, held naked into the unknown, and only he who puts off from him all borrowed furbelows, only he will glimpse the goal, he will be summoned to the goal so that he may ultimately join himself to his name."

"You are Virgil."

"I was once, perhaps I shall be again."

"Not quite here but yet at hand," came like a corroboration from the boy's lips.

It was comfort, to be sure only such comfort as a child has to give, and that was not sufficient comfort.

"This is the house of borrowed names . . . why did you lead hither? It is merely a house for guests."

The smile of compatibility appeared anew, childish, almost mischievous, and yet embedded in a very great, yea timeless intimacy: "I have come to you."

And now, strange to say, this answer sufficed as though it were comfort enough, and it sufficed for the following question, even stranger if possible, strange in its very peremptoriness: "Have you come from Andes? Are you going toward Andes?" Actually he did not know whether he had spoken the question aloud, but he did know that he desired no answer, neither an affirmative nor a negative one, for it was not permissible for the boy to have come from Andes or not to have done so, the first possibility being all too alarming, the second all too absurd. No, there should be no answer and it was right that none followed; however the desire to be permitted to keep the boy here was most intense, most intense the desire to breathe, to breathe toward tranquility, toward divination, ah, the desire was in

61

itself divination. The candles burned obliquely in the gentle
breeze that blew hither and thither like a cool, delicate yet
intense yearning, drifting out of the night, flowing into the
night. The silver lamp next to the couch swung gently to and
fro on its long silver chain and outside the window the emanation of the city, ebbing and flowing above the roofs, was dissolved into purple, from purple-violet into dark blue and black,
and then into the enigmatic and fluctuant.

To breathe, to rest, to wait, to keep silence. Drifting out of
the night, flowing into the night, a stream of silence, and it endured a longish while before he broke it: "Come," he bade the
boy to his side, "Come and sit next to me," and even when the
boy had crouched near him, the silence continued, they remained embraced by silence, given over to the silent night. From
far off came the raging, the raging noise of the crowd frantic to
see, the raging uproar of the feast, the seething of sheer creatureliness, hellish, stolid, inevitable, tempting, lewd and irresistible,
clamorous and yet satiated, blind and staring, the uproar of
the trampling herd that in the shadowless phantom-light of
brands and torches drove on toward the evil abyss of nothingness, almost past saving were there not even within the raging
—and the longer one listened the more audible it became
—, yes, were the song of silence not in it, contained in it from
time immemorial, contained in it forever, the bell-tone of silence
swelling to the brazen din of night and to the din of all human
herds, softly singing the night of the herd, the herd heaving
a sigh in its mighty slumber: deep below the humus of existence,
murmurous with shadows, hidden in childhood, fate-delivered,
untinged by lewdness, dwelt the night; from her sprang everything creaturely, saturated by the murmuring fluids of night,
impregnated by sleep, made fruitful from the source of all fervor, from her sprang plant and animal and man, inexpressibly

interwoven and grown into each other, overshadowing one another, for the curse of reversion was sheltered in the consolation of sleep and the gracious coverlet of being, a dream-nothingness, was spread over the actual nothingness.

Oh, earthly life! The diaphanous world and the world of darkness inhaling and exhaling unceasingly, floating between the twin seductions of too much or too little shadow, the tides of the transient were held inexorably in check between the two poles where time ceased to exist, between the timelessness of the gods and the timelessness of the beast—, oh, in every vein of the earth-bound, in everything springing from the earth the night sprang upward, constantly changed to awakeness and awareness both within and without, shadowily projecting the formless into form, and floating between non-being and being, poised in this equilibrium, the world came to be light and shadow, came to be perceptible in its light-and-shadowhood. Ringing forever in the soul, softly at times, loudly at others yet never silenced, the bell-tone of night, the bell-tone of the herds sounded on, forever, too, the lion-roar of day sounded on, shattering in its light and revelation, the golden storm that engulfed the creaturely—, oh, human perception not yet become knowledge, no longer instinct, rising from the humus of existence, from the seed of sentience, rising out of the wisdom of the mothers, ascending into the deadly clarity of utter-light, of utter-life, ascending to the burning knowledge of the father, ascending to cool heights, oh human knowledge, unrooted, eternally in motion, neither in the depths nor on the heights but hovering forever over the starry threshold between night and day, a sigh and a breath in the interrealm of starry dusk, hovering between the life of the night-held herds and the death of light-flooded identification with Apollo, between silence and the word, the word that always returns into silence. In truth, nothing earthly might abandon sleep, and only he who never forgot the night within him was able to complete the cycle, to come home from the timelessness of the beginning to that of the end, beginning the orbit anew, himself a star in the constellation of time's orbit, arising from dusk and sinking into dusk, born and reborn nocturnally out of the night, received by day whose brightness has entered into the darkness, day, taking on the habit of night: yes, so had his nights ever been, all the nights of his life, all the nights through which he had wandered, the nights passed in wakefulness for fear of the unconsciousness that threatens from below the night, for fear of the unshadowed light from above, fearful of forsaking Pan, full of a fear that knows of the peril of twofold timelessness, yes, thus his nights bound to the threshold of the double fare-well, nights of the obstinately enduring universal sleep, although people rioted on the squares, in the streets, in the taverns, blindly remaining the same in town after town from the very beginning, the sound of their tumult echoing here inaudibly from the reaches of time and therefore all the more keenly recognized, this too was sleep; although the mighty of the world were being toasted amid a surf of torches and music in hall after hall of feasting, smiled at by faces and more faces, courted by bodies and more bodies, they also smiling and courting, this too was sleep; although the bivouac fires were burning, not only before the castles but yonder too where there was war, at the frontiers, at the night-black rivers, and at the fringes of the night-murmuring forests beneath the rutilant roar of the attacking barbarians breaking out of the night, this too was sleep, sleep and more sleep, like that of the naked gray-beards who in stinking hovels sleep the last remnant of wakefulness out of themselves, like that of the sucklings who dreamlessly drowse away the misery of their birth into the sullen wakeful-ness of a future life, like that of the enslaved chain-gang in the ship's belly who lay stretched out like torpid reptiles on the benches and decks and coiled ropes, sleep and more sleep, herds and more herds, lifted out from the indiscriminateness of their ground-soil like the ranging mountains of the night at rest on the plains, set into the unchanging matrix, into the constant regression which is not quite timelessness but which reproduces it in every earthly night; yes these nights, so had they ever been, so they were still, and so this night also perhaps enduring forever, night on the tilted threshold of timelessness and time, of farewell and returning, of herd-solidarity and the loneliest utter-loneliness, of fear and salvation and he, thralled on the threshold, waiting night after night on the threshold, blinded by the twilight at the rim of night and by the dusk at the world's edge, knowing as he did the experience of sleep, he had been lifted into immutability, and as he was taking shape there he was hurled back and aloft into the sphere of verse, into the inter-realm of wisdom and poetry, into the dream that is beyond dream and touches on rebirth, the goal of our flight, the song.

Flight, oh, flight! oh, dusk, the hour of poetry. For poetry was contemplative waiting in the twilight, poetry was the night-foreboding abyss, was lingering on the threshold, was at once participation and loneliness, was intermingling and the fear of intermingling, unwanton in intermingling, as unwanton as the dream of the slumbering herds and yet the fear of wantonness; oh, poetry was anticipation but not quite departure, yet it was an enduring farewell. He felt the shoulder of the crouching boy at his knee, barely touching it, he did not see the countenance but only sensed how it was sunk in its own shadow, however, he saw the dark rumpled hair played on by the candle-light, and he recalled that terrible, joyful-joyless night on which impelled by fate, even then a lover and harassed, he had come to Plotia Hieria who crouched in wintry expectation, wintrily un-budded, and all he did was to read his verses to her—, it was the Eclogue of the Enchantress which had been completed at the wish and order of Asinius Pollio, the Eclogue which would never have turned out so successfully had not his thought of Plotia, his longing and lustfulness for a woman stood sponsor to it, in the writing of which he had been so successful only because he had known from the very start that he would never be allowed to leave the threshold and enter into the night of perfect union; ah, because the will-to-flee had been imposed on him from time out of mind, he was compelled to read the Eclogue to her, and fear as well as hope had been fulfilled, it became their farewell. And it had been the selfsame farewell that once again and on a grander scale had to be experienced later on by Aeneas when, forced by the enigmatic, unfathomably fateful course of poetry, bound for the irrevocable with his departing ships, he had forsaken Dido, forever forsworn from lying with her, from hunting with her, eternally divorced from her who had been his sweet shadow of reality, his sweet shadow of desire, divorced eternally from the night-cave of love beneath the thunders. Yes, Aeneas and he, he and Aeneas, they had fled in a real departure, not only in the lingering farewells of poetry, from whose interrealm they had escaped as if it had no worth for the living, even though it was also the realm of love—, whither was this flight tending? from what depth came this fear of Juno's motherly commands? Oh! love itself connoted sinking under the surface of night, sinking down to the nocturnal ground-soil on which the dream grows to timeliness, sinking under its own threshold to the primal source of the unformed and invisible, which always lay in wait to break out in storm and destruction: it was only the days which changed, time took its course only through days, and it was in movement that time could be beheld by the eye; the eye of night, however, was immovable, enormous, that eye wherein love reposed, and its depth, empty burning stark in the starlight, unchangeably unceasingly night after night throughout time renewing terrestrial timelessness in itself, creating and devouring the world from its deepest eye-pit, no longer beholding, being but the blinding lightning-cleft of nothingness, absorbed all eyes, the eyes of lovers, the eyes of the wakeful, the eyes of the dying, failing for love, failing in death, the human eye failing because it peered into timelessness.

Flight, oh, flight! Taking shape of day, relaxing of night, turned in this relaxation toward the eventuality of timelessness! After a while the candles became encrusted and the gnats swarmed ceaselessly about them with their horrid-monotonous, shapeless-hard humming, ceaselessly the water of the wall-fountain drizzled on, and the drizzling was like a part of its unspeakably timeless, becalmed, oceanic on-flow; motionless the amorini played in the wall-frieze, frozen in an utter-peace, in an utter-silence that ceased to have a shape of its own but that seemed to merge into the wide-spread, austerely reverberating, other-worldly silence of the night, merging into its aeon-bound perseverance which, world-encompassing and breath-encompassed, shadow-bearing and shadow-overborne, erected about itself a cavern from the tide of dreams, the shapeless silence overbalanced by the noiselessness of the thunderbirds beneath the unclouded stars; for whatsoever reposed in the night, drinking in peace and drinking in one another, set a-tremble by shadows, lying in the shadow of one another, soul pressing against soul, husband and wife united, the maiden sheltered in the arms of the youth, the boy in the arms of the lover, whatsoever happened in the night was but the darkness-sharing reflection of its greater darkness, was but the image of its dark flashing lightning, was downfall into the thundery abyss, the coverlet of dreams torn asunder, and even if we cried for our mother to shelter us against the night-storms, she was so far removed, so lost to memory that only now and then a quiver from childhood was wafted to us, no longer a consolation, no longer a shelter, at best the familiar-strange breath of a long since vanished homeland, the breath of peace that preceded the storm. Yes, so it was, and though the night-breeze were ever so warm, ever so mild, though it were ever so cool as it streamed through the windows, even though it gathered all terrestrial things in its tides, olive-groves and wheat harvest and vineyards and fishing-banks, uniting as into a whole the undulant night-breath of lands and seas, bearing and mingling their harvests in the mild hand of the wind, and though this softly-blowing hand drooped ever so dulcetly, stroking across the streets and squares, cooling the faces, sundering the smoke, appeasing the ardor, yes, though this floating breath, with which the form of night was filled to its outermost surface, had even swelled beyond it, transformed into trembling cave-mountains, which beyond all conception, scarcely even external, rested in our innermost depths, within the heart and deeper than the heart, within the soul and deeper than the soul, in our innermost self that had become one with the night, yes, even though all this were so and continued to be so, it was of no use, the time for it was past, it was no longer of use. The sleep of the herds remained pregnant with evil, the earthly raging still unappeased, the fire unquenchable, and love delivered over to the lightning blast of nothingness, while timeless above the cave of night the tempest thunders.

Flight, oh, flight! The mother was past invoking. We were orphaned when the herd came into being, we could invoke no name in our dreams, none had identity in the darkness of utter fusion—, and you, my little night-mate who have attached yourself to me as a guide, are you still there at my call? is it by your fate or mine that you are sent to me that I may talk to you? do you feel that you too are menaced by timelessness? is it hidden under your night as well?—and was it for this reason that you came to me? oh lean against me, my little twin-brother, oh lean against me; I turn away my eyes from the menace, I turn them to you in hope, hoping for the last time to return from my plight, hoping to return with you into the dark cavern which has been built in myself like a homestead I no longer know, oh, be lodged with me in this closeness that beats in my veins like something long estranged and now re-welcomed, and that I would fain have you share with me: then it may come to pass that even the most unfamiliar, that even myself will no longer seem strange to me; oh nestle close to me, my little twin-brother, nestle close, and should you lament your lost childhood, your lost mother, you shall find them again with me as I take you into my arms and into my care. Once more let us tarry in the floating cavern of night, but once again and together let us hearken to its dream-tremors, let us hearken to the "nevertheless" of its interrealm and its sweet reality—, you do not know yet, my little brother, for you are too young, from what profound depths within us the nightly hope mounts upward, so all-embracing, so whole-souled in its tenacity, with such tender-soft promise of yearning in its very distress that it takes us long to hear its hope and its dismay, which surround us like a mountain-chain of echoes, echo-wall on echo-wall, like an unknown landscape and yet like the summoning of our very hearts, yes "nevertheless and nevertheless" and still with such sovereignty as if the complete reflection of a past, long since lived through, would gleam out freshly and yet as unfaltering as though it contained all covenants of consummation—, oh little brother I have experienced it because I have become an old man, older than my years, because I sense every fragility and taint in myself, I have experienced it because I am coming to the end; ah, it is only when we begin to long for death that we really desire life, and in me the undermining, the frame-slackening process of an avidity for death goes on, never pausing, as far back as I can remember, clamoring ceaselessly, thus have I always felt it, anxiety for life and anxiety for death together, in these many nights on the threshold of which I have stood, on the strand of nights and more nights that have gushed past me, the awareness of them gushing and swelling, knowledge of separation and farewell that had its beginning with the dusk, and it was dying, every sort of dying, that coursed past me, grazing me with its mounting flood, saturating me, encircling me, coming from without yet born from within me, my own dying: only the dying understand communion, understand love, understand the interrealm, only in the dusk and at farewell do we understand sleep whose darkest communion is without wantonness, not until farewell do we know that our departure will be followed by no return, not until then do we recognize the seed of wantonness which lies embedded in returning and only in returning; ah, my little nightmate, you too will understand this one day, you will wait on the thresholding shore, on the shore of your interrealm, on the shore of farewell and dusk, and your ship too will be ready for flight, for that proud flight which is called awakening, and from which there is no return. Dream, oh dream! As long as we are at our versing we do not go away, as long as we remain steadfast in the interrealm of our night-day we present one another with every

69

dream-hope, with all longed-for communion, with every hope of love, and therefore, my little brother, for the sake of that hope, for the sake of that yearning, never again depart from me. I have no wish to know your name, your shadow-casting name, I will not summon you, neither for the setting-out nor for the return, but uncallable and uncalled, abide with me so that love may abide in the covenant of its fulfillment, abide with me in the dusk, abide with me on the shore of the stream which we will behold without entrusting ourselves to it, far from its source, far from its estuary, shielded from the dim fusion of inception, shielded from the final, shadowless identification with Apollo's brightness; oh, abide with me, sheltering and sheltered, as I shall bide with you forevermore; once again, love: do you hear me? do you hear what I am asking? is my plea still able to hear your answer, while answering itself, fate-delivered, divested of sorrow?

Or had it become too late?

The night lay without motion, formfast in its near and far apparence, locked here into this room, locked into ever-widening spaces, extending from the vicinity of the tangible to always further frontiers, away over mountains and seas, extended in a constant outflow even unto the unreachable dream-caverns, and this flood, springing from the heart, breaking at the periphery of the dream-caverns and flowing back from there into the heart, received the yearning into itself wave upon wave, dissolving even the yearning for yearning, bringing to a standstill the shrouded swaying of the maternal star-cradle where it began, and encircled by flashes of the dark lightnings below, of the bright ones above, it parted into light and dark-ness, into murk and glare; two-toned the cloud, twofold the source, thunder-close, soundless, spaceless, timeless—oh, riven cave of the inner and outer life, oh, mighty on-going earth!—, thus the night yawned wide, being's slumber was snapped, dusk and poetry had been silently rinsed away, their realm rinsed away, the echo-wall of dreams shattered, and mocked by the silent voices of memory, guilt-laden and hopeless, inundated by the flood, washed away on the flood, life's over-great travail sank to sheer nothingness. It had become too late, there was nothing left but flight, the ship lay ready, the anchor was being lifted; it was too late.

Yet he waited, waited for the night to make its presence known, to croon him something final and comforting, once again with its meandering to awake his yearning. It could scarcely be called hope, rather a hoping for hope, scarcely any longer flight from timelessness, rather a flight from the flight. There was no more time, no more yearning, no more hope either for living or dying; there was no more night. There was scarcely any more waiting, at the most some impatience for the awaited impatience. He held his hands tightly clasped, the thumb of the left one touching the stone of his ring, thus he sat there, feeling the warmth of the boy's shoulder which was shoved within leaning-distance yet not touching his knee, and he had a great longing to loosen his cramped fingers from their increasing spasm so that with imperceptible delicacy he might stroke the night-dark, tousled, childish hair on which he looked down, so that he might let the duskily sprouting night-human in the dark-soft crackling bloom glide between his fingers—night-yearning for yearning; however he made no move, but at length, although it cost him dear to break the tension of expectancy, he said: "It is too late." Slowly, the boy lifted up his countenance full of understanding and questioning as if something had been read to him the sequel of which must follow, and in heed to this questioning, his own face gently approaching that of the boy, he repeated very softly: "It is too late." Was there still some expectation? was he disappointed that the night no longer stirred and only the boy's eyes, gray, childish, steadfast, remained fixed upon him, they too questioning. The impatience which he had wished for suddenly appeared: "Yes, it is late . . . go to the festival." Of a sudden he felt excessively old, and the immediate and earthly manifested itself in the need for sleep and drowsiness, in the need, slumber-wrapt and unconscious, to forget that No-more;

it manifested itself with the slackening of the lower jaw and furthermore with so violent a compulsion to cough that the wish to remain alone and unobserved became imperative: "Go . . . go . . . to the feast," he brought out hoarsely, while his upturned palm only by a gesture and from a growing distance pushed the reluctantly departing boy in short shoves toward the door. "Go . . . go," the words rattled in him again, his breath already failing, and when he was actually alone it seemed as if black lightning struck into his breast from which the coughing broke out mixed with night-blood, robbing him of consciousness; sprawling, shaken and benumbed, cleaving and bursting, a strangling convulsion on the edge of the abyss, and that he had not been hurled into it this time, that it had passed him by once more, that he could hear again the drizzling of the fountain, the crackling of the candles appeared to him afterwards like a miracle. With no little trouble he had dragged himself from the armchair over to the bed, had let himself fall into it, and remained lying there motionless.

Again he held his hands clasped tightly, again he felt the stone of the ring, felt the winged figure of the genius that was engraved into the polished carnelian, and he waited, hearkening whether it would turn to life or to death. Then slowly it was better, he came again, even though still slowly, with much pain and exertion, to breathing, to peace, to silence.

FIRE—THE DESCENT

HE LAY AND LISTENED. FROM TIME TO TIME, ALTHOUGH at greater intervals and with no new showing of blood, the seizure came on again and at first he had even thought he should call the slave from the next room to summon the doctor; but calling cost effort, and to be disturbed by the physician would have been unbearable: he wanted to be alone—, nothing was more pressing than to remain by oneself, again and again to gather all existence within one so that one would be able to listen; this was all-important. He rolled on his side, his legs drawn up a little, his head resting on the pillow, the hip pressed into the mattress, the knees disposed one above the other like two beings alien to him, and very far off in the distance reposed the ankles and the heels as well. How often, oh, how often in the past had he been intent on the phenomenon of lying down! Yes, it was absolutely shameful that he could not rid himself of this childish habit! He recalled distinctly the very night when he—an eight year old—had become conscious that there was something noteworthy in the mere act of reclining; it was in Cremona, the time was winter; he lay in his room, the door which led to the peristyle was cracked, closed badly, and moved a little in an eerie manner; outside the wind rustled over the flower-beds, straw-covered for winter, and from somewhere, possibly from the swinging lantern under the doorway, the faint reflection of a light in pendular rhythm came gliding into the chamber like the last reverberation of an eternal tide, like the last reverberation of eternally changing eras, like the last reflection of an infinitely

75

distant eye, so lost, so broken, so threatening in its remoteness, so fraught with distance that it was a challenge to question oneself as to the reality or unreality of one's own existence—, and just as then, though intensified and made more familiar by the subsequent, sedulous, nightly repetition, even today he felt every single point of support by which his couch carried him, and just as then they were wave-crests over which his ship skimmed, dipping lightly into them, while wave-hollows of unfathomable depth appeared between them. Certainly this was not the main concern, and if now he had wished to be alone it had not been in order to continue childish observations which he could have done without more ado while still retaining the little night-mate; no, it was for something more essential, for something more conclusive, for something the reality of which must be very great, so great that it must surpass even poetry and its interrealm, it was for something that had to be more real than dusk or night, surpassing them by its heightened reality even in earthiness, it was for something that made it worth while to gather all existence within oneself, and it was only to be wondered at that childishness and its irrelevance did not permit itself to be pushed further back, that it was still present with its succession of images just as of yore, that in the chain of memory into which we are forged the first links should be the strongest, as if they, just they, were the most real reality. It seemed almost impossible, nay more, it seemed almost inadmissible that our last-attained, our most real reality could limit itself thus to becoming a mere recollective image! Nevertheless human life was thus image-graced and image-cursed; it could comprehend itself only through images, the images were not to be banished, they had been with us since the herd-beginning, they were anterior to and mightier than our thinking, they were timeless, containing past and future, they were a twofold dream-memory and they were more powerful than we: an image to himself was he who lay there, and steering toward the most real reality, borne on invisible waves, dipping into them, the image of the ship was his own image emerging from darkness, heading toward darkness sinking into darkness, he himself was the boundless ship that at the same time was boundlessness; and he himself was the flight that was aiming toward this boundlessness; he was the fleeing ship, he himself the goal, he himself was boundlessness too vast to be seen, unimaginable, an endless corporeal landscape, the landscape of his body, a mighty, outspread, infernal image of night, so that deprived of the unity of human life, deprived of the unity of human yearning, he no longer believed himself capable of self-mastery, conscious as he was of the separated regions and provinces over which the essential ego had been compelled to distribute itself, conscious of a demonic possession that had assumed direction in his stead, isolated into districts in all their diversity; ah there were the disrupted, ploughed-up districts of the hurting lung, there were those of the distressing fever that wavered up to the skin from unknown, red-glowing depths and there were the districts of the bowel abysses, just as there were the more terrifying ones of sex, one like the other filled with serpents, intergrown with serpents, there were the districts of the limbs with their unbridled innate life, not last there were those of the fingers and all these districts of the demons, some of them settled near him, others at a greater distance, some of them more friendly, others hostile among themselves as well as toward him—nearest to him, belonging most intimately to him were still the senses, the eyes and ears and their districts—, all these domains of the physical and extra-physical, enveloping the hard and earthly reality of the skeleton, they were known to him in their complete strangeness, in their disintegrated fragility, in their remoteness, in their animosity, in their incomprehensible infinity, sensual and supra-sensual, for all together, and he along with them as by their mutual knowledge, were imbedded in that great flood that extended over everything human, everything oceanic, in that homing surge and the heavy swing of its ebb and flow which beats so constantly on the coast of the heart and keeps it throbbing so continuously, image of reality and reality of image in one, so wave-deep that the most

disparate things are swept together within it, not quite unified
but still united for future rebirth; oh surf on the shore of cognition, its ever-mounting tide brimming with the seeds of all
comfort, all hope, oh, night-laden, seed-laden, space-laden flood
of spring; and filled with the empowering vision of his real
self, he knew that the demoniac could be overcome through
the assurance of reality, the image of which lies in the province
of the indescribable yet nonetheless contains the unity of the
world. For the images were taut with reality, since reality was
always to be symbolized only by reality—, image upon image,
reality upon reality, not one of them actually real as long as
it stood alone, yet each a single symbol of an inviolate, ultimate
truth which was the sum of their totality. And if in the many
years past he had followed with increasing avidity and curiosity
the decay and fragility which he felt at work upon his body,
if for the sake of this amazing and amazed curiosity he had
gladly taken on the discomfort of illness and pain, yes, if he had
—and whatever a person did became more or less distinctly
symbolic—continuously borne within him the desire, the seldom
conscious but always impatient desire, for his bodily unity,
which he constantly perceived to be but a seeming unity, to be
finally dissolved, the quicker the better, so that the extraordinary might follow, so that dissolution might come to be
redemption, might come to be a new unity, a consummation,
and if this desire had accompanied and pursued him from
his earliest youth, at least since that night in Cremona, possibly
even since his childhood in Andes, either as a little childish
game of anxiety or as an oppressive, memory-quelling fear,
one as unrecallable now as the other, yet the question as to
the meaning of such occurrences had never left him, it had
been inherent in all of his nightly pre-listening, pre-searching,
pre-sensing, and just as formerly he had lain upon his bed, a
child in Andes, a boy in Cremona, knee pressed on knee, his
spirit sunk into his pre-dreaming, his spirit like his body sunk
into the ship of his being that extended over oceans and over
the broad planes of earth, himself a mountain, a field, the

earth, the ship, himself the ocean, listening into the night inside and outside, perhaps having always had the premonition that his hearkening was directed toward the achieving of that knowledge for which his whole life must be lived through, so now in the same fashion it happened again, it happened here and now, it happened today; and that which had once happened, having constantly become clearer and clearer to him, continued to happen again and again, was happening now; he did that which he had done his whole life long, but now he knew what it was, he knew the answer: he was listening to dying.

Could it be anything else? Man stands erect, he alone, yet he lays him down, stretched out quietly for sleep, for love, for death—, and it is also this threefold nature of his lying down that distinguishes him from all other creatures. Destined to grow upright as long as man stands erect, the human soul reaches out from the dark abyss where her roots are entwined in the humus of existence and strives upward even unto the sun-drenched dome of the stars, bearing upward her cloudy sources from the regions of Poseidon and Vulcan, bringing downward the clarity of her Apollonian goal, and the nearer she comes in this upward growth to being light-drenched form, the more shapely she becomes in her shadowing, branching out and unfolding like a tree, the more is she enabled to unify the darkness and the light in the shadowy leaves of her branches; but when she has stretched out, abandoned to sleep, to love, to death, when she herself has become an outstretched landscape, then her task is no longer the merging of opposites, for in sleeping, loving, dying, the soul is no longer either good or evil, she has become only an unbroken endless hearkening: spread out to infinity, infinitely held in the orbit of time, infinite in her repose, she is absolved from growth, and without growth, along with the landscape which is herself, she persists as the unchanged and unchangeable Saturnian realm throughout the whole of time, persisting from the golden age to the age of brass, aye, even beyond it to the return of the golden age, and by virtue of her nestling into the landscape, by virtue of her imprisonment in the realm of earth and earth's meadows, on the surface of which the spheres of heavenly light and earthly darkness part one from the other, she is like them in being the border, separating and binding the regions above and below, belonging like Janus to both, to those of the wavering stars as well as to those of the weighty stones, to the etheric regions as well as to the fires of the underworld, januslike the double aspects of infinity, januslike the double aspects of the soul, as in her twilight she lies quietly outstretched to infinity so that her hearkening prescience may partake of the significance of both zones without uniting them; however, the circumstance as such has no meaning for her, is not worthy of pre-hearkening or prescience for she feels it neither as growth nor as fading nor as deterioration, neither as a blessing nor a burden, but more as a constant return of the all-encompassing Saturnian era in which the landscape of the soul and the earth are stretched out infinitely, inseparable in their respirations, inseparable in their seasons of sowing and blossoming, in their harvest or growth, in their dying and resurrection, in their boundless seasons, interwoven with the eternal return, surrounded by the circle of eternal sameness and consequently stretched out quietly for sleep, for love, for death—, a hearkening of the landscape and the soul, the Saturnian hearkening to deathless dying, golden and brazen together.

He was listening to dying; it could not be anything else. The knowledge of this had come over him without any shock, at most with the peculiar clarity which usually accompanies a mounting fever. And now, lying and listening in the darkness, he understood his life, and he understood how much of it had been a constant hearkening to the unfolding of death, life unfolded, consciousness unfolded, unfolded the seed of death which was implanted in every life from the beginning and determined it, giving it a twofold, threefold significance, each one developed from the other and unfolding through it, each the image of the other and its reality—was not this the dream-force of all images, particularly of those which gave direction to every life? was not something of the same sort hidden in the cave-images of the universal night which, miraculous and fear-inspiring with timelessness, heavy with stars and presaging eternity, domed death over all existence? What once in boyhood had been a childish and childlike conception of death, the conception of a grave into which the body would be lowered, had unfolded to the great image of the cave, and the erection of the mausoleum beside the Bay of Naples, there near the Posilipian grotto, was more than a mere repetition and visualization of the old childish concept; nay, the whole dome of death was symbolically expressed by this building, perhaps still a little childish when reduced to such earthly dimensions, nevertheless the symbol of the mighty all-embracing domain of death in which he, ever aware of the goal and yet seeking it, he a path-seeker in the dome of death, had day-dreamed a whole life away. For the sake of the all-embracing might of this goal he had long, yes too long, searched for his own vocation; for the sake of this always known yet never known goal, dissatisfied with every profession, he had prematurely broken away from each one, unable to find peace in any, either in the calling of a medical man, a mathematician, astrologer, philosophical scholar or teacher: the demanding but unrealized vision of knowledge, the grave recognizable image of death had stood perpetually before his eyes, and no vocation measured up to that, as none exists that is not exclusively subserviated to the knowledge of life, none with the exception of that one to which he had finally been driven and which is called poetry, the strangest of all human occupations, the only one dedicated to the knowledge of death. Only he who dwelt in the interrealm of farewell—oh, it lay behind him and there was no returning,—only he who tarried in the dusk on the banks of the stream, far from its source, far from its estuary, was in durance to death, serving death like the priest by virtue of his office which stood above any personal vocation, mediating between the above and the below, pledged to the service of death and through this likewise banished to the interrealm of farewell; yes, he had always deemed as priestly the task of the singer, perhaps because of the strange consecration to death inherent in the enraptured fervor of every work of art; until now he had seldom dared to admit it to himself, he had repudiated it, just as in his first poems he had not dared to approach death, but rather had been vigilant to ward off that which threatened and was always at hand by the lovely-loving power of an ardent love for life, more and more futile in his resistance since the poetic power of death had proven itself the stronger, acquiring step by step the privileges of domicile which, in the Aeneid, assumed full sovereign rights, following the will of the gods: the clattering, bloody, admonishing, unchanging sovereignty of fate, the all-conquering sovereignty of death, which by this token also conquers itself and annuls itself. For all simultaneousness was sunk in death, all simultaneity in life and in poetry was forever obliterated in death's complete annulment, and death was filled by day and night, they penetrating each other and becoming the bi-colored cloud of dusk; oh, death was filled by all the diversities that had proceeded from unity so that finally through death these might achieve to unity, death was filled by the initial herd-wisdom of the beginning and by the isolating knowledge of the end—it was comprehension in a single moment of existence, in the very moment which was already that of non-existence; for death was involved in an unending reciprocity with the stream of life and the stream of life flowed incessantly into death, welcomed by death, turned back to the source, the lapse of time changed to the unity of remembrance, to the memory of worlds upon worlds, to the memory of the god: only he who accepted death was able to complete the orbit of mortality, only the eye of him who sought the eye of death would not fail when it gazed into nothingness, only he who hearkened to death had no need of flight, he might remain, because memory had become the well of simultaneousness, and he alone who plunged into memory could hear the harp-tone of that moment in which the terrestrial should open into the immense unknown, opened to rebirth, and to the resurrection of everlasting memory—, landscape of childhood, landscape of life, landscape of death, they 'were one in their indivisible simultaneousness, previsioning the landscape of the gods, the country of the very beginning and the very end, eternally joined by the span of the seven-colored, dewy-breathed bow, oh, the pastures of the fathers. Much took place for the sake of memory, divulging itself at last as a listening to death; and much that was taken for death was only memory, anxious yearning memory that had need to be guarded with care that it might never become lost. It had been so and not otherwise in the case of the tomb near the grotto of Posilipo, caressed by sea breezes, played upon by springlike shadows, entwined in green leaves, this almost playfully built homestead of death full of childhood memories, which he had incorporated into a gardenlike serenity without having been conscious of doing so, in consequence of which everything that had been taken in by the child's eyes at the paternal house in Andes was to be found here on a smaller scale and only slightly altered; for example, the entrance drive to the gate of the courtyard was now the main path through the garden, equipped with the same double curve, bordered on the left by the same laurel bushes, leading on the right to the mound of his childhood games, even though this one was crowned by only a single cypress instead of the ancient olive-groves, while to the rear of the edifice, in great tranquility here as there, the elm trees, shrouded in a twittering of birds, arose today even as in times past, a shelter of solitude and peace; and just as in boyhood it had been possible to pass his hand over the wattled hedge, now it was possible with equal definiteness to dream back, just as definite and valid for all times as it had been to dream forward, to dream toward death and dying, the goal of all dreamy hearken-ing since the days of childhood, the goal and source of his memory, clear, unloseable, knowledge-seeking, although the image of the tomb was only a small, an extremely small frag-ment of memory set in the stream of the past, a quite palpable island, emerging almost by chance in its slight palpability, vanishing, and therefore deserving oblivion compared to the roaring width of the flood which poured itself into his constant hearkening; constantly the flood came toward him, memory-wide, wave-wide, constantly and softly and grandly it advanced, wave after wave of the once-beheld, gleaming in the harp-tone of enduring ineffability—oh, lovely imprisonment of youth, enfolded and ready for freedom—, and it was as if all brooks and ponds of yore poured themselves into this stream of memory, drizzling between the fragrant willows, drizzling between banks verdant with trembling reeds, lovely images without end, themselves a cluster picked by the hands of a child, a cluster of lilies, gilly-flowers, poppies, narcissus and buttercups, the image of childhood in a landscape revealed by wandering and wandering, by song after song, the image of the paternal pastures, the image he had been forced to seek wherever he had been driven, the image of the one and unforgettable land-scape of his life, ineffable-inexpressible image, despite that it was so very luminous, so sharp of contour, sun-drenched, transparent, despite this unfailing clarity with which it had accompanied him, so inexpressible that however often he had depicted it it only resounded in the unutterable, always only there where language is insufficient, where it strikes beyond its own earthly-mortal boundaries and penetrates into the unutterable, abandoning an expression through words and—only singing itself into the structure of the verses—opening up between the very words a swooning, breathless, momentary abyss so that life could be comprehended and death be apprehended in these silent depths, which have become silent to disclose the completeness of the whole, the simultaneous stream of creation in which the eternal rests: oh, goal of poetry, oh, these moments in which speech sublimated itself beyond all description and all communication, oh, these moments in which it plunged into simultaneousness so that it could not be determined whether memory was gushing from speech or speech from memory, these were the moments in which the landscape of childhood had begun to blossom, leaving itself behind, growing beyond itself and every memory, beyond every beginning and every end, transmuted to a simple, rustic, shepherd's order in some golden age, transmuted to the scene of the Latin emergence, transmuted to the reality of the on-marching, commanding and serving gods, not the primordial beginning, surely not the original order, surely not the initial reality but still a symbol of it, not, to be sure, to the voice which was expected to call out from the furthest unknown, out of the inexpressible and extraordinary, out of the unchangeably and utterly divine, but still a token of it, but surely the echo-like symbol of its being and almost an affirmation of it—, the symbol that was reality, reality that would become the symbol in the face of death. These were the moments of resounding deathlessness, the moments of essential life emerged from its twilight, and it was in these moments that the true form of death revealed itself most clearly: rare moments of grace, rare moments of perfect freedom, unknown to most, striven for by many, achieved by few—, but among those who were permitted to retain such moments, to grasp the fugitive evanescence of death's shape, he who succeeded in giving shape to death by incessant listening and searching would find together with its genuine form his own real shape as well, he was shaping his own death and with it his own shape, and he was immune from the reversion into the humus of shapelessness. Seven-colored and divinely mild the rainbow of childhood arched for him over all his existence, daily seen anew, the shared creation of man and the gods, the creation proceeding from the strength of the word with the knowledge of death: had not this been the hope for which he had been obliged to bear the agony of a hunted life devoid of every peaceful joy? He looked back on this life of abnegation, of an actually still continuing renunciation, on this life that had been without resistance to death though full of resistance to participation and love, he looked back on this life of farewell that lay back of him in the dusk of rivers, in the dusk of poetry, and today he knew more clearly than ever before that he had taken on all this for the sake of that very hope; perhaps he was not to be mocked and execrated because life's great travail had as yet not led to the fulfillment of hope, because the task he had wanted to discharge had been over-great for his weak forces, because the medium of the poet's art was perhaps not intended for this after all, however he also realized that this was not the case, that the justification of a task or the lack of its justification was not to be reckoned by its earthly accomplishment, that it was negligible whether his own strength sufficed or not, whether any other man with greater strength were to be born or whether a better solution than the one put forth by poetry were to be found, all this was irrelevant, for the choice had not been his: certainly day after day and countless times during every day he had decided and acted in accord with his free choice, or at least he had thought that the choice was free, but the great line of his life was not of his own choosing nor in accord with his free will, it had been a compulsion, a compulsion on a level with the redemption and the evil of existence, a fate-enjoined yet fate-surpassing compulsion, commanding him to search for his own shape in that of death and thus to win the freedom of his soul; for freedom is a compulsion of the soul whose redemption or damnation is always at stake, and he had heeded the injunction, obedient to the task of his fate.

He shifted upward a little on the pillows to ease his aching chest, very cautiously so that the outstretched landscape of himself which seemed to guarantee him clarity might not fall into disorder and confusion as was the case with those who stand erect; then he felt about him for the manuscript-chest and let his hand finger almost tenderly the surface of its rawhide cover; hot and exciting the feeling of work, the compelling feeling of the discoverer, the great wanderer-sense of creation awoke in him, and were it not that simultaneously there sprang up in him the great fear of the wanderer, the terrible fear of the lost wayfarer who mistakes his path in the impenetrability of night, the same profound fear which accompanies all creation, the hotly happy surge in his breast would have quelled the death-anticipation of the admonishing pains there, would have relieved the lack of breath, would have made him forgetful alike of fever's heat or chill, and nothing would have prevented him from immediately sitting down to work, prepared to begin anew, mindful of the task he had to fulfill to the drawing of his last breath, the task which could bring him fulfillment only with his last breath. No, nothing would have restrained him from work, nothing would have been allowed to restrain him, and yet everything did so, and did it so thoroughly that the finishing of the Aeneid had been at a standstill for months past and nothing remained but flight after flight. And neither the disease nor the pains, long since familiar, long since weathered or outwitted, were to be blamed for that, but rather the inescapable, inexplicable unrest, this alarming sense of being lost with no way out, this sharply-felt foreboding of an ever-threatening, ever-present engulfing calamity, its essence indiscernible, its source undiscoverable, especially as one was ignorant of whether the threat lurked within or without; lying quietly and breathing cautiously he listened into the darkness: the tapers on the candelabrum expired one after the other, only the small, patient light of the oil-lamp next to the couch survived, often swaying to and fro on the faintly ringing chain at the merest breath of a breeze, mirrored on the wall in a butterfly-soft, cobwebby, undulating shadow, and while outside the tumult of the street gradually subsided and the indeterminable noise dissolved into every sort of neighing, grunting, squawking, the drone of the festival receding into a clearer or deeper hum which was dispersed through the kaleidoscopic noise-picture, the even tread of the withdrawing troops became audible as a sort of ground bass, indicating that a section of the guard was retiring to quarters; then it became still, but soon the stillness was animated by a curious vibrancy, curious because the stillness itself was vibrant, as suddenly from afar, from every side—did it come from the fields just outside the city, or from those in Andes?—the chirping of crickets became audible, the myriadfold sound of those myriad creatures, humming endlessly in the hush that was spread over the infinite. Quietly and gradually the ruddy reflection from the illumination of the street-festival paled also, the ceiling of the room grew black except for the bright spot directly above the lamp, which, as it shifted softly, seemed the light's painting of a pendulum, and the stars before the window stood in blackness. What was this unrest, the source of which he was seeking? why was there unrest now when the ebb of the low-despairing clamor should have betokened a general solace for him? No, the evil had remained, and now he perceived it, he was bound to perceive it: it was the evil of man's imprisoned soul, the soul for which every liberation turns into a new imprisonment, again and again.

He stared toward the window, the night circled in its immense space, the orb turned by Atlas resting on the giant's shoulders, strewn with sparkling constellations, the enormous cavern of night from which there was no release; he listened to the rustlings of night, and to him in his utter wakefulness, to him whom fever had brought so low that he burned and froze beneath his covers, there came in sharpened coexistence the pictures, the odors, the sounds, of the present together with those of every lived or livable moment in the twofold remembering toward past and future, so swollen by inevitable, inexplicable weirdness, so uncapturably fugitive, so hidden in mystery despite all their nakedness that he, whipped on and halting at once, was thrust back into the chaotic maze of separate voices—, the shapelessness he had thought to outrun took hold on him again, not as the indiscriminateness of the herd-beginning, but directly, indeed almost palpably, as the chaos of severance, and as a dissolution which by no hearkening or grasping could ever be conformed to unity; the demonic chaos of all separated voices, all separated perceptions, all isolated things, regardless of whether they belonged to the present, the past, or the future, this chaos now assailed him, he was given over to it, yes, this is what it had been since the roaring, indiscriminate noise of the streets had begun to change to a maze of separate voices. This was what it was. Oh, everyone was surrounded by a maze of voices, everyone wandered round in the maze his whole life long, wandering and wandering, yet bound to the spot in the dense forest of voices, entangled in the night-growth, tangled in among the forest roots, which took hold beyond all time and space, oh, everyone was threatened by the anarchic voices and their grasping arms, by voice-twigs and voice-branches which, twining about each other, entwined him, which in branching out from each other shot up erect and crooked into one another again, demonic in their independence, demonic in their separateness, voices of the second, voices of the year, voices of the aeon, which had spread out into a lattice-work of the world, criss-crossed, incomprehensible and impenetrable in their roaring muteness, humid with the groans of pain and harsh with the joyous savagery of a whole world. Oh, no one escaped the primordial roar, no one was spared it, for each one, whether he knew it or not, was nothing other than one of the voices, belonging to them with their insoluble, indivisible, impenetrable threat—, how could anyone sustain hope! the lost one was past saving, imprisoned in the maze, in which no breach or clearing could be discerned, and had he wished to stretch his hope beyond this, to send it over and beyond—there into the inextensible eternity where the unity, the order, the omniscience of the voice-totality was to be divined, to the promise of their great harmony, voice-locked, voice-releasing, to the last reverberating harmonic echo from the furthest spaces of universal unity, universal order, universal perception, to the last echo-solution of the universal task—such hope of a mortal, insolent and abhorrent to the gods, would have burst against the walls of deafness, dying away in the voice-maze, in the maze of perception, in the mazes of time, dying away to an expiring breath; for the voice-source of time's inception was unreachable, it lay beneath the depths of all roots, lying beneath all voices, beneath all muteness, impassable the root-springs of the forests, the root-springs in which the starry map of unity of order and of speech was stored, unbeholdable that symbol of all symbols, for infinite and more than infinite was the variety of their outspreading

courses in the unsurpassable immensity of space, infinite was
the number of identities, infinite the number of paths and their
intersectings and also the multi-compartments of speech and
memory as well as the profusion of their trends, and the infinitude of their private abysses were only very weak, very sparse
reflections woven into the earthly meagerness of that which was
not to be comprehended by thinking, of that which stored in its
breath all starry spaces and would itself be preserved in even
the tiniest point of the spheres, breathing itself in and out,
streaming in and out, the reflection of a symbolization sheerly
unutterable, sheerly unrememberable, sheerly unpredictable, the
salvation of knowledge that by its effulgence outreached every
lapse of time and transformed each split-second to timelessness:
crossroad of all paths, compassed by no one, the immovable,
transported journey's end! even the first, the very first step that
would be taken in any direction of the road-mazes, were it ever
so fleet, would require a lifetime and more than a lifetime for
its consummation, it would require an endless life to retain a
single scanty moment of recollection, an endless life to gaze
but for a second into the profundities that language holds in
its depths! by giving ear unto these depths he had hoped to be
permitted to listen to death, he had hoped to lay hold on a knowledge, even if it were only the divining gleam of an intuition
of that perception-boundary which already was beyond earthly
understanding, but even this hope had proved presumptuous in
the face of the incomprehensibility that pulsed up from the echo-
walls of the abyss, a glint that was scarcely more than a glimmer, now scarcely more than the memory of a glimmer,
scarcely more than the echo of a memory, a fleeting breath so
invisible that not even music would have been able to grasp it,
to say nothing of being able to express this invisibility as a
foretaste of impalpable infinity; no, nothing terrestrial was able
to sunder the impenetrable thicket, no, no earthly means was
sufficient to solve the eternal task, to disclose and announce the
law, striking out toward that knowledge beyond knowledge, no,
this was reserved for supernatural powers and transcendental

means, a potency of expression that left all earthly expression far behind it, a language which would have to stand outside the maze of voices, beyond all earthly linguistics, a speech which would be more than music, a speech which would help the eyes to perceive, heartbreakingly and quick as a heart-beat, the unity of all existence, verily it must be a language still unfound and glowing in the supernal that could undertake this task, and the effort to approach such a language with paltry verses was rash, a fruitless effort and a blasphemous presumption! ah, it had been granted to him to perceive the eternal task, the task of the soul's salvation, it had been granted him to set-to with a spade, and he had not noticed that he had lavished his whole life on it, wasted his life, frittered away the years, squandered time, not just because he had failed and had shown himself inadequate, inadequate to lay bare even a single rootlet, but because the mere decision to attempt the spade-work would exhaust an endless life, all the more since death overtook every soul and was overtaken by nothing, not even by the aid of an overheard language or a pre-heard memory; all-conquering was death, all-conquering the maze that was not to be cleared by anything, and mercilessly confined the lost one, helpless the lost one, himself but a helpless voice in the thicket of separateness. How then could anyone still sustain hope? did not the human event, however and wherever it happened, unhesitatingly disclose itself as a consequence of creaturely fear, from the twilight prison of which one could neither break out nor escape, as it was the anguish of the creature lost in a maze? He became more deeply aware of this anguish, he understood better than ever the unsilenced wish of the lost soul for the death-sublimating annulment of time, he understood better than ever the unquenchable hope of the creaturely masses, he understood what they were aiming at, they down below there, voices and more voices they also, with their wildly despairing clamor, he understood them, when, inviolable and unteachable, clinging to their individual and collective ardor, they screamed out of themselves and to themselves that somewhere in the thicket there must exist an excellent one, a mighty one, an extraordinary voice, the voice of a leader to whom they need only attach themselves so that in his reflected glory, in the reflection of the jubilation, the intoxication, the power of the imperial divinity they might with a gasping, wild, bullish, thundering assault still be able to clear an earthly path for themselves out of the entanglement of their existence, and, aware of this, he saw, he understood, he knew better than ever before, that his own aspirations were different only in form and presumptuousness from those of the frenzied herd's honest though brutal will-to-violation, not however in their objective, meaning, or content; that he had only disguised the simple, creaturely fear that clutched him with the selfsame force, falsified it in a yearning for the omniscient unity of law, falsified it in a vain and therefore doubly sanctimonious listening and fore-listening, that he had simply pushed off to the end of his earthly life the hope for a path-finding, extraordinary, guiding voice, that this most earthly mob-hope was his also, that he had made himself believe it would resound one day from the beyond and would then be supernatural, phantom of his presumption, which was given over to the terrestrial and forfeited to the vanity of all things earthly; oh, now he realized better than before the futility of their herdlike impulse to escape, the futility of their dogging fear, of their attempt at flight, which broke into an uproar with hope and lapsed into silence with disappointment and compelled them to run off again and again into the stark, unshadowed nothingness, lost in time, fixed in time, time unabolished; and he realized that the same lot was assigned to him, quite as inevitably, quite as inescapably,—the fall into the nothingness which does not abolish death, but which in itself is that very death. Oh, erratic and squandered his life, for from the outset the path he had taken had led nowhere, impeded by awareness of its wrong direction, impeded by knowing itself astray, erring and groping in the maze from the outset, a life of false renunciation and false farewell, impeded by the fear of the inevitable disappointment which, even as hope, had been pushed to the limit of life and earthly experience. Had this limit now been reached, so that nothing was left but disappointment? so that nothing was left but icy horror, this crippling and breathtaking horror of death which was perhaps unacknowledged but positive, and possibly even stronger than the dread of disappointment? nothing was left but the numbness which was laid on him like a mysterious penalty determined by his stars, punishing a predestined and unrequitable sin, a sin he had not committed and which was presumptuousness even without being committed, an eternally uncommitted sin standing eternally at his back, forever opposing the eternal task of understanding, the penalty for which was constantly imposed on him so that he might not perceive his task and its fulfillment, an invisible chastisement in a still more invisible numbness, the sin of not awakening and its punishment, time-benumbing, speech-benumbing, memory-benumbing, the drowsy listening benumbed into the void on the dreary field of death; and his body, pining away and aged with weariness, lay quite forlorn in this numbness, extending saturnically and drowsily over the zones of himself which became more and more transparent, more and more evanescent, forsaken even by the demons, continuing to be still more desolate, still more immobile, as if they were blank windows opening upon no view: nothing remained but this, nothing else was even to be remembered, for everything which had once signified life's advantages had failed; the once-pledged, once-timeless memory had become feeble, aging even quicker than he had, lost to him and submerged into what had been barely created, barely lived; and the translucent and glittering pictures of his life's landscape, once so dazzling, had grown dim, had withered and died away; his verses, which he had twined about them had dried up and fallen away, all this had blown away like faded leaves, no longer remembered but merely known about, season-wafted, season-weary, a forgotten rustling; oh, how much there had been; the far past, the near past had existed in thousandfold diversity, in millionfold identities, yet it had never caught up to him, it had never been allowed to become a whole, the circle of memory was not closed, the past would never catch up with him, it was, even in the living, doomed to be unlived and to remain undone, just as the performance of his endless task had been consigned to the unfinished, halted at the very first step, even as this first step, notwithstanding it had already lasted a whole lifetime, remained still untaken as at the very outset, held in a ghastly unshakable paralysis for which there was neither advance nor retreat, consequently no second step could follow the first untaken one, because the distance between each single living second had grown to an immense, empty space which was not to be bridged; and from this point on nothing whatsoever followed, either quickly or slowly, because nothing was able to continue, the done and the undone, the imagined and the unimagined, the uttered and the unuttered, the written and the unwritten, all unable to continue and—, oh ye gods, the Aeneid!—must this also remain unfinished, unable to be continued, unable to be completed like his whole life! Had this actually been determined by the stars? was this actually to be the fate of the poem?! the fate of the Aeneid, his own fate in its unfulfillment! Was this conceivable, oh was this conceivable?! The heavy portal of fear had sprung open and behind it the cavern of horror reared up, mighty and all-encompassing. Something unknown, fearful, ghastly, assailing him simultaneously from within and without, ripped him up; a sudden, malignant outbreak, superlatively painful, tore him aloft with all the devastating, convulsive, stiflingly desperate force inherent in the first lightning-and-thunderclap of a rising storm; thus chokingly it drove into him, death-dealing, death-threatening, yet the seconds following hard upon each other enriched in flashes the empty space between them with that inconceivable thing called life, and it almost seemed to him as if hope blinked up once again in those flashes while, with the fleetness of a breath or a glance, he was being torn aloft in the clutch of the iron hand; it seemed to him that all this was happening so that the neglected, the lost, the unfinished might still be retrieved if only in this instant of renewed second-wind; overcome as he was by pain, by fear, by torpor, he knew not whether it was hope or no-hope, but he did know that every second of new-lived life was needful and momentous, he knew he had been hounded for the sake of this up-flickering of life, whether it lasted a short or a long time, chased up and away from the couch of torpor; he knew he had to escape the breath-lack of the narrow-walled and shut-in room, that once more he must send his glance outward, turned away from himself, turned away from the zones of his self, turned away from the dreary field of death, that just once more, for a single time, perhaps for the last time, he must come to comprehend the vastness of life, he must, oh he must again behold the stars; and starkly lifted up from the bed, held in the clutching fist that gripped into his whole body and yet grasped him from without, he moved himself with stiff-jointed legs, like a marionette convoyed on wires, uncertainly as though on stilts, back to the window against the frame of which he leaned exhausted, a little bent over because of his weakness but despite this held upright so that, as with elbows drawn back he satisfied his hunger for air with deep regular breaths, his being might disclose itself anew, participating in the breath-stream of the yearned-back spheres.

I T WAS the necessity for air, the animal necessity to breathe that had driven him to the window, but at the same time it was a necessity not of the body, a longing for the visible, for the visible world, for what could be breathed in from the assurance of the visible universe. Numbed and stifling he stood at the window, held by the mighty and embracing hand, and he knew not how long he stood there; it may have been only a few seconds or as many minutes, and the awareness of time flowed back into him incompletely and in snatches, long passages of time being obliterated by the fear and pain of strangling; the world rebuilt itself, knowledge came to be knowledge only in fragments, and in the same way he became attentive to what had occurred, realizing bit by bit that it had occurred not merely for the sake of the Aeneid, but for something he had yet to find.

Now the world lay still before him, after all the previously endured pandemonium amazingly still, and it appeared to be late in the night, apparently past its middle; the stars glowed greatly in their great courses, comforting and strong and quietly a-shimmer with reassuring recognition although disquietingly overcast despite the complete absence of clouds, as if a so-to-speak unyielding and impenetrable, cloudily-crystal dome through which the glance could barely pass were stretched midway between the starry spaces and that of the world below; and it almost seemed to him as if the demonic partition into zones to which he had been subjected during his recumbent listening and his listening recumbency had been carried here to the outside world and that here it had become sharper and more extensive than when it had been imposed on himself. The earthly space was so cut off and insulated from the heavenly ones that nothing more could be felt of that longed-for wind blowing between the worlds, and not even the hunger for air was appeased, even this pain was not lessened because the fumes, which earlier had enshrouded the city and which had been sundered but could not be blown away by the evening breeze, had changed to a sort of feverish transparency, thickened under the burden of world-segregation to a dark jelly which floated in the air, unmoving and immovable, hotter than the air and so impossible to breathe that it was almost as oppressive as the stuffiness within the room. Ruthlessly that which could be breathed was separated from that which could not, ruthlessly, impenetrably, the crystal shell was spanned darkly overhead, a hard, opaque partition barring off the fore-court of the spheres, the fore-court of the breath, the fore-court of the universe in which he stood, set upright by the iron hand, supported by it; and whereas formerly, ensconced in the earth's surface and stretched out over the Saturnian meadows, he had constituted the boundary between the above and below, in immediate contact with both regions and involved with both, now he tow-

ered up through them as an individual soul, predestined to her
growing, who, lonely and single, knew that if she wished to
hearken into the depths above and those below she had to
hearken to herself: immediate participation in the greatness of
the spheres was not granted to one who stood in the midst of
earthly time and earthly-human growth, endowed again with
both; only with his glance, only with his knowledge might he
penetrate the infinite detachment of the spheres, enabled to grasp
and hold them only with his questioning glance, enabled to restore the simultaneous unity of the universe in all of its spheres
by his questioning knowledge alone, achieving only in the
streaming orbit of the question the vital immediacy of his own
soul, her innermost NECESSITY, the task of preception laid on
her from the very beginning.

Time flowed above, time flowed below, the hidden time of
night flowing back into his arteries, flowing back into the pathway of the stars, second bound spacelessly to second, the re-
given, re-awakened time beyond the bonds of fate, abolishing
chance, the unalterable law of time absolved from lapsing, the
everlasting now into which he was being held:
Law and time,
born from each other,
annulling, yet always giving birth to each other anew,
reflecting each other and perceptible in this way alone,
chain of images and counter-images,
noosing time, noosing the arch-image,
neither wholly captured, yet for all that
becoming more and more timeless
until, in their last echoing unison,
in a final symbol,
the image of death unites with the image of life,
portraying the reality of the soul,
her homestead, her timeless now, the law
made manifest in her, and hence
her necessity.
Everything had been brought to pass through necessity, even the

traversing of the perceptive path where the inner and outer worlds were dissolved to an unrecognized infinity, detached and divided to complete strangeness. Yet did not this unavoidable, inescapable necessity contain the hope for the restored harmony of existence, for the confirmation of what was occurring and what had already occurred? the images had emerged through necessity and through necessity they pressed on, coming nearer and nearer to reality! Oh, nearness of the arch-image, nearness of the arch-reality in the fore-court of which he was standing—, was the crystal cover of the heaven-secret about to be rent? was the night about to unveil its final symbol to him whose eye must falter when the night's eye opens? He stared upward to the stars whose two-thousand-years' revolution was soon to be rounded off, following fate orbit by orbit, bearing fate on from father to son in the generations of time, and he was greeted by the pulsing now of the heavens, extending from the visible into the invisible and filling the complete cycle of re-given conscious-ness, greeted from the southwestern horizon by the familiar and uncanny image of the Scorpion, the dangerously crooked body laved by the mild stream of the Milky Way, greeted by Andro-meda, nestling her head on the winged shoulder of Pegasus, by that never-vanishing presence shining forth in invisible wel-come, and from the aeons preceding the creation of the ancestors the constellation of the dragon sent forth its ten-fold illumina-tion, the dragon deprived of its erstwhile throne; he gazed up-ward into the stony chill where the image of law was circling, cut off from the dark-gleaming breath, cut off from the never-descending but always surmised truth, necessary to itself in a sphere removed from mankind; and seeing its image, sensing its image in the abundance of images which comprise it, he felt perception at work in himself, knowing it was beyond chance, knowing that the power of his perception allowed him to wait without expectation, freed from all impatience, and in knowing this he became ready for the necessary completion in the uncom-pleted. Thereupon the hand that upheld him became soft and softer, came to be safety. And upon the roofs of the city the light of the easterly moon lay like a cool, greenish dust; earth things drew nearer. For he who has left the first portal of fear behind him, enclosed in the fore-court of a new and greater mystery, enclosed and caught by a new apprehension which places him again in the midst of his own development, in the midst of his own law, absolved from returning, absolved from the Saturnian lapses, absolved from his own impatient hearkening, he is the one again made to stand erect and to grow upright, to find the way back to himself; and his bark glides on but only with oars drawn back, drifting softly and unexpectantly in the time granted to him, as if the landing were just in front of him, as if he were about to be landed on the shores of the chance-delivered and final reality:

for he who has left the first portal of fear behind him
has entered the fore-court of reality,
now that his perception, discovering itself and turned towards itself,
as if for the first time,
begins to comprehend
the necessity inherent in the universe, the necessity of every occurrence,
as the necessity of his own soul;
for he to whom this befalls
is held into the unity of existence,
into that pure now common to man and the universe,
the inalienable possession of his own soul,
by virtue of which she floats, as float she must,
over the abyss of nothingness, opened and threatening,
and over the blindness of man;
for he is held into the everlasting now of the question,
into the everlasting now of man's knowledgeless-knowing,
into man's divine prescience,
knowledgeless in that it asks and must ask,
knowing in that it precedes the question,
divine prescience, divinely bestowed before birth on man and man alone

as his innermost human necessity,
for the sake of which
he must put his perception to the test again and again
and be proven by it again and yet again,
man trepidant for the answer, perception trepidant for the
   answer,
man bound to perception, perception bound to man,
both held together and trepidant for the answer,
overcome by the divine reality of fore-knowledge,
by the magnitude of reality embraced by the knowing question,
a question never to be answered by the truth of earthly
   knowledge, and yet
which can be answered, must be answered here alone in the
   realm of earth,
realized on earth
as the counterplay of a dual world-shaping,
reality conformed to truth, truth conformed to reality,
complying with the law of the soul,
her necessity;
for, tense with questioning, the soul
is held into her salvation, saved by truth,
enjoined to perception, to questioning, to shaping,
stretched between her certitude of knowledge and her capacity
   for perception,
in search of reality,
and summoned in this manner by primal knowledge,
summoned by the knowing question which suggests
something chanceless establishing unity in all that exists,
called hither to the realization of knowledge,
to the knowledge born of perception,
to perception of the chance-delivered law,
the soul is caught constantly setting out,
ready for departure and departing toward her own essence,
toward her incarnation and beyond her incarnation,
her start and goal united in the spheres,
bringing man into his humanity;

for man is held into the perceptive ground of his knowing soul,
into the perceptive ground
of his doing and searching, his willing and thinking, his dreams,
he is laid open to the infinite and the chanceless within the real,
this most comprehensive and forceful
most relentlessly gentle, most actual image of himself in his
    own reality,
to which he will come home, to which he is coming home
forever,
held into the now of his own symbol
in order that it may come to be his constant reality;
for it is the defiance of its summons
into which man is held,
the defiance of the imprisoned one,
the defiance of his inextinguishable freedom,
the defiance of his inextinguishable will for knowledge,
so unyielding,
that he becomes greater than all earthly shortcomings,
growing beyond himself,
the titanic defiance of humanity;
verily man is held into his task of knowing,
and nothing is able to dissuade him,
not even the inevitability of error,
the bound nature of which vanishes before
the task beyond all chance;
for even though man was so imprisoned in his earthly shortcomings—and before all, this one who leaned painfully clutching
the window-sill, a sick man grievously struggling for breath—,
for even though man was so fated to disappointment, delivered
over to every sort of disappointment in great things as in small,
his labor in vain, fruitless in the past and hopeless in the future,
and even though disappointment might have chased him on from
impatience to impatience, from restlessness to restlessness, fleeing death, seeking death, seeking work, fleeing work, harassed
and loving and again harassed, fate-driven from one perception
to another, driven away from the erstwhile life of simple cre-

ative work toward all the diversity of knowledge, driven on toward poetry and to the further exploration of the oldest and most occult wisdom, impatient for knowledge, impatient for truth, then driven back to poetry as if it could be related to death in a final fulfillment—oh, this too was disappointment, this too the wrong path—, oh, even though this had been such an utterly wrong path, aye, simply a wrong path that was and is, aye, even less than a wrong path with hardly an attempt toward the first step and that gone astray before the start, oh, even though his whole life seemed so utterly shipwrecked and remained so ship-wrecked, so clogged by shortcomings from the very beginning, damned to founder for ever and aye, since nothing was fitted to penetrate the thicket, since the mortal never came through it, since fumbling about motionless on the spot, bound to despair and disappointment, he remained in bondage to every frightful-ness of error, oh, nevertheless and nevertheless, nothing had occurred without necessity, nothing occurs without necessity, be-cause the necessity of the human soul, the necessity of the human task overruled every circumstance, even the wrong road, even the error;

for only amidst error, only through error
in which he was inescapably held,
did man come to be the seeker
that he was,
the seeking human;
for man needed the realization of futility,
he must accept its dread, the dread of all error,
and recognizing it, he must drain it to the dregs,
he must assimilate it,
not in self-torment, but rather
that through such conscious assimilation
the dread might be expunged,
only thus might one pass through the horny portal of dread
and achieve existence;
this was the reason why man was held into the space of incer-
    titude,

102

held thus, as if no boat were bearing him now,
even though he floated forward on a floating bark;
this was why he was held into space after space
of his own awareness,
into the spaces of his self-realizing self,
self-realization—fate of the human soul;
but he, behind whom the heavy wings of dread's portal had
  closed,
had arrived at the fore-court of reality,
and the unknown stream on which he was being floated onward,
this unperceived element became the source of his knowledge,
being, as it was, the streaming growth of his own soul,
the uncompleted within himself, and unable to be completed,
which for all that developed to a whole
as soon as the self was self-assimilated,
made indestructible by growing into the streaming oneness of
  the universe,
realized by him, seen by him
in a concurrence which by its everlasting immediacy
forced all the spaces into which he was held to a single space,
to that unique space of the source, likewise
sheltering the self, only to be sheltered by it,
embraced by the soul while yet embracing it,
at rest in time, conditioning time,
bound by the law of perception and creating perception,
floating along in its streaming growth,
swimming with it as it floats and grows and develops,
the sole source of reality;
oh, so supernally great
were these tides of the self and the universe
flowing out of and into each other,
that floating and being held, liberation and imprisonment,
were merged in this tide to an inseparable common
  transparency,
oh, so eternally necessary,
oh, so immeasurably transparent,

that in the severed upper spheres,
accessible only to the glance, accessible only to time,
familiar to both,
reflected in both, reflected in the opened human countenance
tilted upward by the gentle-unyielding hand,
encircled by fate,
encircled by stars,
the promised gift of confirmation shone out,
the gift of time, delivered from chance and enduring forever,
opened to perception, the comfort upon earth—,

and, consoling in a universe flooded in moonlight, the spheres
joined each other, the spheres of heaven and earth united forever, consoling as the breath that shall return to the breast from
over there, announcing as solace that nothing has been in vain,
that whatever had been done for the sake of understanding was
not done in vain, and could not have been done in vain because
of its necessity. Hope lay in the unaccomplished as well as in
what was impossible of accomplishment, and pressing close,
very timidly, the hope of finishing the Aeneid. Hope-resounding
echo of the promise upon earth, reverberating in earthly confidence; and the mortal surrounded by earthly existence was
ready to receive it.

Solace and confidence indeed, the solace of confirmation,
although the crystal cover of the heaven-secret had not parted,
no image had appeared there, least of all the ultimate image;
the eye of night remained veiled, his own eye had not faltered,
and now as before the zones of immensity were to be joined only
in reflection and counter-reflection, now as before the vast separation above and below were to be brought into a unity only
by glimpse or surmise, now as before it was only the fore-court
of reality in which he stood, it was merely the place of the
earthly question in the immediacy of which he was held, de-
barred from reality in its fullness and unity, and nevertheless
—solace and confidence. The moonlight streamed like a cool
dust through the heat of night, saturating it without lessen-

ing it, without merging with it, a blind-cool reflection of the heaven's stony gleam painted upon the heated darkness. Oh, human certainty, knowing that nothing has happened in vain, that nothing was happening in vain, although disappointment seems to be all, and no way leads out of the thicket; oh, certainty, knowing that even when the way turns to evil the knowledge gained by experience has grown, remaining as an increment of knowledge in the world, remaining as the cool-bright reflection of that estate beyond chance to which the earthly action of man can penetrate whenever it conforms to the necessity determined by perception and attains in this way a first illumination of earthbound life and its herdlike sleep. Oh, certainty full of trust, not streaming hither from heaven but arising as from earth in the human soul because of the perceptive task laid on it—, then must not the fulfillment of certain trust, if fulfillment be at all possible, be realized here on earth? the necessary is always consummated in the simple way of earth, the streaming round of questions will always find its closure only upon earth, even though the perceptive task may concern itself with uniting the separate spheres of the universe, still there is no genuine task without earthly roots, none possible of solution without an earthly starting point. The world of earth spread out before him had escaped into moonlight, humanity had withdrawn under itself, escaped into sleep, hidden in the sleep-sated houses and fallen below itself, separated from the up-sunken stars, and between the upper and lower zones the stillness of the world was doubly desolate; no voice broke into the breathless silence, nothing could be heard except the soft rise and fall of the crackling bivouac-fires and the heavy bored steps of the guard on patrol along the outer wall coming nearer in his rounds, then dying away again, and if one listened intently it seemed as if here too a soft echo from somewhere was vibrating in unison, an accompanying sound, scarcely an echo, scarcely refracted, only diffused in order to be refracted against the house walls at the edge of the plaza, refracted in a net-work of streets and dwelling-caves, against the stone fields of town after town, refracted on the walls of mountains and seas, re-fracted on the murky crystal vault of heaven, refracted on star-light, refracted on the inscrutable, breathed hither and diffused by refraction, swinging, swinging to this side, but vanishing at once if one attempted to capture it. But earthly and at hand, yet strangely connected to the spheres, the fire behind the walls continued to crackle faintly, and though often it too ebbed off into something like echo, and into the invisible, it too taking its place in the chain of images and more images, it was like a pledge confirming the human effort, pointing to the earthly source of the titanic will for unity born into the human soul; it was like a demand upon perception to turn toward earth and earthly things in order to find there its strength for renewal, the Promethean element that stems from regions here below and not from those above. Yes, he had to direct his attention to the realm of earth, and he waited attentively, tired of breath-ing, bent over the window ledge, awaiting that which was neces-sary and would have to come.

Below him the narrow space between the palace and the outer wall yawned in moat-like blackness, the windows giving on it were unlit and dead, the black bottom of the shaft unfath-omably deep, while behind the wall, completely overshadowed by it, visible only by its reflection, one of the bivouac-fires was burning, and when the watch on guard crossed the small flicker-ing region on his path, one could see the shadow of the man gliding indistinctly over the dull, ruddily-lit, stone pavement, a dark breath of shadow that often sprang up jaggedly on the walls of the building opposite, lasting for the flicker of an eye-lid, unreal in its strange, unexpected movement. What went on there, though hidden by the walls, was the merest discharge of a military duty, but nonetheless, like every human performance of duty, strangely connected with the basis of perception, with the simple task of perception itself, and therefore not in vain; what happened there preceded itself in the fore-court of reality, near to the realm of consummation. Yet the breach into the ulti-mate reality would not be made from the sphere of the stars, nor from the spheres in the interstellar spaces; not there would the promised confirmation redeem itself, but rather from the sphere of humanity; the impetus to break through the boundaries would proceed from man; for this was man divinely destined, for this, confidence was bestowed upon him, for his divine necessity; and although the great moment for the attainment of reality might not be fixed in time, undiscoverable in the obscurity of fate, and whether the event took place in a not-to-be-lived future or in the immediate present, if indeed it might not already have come to pass, the command to vigilance was heard, ringing out peremptorily from an occult fate, urgent and admonishing, the command to hold fast to every moment in preparation for the moment of revelation, revelation in the realm of the chanceless, in the realm of law, in the realm of humanity. The order rang out from the realm of the unsearchable and it resounded, inaudible and lost, from out the clamorous ringing of the heat-weary, feverish, moon-drenched black glair encircling the earth and flowed impassively across the roofs, flowed toward the windows and held in embrace even him who stood there, enveloping him in the command to vigilance, as if this very command were a part of the fever. And feverishly he directed his vigilance to the visible in sheer yearning for the sight of a living creature somewhere. Nothing appeared. Toward the land at the southwest the warning, brightly-lustrous image of the Scorpion stood over a glimmering earth, the border between the city dwellings over there and the half-hidden, wavering night-hills of the landscape glimmered out; the rising and falling surf of fields and groves and meadows, their grass-waves, their leaf-waves drenched by the stone-cool flood of moonlight glimmered out, overcast in the final blackness of immensity; they glimmered out in the stonily-resounding, stonily-chilling, stonily-trembling fever-waves of the enflooded starry spaces, night-drenched, light-drenched, gliding hither and yon, streaming to and fro, and the pale sheen did not end with invisibility. Thus it flowed out and back again, hot and cool, shadow and light from a twofold source, submerged in blackness, flowing down into the shaft of the courtyards, the squares, the streets, spread out over the visible-invisibility of all things earthly. Obliquely opposite a street opened into the square; it was swept through brightly by the moon in that straight track open to the view, darkened only here and there by higher houses, and it could be ascertained by the sweep of the roofs that in its far straying the street extended to the outskirts of the town in a slight double-curve like that of the Scorpion to which it led, seductive in the similitude of its form, seductive in its ongoing, indeed so seductively alluring that it became a trepidant yearning to be allowed to wander through the street, hurrying lightly through its turns, out into the country toward the constellations, wandering through homeland after homeland, crossing the groves of fever-light and fever-shadow—blithe the dream-step that flits through them—oh to wander out there, over those glimpsed streets containing their origins in their goals, to wander out there and never to turn back! One needed no guide on such an easy path, and also no stern awakener, for the incandescent, shimmering sleep of the world endured without interruption; one needed only to stride forth, to wander out into the realm of the unrecallable; all boundaries were opened and nothing was able to halt the wanderer, nothing would overtake him, nothing confront him, the divine would not precede him and he would not encounter the bestial, his foot unhindered by either, but the path that he followed would be that of comfort and confidence, the path of necessity, the path of the god. Was this really so? Was there no longer an alternative course? Would there really not be another path leading back to the animal, falling back into the sub-animal?

This meant waiting, waiting with great patience, patience that lasted a long, unbearably long time. Then, however, something presented itself, and, strangely enough, that which was approaching, even though the opposite of everything which could have been expected, seemed as if called here by necessity. At first it came as a sound-image, that is as the sound-image of shuffling steps and indistinct murmuring detaching itself slowly from the silence, and it remained hidden in the shadows for some time before there emerged the shapes to which the sounds pertained, three indistinct white spots, staggering and often at a standstill, closing in together and then wandering apart, visible in the moonlight, drowned in the darkness, pushed on as if against their will. Breathless from the strained vigilance, breathless from the oppressiveness of the stuffy nightglair, his hands clasped together, his fingers clasped convulsively over his ring, he leaned stiffly out of the window and stretched out his head, intent on the approach of the three apparitions. Now for a time they remained speechless, then, however, in contrast to the previous indistinct murmuring, a voice broke out, sudden, sharp and extremely distinct, a crowing tenor voice, almost shouting as if its bearer had roused himself to an irresistible, final decision, announcing: "Six sesterces." Again there was silence, and it seemed as if such finality permitted of no further reply, still, for all that, it was imparted: "Five," came in a quiet, almost sleepy bass, from a second voice, the malicious yet jolly voice of a man who intended to cut short further negotiations: "Five."—"Shit, six!" cried the first voice, undaunted, whereupon the bass voice, after some unintelligible haggling settled quietly on the last offer: "Five, and not a dinar more." They halted. Until now it could not be ascertained for what they were bargaining, now, however, a third voice intervened, the voice of a drunken female. "Give him six!" she ordered in a tipsy, greasy sort of shrieking, and something servile and soliciting lay behind its impatient, pandering urgency, without accomplishing much, to be sure, for now the answer consisted only of a throaty, scornful laughter. And irritated at once by the laughter and the unassailable mockery, the female voice pitched into fury: "Guzzling the most and paying nothing . . . meat you want, and fish you want, and everything else . . ."; and as there followed only the yelping male laughter, she went on: "Flour I should buy and onions and the rest of it, and eggs and garlic and oil, and garlic . . . and garlic . . ." panting drunkenly to the accompaniment of the inciting male laughter that was suppressed to a broadly-chuckling gurgle, she stuck to the exorbitance of garlic—, "garlic, you want . . . garlic . . ." "Right you are," crowed the tenor, interrupting, and with an immediate change of thought decided on a "shut up!" She, however, as if the word possessed some clarifying power, went right on: "garlic . . . garlic I'm supposed to buy . . ." Once more they were engulfed by the darkness, and from out the darkness the cry for garlic continued, and really, as if responding to a cue, the feverish gloom was laden and impregnated at once with all the combined kitchen odors that the city was able to emanate—heavy, sated, rank, oily, settled and horribly digested and decomposed, scorched, unsavory, regurgitated—the sleep-inducing nourishment of the city. For a few moments it became still, strangely stifling as if even the three down there had been swallowed in the stale fumes, and even after their re-entry into the light they had nothing more to say; the argument over the garlic was exhausted, they approached silently, becoming more and more distinct, yet for all their silence having become in no way peaceful: to the forefront there appeared a conspicuously lean fellow with hunched-up shoulders, limping on a stick which he raised threateningly whenever he had to stop for the other two to catch up with him; at some distance behind him followed the woman, fat and compact, and finally, fatter if possible, more drunken if possible, in any case more ponderous, the other man, a broad-bellied tower, who being unable to make up the constantly increasing distance between himself and the woman, attempted to stop her at last with a whiny sort of whistling and a childish holding up of hands; so they came on, a staggering doubtful spectacle that became even a little more doubtful when they arrived at the mouth of the street in the flickering light of the camp-fire; in this manner they brought up before his very eyes, in the midst of a fresh outbreak of their haggling, as their hobbling ringleader with a left turn toward the harbor tried to cross the square, whereupon the woman yelled after him "Stinker!" so that, arrested and desisting from his purpose, he turned about to attack her with his brandishing stick, not, however, intimidating the undeterred woman who continued with her carping, but seeming to perturb the fat tower who, whimpering to himself, turned to flight, and thus compelled the woman to run after him and drag him back —, her success proved so gratifying to the other one that he dropped his stick and now really succumbed to that yelping, thick-throated laughter that once before had driven the woman into a rage. Immediately the same thing occurred, the woman became enraged: "Go home," she dictated to the lean laugher, and as he with a wagging outstretched finger pointed to his former destination in the direction of the harbor, she stretched out her arm in the opposite direction, panting with excitement and babbling the while: "See to it that you get home, you've no business in the city . . . You don't fool me, I know what you've got there, I know all about your slut . . ." "Ho?" the wagging finger came to rest, the hand shaping itself to a cup and to the gesture of drinking. This meant so much to the fat one who leaned against the house wall that he found his way back to his last decision. "Wine," he chuckled, transfigured, and started to move. The woman barred his way. "Hmm, wine," she bickered, "wine? . . . he should go to his slut and I'm supposed to cook for him . . . he wants to have pork and what not . . ." "Piggy-meat," crowed the tenor. Contemptuously she pushed him back against the wall, but almost tearfully she approached the other one: "You want everything of me but not to pay for it . . ."—"I pay him five. I've said it . . . come along, you'll get some wine."—"A hoot for your wine . . . six is what you pay him."—"He gets wine too."—"He don't need your wine."—"That's none of your dirty business, you carrion; I'll pay him five and not a dinar more, and he gets his wine."— "Five," commented the fat-paunch at the wall with dignity. The woman flew at him: "What 'dya say? what 'dya say?" Alarmed he sought for a subterfuge: at last he observed with friendly courtesy: "Shit."—"What 'dya say t'him?" She did not let him loose, and driven into a corner he repeated with forced courage in accord with his new conviction: "Five."—

"You dare say that, you sluice, you wine-belly . . . and I'm supposed to produce your fodder . . . without cash I'm supposed to get it . . ." This made no impression on the fat one: "Wine . . . you get wine, too," he piped blissfully, as if now he would have to be praised for his courage. She had clutched his tunic: "He takes all his money to that slut . . . he must pay six, do you hear, six . . ."—"Six," said the tower, obediently, and made an attempt to sit down, which to be sure, was not successful as the woman still gripped him. For the lean one this was the source of unending, boisterous, stick-brandishing pleasure: "Five is what he said, and five I'll pay him; I stick to that!"— "That's not true," she hissed, still holding the fat-paunch by the tunic, she screamed in his face: "Tell him it's six, tell him!" With all this her voice, even though it was so very unbalanced, did not lose its insinuating, wooing undertone; only one could not determine toward whom this was directed. At all events, the lean one interrupting his hilarity became a shade more conciliatory: "What do you want anyway? As it is, you get your flour for nothing from Caesar . . ." She stopped short, and this afforded the fat one who twisted under her tugging grip not only a pause for breath but also an opportunity to get away from the troublesome matter of the sesterces: "Hail to Augustus!" he crowed toward the imperial residence, and with high-brandishing stick the other one, who likewise turned toward the palace, stressed the joyful, quavering shout with a rousing "Hail to him!," and again, quavering with enthusiasm there resounded, "Hail to Augustus!" and still again the lean one saluted with a rousing "Here's to him!"—"Shut your mouths, shut your mouths, the both of you," interrupted the woman, disgusted and angry, and actually for a few moments this had an effect: not exactly out of respect for the woman's command but more out of respect for the Caesar who was being celebrated, the two became speechless, yes even transfixed, the fat one with open mouth, the lean one with stick held high, and while the stick-armed shadow flickered upon the wall in the crackling firelight and the woman, with heavy arms akimbo, observed the fine effect, one could have thought that this lull would endure for all eternity, even as it was being shattered by a fresh outbreak, a fresh rumbling up of the yelping derision, abruptly cut off by a laughter in which the lubberly pair joined, a laughter at first tenorishly clear, followed by the gleeful warbling of the fat-paunch after which came the uncontrollable, giddy, babbling cackle of the woman, while the stick beat the time: three-mouthed the shaking laughter that gurgled up from an unknown fiery depth and shook them, three-headed the scorn with which they derided themselves and each other, three-bodied the un-known, the most unkown god. The laughter mounted to a climax and the thin one caused it: "Wine," he shouted, "You'll get yours, Fatty, wine for everybody, wine to toast Caesar!"—"Hee, hee, hee," cackled the woman, and her laughter tumbled into anger and then really into whorish lewdness, "Your Caesar, I know about him . . ." "Flour from Caesar," the patriotic tower informed her graciously and began to move away from the wall, "flour from Caesar, you heard it yourself . . . here's to him!" It was such a circling round the same old point that one almost expected her to belch out again her cry of "garlic," and when in addition the other one, bawling and gulping, drew near with the corroboration: "Yes, indeed, they'll dole it out tomorrow, tomorrow he'll let it be distributed . . . cost you nothing!" then her patience failed: "Filth is what they'll dole out," she screamed so that it resounded over the whole plaza, "filth is what Caesar is going to give us . . . and filth is what your Caesar is, filth, that's what he is. All he knows is dancing and singing and fucking and whoring, your fine Caesar, but that's all he can do and he won't give a speck away!"— "Fucking, fucking, fucking . . ." repeated the fat one raptur-ously, as if this one chance word had disclosed all the lewdness of the world and all its lust, "Caesar is fucking, hail to Caesar!" Meanwhile the lean one had limped along a few steps, possibly worried that the guard might come nearer, and though his night-laughter held now as before to its throaty bawling, he sounded uneasy as he called back over his hunched-up shoulder: "Come on . . . you're getting wine, come on!" To be sure this accomplished nothing, and it is possible that nothing could have been accomplished anyway, for the fat-paunch, obstinately enchanted by the dancing and fucking Caesar, was unmistakably set on imitating the sublime one, patriotically careful to support his amorous efforts by hailing Augustus the father, Augustus the Caesar, Augustus the savior, as he attempted, hands outstretched in lewd imploring, to lay them on the scolding, cursing, retreating woman, clumsy and droll and emitting little crowing sounds—a contented, twittering Colossus, ready for copulation, who in the course of his drunken desire had fallen into a hopping, almost light-footed dancing, deaf and blindly set upon his goal, and certainly not of a mind to abandon it, had not an unexpected blow from the stick of the softly approaching limper put a sudden end to the game: it all happened with such indescribable speed and silence that one heard nothing, it was as if the stick had struck into a heap of down and not even a single sound of pain or fright had been audible, no groan and no sigh was to be heard, the fat one had only plumped down, turned over a little and then lay quiet—, the murderer, however, gave him no further concern, and taking himself off without even looking back, he limped calmly away, but still not in the direction of the port or the wine or the slut, but followed the homeward path as bidden him by the woman, paying no attention to her who, undecided—perhaps struck and moved by the suddenness of the extinguishment or by the so suddenly extinguished chance lust—had lingered, bent over the corpse, before she deserted it after a few seconds, and with quick decision hurried to overtake the vanishing cripple; all this happened with such speed and yet with such remoteness, so deeply implicated in the febrile, impassive night-glair that perhaps no one—least of all an invalid who, bound by his pain, bound by the imposed vigilance, had been compelled, bound and transfixed, to follow the occurrence from the window —would have been able to prevent it by an outcry, a beckoning or by any sort of interference; but even before it had been possible to become conscious of it all, even before the murderous pair had vanished behind the pinnacle-crowned, sharply protruding corner of the outer wall, the fallen one stirred, and after he had succeeded in turning round on his belly he started crawling hurriedly on all fours after his companions like an animal, like a big clumsy insect that had lost a pair of its legs. Not comedy, no, but terror and awe hovered about the grovelling beast, and the terror and awe still went on when he stood himself at last upon his hind legs to urinate on the house wall, afterwards, however, losing his balance with every step and pawing the wall as he staggered along beside it. Who had the three been? had they been sent out from Hades, sent out from those miserable slums into the windows of which he had looked, pitilessly impelled to it by fate? What else must he witness? what else must he encounter? was it not yet enough? Oh, this time he was not the butt of insult, the sneers and laughter that shook the three were not meant for him; this bawling, yelping, compelling male laughter had nothing in common with the female laughter of Misery Street, no, this laughter contained something worse, terror and awe, the awfulness of the matter-of-fact that did not concern itself with the human, neither with him who looked on and comprehended here from the window, nor indeed with any human being; this was like a language that is no longer a bridge between people, like an extra-human laughter, its range of scorn playing about the factual worldly-estate as such, that in reaching beyond the realm of all things human no longer derides humanity but simply destroys it by exposing the nature of the world; oh, this was what the laughter of the three apparitions had accomplished, expressing horror, bringing horror to pass, the male laughter, the bantering, bawling laughter of horror! Why, oh, why had it been sent to him? Through what necessity had it been sent here? He leaned out of the window to listen after the three—there on the southern heaven was Sagittarius, unmoved and mute, his bow bent toward the Scorpion; the three had vanished in the direction of the Archer and from out the silence there fluttered now and then, at first rudely torn then delicately fringed, at first highly colored then becoming gray, the filthy rags of their insults, fluttering off at last as a slimy, greasy, carping guffaw of the female voice, wooing and servile in its whining lament, as a few words in the throaty bass of the cripple, his laughter yelping out now and again, finally as a mere vague cursing, becoming almost nostalgic, almost gentle; and this was absorbed into the remaining sounds of the nocturnal distance, spun into and unified with every tone that the night released as a last reminder, unified with the dreamy crow of a cock in silvery sleep, unified with the forsaken yelping of two dogs that somewhere beyond in the shimmering distance, perhaps on a building lot, perhaps at a country house, acclaimed their moon-existence to one another, the animal dialogue joined over the gap with the tones of a human song coming in snatches from the harbor district, its source indeed recognizable as blown from the north and yet almost without direction, tender this too, although probably just part of a song sung by an obscene sailor roaring with laughter in a tavern reeking of wine, yet tender and nostalgic, as if the silent distance, as if the benumbed other world inherent in it were the spot where the unspoken language of laughter and the unspoken language of music— the one, a language above the border of human limitation, the other, one that is below this border, both languages beyond that of speech—had joined to form a new speech, joined to a language in which the dreadfulness of laughter was absorbed into the graciousness of beauty, not nullified but intensified with a double dread, to the mute language of the most benumbed distance and desolation, unspeakably removed from humankind, to the tongue beyond any mother-tongue, to the inscrutable speech which is completely untranslatable, sent inarticulate into the world, penetrating the world unintelligibly and inscrutably with the sense of its own remoteness, existing in the world by necessity and hence doubly unintelligible, unspeakably unintelligible as the necessary unreality within the unaltered real!

For nothing had changed: form-fast and mute, unchanged in the visible world, sunk deeply under the surface of heaven

116

were the multitude of stars; to the north was the serpent overcome by the arm of Hercules, to the south stood the threatening
Archer; unchanged in the invisible realm stood the forest rigid
in darkness, criss-crossed by serpentine, moon-shot pathways
through which the dream-sated deer were running in search
of the sparkling water-holes; unchanged in the distant and yet
almost homelike realm of the invisible were the mountain-
peaks, gleaming with silence and greeting the mountainous
splendors of the moon, and far beyond anything that could be
seen was a silver rustling—the sea; thus the night was disclosed
to him, unchanged in its visible and invisible realms, one of
a myriad nights continuing immutable since the very beginning,
the world opened in its most invisible realms, sphere after
sphere separated from each other, the fore-court of reality unchanged; oh, nothing had changed and yet everything was
moved into a new distance which cancelled all nearness, penetrating the near and transforming it into an inscrutability which
made one's own hand strange to one, which drew one's own
glance out into the invisible, into an omnipresent remoteness
that sucked up light, even the wall-shadowed, crackling firelight
below into its nowhere, a remoteness that drew every tone of
life, even the lonely, infrequent step of the sentry down there,
out of the realm of the senses and took it all home into the
inaudible, distance brought into proximity, the unreal element
still in the reality of both, and in both, transported by distance,
—beauty. For
on the most transported horizons beauty shone forth
streaming out into mankind,
removed from perception, removed from the question,
effortless
only to be glimpsed
the unity of the world established by beauty,
founded on the beautiful balance of ultra-distance,
which saturated all points of space, sating them with distance,
and—sheerly demonic—not only resolved the most incongruous
    things

into equal rank and meaning,
but also—still more demonic—filled the remoteness
of every point in space with the remoteness of time,
bringing the quivering scales of time everywhere to a standstill,
repeating its Saturnian suspension,
not the annulment of time, far more its enduring now,
the immediacy of beauty, as if by gazing upon it
man, although set erect and growing upright, were permitted to
    sink back
into his drowsy, recumbent listening,
stretched out anew between the depths above and the depths
    below,
newly at one with his listening-looking, which he sent forth
as if the depths allowed a new participation,
one free from knowledge and questioning,
one which might be foregone as it was in the dawn of time or
    in its night,
as if one might forego the choice between good and evil,
fleeing the human duty of perception,
fleeing into a new and hence false innocence, letting
the abandoned and the duty-bound, evil and redemption,
the cruel and the kind, life and death,
the comprehensible and the incomprehensible
be brought into a single indiscriminate unity,
bound in the cestus of beauty,
streaming out blithely into the beauty-embracing glance.
Wherefore beauty was a bewitchment, enchanting and enchanted
    beauty
demonically absorbing everything, gathering all into its
    Saturnian poise;
wherefore beauty was a reversion to the pre-divine
lingering in man as a memory of something that existed before
    his prescience,
a memory of the tentative time of the creation, prior to the gods,
a memory of the amorphous, dusk-enshrouded semi-creation,
lacking the pledge, lacking development, lacking renewal;

118

nevertheless recollection and as such pious, albeit

with a piety impervious to the pledge, to development, to renewal,

the demonic piety of the transported being who looked on beauty, on the threshold of ecstasy

but without the will to go beyond it,

turned back to the pre-creation,

to the fore-show of the divine which resembles divinity,

to beauty;

for so all-embracing was the night spread out before him, so very remote, so filled with the silver dust of echo ringing back from the last reaches of the world, that the night and all that was buried within it became inseparable, whether a song, a yelping laugh, a hint of the animal voice, a rustling of the wind, one could not tell which. And this ingenuousness, this antagonism to knowledge with which beauty—as if to protect its frailty and tenderness—veiled itself, yes must veil itself, because the world-unity founded by it was much more evanescent, less resistant, more vulnerable than that of perception, one which furthermore and in contrast to the latter could be injured at any point by knowledge, this impercipience was radiated to him from the whole cycle of the visible world along with beauty, gentle and at the same time demonic in its allure, in its arrogant seduction to equivalence, demonically whispered to him from the outermost borders and penetrating to the innermost, a shimmering oceanic whisper streaming into him with the drenching light of the moon, balanced like the floating tides of the universe which interchange the visible and invisible in their whispering might, binding the multiplicity of things into the entity of the self, binding the multiplicity of thoughts into the unity of the world, both, however, denatured in becoming beauty: knowledge of beauty was lack of knowledge, perception of beauty was lack of perception, the one without vantage of thinking, the other without the full measure of reality, and in the rigidity of beauty's equilibrium—rigid the floating balance between thinking and reality, rigid the reciprocity of question and answer, of askable and answerable from which the world was born—the flood-scales of inner and outer worlds were brought to a standstill, becoming in this rigid balance the symbol of the symbol. Thus the night arched about him, the dark-gleaming space balanced in harmonious beauty and spread out Saturnically over all time, therefore surely remaining in time and not extending beyond the realm of earth, stretched from boundary to boundary while constituting at every point of itself the innermost and outermost of limits; thus arched the night about and within him, and beauty, the symbol of the symbol, was floated to him from the night, balanced over the world, bringing with it all the strangeness of inner and outer remoteness and withal curiously familiar, veiled in impercipience and yet curiously unveiled, because now it revealed itself to him suddenly as under a second magical illumination, the symbol of his own image, as clearly as though he himself had created it, the symbolization of the self in the universe, the symbolization of the universe in the self, the interlocked dual symbol of all earthly existence: illuminating the night, illuminating the world, beauty spread to the borders of unbounded space and, immersed with space in time, carried on with time through the ages, it became the ever-enduring now, giving boundaries to boundless time, the perfect symbol of earthly life limited by time and space, revealing the woe of limitation and the beauty of life on earth;

thus in mournful sorrow,

thus beauty was revealed to man,

revealed in its self-containment which was

that of the symbol and of equilibrium,

the self gazing at beauty and the beauty-filled world

enchantedly facing each other,

each a-float in the place allotted to it,

both limited, both self-contained, both in equilibrium

and therefore balanced in their apposition in the space common
    to both:

thus was revealed to man

the self-containment of earthly beauty,
the floating expanse and the magical beauty
of self-contained space, borne on and benumbed by time,
incapable of renewal by the question,
incapable of expansion by knowledge,
the constant completeness of space held in balance
by the influence of beauty within it, yet without renewal or
    expansion;
thus space in its completeness and self-containment
revealed itself in every one of its parts, at every point,
as if each of these were its innermost core,
revealing itself in every single figure, in every thing, in every
    human work
as the symbol of its own spatial finitude
at the innermost limit of which every created thing annuls itself,
the symbol annulling and subliming space, beauty annulling
    and subliming space
by the unity maintained between its inner and outer boundaries,
by the infinitude of the self-containing boundaries,
infinity—but bounded, the sorrow of man;
thus beauty was revealed to man as an occurrence on the
    boundary,
and this boundary, the inner like the outer,
the boundary of the remotest horizon or that of a single point,
was spanned between the finite and the infinite,
utterly remote while still of earth and within earthly time,
yea, bounding time itself and causing it to linger,
space lingering at its own border with time, but not annulling
    time,
this being but a symbol, an earthly symbol of time's annulment,
a mere symbol of death's abolishment, not the abolishment itself,
the boundary of human life that never reached beyond itself,
wherefore it was also the boundary of inhumanity—
thus it was revealed to man as an event of beauty,
revealing beauty for what it was, as the infinite in the realm of
    the finite,

as an earthly sham-infinity,
and hence a game,
the game of earthly men amidst their earthliness, playing at
    eternity,
the symbolic game on the periphery of earthly life,
beauty the essence of the play,
the game that man played with his own symbol in order that
symbolically—since otherwise it was impossible—he might
    escape his fear of loneliness,
repeating the beautiful self-deception again and again,
the flight into beauty, the game of flight;
thus there was revealed to man the rigidity of the beautified
    world,
its incapacity for all growth, the limitation of its perfection,
this world which survived only by repetition and
which, even for this sham-perfection, had always to be striven
    for anew,
it was revealed as the play of art in its service of beauty,
as art's despair, its despairing attempt
to build up the imperishable from things that perish,
from words, from sounds, from stones, from colors,
so that space, being formed,
might outlast time
as a memorial bearing beauty to the coming generations, art
building space into every production,
building the immortal in space but not in men —
wherefore it lacked growth,
wherefore it was bound to the perfection of mere repetition
    without growth,
bound to an unattainable perfection and becoming more
    desperate as it came nearer to perfection,
constrained to return constantly into its own beginning which
    was its end,
and hence pitiless,
pitiless toward human sorrow which meant no more to art

than passing existence, no more than a word, a stone, a sound,
    or a color
to be used for exploring and revealing beauty
in unending repetition;
and thus beauty revealed itself to man as cruelty,
as the growing cruelty of the unbridled game
which promised the pleasure of infinity through the symbol,
the voluptuous, knowledge-disdaining pleasure
of an earthly sham-infinity,
hence thoughtlessly able to inflict sorrow and death,
as happened in the realm of beauty at the remote periphery,
accessible only to the glance, only to time,
but no longer available for humanity and the human task;
thus beauty revealed itself to man as the law that lacked per-
    ception,
beauty in its abandonment proclaiming itself as a law
unto itself,
self-contained, inextensible, incapable of development or
    renewal,
pleasure the rule of the game,
self-gratifying, voluptuous, unchaste, unchangeable,
the beauty-saturated, beauty-saturating game in which
beauty was at play with itself,
passing the time but not annulling it,
playing out fate but not controlling it,
the game that could be repeated endlessly, continued endlessly,
yet one that had been destined from the beginning to be broken
    off,
because only humanity is divine;
and thus the intoxication of beauty revealed itself to man
as the game forlorn from the outset, forlorn
in spite of the eternal balance in which it was established,
in spite of the necessity which compelled it to be resumed again
    and again,
forlorn, because the unavoidable repetition brought with it

the unavoidable loss,
forlorn, because the intoxication of repetition and that of the
    game
were inevitably reciprocal in their affects,
both caught in the twilight,
both subject to lapse,
both without growth though assuredly waxing in cruelty—
whereas the true growth,
the increasing knowledge of perceptive mankind,
undeterred by lapse and freed from repetition, unfolded itself
    in time,
unfolded time to timelessness, so that
time, as it consumed all lapse by force of growing reality,
might break through and pass beyond boundary after boundary,
the innermost like the outermost, leaving behind symbol after
    symbol,
and even though it left the final symbolic nature of beauty
    undisturbed,
untouched the necessity of its consummate harmony,
yet the earthly quality of this game had nonetheless to be
    uncovered,
the inadequacy of the earthly symbol be revealed,
the sadness and despair of beauty laid bare,
beauty stripped of intoxication and sobered,
its perception forfeited and itself lost in impercipience,
and with it, the sobered self,
its poverty—,
and he, to whom the symbolic nature of the self, of beauty, of
the game, of time's passing, had come as an illumination,
streaming to him by unavoidable necessity from the innermost
and outermost limits of the world, from the innermost and outermost spaces bound by the night, so that he bore the whole occurrence within himself, buried in himself even though he was confined in it, held within the bounds of necessity, held into the
limited space of his own ego, within the spatial boundaries of
the world and within the symbol of its boundlessness, held with-

in the scope of the game, within the compass of an overdistant nearness, the compass of beauty, the compass of the symbol, which was questionable at every point and yet which warded off and transfixed every question, held in the constriction of every kind of rigidity, he himself rigid, stifled by the rigidity, he sensed, he grasped, that none of these spaces reached beyond the transparent cover which was spanned between the realms above and those below, that all of them lay in the interrealm of the still-unachieved infinity, that their borders were those of the infinite while yet belonging to the realm of earth: the still-earthly, the realm of beauty, the terrestrial, still terrestrial, infinity! it was within this sphere that he was held, confined within it; he was confined in the space of the earthly breath, but expelled from the space of the spheres, from that of the true breath. And sensible of the confinement, aware that in it lay the cause of all rigidity, the cause for all holding of the breath, he felt on all sides a force at work to shatter this constriction, feeling the necessity, the inevitability, of such a shattering in the depths of his being, in the depths of his soul, in the depths where he breathed or did not breathe; he felt this bursting and he knew what it was, sensing and realizing how it had been made ready in him and in the world, how it dwelt in him even though it surrounded him; he was aware of it as something physical, lying in wait to gag and choke him, robbing him of breath as it robbed the visible-invisible world, but nonetheless aware that it was a demonic temptation weaving within and about him, surging high within him and breaking over him, bodily-disembodied, the temptation to destroy until all was destroyed, to shatter until all was shattered, the temptation to self-surrender and self-derision, to self-destruction, choking him, shaking him through and through, but still promising deliverance; thus it was that he felt something in him, lurking, ready to spring and burst him asunder, the proximity of an inscrutable feeling so ancient that it was beyond recollection, thus he realized it and thus he wished it to come about, in a sheerly atavistic opposition to the numbness, to its further development, to the restriction of the limited

space, to existence and its still-existing incongruities, but furthermore to the residual sorrow behind all play and all beauty, oh, it was the temptation of an immense, primitive lust, it was an immense, itching lust, the itch to burst everything, to shatter the world, to explode his own ego, shaken as he was by the lust of a still greater, still earlier knowledge, oh it was such an intensification of feeling, of experiencing and of knowing that it became enlightenment, an enlightenment that came to be perception, yes even self-perception, flooding up to him from the deepest repository of the prescience in which he was held, a last comprehension streaming to him, and in a flash he perceived that the bursting of the beautiful was caused by nothing but naked laughter and that laughter was the predestined explosion of worldly beauty, of which it had been an attribute from the first, inherent in beauty forever, shimmering out as a smile at the unreal borders of utter-distance, but bawling out noisily on that curving horizon which marked the turning point of beauty's duration, breaking out as the booming, thundering demolishment of time by laughter, as the laughing, demonic force of complete destruction, laughter being the necessary counterpart of world-beauty, the desperate substitute for the lost confidence in wisdom, the end of the intercepted flight into beauty, the end of beauty's interrupted game; oh sorrow for sorrow, making game with the game, pleasure in the very expulsion of pleasure, a doubling of sorrow, a doubling of the game, a doubling of pleasure, this was laughter, a constant flight from the haven of refuge, beyond the game, beyond the world, beyond perception, the bursting of world-sorrow, the eternal tickle in the masculine gorge, the cleaving of beauty-fixed space to a gape in the unspeakable muteness of which even the nothing became lost, enraged by the muteness, enraged by the laughter, divine even this:
for
the prerogative of gods and men was laughter,
springing first from that god who recognized himself,
springing dumbly-aware from his intuition,

from the intuition of his own destructibility,
from his intuition of the destructibility of the creation
in which, as a created and creative part, he prevailed
a god, growing by virtue of worldly wisdom toward self-perception and beyond it, back
to intuition,
whence arose laughter;
oh divine birth and human birth, oh death of the gods and
of men,
oh their common beginning and ending, eternally implicated
with each other,
oh, laughter stemmed from the knowledge that the gods are not
divine,
from the knowledge common to gods and men
originating in that unquiet and disquietingly transparent
zone of communion
which was spanned demonically between this world and the one
beyond,
in order that in its beclouded zone of demons
gods and men could and might encounter each other,
and though it were Zeus who struck up laughter in the circle
of the male gods,
it was the human being who aroused the laughter of the gods,
just as
the laughter of men was aroused by the behavior of animals
in the endless cycle of drolly serious recognition,
just as
the god found himself again in man and man found himself
again in the animal,
in order that the animal might be raised through man to the god,
the god, however, returning to men through the animal,
god and man united in sorrow though overcome by laughter,
because
this was the farcical game of that first sudden confusing of all
spheres,
the game in the fatal rules of which

they had been caught,
the farce of the first sudden disclosure of native nearness,
the great farce of intermingling the spheres,
a vagary of the gods, a beauty-destroying, order-annulling game,
the divine in creation and the creature frightfully commingled,
and both cheerfully surrendered to chance,
the abomination and scorn of the knowing mother-goddess,
the sport and hazard of the gods who, delivered from percep-
    tion and disdaining it,
were flooded by laughter,
because this joke of abruptly uniting the spheres,
perpetrated without the faintest trace of perception or
    questioning or any kind of effort,
executed itself as self-abandonment, as a jovial, frivolous
surrender
to chance and to time,
to the unpredictable surmise, to the surmised unpredictable,
to the delightful immediacy of a guess,
unconcerned that it be so,
even as to death;
a joke of the inscrutable, a joke so huge that
with the sportive destruction of the last remnants of lawfulness,
with the ludicrous collapse of order, of the boundaries and
    bridges,
with the breakdown of the fixed spaces and their beauty,
with the collapsing sphere of the beautiful,
there followed the final and ever-valid reversion,
the reversion
into a boundless realm without knowledge, without name,
    without speech, without connection, without dimension,
the partitions tumbling down,
the intuitions of the gods thrown in with that of men,
breaking down their common creation but also
laying bare the nature of the ageless pre-creation,
reversed by this disruption to immediate proximity,
the vision of the pre-creation laid bare in an impression

so remote that it was no longer memory,
an impression inaccessible even to the divination of the god,
laying bare an amorphousness in which
the real and the unreal,
the living and the lifeless,
the significant and the atrocious
were coupled into a sameness beyond conception,
laying bare that unconjectured nowhere, in which
the stars float at the bottom of the waters
and where no thing could lie so far from another
as not to disclose itself as interlocked with it,
waggishly turned inside-out and outside-in,
thrown together by chance and branching out from each other
    by chance,
waggish
these indiscriminate chance-creations of time's passing,
herds of gods, of men, of animals, of plants, herds of stars
containing each other,
the nowhere of laughter exposed,
the very world-inversion exposed in a laugh,
as if that pledge of creation had never existed,
the pledge by which gods and men had mutually bound
    themselves,
duty-bound to perception and to an order which creates reality,
bound to helpfulness—the duty to duty:
oh, this was the laughter of betrayal,
the laughter of unburdened, carefree faithlessness,
this was the unkindness and irresponsibility of the pre-creation,
aye, that it was,
the unkind inheritance, the bursting seed of withheld laughter,
inherent in the creation of all worlds from the outset,
    ineradicable,
already shining out from the smiling, serene reticence
by which, in premature loveliness, it offered to charm,
shining out in the premature-pitiless knowledge by which
even horror, dissipated by beauty, was transfixed

at a pity-lost, pity-frozen distance,
and beyond that, beyond all distance whatsoever, where the
    innermost and outermost unite,
shining out in the dimensionless un-space of the ironic and
    terrible surface,
the surface of beauty, to which it would topple
when the borders of time were reached, showing forth its inner-
    most and underlying nature,
the inborn nature of beauty, born out of beauty again and again,
its unformed lack of creativeness, impervious to form,
born out of, tumbling out of, hurled out of beauty,
laughter:
the language of the pre-creation—,
for nothing had changed, oh nothing: form-fixed and mute, sunk
deeply into the dome of heaven, perjury still lowered, redolent
of laughter; there in the inviolable song of the stars, impregnating the earth with quietude, impregnated with the earthly
quiet, there in the shining continuance of the world, in the
realms of the visible and invisible and in the beauty that turns
to song, there, trembling from restraint and ready to break out,
forcibly tickling and strangling, lurked the sultry laughter akin
to beauty, the lowering, tempting desire for destruction was
there within and about him, it embraced him yet lurked within
him, expressing horror and bringing it to pass, the language
of the pre-creation, the language of the void, to bridge which
nothing has ever existed, nameless the space in which it func-
tioned, nameless the stars which stood above it, nameless, unrelated, expressionless, the solitude of the space kept for language
amidst the spheric confusion, the unavoidable place of dissolution for all beauty; and gazing at beauty while already held
into a new space—the space feverish with horror and he also
feverish with horror—he perceived that no further entrance to
reality presented itself, that there was no return and no renewal,
nothing but the laughter that destroyed reality, indeed that the
wordly existence laid bare by laughter could hardly claim to be
considered as real, question and answer annulled, the duty of

perception cancelled, and cancelled the great hope that the pledge of knowledge would not be in vain, not merely because truth was futile but rather because it was superfluous within the range of petrifying beauty, within the range of its collapse, within the range of laughter—, worse and more malign than the herd-sleep was laughter, no one laughs in dreams unless under pain, unless under death from the growing cruelty juggled so jestingly before him by beauty; oh, nothing was so near to evil as the god tumbling down into a false-humanity or the man catapulted toward a false-divinity, both lured toward evil, toward calamity, toward the uncreated state of the animal, both playing with destruction, with a demonic self-destruction from which they were perchance separated only by a hand's breadth, since anything might be expected in the ceaseless flow of time, both laughing over the uncertainty and the brevity of this time-span surrendered to fate, both prey to a laughter that took pleasure in the lightly abandoned duty and the lightly broken pledge, both tickled and excited by the risk, laughing over the cancellation of the divine as well as the human element in the irrelevancy of all knowledge, laughing over the propagation of evil which is born from the beautiful evil, laughing over the reality of the unreal, jubilant because the pledge of creation has been broken, become maniacal with exultation over the success of their deed, a treacherous undoing and not a deed, the fruit of the broken pledge. Then he understood: the three staggering below had been witnesses to the perjury.

And they had become witnesses against him. That was why it had been necessary for them to come. That was why he had had to await their coming. They had appeared as witnesses and complaints, to accuse him of sharing in their guilt, alleging that he was one of them, an accomplice, a perjurer, and guilty even as they, because, like them, he knew nothing of the pledge which had been broken and continued to be broken, because from the outset he had been oblivious of the pledge and of duty, aye, and it was this that increased his guilt, notwithstanding the necessity by which his life, just as theirs, was fate-ordered to reach this point, the point of relinquishing the creation again: the creation was once more relinquished, gods and men again abandoned to the unborn state of the pre-creation in which life and death are equally doomed to be meaningless, for duty derived only from the pledge, for meaning derived only from the pledge, and nothing retained meaning when, duty being forgotten, the pledge was broken, the pledge given at the obscure beginning, the pledge which must be kept by gods and men although no one knows what it is, no one except the unknown god, for all language stemmed from him, the most hidden of heavenly creatures, only to return to him, the guardian of the pledge of prayer, of duty. It was to await him, the unknown god, that his own glance had been compelled earthward, peering to see the advent of him whose redeeming word, born from and giving birth to duty, should restore language to a communication among men who supported the pledge, hoping thereby to retrieve language from the regions above and below speech, the regions into which man—this too his prerogative— had plunged it, seeking to rescue it from the cloudy state of beauty and the tatterdom of laughter, that it might be led out of the thicket of opacity, in which it had been squandered, and reinstated as the instrument of the pledge. This hope had been a vain one, and the world, sunk back into amorphousness, into meaninglessness, sunk back into an unborn state, encircled by the shadowy mountains of its pre-natal death over which it could not be lifted by the wings of any earthly death, lay spread out before him, the world threaded with beauty and sundered by laughter, its language lost and without human brotherhood, because of the broken pledge of which it too was guilty; instead of the unknown god, instead of him bearing the pledge that led to duty, these three had come hither: the bearers of dereliction.

The one duty, earthly duty, the duty of helpfulness, the duty of awakening; there was no other duty, and even man's duty toward divinity and the god's duty toward humanity consisted of nothing other than helpfulness. And he, whom fate had necessarily and inevitably made fellow to the bearers of dereliction, was just as unwilling for duty and helpfulness as they; and probably the apparent modesty of his needs was no more than disdain for the help that came to him from all sides, and which he accepted without gratitude, for he resembled the mob in this respect also, the mob which demands all sorts of favors but repulses all real help in consequence of its own incapacity for helpfulness: one who from the beginning has yielded to perjury, who has grown up and lived in stony caves, who therefore starts out saddled with the perjurer's fear, such a one from his youth on is far too knowing, far too tricky, far too pleasure-loving and quick-witted to take stock in anything that does not promise immediate gratification of his dawning greed, that does not point to licentious coupling in an all-permitting lawlessness or, if not this, then at least to an advantage measurable in sesterces; it was all one whether these three down there demanded wine, flour, or garlic, or whether others cried out for circus games in order to deaden their fear with these bloody burlesques, with these murderous distorted games which were played on the perilous border where beauty and laughter meet, bringing them in self-betrayal and god-betrayal to the heavenly powers, in a sham penance for their perjury; it was all one whether this was done for pleasure or in placation of the gods, since it was not for an awakening, not for help, for real help that they sued but only for advantage, real advantage; and if Caesar wished to tame these lawless ones to lawfulness again, then circuses, wine and flour were simply the price he had to pay for their obedience. And yet, strangely unaccountable, they even loved him, although in reality they loved no one, although they knew no solidarity save the spurious solidarity of the mob, in which, lacking a common perception, none loves the other, none helps the other, none comprehends the other, none trusts the other, none hears the other's voice, theirs being the non-solidarity of those who lack a common speech, the speech-robbed non-solidarity of unrelated beings: not only had their tricky fear and cocksure suspicion made perception seem sheer superfluity to them, an empty swindle with words, productive of neither pleasure nor advantage, and which, moreover, could be outdone at any time by the play of still slyer words, not only had love, helpfulness, communication, trust, and language, each dependent upon the other, been dissolved by such means to an empty nothingness, not only, in consequence of all this had a simple calculation come to seem their one remaining and reliable hold, but even that appeared no longer reliable enough, and their fear, despite their passionate preoccupation with counting and reckoning, had not been allayed thereby; they saw through it now as a windy nothing and therefore they felt themselves driven to despair, even though despair expressed itself in a wittily-knowing, voluptuously-witty self-mockery; shaken by laughter, because nothing is able to withstand a fear so deep as theirs, because even what could be counted did not become credible or reliable until one had spat upon the coin, using the appropriate magic formula; though believing every miracle—basically their most human and even their most likable characteristic—they were skeptical of truth, and it was this which made them, who believed themselves such excellent accountants, entirely unaccountable, made each of them, cut off in his fear, simply dense and finally unapproachable. Had he, according to the plans of his youth, approached them as a physician, they would have derided and disdained his help were it ever so gratuitously offered, preferring the ministrations of any herb-witch; that had been their standpoint and conditions had not changed and his recognition of this was one of the reasons why he had finally changed his profession; but convincing as these reasons had once seemed to him, today it became clear that they had been the beginning of his own descent to the mob pattern, that he had never been entitled to abandon medical science, that even the doubtful help which it could offer would have been more honorable than the delusive hope of helpfulness with which he had subsequently decked out his profession as poet, hoping against his inner conviction that the might of beauty, that the magic of song, would finally bridge the abyss of incommunication and would exalt him, the poet, to the rank of perception-bringer in the restored community of men; lifted out of the mob pattern and therefore able to abolish that pattern, Orpheus chose to be the leader of mankind. Ah, not even Orpheus had attained such a goal, not even his immortal greatness had justified such vain and presumptuous dreams of grandeur, such flagrant overestimation of poetry! Certainly many instances of earthly beauty—a song, the twilit sea, the tone of the lyre, the voice of a boy, a verse, a statue, a column, a garden, a single flower—all possess the divine faculty of making man hearken unto the innermost and outermost boundaries of his existence, and therefore it is not to be wondered at that the lofty art of Orpheus was esteemed to have the power of diverting the streams from their beds and changing their courses, of luring the wild beasts of the forest with tender dominance, of arresting the cattle a-browse upon the meadows and moving them to listen, caught in the dream and enchanted, the dream-wish of all art: the world compelled to listen, ready to receive the song and its salvation. However, even had Orpheus achieved his aim, the help lasts no longer than the song, nor does the listening, and on no account might the song resound too long, otherwise the streams would return to their old courses, the wild beasts of the forest would again fall upon and slay the innocent beasts of the field, and man would revert again to his old, habitual cruelty; for not only did no intoxication last long, and this was likewise true of beauty's spell, but furthermore, the mildness to which men and beasts had yielded was only half of the intoxication of beauty, while the other half, not less strong and for the most part far stronger, was of such surpassing and terrible cruelty—the most cruel of men delights himself with a flower—that beauty, and before all the beauty born of art, failed quickly of its effect if in disregard of the reciprocal balance of its two components it approached man with but one of them. Wherever and however art was practised, it had to follow this rule, indeed the following of it was one of the artist's essential virtues, and very often, though not always, that of his protagonist: had the virtuous Aeneas remained as soft-hearted as might once have been expected of him, had he, either in the upsurge of his compassion or for the sake of the poem's beautiful tension, been reluctant to kill his mortal enemy, had he not, with better judgment, decided in that moment to do the terrible deed, he would by no means have become the example of gentleness which had to be emulated, but instead he would have become a tedious and unheroic figure unworthy of portrayal by any poem; whether the hero and his deed were Aeneas or another, the concern of art was how to maintain equilibrium, the great equilibrium at the transported periphery, and its unspeakably floating and fugitive symbol, which never reflected the isolated content of things but only their interconnections, this being the only way in which the symbol fulfilled its function, since it was only through this interconnection that the contradictions of existence fell into a balance, in which alone the various contradictory trends of the human instincts were comprehended—were it otherwise, how could art be created and understood by men!—gentleness and cruelty comprehended in the equilibrium of beauty's language, comprehended in the symbol of the balance which they maintained between the ego and the universe, in the intoxicating magic of a unity which endured with the song, but no longer. And it could not have been otherwise with Orpheus and his poem, for he was an artist, a poet, an enchanter of those who hearken, singer and hearer enshrouded in the same twilight, he, like they, demonically caught in the spell of beauty, demonic in spite of his divine gifts, the enchanter, but not the savior of man—a privilege never to be his: for the grace-bearing savior was one who has cast off from himself the language of beauty, he has reached beyond its cold surface, beyond the surface of poetry, he has pushed on to simple words which, because they come close to death and to the knowledge of death are able to knock on the imprisoned souls of his fellowmen, to appease their fear and their cruelty, and make them approachable to real help; he has attained the simple language of spontaneous kindness, the language of spontaneous human virtue, the language of awakening.

Was it not this very language for which Orpheus had striven when, in search of Eurydice, he made ready for the descent into the realm of the shades? Was he not also in despair, one who perceived the impotence of the artist in his discharge of human duty? Oh, when fate has thrown one into the prison of art, he may nevermore escape it; he remains confined within the unsurpassable boundary on which the transported and beautiful occurrence takes place, and if he is incompetent he becomes a vain dreamer within this enclosure, an ambitious trifler with un-art; if, however, he is a real artist he becomes despairing, for he hears the call beyond the border, and all he may do is to capture it in the poem but not to follow it, paralyzed by the injunction and bound to the spot, a scrivener this side of the border, although he has taken on the vocation of the sybil and, piously like Aeneas, has touched the high altar of the priestess, thus accepting the pledge—

—easy the pathway that leads down to Hades, and the gateway of Pluto stands ever open, but the road back is sorely beset, threatened by the swift turns and the whirlpools of the river Cocytus; only those crowned by their virtue, or of a lineage divine and hence favored by Jupiter, may return from grim Tartarus and its terrors; yet if your courage constrains you to cross the Styx twice in your rashness, listen to all that is needful: sacred to her who reigns in the regions below, deep in the dark valleys, growing amidst the wild forest, in the heart of the densest of thickets, there is a branch that is shimmering and golden, putting forth a wealth of gold leaves; and never shall you succeed in making the downward journey until, in honor of Persephone and in obedience to her will, you have broken a gleaming shoot from that self-renewing, golden tree; hence you must be ever alert to espy this branch, you must search for it always, and if destiny be gracious you shall pluck it with the lightest touch of your naked hand; yet no might is so strong, no weapon of steel so compelling, that it could tear this bough from its stalk if it be not the will of fate, the all-commanding, who has in reserve another duty for you—, that first, in expiation, you take care of the unburied body of your friend whose soul has flown, the body which asks for the grave, his right, and your duty—

—, then, called both from fate and the god, their will being one, the border shall be opened for him whose privilege it is to assume the holy duty of helpfulness; but he who is destined by the double will of fate and the god to be an artist, damned but to know and surmise, damned but to write down and speak out, he is denied the purification in life and in death as well, and even his tomb means no more to him than a beautiful structure, an earthly abode for his body, providing him with neither entrance nor exit, neither entrance for the illimitable descent nor exit for the illimitable return; destiny denies him the golden bough of leadership, the bough of perception, and in consequence he is condemned by Jupiter. Hence he too had been condemned to perjury and to the abandonment of the perjured, and his glance, forced earthward, had been allowed to encounter only the three perjuring accomplices staggering over the pavement, bringing him the sentence of guilt; his glance had not been permitted to pierce deeper, not beneath the surface of the stones, not beneath the surface of the world, neither beneath that of language nor of art; the descent was forbidden him, most forbidden the titanic return from the depths, the return by which the humanity of man is proven; the ascent was forbidden him, the ascent toward the renewal of the creative pledge, and he knew now more clearly what he had always known, that once and for all he was excluded from those to whom was pledged the help of the savior, because the help of the pledge and human help implemented each other, and only through their conjunction could the Titan fulfill his task of establishing community and, beyond that, humanity, which, though born of the earth aimed toward heaven, because only in humanity and true community which reflected the whole of man's humanness and humanity as a whole did the perception-borne and perception-bearing cycle of question and answer become perfected, excluding those unfit for helpfulness, for duty, and the pledge, excluding them because they had excluded themselves from the titanic task of mastering, realizing, and deifying human life; verily this he knew,

and he also knew that the same thing held true in the realm of art, that art existed—oh, did it still exist, was it allowed to exist?—only insofar as it contained pledge and perception, only insofar as it represented the fate of man and his mastery of existence, insofar as it renewed itself by fresh and hitherto unaccomplished tasks, only insofar as, in achieving them, it summoned the soul to continuous self-mastery, compelling the soul to reveal level after level of her reality as, descending step by step, penetrating deeper and deeper through the inner thickets of her being, she gradually approached the unattainable darkness which she had always surmised and been conscious of, the darkness from which the ego emerged and to which it returned, the dark regions where the ego developed and became extinguished, the entrance and exit of the soul, but likewise the entrance and exit of that which was the soul's truth, pointed out to her by the path-finding, the goldly-gleaming bough of truth which was neither to be found nor plucked by means of force, since the grace of finding it and the grace of the descent were one and the same, the grace of self-knowledge, which belonged as much to the soul as to art, their common truth; verily, this he knew,

and he knew also that the duty of all art lay in this sort of truth, lay in the self-perceptive finding and proclaiming of truth, the duty which has been laid on the artist, so that the soul, realizing the great equilibrium between the ego and the universe, might recover herself in the universe, perceiving in this self-recognition that the deepening of the ego was an increase of substance in the universe, in the world, especially in humanity, and even though this doubled growth was only a symbolic one, bound from the beginning to the symbolization of the beautiful, to that of the beautiful boundary, even though it were but a symbolic perception, it was precisely by this means that it was enabled to widen the inner and outer boundaries of existence to new reality, even though these boundaries might not be crossed, widening them not merely to a new form but to the new content of reality which they enclosed, in which the deepest secret of reality, the secret of correlation was revealed, the mutual relation existing between the realities of the self and the world, which lent the symbol the precision of rightness and exalted it to be the symbol of truth, the truth-bearing correlation from which arose every creation of reality, pressing on through level after level, penetrating toward, groping toward the unattainable dark realms of beginning and ending, pushing on toward the inscrutable divinity in the universe, in the world, in the soul of one's fellow-man, pushing on toward that ultimate spark of the divine, that secret, which, ready to be disclosed and to be awakened, could be found everywhere, even in the soul of the most degraded—, this, the disclosure of the divine through the self-perceptive knowledge of the individual soul, this was the task of art, its human duty, its perceptive duty and therefore its reason for being, the proof of which was art's nearness to death, and its duty, since only in this nearness might art become real, only thus unfolding into a symbol of the human soul; verily this he knew,

but he knew also that the beauty of the symbol, were it ever so precise in its reality, was never its own excuse for being, that whenever such was the case, whenever beauty existed for its own sake, there art was attacked at its very roots, because the created deed then came to be its own opposite, because the thing created was then suddenly substituted for that which creates, the empty form for the true content of reality, the merely beautiful for the perceptive truth, in a constant confusion, in a constant cycle of change and reversion, an inbound cycle in which renewal was no longer possible, in which nothing more could be enlarged, in which there was nothing more to be discovered, neither the divine in the abandoned, nor the abandoned in human divinity, but in which there was only intoxication with empty forms and empty words, whereby art through this lack of discrimination and even of fidelity, was reduced to un-art, and poetry to mere literarity; verily, this he knew, knew it painfully,

and by the same token he knew of the innermost danger of all artists, he knew the utter loneliness of the man destined to be an artist, he knew the inherent loneliness which drove such a one into the still deeper loneliness of art and into the beauty that cannot be articulated, and he knew that for the most part such men were shattered by this immolation, that it made them blind, blind to the world, blind to the divine quality in the world and in the fellow-man, that—intoxicated by their loneliness— they were able to see only their own god-likeness, which they imagined to be unique, and consequently this self-idolatry and its greed for recognition came more and more to be the sole content of their work—, a betrayal of the divine as well as of art, because in this fashion the work of art became a work of un-art, an unchaste covering for artistic vanity, so spurious that even the artist's self-complacent nakedness which it exposed became a mask; and even though such unchaste self-gratification, such dalliance with beauty, such concern with effects, even though such an un-art might, despite its brief unrenewable grant, its inextensible boundaries, find an easier way to the populace than real art ever found, it was only a specious way, a way out of the loneliness, but not, however, an affiliation with the human community, which was the aim of real art in its aspiration toward humanity, no, it was the affiliation with the mob, it was a participation in its treacherous non-community, which was incapable of the pledge, which neither created nor mastered any reality, and which was unwilling to do so, preferring only to drowse on, forgetting reality, having forfeited it as had un-art and literarity, this was the most profound danger for every artist; oh how painfully, how very painfully he knew this,

and by this token he knew also that the danger of un-art and literarity had always encompassed him, and still encompassed him, and that therefore—although he had never dared face this truth—his poetry could no longer be called art, since, devoid of all renewal and development, it had been nothing but an unchaste production of beauty without real creativity, and from beginning to end, from the Aetna Song to the Aeneid, it had been a mere indulgence of beauty, self-sufficiently limited to the embellishment of things long since conceived, formed, and known, without any real progress in itself, aside from an increasing extravagance and sumptuousness, an un-art which was never able of itself to master existence and exalt it to a veritable symbol. Oh, in his own life, in his own work, he had experienced the seduction of un-art, the seduction of all substitution which puts the thing created in the place of that which creates, the game in the place of communion, the fixed thing in the place of the living, ever-vital principle, beauty in the place of truth: he knew all about this substitution and reversion, knew it all the more as it had been that of his own life's path, this erring path which had led him from his native fields to the metropolis, from the work of his hands to self-deceptive rhetoric, from a humane and responsible sense of duty to a pretense of compassion, which observed things from above and aroused itself to no real help, borne along in a litter the whole way, the way leading down from a community regulated by law to a chance seclusion; the way, no, the fall into vulgarity and there where vulgarity is at its worst, into literarity! Although he had seldom been aware of it, he had succumbed again and again to intoxication, whether it had been offered to him as beauty, as vanity, as artistic dalliance, or as a game of forgetting; these things had ordered his life and constricted it as though in the wreathing, gliding coils of the serpent, vertiginous, this intoxication of constant revolving and reversion, the seductive intoxication of un-art; and although now, on looking back at this life he might feel ashamed, although now, the limit of time having been reached and the game about to be broken off, he had to admit to himself in cold sobriety that he had pursued a worthless, wretched, literary life, not a whit better than that of a Bavius or a Mavius or others of their sort whom he had despised as mere phrase-makers, and although such an admission might reveal again that all contempt contains some self-contempt, now

142

as this rose up in him so disturbingly, with such shameful stabs of pain that it seemed there could be but one possible or desirable solution, namely self-extinction and death, nevertheless that which had overcome him was something other than shame and more than shame: he who looks back on his life, sobered, and because of this sobriety perceives that every step of his erring path has been necessary and inevitable, yea, even natural, knows that this path of reversion was prescribed for him by the might of destiny and the might of the gods, that therefore he had been bound motionless to the spot, motionless despite all his aspirations to go forward, lost in the thicket of images, of language, of words, of sounds, commanded by fate to be entangled in the ramifications within and without, but denied by fate and the gods the one hope of those who lack a leader, the hope of seeing the golden, shimmering bough amidst the wilderness of these prison walls; he who has perceived these things, he who perceives them is no longer ashamed, he is horrified, for he perceives that everything happened simultaneously for the Olympians and that consequently the will of Jupiter and that of fate had come to be unified in a terrible concurrence, revealed to earthly man as an indivisible union of guilt and punishment. Oh, virtuous alone is he whom fate has destined to discharge the dutiful service by which the human community is established, he alone is chosen by Jupiter to be led out of the thicket by fate, but when the common will of fate and the god does not permit this discharge of duty, then inability or unwillingness to help are held to be one and the same, and both are punished by helplessness: unfit for help, unwilling to help, helpless within the human community, shy of communion and locked in the prison of art, this was the poet, without a leader and, in his defection, unfit for leadership; and should he wish to rebel, should he wish to become a helper, an arouser from the twilight, in order to win back to the pledge and to brotherhood, these aspirations of his were condemned to fail from the start —and the three had been sent to him so that he might realize this with horror and shame: his help would be a sham-help, his truth but a seeming truth, and even were they to be acceptable to mankind they would be misleading and calamitous, far from leading to salvation, far from salvation itself, aye, this would be the outcome: the one lacking perception would bring perception to those unwilling for it, the word-maker would be calling out speech from the mute, the derelict would impose duty on those ignorant of duty, the lame would guide the halt.

He was again abandoned, abandoned to an abandoned world, oh, no hand held him now, there was nothing there to shelter or sustain him; he had been let fall, and he hung brokenly over the window-ledge, clinging lifelessly to the dusty, hot, inanimate bricks, feeling the sharp dust of their overheated, primordial clay under his fingernails, clinging to the primordial earthliness of which they were composed; he heard the stifled laughter in the stone-heated, form-fixed silence of the surrounding night, he heard the taciturnity of consummate perjury, the obdurate hush of a guilty conscience, robbed of speech, of knowledge, of memory, the silence of the pre-creation and its increasingly cruel death, the conditions of which allowed no rebirth or renewal for the created world, for such a death bore no traces of divinity: oh, no other creature was so unconditionally and undivinely mortal as man, for none was so capable of perjury, and the more abject he was the more mortal he became, but most perjuring and most mortal was he whose foot had estranged itself from the earth and touched nothing but pavements, the man who no longer tilled and no longer sowed, for whom nothing took place in accord with the circling of the stars, for whom the forest no longer sang, nor the greening meadows; verily nobody and nothing was so mortal as the mob in the great cities, grovelling, sneaking, swarming through the streets, having staggered so long that it had forgotten how to walk, upheld by no law and upholding none, the re-scattered herd, its former wisdom forfeited, unwilling to have knowledge, submitting like the animal, like something less than the animal, to every chance, and at last to a chance extinction without memory, without hope, without immortality; the same thing had happened to him, to him in conjunction with the re-scattered mob-herd of which he was a part, so had it been laid on him as a necessity of fate, inevitable. He had left the region of fear behind him, but only to see with horror how he had fallen to the level of the mob, fallen to a surface which offers no ingress to any kind of depth—, would this fall go still further, must it go further? from surface to surface, down to the final one, the surface of sheer nothingness? to the surface of final oblivion? The Plutonian doors were always open, the fall was inevitable, the fall from which there was no return, and in the intoxication of falling, man was prone to believe himself propelled upward, believing it until he was there where the timeless event of the heavens revealed itself simultaneously as an encounter in the realm of earth, until on the boundary of time he met the un-deified god, who had caught up with and outrun him and who, wrapped in the fluttering mantle of cosmic laughter, hurtled downward even as he, both of them cast into the same state of sober self-abandonment, surrendered to a horror which, even though it was expressed by a doggedly stubborn laughter, was dimly aware of a still greater horror to come and hoped to laugh it off; this fate-driven journey, this fall proceeded toward a horror, a shame, a denudation still more naked, going on in a fresh access of destructiveness and self-destructiveness, worse than before, in a new isolation which was meant to surpass all former loneliness, all the loneliness of night and the world, deserted by not only all that was human but moreover by all that was substantial; here the empty surface of unmastered existence was suddenly laid bare, and the night in the inaccessible inner and outer spheres, although unchanged and radiant in the full circle of its darkness, had dissolved into a nowhere which was so delivered over to chance that all perception and knowledge had become superfluous, and being useless was allowed to vanish; memory like hope had vanished, vanishing before the might of unmastered chance, for it was that which was revealed in the foregoing experience; inescapable this chance which held sway over the uncreated, enveloped by in-

145

toxication and the unremembered abandonment of the pre-creation, threatened by its cold flames, by its amorphousness and pre-natal death, making itself known as naked chance which spelled utter and nameless loneliness, and claimed the right to be supreme—, this was the journey's end, the now visible end of the fall, the very essence of anonymity.

The nameless loneliness of chance, yes it was that which he saw before him as, ready for the fall and already falling, he stood there at the window. Unconquered and unconquerable in its abandonment, the estranged night lay open to his fevered glances, unchanged, immobile yet strange, brushed by the gently-unyielding breath of the moon, unchanged, immobile, and flooded by the gentle flow of the Milky Way, submerged in the silent song of the stars, submerged in the beauty and the magical unity conjured by beauty, submerged in the dissolving unity of a world become beautiful, submerged in its vast remoteness, benumbed and benumbing, and, like space,—beautiful, rigid, and vast, and demonically enchanted to strangeness—it was carried along through time with space, night, and yet immortal in time, aeonic yet not eternal, estranged from humanity, strange to the human soul, because the quiet unification which took place here, saturated by distance and saturating distance, no longer allowed of participation; the forecourt of reality had changed to the forecourt of unreality. Extinguished was the order of the spheres in the universe; their mute-ringing silver spaces, enclosed and estranged by utter incomprehensibility, became silent, including in their strangeness the utter incomprehensibility of all things human; sun and stars and Milky Way had no longer a name, they were alien to him in their remoteness, in their seclusion, which was without bridge or communication and yet which weighed upon him, subduing and threatening, transparent and hot, the overheated chill of universal space; whatever was about him enclosed him no longer, he stood outside the cave of night even though within it, cut off from his own as well as from all alien destinies, cut off from the fate of the visible-invisible world, cut off from divinity, from humanity, from perception, from beauty, for even the beauty of the visible-invisible world had vanished into namelessness, and even the knowledge of it, the meaning of it, had faded—

— oh Plotia, do I still remember your name? in your tresses dwelt the night, spangled over with stars, presager of longing, promiser of light; and I bowed over their duskiness, drunken with night's lambent breath, I did not sink into them! Oh lost life, most intimate strangeness, strangest intimacy, you the furthermost nearness, the nearest of all things far, first and ultimate smile of the soul in its earnestness, you, oh you who were and still are everything, close and strange and a near-far smiling, you, fate-bearing blossom, I could not let your life enter into mine because of its overwhelming remoteness, because of its overwhelming strangeness, because of its overwhelming nearness and intimateness, because of the burden of its nocturnal smile, because of fate, your fate which you bear within you and must bear forever, not to be consummated by you, not to be consummated by me, the fate which I dared not take upon myself because the utter impossibility of its consummation would have riven my heart, and I have been witness only to your beauty, not to your life! oh, you, reluctant departer whom I did not call back, you, graced by longing, whose recall was not permitted me, you, who will not return, your step, alas so light in the inscrutable and inaudible, you, the lost shining behind the shadow, where is your homecoming? where are you? you did exist; and you let me have the ring from your finger, placing it on my hand, and there was a time that encircled us darkly, time that rushed on, enshrouding the darkness, enshrouded by it, oh Plotia, I no longer know what it was—

— scarcely a memory now was that which had vanished, that which had been real and more than real, scarcely more than a name was the woman he had loved, scarcely a glimmer, scarcely a shadow, she had sunk away from him into the inscrutability of chance, and nothing remained but an astonished remembrance of something having existed, of beauty's dying music, the remembrance of a whilom wonder and a once inexplicably powerful oblivion that he had pursued with all the amazing perseverance of a narcotic, oh, still bemused even in remembering that it had ever been, in remembering that beauty had resounded, had been able to resound, that, imbedded in the human countenance like a soft breath issuing from eternity and breathing of eternity, it had shone out from the human countenance again and again, distantly intimate, strangely near, nocturnally smiling, glowing and fading, fragile as the white privet—a delicate tissue-veil of death spread over all things human, the veil of humanity, made dense in beauty while having at the same time become more transparent therein, as if oblivion had crept into the soul, as if the soul had lost itself to its earthly immortality in beauty, in the simple oblivion of beauty, as if a last remnant of hope still flickered in human beauty, that long-lost hope which is turned toward the inaudible, unattainable knowledge of death: nothing was left of it save invincible death standing behind the death-sweet shape which would not return; invincible and grandly erect, death reared up in immensity, raised up to the stars, filling the spheres and binding them, and along with death, evoked by its muteness, moved by it, fulfilling it, seeming to be its very essence, there was a sudden upsurge of all that death comprised, death surging up mutely with all that it contained, the death-stricken, the death-bound, the chance-born, the chance-bound, the hordes of human shapes waiting for death, multitudinous the lame ones, manifold the fat-bellies, the jabberers and carpers, multiplied to such a dense horde that the empty stone receptacle of the plaza overflowed with them, pushing them on into all the spheric spaces without, altering the emptiness of the plaza or that of the spaces, a horde so dense that it was like the outburst and outpouring of time itself, a death-herd of concurrent identities, the earthly-human multiplicity, the earthly man in the cyclic multiplicity of his transformations together with his skeleton and skull—his round skull, flat skull, pointed skull, covered in wool, straw or flax, bald or braided,— skull after skull; the

skull-bearing human with its multiplicity of faces—the animal
face, the plant-face, the stone-face—curiously covered with skin,
either smooth or pimpled or wrinkled, full-fleshed or slack, with
jaws for chewing and speaking, the face's cavern stonily beset
with teeth; the face-bearing man with his various odors of skin
and cavities, with his smile—silly, shrewd, defiant, defenseless
—with his smile which even at its meanest is divinely touching
and opens his countenance before it is closed again in laughter,
lest his eye behold the inhumanity of the shattered creation;
the human being blessed with the gift of sight—enlarged, transfixed, clarified, clouded, made vital, through the eye—revealing
his destiny in his eye, hidden to himself in his eye; the fate-
bearing human being, fate-destined by the very power of his
eye to know shame, and yet the only creature who speaks, his
human voice shamelessly and moistly articulated by the jaws,
the tongue, the lips, the breath-bearing voice, the communion-
bearing voice, the voice which issues from him—harsh, unctu-
ous, flattering, threatening, flexible, stiff, gasping, flaccid,
squeaking, bellowing—the voice which can be all of these but
is always able to transfigure itself into song; the human being,
this wonderful, terrible and yet miraculous entity of atomic
being, of language, of expression, of perception and imperception, of dull drowsing, of calculations in sesterces, of desires,
of enigmas, this creature indivisible yet divided into an infinite
number of individual parts, individual abilities, individual
spheres, divided into organs and living-zones, into substances,
into atoms, multiplied over and over again; all this multiplicity
of being, this maze of human particles, not even well composed,
this creaturely thicket, as earthly in its reality as earth's stony
ribs, earthly as death's skeleton, this underbrush of bodies,
limbs, eyes, and voices, this thicket of the half-created and the
unfinished which issues from chance lust and is forever sprouting out, one from the other, indiscriminately coupled in constantly renewed lust, carelessly commingled, copulated, interwoven, ramified, continuing to branch out and renew itself
while constantly withering, so that what was withered, dried-up

and faded might fall back to the earth; this human thicket, alive
with the elements of the plant and the animal, this thicket
of the living consecrated to death, this it was that flooded up
with the shape of death, surging up with its booming and its
silence, it was death itself filling the spheres, the human chaos
of chance, so accidental and so mortal that we scarcely know
whether he who happens to appear before us as living has not
long since died, or perhaps has never been born, still in the state
of the pre-natally dead or unborn——, Plotia, oh Plotia, never
yet found, undiscoverable! oh, she remained undiscoverable in
the underbrush of death, she had sunk away from him into
the reabandonment of the underworld and he had less communion with her than with one who is dead; for he himself was
dead, died off into the fore-death of uncreativeness, died off
into perjury, into lameness, into crookedness, died off into the
reabandonment of a vulgar, urban literarity which includes
even death in the illusory path of its false reversion, adulter-
ating death with beauty and beauty with death, trying to attain
the unattainable by means of this lewd, corruption-seeking
equalization, to substitute it self-deceptively for the inaudible
knowledge of death, but also certainly to extend the pleasure
of this sort of intermingling to love, indeed by love to push
this playfully-lewd game to its actual climax; for he who is
unable to love, who is unfit for love's communion, he must
rescue himself from his bridgeless isolation by means of beauty;
titillated by cruelty he becomes a seeker of beauty, a devotee
of beauty, but never a lover, far rather an observer of beauty
in the midst of love, one who desires to create love through
beauty, because he confuses what is created with that which
creates, but also because he sniffs and follows hard on the
intoxication to be found in love, the intoxication of death, the
intoxication of beauty, the intoxication of oblivion, because in
the drowsy absorption of his dalliance with beauty and his love
of death he creates for himself the pleasure of oblivion, eager
and willing to forget that love, even though blessedly able to
create beauty, never has beauty as its goal, but heads solely

toward its own immemorial vocation, that most human of all vocations which always and without exception implies assuming the other's burden of fate; oh, the dead hold no communion among themselves, they have forgotten one another—

— oh Plotia! unforgotten and unforgettable! you who were swathed in beauty! oh, if love existed, if the discrimination of love could exist in the human thicket, it would portend that together we might descend to the obliterating fountain of nothingness, to the sobering depths of the underworld, that we might descend, we sober and without illusions, going down to the primal base, not through the beautiful ivory portal of dreams which never opens for the return, but through the sober entrance of horn which would permit us to come back, retrieving in our common ascent a new fate from the last fate's embers, retrieving from the last lovelack a new love, a newly created fate, fate in the making! oh Plotia, childlike yet no longer a child! only the unfolding fate may we take upon ourselves, not fate that is fixed; only as it unfolds does this fate become love's reality which we seek for in kernel and bud of all that breathes of spring, in every grassblade, in every flower, in all young and growing creatures, but most fervently in the child, assuming the unfolded fate and its readiness to be formed, for the sake of which we bow to all that is still untouched, subsuming what is coming to pass in that which has already come to pass, taking the boy into the formative strength of the man, oh, Plotia, it is this unfolding fate, it is this which would be bestowed upon us if love existed, if its discriminative force, freed of all chance lust, could assure us the real certainty of loving, then fate itself would be love, love in its unfolding and its being, love as the descent into the depths of unremembrance and the ascent once more in complete recollection, as the extinction to nothingness and as the homecoming into an unchanged sameness, were it in the form of grassblade and blossom and child, as unchanged as these always are, and yet changed to love, enhanced by the gleaming shadow of love's golden bough, the undiscoverable—

— oh, the dead are without communion among themselves, under no bright shadow of a golden bough, they have forgotten one another; and Plotia's figure, Plotia's unforgotten-forgotten existence, which had once been his shimmering light behind every shadow, had lost itself in the shades and had become indistinguishable in the shadowy realm, sunken into the hordes of the dead, a particle yet scarcely a part of the collective dead, the mass of whose faces, skulls and figures were nameless and indistinguishable for him, all together having disappeared and evaporated because, from the beginning, they had been as dead for him, nameless because he had never once wanted to be of actual help to the living, aye more—condemned by the gods and fate to such unwillingness, innocent and yet guilty—because he had needed a whole lifetime even for the first attempt at help, for the first untaken step, for the first untaken start of such a step, reluctant to join any living community in service, to say nothing of taking the fate of a single living creature upon himself for this purpose, oh, he had misused his life in the non-community of the dead, he had always lived with the dead only, among whom he reckoned the living, he had considered human beings as lifeless building blocks with which to erect and create a death-fixed beauty, and therefore human beings as a whole had disappeared for him into the realm of the unaccomplished, into the oblivion of the eternally uncreated. For only in the task that the human being assumed because of his humanity was the saving perception also to be found, and in shirking the task he robbed himself even of salvation. Unfit, that is what he was, unfit for real helpfulness, unfit for the loving deed; he had looked on human sorrow and been unmoved by it, he had looked on the horror of events merely as something to be remembered unchastely and without chastity recorded in beauty, and this was the very reason why he had never succeeded in depicting real human beings, people who ate and drank, who loved and could be loved, and this was why he was so little able to depict those who went limping and cursing through the streets, unable to picture them in their bestiality and their great need of help, least able to show forth the miracle of humanity with which such bestiality is graced; people meant nothing to him, he considered them as fabulous beings, mimes of beauty in the garments of beauty, and as such he had depicted them, as kings and heroes of fable, as fable-shepherds, as creatures of dream in whose unreal god-likeness, played out and dreamed out in beauty, he also — resembling the mob even in this — would gladly have participated, in which perhaps he might have participated had they been visions of the real dream instead of mere word-creatures, barely alive in his poetry but dead as soon as they turned the next corner, emerging from the dark thicket of language and disappearing into limbo, into unlovedness, into numbness, into death, into silence, into unreality, just as those three who had vanished, never to be seen again. And out of their vanishing there boomed the evil, world-shattering muteness of derision with which these three had been shaken, boomed maliciously as a second silence through the silence of the plaza and the streets below, boomed through the stillness of the night, a chance laughter full of strangeness, booming, bursting and annulling space though not annulling time, the laughter of consummate perjury, the mute booming of the shattered creation at the mercy of chance.

Nothing remained but the scorn-blinded shame of an extinguished memory, which had turned to the unchastity of a dead sham-memory. Aroused by no earthly flames the fires of heaven had died down into namelessness; the middle was silent, covered by the paving-stones of cities, it had merged with the most distant boundaries, grown cold under the breath of nothingness, and now the simultaneous stream of the creation in which the eternal reposes, it too was benumbed: woe to the sham-reversions of the false path, for they but imitated the vast orbits which have the power to bind past and future into the eternal now of timelessness; woe to this seeming timelessness which was the essence of all intoxication and which, to maintain such diversion, must needs continue to substitute the thing created for that which creates, beauty-thirsty, blood-thirsty, death-thirsty, betraying and perverting the sacrifice for the voluptuous intoxication of pleasure; woe to this unchaste vanity of memory for which the reality had never existed, and which remembered simply for the sake of remembering; woe to this reversion of being, for the pledge could not be renewed, the flame could not be rekindled, for dalliance failed and must fail, no matter how much beauty, blood and death was contributed to it, it remained ineffectual at the turning point of time on which all earthly immortality was shattered; verily, so long as the sacrifice failed to be a real sacrifice, disaster was inevitable, there was no awakening from the sleep of twilight, and the presumptuous one, caught in a vicious circle, remained imprisoned once and for all, the presumptuous one, who regarded himself as justified in neglecting his pledge because he interpreted the enchanting concurrence inside and outside, the ebb and flow of the world's tides, the tempting view at the beauty-hemmed boundaries of the world, because he interpreted seduction itself as permission for that unreal reversion, which held just as much intoxication as forgetting or remembering, both spelling the loss of reality—woe to the intoxicated one, who presumptuous and obstinate lingered in his perjury and, whether overcome by remembrance or not, forgot that he was human; he had lost the fiery core of being and no longer knew whether he toppled upward or downward, whether he peered forward or backward, his cyclic path was without direction, but his head was screwed stiffly and absurdly onto his neck. The dead are inert, she who was dead could not be aroused, the space of oblivion had closed above her in a gray flood, and it seemed as if the women in Misery Street had known that one who had not realized his life was being carried there into his final disillusion, into his last oblivion. Had their scorn now really justified itself? Was there nothing left for him save the shameful plunge into nothingness and into the regions of the empty surface which stretch out subterraneously beneath the borders of oblivion? Oh, they had judged rightly and he was meant to accept the scornful curses with horrified shame, for the unchastity of which he had innocently made himself guilty was more debased than the most shameless, passing lust of the mob, since his guilt was the unchastity of a voluntary downfall, since, even though at fate's bidding, he had been a willing part of a perjured and lost race, a race which reeled over the flag-stones of the void, the Titanic deed forgotten, a race as fireless as the animal, as cold as the plant, as inert as the stone, lost in the underbrush, itself mere underbrush, sunk into the indiscrim-ination of final petrification: he had fallen prey to the threat which encircled the degraded, he degraded along with them, lost with the lost ones, and the threat—fate-empowered by a higher threat, not to be held back by the roaring of any laughter, silent with an absolute silence, tone-benumbing, light-benumb-ing, in the crystalline darkness of the stonily inevitable, diffused and benumbed along with the night—the threat mounted higher and higher. Everything was threatened, everything had become unsure, even the menace itself, since the danger had changed, transposed from the zone of incidence to that of permanence. The night endured unshaken, coldly glowed the darkly trans-parent gold of its pinions spread over the human dwellings, which on all sides rested stonily upon the rigid earth, painted over by the arid light of the moon; and the rigidity, drinking in the light from the stars, was transformed into transparent stone unto its deepest, fiery depth, was turned into a transparent stone-shadow in the opened crystal shafts of the world, turned to a crystal echo of the inaudible, until it was like petrification's last breathless struggle for breath, a stony gasp praying for the breath of life; shadow-petrified, shadow-petrifying, it roamed up and down, even the sentry's steps beyond the wall, after marking off time as permanent, became part of it; they had turned into stone, a resounding, solemn shadow-tread of noth-ingness, growing out from the ringing pavement and back into it; and as the stiff-pointed, sharp-shadowed apex of the iron cupola surmounting the wall-turrets now became visible under the continual intensification of light, the shaft between the wall and house opened up no less candidly, its shadows sharpened and cleared by the light unto its final depth, silver-green from the flow of spheric brightness, light-petrified, light-dry, light-ringing, from very muteness down to the sandy grit of its floor, down to the absolutely immobile vagueness of the shaft-bottom where, in the dry shadow of some brush, all sorts of oddments, scarcely describable, became visible, half-hidden by the silver-green branchings of the thicket, with planking and tools, these also casting shadows, but in a fashion so terribly solemn that it was like a lonely and strangely unworthy echo of the stony, universal muteness, mirroring danger, revenge and threat, because here the nothing was reflected in nothingness, the transparent in dust, one like the other grazed by the motionless pinion, both paralyzed by melancholy and in both, hunted and torn, the unheard hissing of death—

— but the Ciconean women, whom he had offended out of love for her who was dead, had torn the man into pieces during their bacchantic orgies at the feast of the gods, and scattered far and wide in the fields the limbs wasted away; the head too was torn from its marble neck, but still it retained its voice and, already seized by the paternal Hebrus in its swirling eddy, the head called back with its failing breath, "Eurydice, thou poor one," and from the bank of the stream came back the echo, "Eurydice"—

— yet he was echoless, a dead reverberation in the desert mountains of Tartarus which had shot up to remain there forever, he was a mute echo in both worlds which were fading out without moving, a mute echo of a breath-wringing gasp in the dry chasms and in the crystal shafts of petrification; he was a sightless skull, rolled out into the stone rubble on the shadowy shores of oblivion, rolled under the dry, dense shrubbery on the shores of the shadowy stream, rolled toward a void so totally without egress that it extinguished oblivion itself; he was nothing but a blind eye, without trunk, without voice, without breath, emptied of breath, and thus he was thrown out to the vacuous blindness of the underworld: his task had been the casting off of shadows, instead of which he had created shadows, the great pledge of allegiance to earth had been laid upon him and he had been perfidious to it from the first, oh, he had been charged with the task of moving the stones from the sepulchre once again, so that humanity might rise to rebirth, so that the living creation as law, manifested in an ever-recurring contemporaneousness despite all changes of time, might not be interrupted, so that the god might again be awakened to this eternal presentness by the everlasting now of the sacrificial flames and forced back to the pledge of self-creation,— the god shaken by the pledge, torpidity checked by the pledge, the flames kindled by the pledge, oh, this had been his task and he had not accomplished it, he had not been allowed to accomplish it; even before he had been able to move the gravestones in order to fulfill the unknown pledge, aye, even before he could touch them, even before he had been able to lift his arms, these had become heavy, paralyzed and transparent, grown into the stony petrification, grown into the motionless, heterogeneous, dry and transparent stone flood, and this immobile flood, petrifying and petrified, penetrating from all the spheres toward the middle and shivering back again as far as the borders of the spheres, absorbing the living and unliving in its shadowy crystal, became a single stone, the sacrificial altar of the universe, ungarlanded, unwarmed, unshaken, immovable, became the grave-stone of the world, denuded of sacrifice, covering the inscrutable and itself inscrutable. OH, THE LOT OF THE POET! LOVE'S POWER OF REMEMBRANCE HAD FORCED ORPHEUS TO ENTER THE DEPTHS OF HADES, ALTHOUGH AT THE SAME TIME IT PREVENTED HIM FROM GOING FURTHER, SO THAT, LOST IN THE UNDER-WORLD OF MEMORY, HE WAS PREMATURELY IMPELLED TO RETURN, UNCHASTE EVEN IN HIS CHASTITY AND RENT IN HIS CALAMITY. HE, UN-LIKE ORPHEUS, HE, LOVELESS FROM THE BEGINNING, UNABLE TO SEND FORTH THE LOVING RECOLLECTION AND GUIDED BY NO MEMORY, HE HAD NOT EVEN REACHED THE FIRST LEVEL UNDER THE IRON RULE OF VULCAN, EVEN LESS THE DEEPER REALM OF THE LAW-FOUNDING FATHERS, AND STILL LESS THE MUCH DEEPER ONE OF THE NOTHING,

157

WHICH GIVES BIRTH TO THE WORLD, TO MEMORY, TO SALVATION, HE HAD REMAINED IN THE TORPID EMPTINESS OF THE SURFACE. The unmastering, once having taken place, leaves nothing behind to be mastered, and the great life-bearing tides of enkindling and extinguishing, absorbed by the vast silence of the perception-drained, law-drained ignominy, these too were silenced; likewise the tides of beginning and ending, the tides of blazing perturbation and mildly-trickling reassurance, their mutual regeneration, that turns one into the other, were silenced; the universal entity, having forever lost its breath, its substance, its movement, its cohesion, was now stripped down to a silent glance amidst the universal silence, stripped to an encompassing view of pure nakedness in its visible invisibility, stripped to its glanceless-glancing, unalterable, final non-existence: stony the staring eye above, stony the staring eye below, oh, now it had come, the long-awaited, the always-feared, it had come at last, now he beheld it, now he must look into the namelessly inconceivable, into the inconceivable namelessness, for the sake of which he had fled through a lifetime, for the sake of which he had done everything to prepare for a premature ending of this life, and it was not into the eye of night that he looked, for the night had vanished into the petrification, and it was not fear, not horror, for it was greater than any fear or any horror, it was the eye of stony emptiness, the torn-open eye of a fate, which no longer participated in any occurrence, neither in the passing nor in the annulling of time, neither in space nor in spacelessness, neither in life nor in death, neither in creation nor in discreation, an unparticipating eye in whose glance there was no beginning, no ending and no concurrence, released from subsistence and survival, bound to subsist and survive only through the threat and the looming suspense, only by the element of time in the waiting interval that still continued, reflected in the continuing existence of the threatened one and in his threat-fearing glance, the threat and the threatened cast out to one another in the dregs of time. And flight was no longer possible, only its breathless gasping, and there was no going on—whither could it have led now?—and the gasping was like that of a runner who, having passed his goal, knows he has not met it and will never meet it, because in the no-man's-land of perjury, this perjured un-space, through which he had been driven, only to be driven on and on, the goal could not be pledged and remained unvouched-for, aimless the creation, aimless the god, aimless the human being, the creation without echo, god and man without echo in the lawless reabandonment that gives birth to un-space. That which surrounded him no longer symbolized anything, it was a non-symbol, the very essence of the unreflectable and beyond reflection; it had the dolor of symbol-impoverishment, the dolor of vacuity, that was spacelessly submerged into every thing created in space and even dreamily submerged into the dormant humus of existence, divested of all symbol and yet containing the seed of every symbol, voided of space, yet like a final trace of time-borne beauty conditioned by space, the dream-sadness that dwelt in the depths of every eye, in the eye of the animal as in the eye of the man, and the god, indeed, shimmered even in the universal eye of emptiness like a last sigh of the creation, mourning and mourned in the throes of a scarcely remembered chaos, as if vacuity originated in sorrow and sorrow likewise continued to stem from vacuity, as if in their oneness were implanted the primal doom of all incarnation, the evil that threatened everything human and divine, their common fear of fate, their common punishment by fate; on the one hand the fear of the perjurer condemned from the outset to perjury, on the other hand the punishment with which fate overruled even the gods, the punishment for the deed undone, the uncommitted wrong, the punishment determined by the unknown law, which was the loss of perception, and languishing in the prison of a blindly-compelled drowsiness, the HOPELESSNESS OF IMPERCEPTION IN ITS IMPERCEIVABLE NECESSITY: near and nearer it moved, driven by the mutely-gasping, breathless, unredeemed sorrow, yet so slow as to be immobile, lost in sorrow and evil, lost in an emptiness which absorbed even the sorrow and the evil; stony and leaden it arose from all the

shafts of the inner and outer worlds, as if the threat were about
to be consummated, the peering emptiness mounting like a thun-
derstorm; more and more threatening became the not-yet-encoun-
tered, stonier the compulsion of the glance, pushed near like a
wall of silence, pushed nearer in a stupefying muteness which
was his as well as that of all the spheres, burdensome and more
than burdensome, more and more oppressive, the glance-widen-
ing gaze of terror which approached the lifeless middle; and
the ego, caught and encircled by the middle, caught between
the glance-walls, forced into the indiscrimination of inner and
outer worlds, stifling in this double sadness, in the boundless,
universal sorrow of the still-surviving existence, which lifts all
multiplicity and all duplication into the vastness of its own
immensity, thereby annulling it, the ego, too, was annulled,
absorbed and crushed by immensity with its doleful emptiness,
with its terrible foreboding that carried the twofold fright and
the twofold horror while dissolving them; the ego, too, was dissolved, dissolved yet frozen into the glance of the surrounding
threat, the glance-threatened ego having long since become no
more than a blank stare; the threat-subjected ego was compressed
to the last trace of its existence, was annihilated to the un-space
where it was inchoate and unthinking, was thrown back to the
minimal point of life at its ebb, unresistingly delivered to the
clasp of emptiness; oh, it was thrown back, hurled back, propelled into the abasement of itself, flung into contrition, into
utter contrition, humbled to a necessity from which there was
no escape, to ITS OWN NECESSITY FOR CONTRITION, humiliated
in the abjectness of the void which is the sheer ceasing of existence; the ego had lost its selfhood, had been stripped of its
human qualities, nothing more remained to it save the naked
soul's most naked guilt, so that even the soul, having no more
selfhood though yet immortal as the human soul, existed only
in its contrite and empty nakedness, forced down and absorbed
by the unmirrored emptiness of the threat-silent eye, unwitnessed the contrition, unwitnessed the ego, unwitnessed the
soul, blankly abandoned to the power of the extinguishing

160

glance, itself extinguished—; silence, emptiness, vacuity, muteness, yet behind the black-crystalline walls of the universal
muteness, in the distanceless utter-distance of unbordered immensity, fading, inaudible, like a most desolate sound-image
of existence, already beyond existence, thin, bright and female,
frightening in its unspeakable smallness, a single point took
sound, vibrating from the most inaccessible point of the spheres,
its core of terror taking sound in a tiny titter, the vacant titter
of emptiness, the tittering of the empty nothing. Oh, where was
there help?! where were the gods?! was this which had happened
the last emanation of their power, their revenge and retaliation
for their abandonment again by abandoned mankind?! were the
women-kind of the gods exulting over lost humanity and the
inescapable perjury of the world?! Deafened now to any answer,
he listened into the chaos, but the answer did not come, for the
perjurer was not able to pose questions, as little able to question
as the animal, and the stone was dead, dead without an echo
to the unasked question, dead the stony labyrinth of the universe,
dead the shaft on the very bottom of which the naked ego, abased
to extinction, divested of both question and answer, barely
existed. Oh, back! back into darkness, into dream, into sleep,
into death! Oh, back, just to be back once more, fleeing and fleeing backward once again into the sphere of recognition! Oh,
flight! but flight again? if there was still flight, if flight were
actually possible, if he was actually meant to escape? he did
not know, perhaps he had once known but now he knew nothing,
he was beyond all possibility of knowing, seeing that he was in
a void without knowledge, in the universal emptiness, beyond
the agitation of flight, alas, the penitent is already beyond
escape—, but dejected by his perjury, as if the perjurer himself must be broken, as if he should nevermore be allowed to
stand erect, he felt himself flung to his knees, and bowing deeply
under the immense burden of the blind-unmoving, invisibly-
transparent universal emptiness, flight-benumbed, flight-para-
lyzed, the laden shoulders bent down, he sought with dry and
lifeless hands blind-fingered for the wall of the room, touching

with blind fingers the blind-fingered shadow on its moon-lit, moon-dry surface, he groped his way along it, accompanied by his deeply-bowed shadow, gliding near him, groped his way with violent trembling back into the darkness, unmindful of what he was doing or not doing, he felt his way to the wall-fountain, allured like an animal by the water, hankering for what was still earthly, still living, still moving; with hanging head he crept like an animal through the benumbed aridity toward the most animal of all goals, toward water, so that bent over in the sheerest animal necessity he might lap at the silver-trickling moisture.

Woe to that man who has not shown himself equal to the grace again bestowed upon him, woe to the penitent who cannot bear his penance, woe to the creaturely remnant of existence who will not put off his existence, alas, who cannot do so, because the extinguished memory persists in its emptiness; woe to that man, who despite his contrition remains unalterably un-delivered, condemned to creatureliness! about him the laughter breaks out anew, and it is the laughter of horror, a laughter neither male nor female, neither that of the gods nor the god-desses, it is the empty tittering of the void, it is the remnant of vitality in the void that does not disappear for the mortal, that titters and breaks into laughter, the remnant which unveils itself as existence in nothingness, nothingness in existence, as the union of sham-life and sham-death, as the hilarious knowledge of this sham-dead existence, as the terrible and fearful remnant of knowledge amidst the emptiness, maniacal and inducing madness, becoming more and more intense until the emptiness is turned into naked horror. For the more that remorse gains ascendancy over the human being and strips him of his human essence, the more directly it takes hold on the creaturely and the bestial in human nature, the quicker it comes to grips with animal fear, the horror-hounded fear of the human being who has been hurled back into his creaturely loneliness and like a stray-

162

ejected part of the flock cannot find its way back to the herd; this was the horrible fear implanted in all the herd-born from the beginning of things, the fear of a discarnate death-emptiness, and—at the final peak of fright, in the final deliverance to fear, almost beyond death—it was the mute terror of the beast that, alone in its littleness, invisibly overcome, bereft of consciousness, creeps trembling under some dark shrubbery so that no eye may watch it dying. Woe to the penitent whose soul is incapable of bearing the little loneliness laid upon it, its smallness comes to be unconsciousness, and the grace of humility becomes an empty degradation for him. Had it gone so far? His thinking was lowly, insofar as it still existed, his actions were those of an animal, insofar as there were any, and laughter, blindly hidden, waited within the inaudible; suddenly and without deliberation he had reached the bed and was crouching in it pitifully, his throat constricted, a dry coldness in his limbs, surrendered unconscious to the black-invisible omnipotence spread out doubly over the contrite and the creaturely, surrendered unconscious to a realm beyond fear, beyond terror, beyond horror, beyond death, yet he felt fear, terror, horror and death break out anew, feeling the horror in the intangible, perceptible, even in imperceptibility; he was let fall while yet being held, still held, held into the empty space of horror, oh, he was held into the horror and at the same time filled with horror: first and last memories touched each other, both lost and locked in loneliness within the thicket of life, the thicket of voices, the thicket of images, the thicket of memory, the beginning never dimmed, even though overshadowed by so many years, never dimmed the memory of the straying herd-animal, the memory of its primal horror, the only one which had remained, all others being but transformations of this solely terrible one that sat on every branch in the thicket of memory, tittering scornfully, laughing scornfully, laughing over the motionless encirclement of him who was hopelessly lost in the thicket, encircling him, itself the thicket, itself the impenetrable; the journey of memory was without movement, a journey of ceaseless beginnings and ceaseless endings, a journey across the un-space of memory, across the un-space of stagnated straying, across the un-space of the unrecallable trance-life; it proceeded without movement, a whizzing journey through all the transformations of un-space, inevitably accompanied and encompassed by them, dimensionless in their trance-stagnation, dimensionless in their trance-movement, always however within the undimension of horror, because it was the inescapable, the ever-present, the never-forsaken prison of the leaden trance of death, in the shadow of whose horror the sham-life of mankind plays itself out—he was held into the undimension of a trance-death. And even though he lay still, without moving a finger's breadth in any direction, and even though the room about him did not change in the slightest, it seemed to him that he was being carried forward, yes, that he was being carried forward, drawn forward into the invisible by the invisible, by his fore-knowledge, by his fore-remembrance; now memory in all its diversity scurried past him as if to lure him on, as if by its means the journey could or should be accelerated, he was being carried forward to the goal of horror which had been there from the beginning, and the room floated with him, unaltered and yet disarranged as in travel, time-fixed and yet constantly in flux. Rigidly the amorini released themselves from the frieze and despite this they remained a part of it, the acanthus leaves, freed from paint and plaster, became human-faced and the stem, grown out to the crooked claw of an eagle, floated near the bed, opening and closing its talons as though wishing to test the strength of its grip; beards grew out of the leaf-faces and were sucked back again, they floated on in immobility, often turning over, often rotating in a motionless whirlwind; there came to be more and more of them, far more than the wall-painting contained even though it renewed itself constantly, they fluttered out of the frieze, they fluttered out of the bare wall, they fluttered from a nowhere, vomited forth from the bubbling cold volcanoes of nothingness, which were erupting everywhere in the visible and invisible, within and without, they were the lava of these volcanoes, the breathy detritus of a former existence and disintegration, becoming more diverse as they increased, shapes forming and being formed out of emptiness and, for all that, changing into one another as they fluttered along, transformed and untransformable stuff, fluttering like leaves and butterflies, some like arrows, some fork-tailed, some with tails like long whips, some so transparent that they only floated about, invisibly-mute like silent shouts of terror, many, on the other hand, as harmless as an idiotic-transparent smile, as numerous as sun-motes, as cumberless as ants, they swarmed vacantly about the candelabra in the center of the room, nipping at the spent candles, making way immediately, to be sure, for things that came storming, buzzing and dancing in their wake, more than pushed out by a press of hollow shapes in which, next to faces and non-faces, next to the twin-bodied Scyllas, strange seals, and bristling Hydras, next to the bloodily-hissing, bloodily-bound heads of tousled, snake-like hair, all sorts of deformities were scampering, and all kinds of hoofed creatures, half-starved or unfinished Centaurs or fragments of Centaurs, winged and unwinged, whizzed past, the orcus-pregnant space bursting with grotesque animal-life; toadish, lizardish, dog-footed creatures emerged, reptiles with innumerable legs, with no legs, with one, two, three, a hundred legs, at times wobbling in the bottomless pit, at others sailing past woodenly, stiffly a-sprawl, often pressed close together as if, with all their sexlessness, they meant to mate in flight, often entering each other with arrow-like swiftness, as if they were hollow creatures of air, ether-born and ether-carried, surely that is what they were, for their winged horde, staggering, creeping, tumbling over one another, although they covered and concealed one another, could be seized and held easily by the glance even unto the last single speck and into the furthermost limits of the room packed full of them; oh, they were ether-scaled, ether-winged, ether-bred, abruptly spewed up from the volcanoes of the Aeons, torrential, voluminous, constantly evaporating, constantly vanishing, so that the room became empty again and again, as empty as the spheres, as empty as the whole world, with an emptiness through which trotted only a single horse, stamping alone high in the air with bristling mane, through which floated only a single male torso whose flatly transparent head, turned toward the bed, was distorted by hollow, scornful, mirror-laughter before it was once again swallowed in a newly-risen vermin-flood of horror—and not one of these creatures breathed, for there is no breath in latency; the room had become a chamber of furies and it offered space enough for the whole terrible occurrence, even though this waxed without let or hindrance: the ceiling had no need to lift, although the candelabrum had spread out to a gigantic tree, the candle-holders stretching immeasurably to become the towering, moist-leaved branches of an ancient, shade-giving elm, and in its foliage, leaf by leaf, thickly gathered as dew-drops, sat the hypocritical dreams; the walls had no need to widen although all the cities of the world lay between them, and all of them burning, the cities of the remotest past and remotest future, man-blatant, man-tortured cities, cities with foreign names which nevertheless he recognized, the cities of Egypt and Assyria and Palestine and India, the cities of the dethroned gods, come to helplessness, the pillars of their temples crashed, their walls shattered, their turrets broken, the paving-stones of their streets cracked open; and the smallness of the chamber sufficed for the vastness of the whole world, although city and field and sky and forest had not lessened in size, and everything, great and small together, revealed itself in an almost overpowering sameness of significance, this sameness suggesting that under the elm branches, as if their leafy shadows were high-flying thunder-clouds, the most terrible of cities, the largest and most accursed, were rising up in immeasurable vastness in the midst of ever-returning havoc—Rome, but humiliated, through whose streets, sniffing for prey, the wolves strolled to take their city again into their possession; the room encircled the globe, the cities encircled each other, not one of them was either inside or outside, all of them floating, while overhead, high above the volcanoes, high above the petrification, high above the foliage, cut off from everything, in the lofty gray dome of the sky, with a furious clatter of motionless, iron pinions, glinting and whirring like contraptions of steel, noiseless the birds of hate soared in wide, deep circles over the lands of abomination, ready with grim cowardice, with joyful fury, to swoop down with opened talons and sink their claws into the bloody fields, the bleeding hearts of the peasants, tearing at their entrails and devouring them, prepared to take their place in the train of wolves and butterflies passing the bed, fleeing with them to the outposts of defencelessness and comfortlessness, to the edge of the fiery craters and dragon-plants, never recognized, never named but always known, the snaky borders of animality. What further volcanoes of the pre-creation had now to be opened? what new monsters would they still disgorge? was not everything stripped to its final nakedness without that? was not the high peak of every conceivable horror already inherent in the encircling beastliness? Or was the transparency of fear leading on to a fresh knowledge of fear, to new fear on inconceivably new levels of primitivity? Everything was exposed, nothing could be grasped, nothing was allowed to be kept, all that remained was the trance-movement of the things in flight, all that persisted was the dusky gray light of a cold aimlessness in which nothing near or far, above or below, could be seen, while he, fleeing with the train of monsters, flying with them through the cold light, through the aimlessness, he was seized and held, held by a bodiless, flying plant-hand with wild, untamable fingers, and he recognized the trance-death, the gray rigidity through the un-space of which he was being carried: icy horror, devoid of symbols, such were the images which floated about him, these tailed things that were not animals, these gaping jaws that did not clutch, this lifted crest that did not strike, this spraying poison that did not land, attacking and encircling from the rear, transparency assailing transparency, empty in their threatening and, despite that, more terrible than any shout or seizure; horror itself had become transparent, the organic nature of naked horror had revealed itself, and in its depths of depths, in its furthest well-spring lay the serpent of time, closed to a circle, icily coiling about the trickling of nothingness. Yes, this was the rigid horror of trance-death, and the animal face was scarcely a face now, all that remained of it was the transparency of plant life, sprouting in stems, entangled in stems, twisting in tail-stems, controlled by snakestems, shooting up from some immeasurable, undiscoverable lattice-work of roots, its subanimality incorporated in it, the animal-face denuded to the horror of blankness, fed by the nothingness of the middle. No horror of death could compare with this fullness of horror, for this was the horror of trance-death, surrounded by subanimality, by the pre-animal; no fear of being wounded, of pain or of suffocation could equal this stifling horror, in the very intangibility of which nothing remained to grasp, because in the not yet created creation, in its no-breath, in its breath-need, there was nothing which one could grasp: this was the breath-need of the unfinished, the unborn creation, its absolute transparency in which animal, plant, and human, all of them transparent, resembling each other to sameness, were forced to suffocate one another because of their breath-robbing terror, because of their undelivered and undeliverable bondage to the nothing, because of their unlived, transparent lack of identification, because of their extreme sameness and hostility—all of them filled with the horrible fear of the animal, which recognizes the utterly amorphous animalhood of its own non-being, oh, the stifling horror of the universe! Oh, had this fear always existed? had he ever been free of it? Had it not always been a vain defense against the storm of horror? Oh, it had gone on night after night, year after year, as far off as youth, as near as yesterday; night after night in idle self-deception he had thought to listen to dying, but it had been only a defense from the horror of trance-death, a defense from the images of trance-death which had appeared night after night and of which he wished to know nothing, which he had refused to see and which had remained for all that—

Oh, who wants to sleep while Troy is burning! again and

again! now are the waves of the sea set to foaming, churned by the oar-strokes, cut by the furrowing ships, as their triple-beaked prows cleave the waters . . .

—, the images persisted and were not to be banished; night after night terror had lifted him through the silence of the spectre-filled craters, through the unremembrance of the pre-creation, through the re-abandoned, aeon-far existence reversed to immediate proximity, across the gnarled, weary fields of complete desolation, deserted by all men and all things, creation abandoned anew. Night after night he had been led up to the cold unshakeable force of reality, to that unreal reality that comes before all the gods and outlasts all the gods and that puts the seal on their helplessness; he had caught sight of Moira, waiting gruesome and three-bodied, she in whose images all forms of sham-death are suggested, and he had tried to close his eyes to her paralyzed-paralyzing, powerless power, blind in his distraction, deaf to the coruscating giggling scorn of the nothingness which the helplessly sobered one is nevertheless unable to escape, deaf to the fateful, flat laughter of the pre-creation which makes him aware of the impossibility of mastering the nameless, the indiscriminate, the unformed, and prompts him to contrition; oh, thus had it been, bearing the inevitable threat, warding off the inevitable; the years were like the flowing on of a single night, flooded with images, bedevilled with images, capering with images, borne along by images in a standstill of horror, and the thing that unremittingly and irresistibly had announced itself night after night could no longer be averted; it was a horror-cramp of tranced prostration in which he would lie, constrained by his coffin, constrained by his grave, stretched out for the immobile journey, he alone, without support, without intercession, without succor, without mercy, without light, without eternity, surrounded by the imperturbable, stony slabs of the sepulchre which would open for no resurrection. Oh, the tomb! it was here also in the narrow chamber, also touched by the elm-branches, danced about by furies, stormed by the fury-scorn, ah, even the tomb seemed to scorn itself as well as the self-deception to which he had clung, scorning his childish hopes which had betrayed him into believing that the quiet immutability of the Bay of Naples, that the serene sunny majesty of the sea with its far-reaching memories of home, that the power inherent in such landscapes would gently attend the act of dying and change it to an unsung, unsingable music, a music which would awaken life, forever hearkening, forever hearkened to, awaken it to death; oh, scorn and more scorn, now that the edifice stood devoid of space, devoid of landscape, with nothing opening beyond it—no sea, no coast, no fields, no mountains, no stone, not even the amorphousness of the primodial clay—nothing but the intangible waste, incomprehensibly horrible in its very nothingness, a naked scorn-edifice, surrounded by that ever-undulating flood in which he floated and was carried along with the grotesque animals on every side, swirled into and borne floatingly onward by the stuffy, breathless, parched, undrinkable ether-glair, which was neither air nor water, borne onward by the transparent fumes of every flaming fear, by this no-breath of the whole pre-creation which vanished like a sort of dry sifting between the fingers; and even in this terribly animal-sated, animal-pregnant, animal-dripping, ethereal element—absorbing him who had fallen back into animality—half-birds were perching on the roof-top, terrible grave-birds with fishy eyes in a crowded row, owl-headed, goose-beaked, pig-bellied, gray-feathered with feet that were merely human hands webbed for swimming, brooding birds flown from no countryside, whose flight was unfit for any land. Thus they crouched in the nakedness of terror, glowering and perching close to one another, and thus also stood the tomb crowned by them, as much within the bay-window as outside there in the unreachable, sought-for distance. Layer on layer, one above the other, the bareness of a no-heaven was covered by the round bow of the bay-window, both arching over the sepulchre, both permeated by un-space even though shot through by the velvet blackness of the whole star-studded round of the sky, and the domes of the universe were intergrown by elms in an immeasurable expansion of all discrepancies and distances which, at the same time, was an immeasurable contraction of them; the landscape-lack pierced the landscape and was pierced by it, the un-space pierced space and was pierced by it, symbolic in its lack of symbol, just as the animal element penetrated the trance-death and was penetrated by it in turn; the symbols of life had died away, spent like the starry animal formations of the heavens, their meaning fulfilled and full of meaning; they had grown cold under the bareness that covered them, but the symbols of death remained, if only in the symbolic bareness of the inexpressible, unthinkable, unimaginable pre-creation; they remained in the creaturely, expressionless, animal grimace, in these images of horror creeping out of trance as if stemming directly from emptiness, reflecting nothing and reflected in nothing, image and counter-image united in the nullity of expression inherent in every deep, primal loneliness which, never-comprehended, always known, always feared, coils in the aeonic depths of time and creaturely animality; the cycle of the symbolic closes itself in latency, closes itself there in the pre-creation's mingling of the spheres, closes itself there where nothing has a connection with anything else and where the empty, aeonic distance revolves to become visible in the vacant grin of the animal, as if the conscious image of primal loneliness had been carried through endless cycles of images, from semblance to semblance, in order to reveal itself in ultimate nakedness at the very imageless end; and in this revelation, in this mutely thundering outbreak of the uncreated and its loneliness, breaking out with all the malice which corresponds to the baffled, displaced aggressive greed in the blank animal grimace, the evil becomes manifest, the evil behind all creation and uncreation, behind the pre-creation and all lonely distance, threat-boding and disclosed in the oppressiveness of the trance-death, implying ominously that all paths of reversion, that all ways of insensitivity, of dalliance, of intoxication lead unhesitatingly to animality, that all ways of beauty end squarely in the grotesque. And on the roof of the sepulchre which was to have transformed death into beauty sat the chain of evil birds. On every side the cities of the globe were burning in a landscape devoid of scenery, their walls crumbled, their flag-stones cracked and burst asunder, the fumes of decay on their fields reeking of blood; and the godless-godseeking lust of sacrifice raged everywhere, sham-oblation after sham-oblation was heaped up in a frenzy of sacrifice, men mad with sacrifice raged all about, slaying the next in turn in order to shift their trance onto him, razing their neighbor's house and setting it in flames in order to lure the god into their own; they stormed about in evil vehemence and evil rejoicing,—oblation, slaughter, brand and demolition giving honor to the god in the way he willed it, in order to deafen his own horror and his own knowledge of fate, he who, to this end, being greedy for laughter and destruction, had unchained human belligerence, the belligerence of intoxication and of sacrifice and, having become impotent, participated in and enjoyed it, gods and men driven and more than driven by the same furiously destructive fear, the fear of being petrified in stony isolation, the fear of trance, the fear of insensibility, driven into a dead-lock by the murderous, merry-making pandemonium of the gods, by the murderous game of men, by the volcano of nothingness in the soul, from which the fire flooded out in a flowing un-element and stood still; the cities burned without ashes, the flames licked like stiffly-erected tongues, like upstanding scourges lashing up from no depths, indeed, below the torn, frayed surface which had opened out of itself, there was no second surface, there was no depth at all, the flames being composed of the hard, serrated surface itself, and about them roared the stark-yelling thicket of paralyzed voices, their cries nothing more than terrible, fanglike shadows, roared the mute storm of the re-abandoned and shattered creation: rigid new structures rose out of the ruins on every side, they grew upward into the drab, gray light, into the lightlessness of the light-stripped waste, growing out of the emptiness and yet having always been there, hopelessly standing there since time out of mind for the glori-fication of lasting murder, for the perpetuation of evil, struc-

tures of spurious life, of spurious death, their cornerstones
drenched in blood, leaning heavily on life, and no amount of
blood was able to fuse the constructions, the encirclements, the
petrifications of evil with the law and into the stream of creation, no exorcism was able to uncoil the icy serpent by the
renewal of the pledge; pre-creation was stronger than creation:
the trance was the state of the unborn, it was the obstacle in the
orbit of creation, evading and opposing the creation, itself a
state of uncreation, desiring to perpetuate itself to the exclusion
of all else, setting itself up as a monument and making itself
into a tomb; it remained robbed of speech, conscious of guilt
and with subsided breath; it remained despite its stony monu-
mentalness unperpetuated and without permanence and, having
shaken off the creation, it had come to be a grave from which
there was no rebirth. Thereupon the dome of the un-space, the
dome of the no-heaven itself became a single cavernous tomb,
imbedded in the serpentine windings of the celestial viscera,
imbedded in the god-rejected viscera which bear the humus of
existence, where fate is astir and makes itself known regardless
of time; and he was being carried into this cave as to a homecoming; the journey was leading there and, although he was cast
out of heaven, himself intergrown with serpents, nevertheless
he lay imbedded in the celestial viscera. What a shuffling of
inside and outside! What a terrible reversion! On every side
the tomb-streets and tomb-cities of the death-inhabited world
were ablaze, on every side the stony aimlessness of human fury
glared forth, as did the jubilation, the sacrificial madness of
men; on every side the cold flames of human passion stood
stiffly erect, and humanity was being discreated, the creative
gods were being dethroned amidst the stony snarling of the
dying creation, denuded by death—, the decree of the dis-
tracted gods confused by their belligerent fear, the decree which
had to be enacted for purposes of their own. For creation demanded continual resurrection; creation consummated itself
only in continuous rebirth, enduring only as long as there was
resurrection and not a moment longer; oh, only he might become

a creation, only he might be called a creature, who descended again and again to the fires of rebirth, taking unflagging care lest the unvanquished should rise again, lest the maternal uncreated should break out to stony muteness; oh, only he was created who gave issue to creation, who, in ascending, brought himself as offering, without reservation and absolved from reversion, without reverting to intoxication, aye more, without any turning back for verification or identification, putting off from himself all carnal fear, putting off also the last carnal desire; oh, only then are we creatures of creation, when we have stripped off all carnality, when we have learned to separate ourselves from even the knowledge of carnality and what lies behind it, when we have roused ourselves to accept our final penance with humility, when we are able to obliterate our own graves! And when, uneasily and dream-far, this realization came to him, who lay there as if in a dream, and when a voice from a second dream whispered into the first one, as if breaking once more through the fear, revengefulness, and impotence of the gods, as if yet again and perhaps for the first time they were exercising a bounteous mercy, as if that mysterious, wordless whisper issued directly from the horrible, once again shattered fear of the gods themselves, murmuring that he was to have courage—courage for extinction, courage for belittlement, courage for submission, courage for the redemption of contrition—he could hear in this whispering wordlessness, that was like a language beyond language, a much narrower condensation of meaning, a wordless word from a dream still more remote than the second one, a softer, more urgent murmuring, incomprehensible although summoning to action, scurrying off and dying away, yet being the strictest order, the imperative command that everything which had served a false life, and confirmed it, must disappear so completely as never to have been, evaporating into the inconsequential, disintegrated into the nothingness, divorced from all memory, divorced from knowledge, forced back from everything that had existed in men as well as in things, oh, it was the command to abolish everything that had been done, to burn everything that he had ever written or composed, oh, all his writing would have to be burned, all, and the Aeneid besides; that is what he heard within the inaudible, but before he had extricated himself from the stupefaction with which he had stared toward the motionless chain of half-birds crouching on the eaves of the building, a gradual wave seemed to flow over the blanched plumage, flowing and drifting airily, one wave and then another, and suddenly in a spume of noiselessness the swarm had flown aloft, as though lifted up without flight and dissolved to invisibility, so that the familiar housetop could be seen for a second, just for this single second however, for in the next one the building crashed down, not less noiselessly than the wing-beats of the birds which had flown away, not less airily transformed into invisibility; sucked into the nothingness. And when he had realized this the lack of sound began to change, and it changed to stillness; the torpidity turned to calmness, the motionless journey which had carried him on came to an earthly halt, the spectres—in the shapes of plants and animals, and finally in that of a single, flaming-haired fury with pale transparent body and streaming locks—no longer accompanied him, instead they glided past him; they glided thither where the sepulchre had sunk down and they sank after it, one after the other absorbed in the empty duskiness of the shadowy crater; and even though this emptiness stared back at him horribly like a threatening counter-eye, and yet his own, a final threat of horrible emptiness, when the last of the harpies had vanished within it, it too was seized by dissolution; the sucking force came to be an all-inclusive peace, came to be profundity, came to be the eye of earthly night, the eye of dream, large and heavy with ethereal tears, resting on him its dark-gray velvety gaze, lightly embracing him who was delivered from dream while yet in a dream; opened in returning, the night was again to be seen, and in the uttermost depths of its glance the small yellow-tipped flame of the oil lamp flickered up again—oh, a star, and near at hand—, beaming in the moonless, nocturnal peace of the chamber, its peace regained and in readiness for sleep, the frieze scarcely recognizable, the walls darkened which encased only the familiar earthly furniture as if it had never been otherwise; this was coming back though not home-coming, this was recognition without remembrance, it was a mild revival, and yet, it was an extinguishment even milder, it was deliverance and imprisonment indescribably merged into dissolution, becoming miraculous by being accepted. The wall-fountain drizzled softly, the darkness became mildly moist, and though nothing stirred in any shape or manner, the muteness was un-muted, the numbness un-numbed, time became more yielding, more living, released from the silvery-cold stare of the moon and free to move once more, so that he, likewise freed of his fixation, was able to raise himself slowly, albeit with utmost effort; resting on palms whose outstretched fingers probed into the mattress, with his fever-hot head sunk a little between his hunched shoulders, thrust slightly forward and trembling a bit from his effort, he listened into the softness, and his listening pertained just as much to the clemency of the re-turning life-stream, which was not to be checked by any fever, as to the scarcely-emerged, scarcely-captured, now scarcely-capturable command from the dream, the command which had bidden him destroy his writing and which he now wished to hear in reality, which he must hear, so that he might be more certain of salvation: much as he wished to hear and fulfill it, the hidden command was unfeasible, it remained unfeasible until a wording for the whispering wordlessness could be found, and in the mysterious, great uncertainty that encompassed him the command to get back to words was forcibly at work; the walls of silence still surrounded him but they had ceased to be threatening; the fright still continued but it was a fright without fear, it was fearlessness within fright; the innermost and outer-most borders still turned in toward and into each other, but he sensed how his listening dissolved or united them, not, to be sure, to an earlier order of understanding, certainly not to a human order, an animal order, a material order, not to a world-order in which formerly he had moved and which, extinguished along with his extinguished memory, no longer existed and never would exist for him again; and neither was it the unity of the beautiful nor that of the world's shimmering loveliness which disclosed itself, no, it was none of these, but rather that of a ringing tide within the incomprehensible, streaming in and out with the night, the unremembered-remembering of a sojourn in which the uncompleted had completed itself, connected with a longing for creation in a last arch-loneliness unspeakably beyond attainment, in an unimaginably fresh recollection of utter cleanliness and chastity; and that which his listening perceived was contained in the flood of longing, coming from the outermost darkness and vibrating simultaneously in his innermost ear, in his innermost heart, in his innermost soul, wordless within him, wordless around him, the hailing and humbling, quietly great power of the twofold, runic first-cause, holding him and fulfilling him as his listening became more profound; but soon it was no longer a crooning or a whispering but rather a mighty booming, a booming, however, which was carried to him through so many layers of present-experience, past-experience, future-experience, through so many layers of remembering and not-remembering, through so many layers of obscurity, that it did not even reach the strength of a whisper; no, it was not a whispering, no, it was the unison of countless voices, and beyond that it was the unison of all voice-herds, ringing up from all the reaches and recessions of time, singing and clanging and booming of safety and seclusion, perturbing by mildness, comforting by sadness, unattainable in its longing, inexorable, irrefutable, unalterable in spite of its great remoteness, becoming more and more commanding, singing more and more alluringly the more meanly his ego abased itself, the more his resistance gave way and he opened himself to the sound, the more he despaired of actually comprehending the greatness of the voices, the more his knowledge of his own unworthiness grew; and overcome by the bronze omnipotence, overcome by its gentleness, overcome by anxiety for his work that was to be snatched from him, overcome to desiring the judgment that would demand just that, overcome by fear as well as hope, overcome to the point of extinction and self-extinction for life's sake, imprisoned and liberated within the compass of his own insignificance, unconsciously-conscious under the power of the unformable, yearned for, universal chorus, that which he had long known, long suffered, long understood was wrung from him, escaping him in a tiny, inadequate expression of the inexpressible, looming large as the aeons, escaped him in a moan, in a cry: "Burn the Aeneid!"

HAD THE words formed themselves in his mouth? he scarcely knew, he did not know at all, and yet he was not surprised by an echo, almost an answer: "You called?" sounding so tender and familiar, almost homelike, from a nowhere unbelievably near or unbelievably far, a sound floating into indistinctness if not into infinity, if not into the longed-for place of the universal chorus, and for a moment he thought it was Plotia, he thought he heard the floating darkness of her voice, as though he might, as though he must expect her in the re-calmed, re-dewed, re-assembled night, perceiving, however, with even greater certainty and in the next moment, that it had been the voice of the boy, and the unsurprised naturalness with which he accepted his return was so lightly mundane in its nature, flowing so easily between earthly shores and for this very reason unconcerned whether they betokened joy or disappointment, that he became quite worried lest he should interrupt this flow by even a glance or turn of the head; he lay there with closed eyes and he did not stir. And he was unaware how long this lasted. But then it seemed to him as if again words were forming in his mouth, as if he said: "Why have you returned? I wish to hear you no longer." Once again he did not know whether he had spoken aloud, whether the boy was actually in the room, whether an answer could be expected or not, this was a floating sort of expectation, like that when a lyre is being tuned somewhere before the song rings out, and again there resounded quite near and yet remote as if coming hither from the sea, encompassed and glistening softly in the moonlight: "Do not push me off."—"But," he countered, "you are in my way. I want to hear the other voice, you are only a sham-voice, I want to get on to the other one."—"I was your path, I am your path," came the answer, "I am the overtone of yourself that was yours from the very beginning, vibrating beyond every death unto eternity." This was like a temptation full of sweet allure, full of simplicity, full of dream, the call of dream to make him turn back again, an echo from childland. And the soft, far-near, homelike, sorrow-dispelling voice of the boy went on: "The reverberations of your poem are eternal." Whereupon he said: "No, I no longer want to hear the echo of my own voice; I await the voice that is beyond mine."—"You can no longer silence the overtones of the heart; their echoes remain with you as irrevocably as your shadow." It was temptation and he was enjoined to cast it off: "I no longer wish to be myself. I want to vanish into the shadowless depths of my heart and into its profoundest loneliness, and therefore my poem must precede me." No answer followed, something was wafted like a dream from invisibility, dream-long dream-short, and finally he heard: "Hope desires co-hope, and even the loneliness of your heart is but the one lone hope of your beginning." "Yes," he admitted, "but it is hope for the voice which will companion me in the solitude of my dying; if it should fail me I shall be without absolution and forever bereft of consolation." Again there was an indefinite pause until the answer came: "Never again can you be alone, never and nevermore, for something has sounded out of you that is greater than yourself, greater than your loneliness, and moreover you are unable to destroy it; oh, Virgil, in the song of your solitude are all the voices and all the worlds, they are with you together with their reverberations, they have broken through your loneliness forevermore and have been woven into all the futurities forever, for

from the beginning, Virgil, your voice was the voice of the god."
Oh, this is how it had been fore-dreamed once upon a time in
some place or other that lay in a long-lost past, it was turning
back to a former pledge that he once made to himself, a pledge
now being fulfilled, sorrow-dispelling and happily hopeful in
its self-evidence, and withal the hope was a false one, the make-
believe hope of a boy, of a child, a hope that was dissolving
into self-mockery. And immediately he went on: "Who are
you? what are you called?"—"I am Lysanias," came the
answer, this time moved perceptibly nearer and from a direction
easier to ascertain, from where the entrance door was likely to
be. "Lysanias?" he repeated as if he had not understood aright
and as if actually he had been expecting another name, "Lysanias . . . ," and lying there motionless, murmuring the name
to himself, still amazed despite all the substantiality of the
occurrence, astonished not only at the strange unfitness of the
name but also that he had put the question: had he not previously
decided to leave the small night-companion in the floating namelessness from which he had been sent? had he not for the sake of
this namelessness sent him away? And amazed, he questioned further: "I sent you away . . . why did you not go?"—"I did go,"
sounded back and this time quite near and in the familiar,
cheery, somewhat rustic voice of the boy, behind whose modesty
a little peasant slyness was lurking, on guard for the next question; unaware of this he challenged him: "So you did go and
for all that you are still here."—"You did not forbid me to
watch beside your door . . . and now you have called." That
was true and still not wholly true, a lie flickered through it,
although a small and childish one, and more like an echo of
the great one slinking through his own life, that sly and more
than sly half-truth that sticks to the word and never does justice
to actual reality, a seeming truthfulness that he had always
practised, ah, already as a child, as he began to dream of
overcoming death; truth and falsehood, calling and not calling,
nearness and farness flowed into each other, they merged
together just as they had ever done; it became incomprehensible

that the boy should have kept watch behind the door, while simultaneously, as if summed up for all eternity, the encircling horror had been manifested on the street beneath his window, incomprehensible that the monsters had staggered about there; ah, it was enigmatic, it remained enigmatic, incomprehensible as a simultaneity which having taken place still lasted, like a second reality without continuance, without past, without future, and which for all that reached into the newly-won earthliness, almost like a sham reality under a false name, devoid of that other-worldly compensation inherent in all loss; and fearful of this kind of paradox in the turns of fate, fearful of the laughter that had rung out there, shattering fate, fearful of anonymity and constraint, asking for the name which must again and again prove to be a random and untrue one, oh, fearful of the riddle of recognition, it was as a defense from the experience of simultaneity, it was as flight from what had happened and what was happening, it was as escape into the obviousness of the present and its physical immediacy that he opened his eyes; yonder on the window-panes strips of the receding moonlight were still showing, the room was enclosed in a wall of shadows, and though it was still unadvisable to disturb this quiescence and to turn his head, from the shadowy outlines of the door—were one to glance sidewise in that direc- tion—the figure of the boy was emerging, delicate and barely discernible; all this was floating, a strangely floating, strangely lightened, earthly-present, lifted out of simultaneity, lifted out of the past, lifted out of the future into a here-and-now, into an undefined earthliness that had no name. The boy had led him to this point—, did he intend to lead him back a little way, now that he had again announced himself, unsummoned and under a strangely unfamiliar name? The guidance of earthly life was at an end and there was no further need of guidance for the earthly life without a future; but should such guiding help still exist, it was not the office of the boy to dispense it, for only the implored help is effectual and it cannot be granted to him who cannot call it out by name. And, as the boy's shape disengaged itself further from the shadowy door-way, he warded him off again as if to reaffirm himself: "I have not called for your help . . . you are mistaken, I have not called . . . ," and then added in a softer tone, "Lysanias." The boy thus addressed, unabashed by the rebuff, had walked out from the dark background into the calm circle lighted by the oil-lamp; at the mention of his name the overcast, young face opened to a brightly-candid, trusting smile: "Help you? Help the helper? You give help even as you ask for it . . . only permit that I mix the wine for you"; and he was already busying himself at the buffet. What did the boy know of help-ing? what did he know of a lifetime's incapacity for help? what did he know of the horrible sobering of the helpless one who is not even able to call out the name for help, in conse-quence of which it is denied him forever? Or did he know that perjury shuns help and must be expiated by being expunged? or did he want to urge him to still another reversion, the fatal, inescapable false turn to intoxication? this thought was like the return of horror, and disregarding his feverish thirst he declined with an abrupt and frightened gesture: "No wine, no, no, no wine!" Again strange, and in fact strangely surprising, was the subsequent response of the boy; it is true that on meeting a hasty rebuff he had lowered the mixing-jug, only to lift it again immediately, and weighing it between his hands he remarked in a contentedly-calm and strangely calming manner: "Oh, there will be more than enough left over for the drink-offering." Oh, for the offering! Now he had uttered it! Yes, the offering had been at stake and was still at stake! the restoration of sacrificial purity, the restoration of that symbol-ism in which unity is reflected, the regaining control over the intoxication of sacrifice, of butchery, of wine, all these depended on the offering, depended on the complete sacrifice of self-eclipse, depended on the creative obliteration of what had been lived through and done with, through which he, simultaneously offering and officiant, father and child, man and his works in one, should himself become a supplication lodged in the con-

summate vigilance of the father and the consummate littleness
of the child, helping by desiring to help, encircled by shadows
and merged into the shadows to his complete extinction, so that
with the earthly rounding-in of the image-sequences, so that
in the final up-rush of the deepest darkness, arising twofold
in the beastlike-plantlike creature, blood reflected in wine, wine
reflected in blood, the age-old enigma might disclose itself like
a light-ringing echo from the spectacle. The repurification of
the sacrifice was at stake, and if he who was charged with it
should try to carry out this chaste office in the fury-infected
room, yes, if he who had barely escaped the horror should
touch even a single drop of wine while here, it would be terribly
transmuted to a blood even more terrible, the sacrifice would
remain unclean, and the destruction of his work would be nothing but a senseless, insignificant burning of a manuscript; no,
the place of the offering must be chaste, chaste the gift-offering,
chaste the officiant, chastity enclosed in chastity, while the pure
wine is poured, offered in salty blood in the rays of the rising
day-star, the shell of the early morning sky quivering open in
pearly iridescence; thus it should come to pass on the seashore,
the poem consumed in the trembling flame—, but was such an
intention not the grievous revival of that slick, aesthetic playing
with words and events that had constituted the fateful treachery
of life? Was not this arrangement of seashore, dawn and
sacrificial-flame nothing but that somnambulistic game in which
the world moves, unchastely impregnated with blood and murder, whenever it surrenders to beauty? Was this not conformity
to that murderous sham-sacrifice enjoined by the gods, themselves enjoined to it, in which the inevitable sham-life is again
resurrected in its changed sham-reality, the inevitable sham-
real interrealm of poetry? No, a thousand times no! it must
happen at once, without sacrificial arrangements, without wine-
pouring, without aesthetic rites, he had not a minute to lose,
under no circumstances should he wait for the sunrise, no, he
must do it now, and with a desperate effort he sat up: he
wanted to go immediately into the open, anywhere where a

fire was burning, he wanted to move the weight of the manuscript rolls thither, maybe the boy would help him with this,
and somewhere in the starry night their words would turn to
ashes; the sun should see the Aeneid no more. This was his
charge. He kept his eyes fixed on the manuscript-chest—however: what had happened to the chest? as if it had been removed
to a great distance, the chest had become dwarfed, a dwarf's
chest, lost amidst the furniture which had likewise dwindled,
and although the thing stood on the same spot as before, one
was unable to come near it, to reach for it. And besides, the
boy stood in between, undiminished in the midst of so much
that had shrunk; in his hand was the full beaker, and he said:
"Take one gulp, just as a sleeping potion." This was said
with all the docile solicitude with which a son, unexpectedly
grown to full responsibility, might address his father, but with
a childish overtone that was even slightly touching, because
the boy's capacity for responsibility being unequal to his willingness for it, the result was a small arrogance which in its
disparagement was a trifle comic: a sleeping potion was being
offered him as if combating the fear of awakening, the fear of
gods and men, were of no importance, as if this vigilance were
not absolutely essential now in order to take on for the last
time the duty of creation! Or might this disparagement be
justified? Was this shrinking of the Aeneid to dwarf proportions, was this shrinking of his surroundings, which nevertheless
did not affect the boy, not a sign that he was justified in his
presumption, was this disparagement not the reflection of a
higher one which stemmed from the beyond, one that intended
to show once and for all that he had been proven unworthy to
assume the priestly-paternal office? Consequently was he not
compelled to remain confined in his dream—forbidden to
descend, forbidden to return, the ivory portal bolted against
him, but still more the one of horn? And nevertheless! nevertheless there was still hope, oh nevertheless even he, he the
erring one, could still be led to the chastity of that grace!
Certainly the corruption was still unabsolved despite his tor-

ments, but he had been released from the fore-hell of trance-death, and perhaps the boy, now that he was grown, would be the right leader who would carry him, the weak and ailing one, through the portals of grace! Oh, like a gleaming vessel of light the beaker was being held aloft by the boy, and he stretched his hand toward it. But before he could reach the gleaming thing, all maturity seemed to desert the boyish form; either the shrunken surroundings had won back their former dimensions or—this was not easy to decide—the boy himself had become dwarfed? did this portend that the boyish figure was not permitted to grow? was it threatened by all this dwarfing? But as for himself, he was left alone, without help, without guidance, so that he must bear the burden of decision alone to the end, and he was not permitted to accept the potion: "A sleeping-draught? No, I have slept enough, all too long; it is time to stop, high time to be up . . ." Again all was weariness and earthliness; no, the boy would not grow again, would not lend his help, would not support him, either at the departure or at the sacrifice, to say nothing of later—oh, disappointment, oh, fear, oh, plea for help! And nothing remained but to sink back into the pillows, tired from the disappointment, breath-robbed and voiceless, whispering: "No more sleep." Yet now for the third time, as if in succor, came an astonishing reply: "No one has been so watchfully awake as you, my Father; rest now, for rest is due you, my Father, rest and watch no more." His eyelids closed softly upon being called father, which was like a gift, like a reward for his self-abnegation, a dispensation for his vigilance, which had become valid, valid only now that its readiness had changed to the unreserved readiness of contrition, and his watchful service to past and future changed into voluntary submission, accepting the present; it was the dispensation of an ever-new start which, like atonement, lay eternally before all birth and beyond all deeds. For sacrifice and absolution were one, they did not proceed one from the other, instead they issued from each other, and he alone might become worthy to be called father, who was graced to go down into the shadowy abyss, graced therefore, having brought himself in sacrifice, to receive the priestly consecration of his sacrificial office, graced by being incorporated into the august and endless line of the fathers, which reached back to the exalted and inaccessible beginning and there received from the first ancestor, powerful in abnegation, enthroned amidst his shadowy court, the strength for perpetual renewals, the continuous blessing of human life, the grace bestowed by the ancestor, the city-founder beyond petrification, the name-giver, he who upheld the law, exempt from all beginning and all ending, exempt from birth, exempt from all desinence. Was he really chosen to appear before the exalted countenance? Was a mere boy, this boy, actually able to unlock the portals? As if they were one and the same, the doubt of himself was strangely involved with that of the boy's vocation, a doubt curiously apart from time; the glance which searched the youth's features once more was a question, and it was with a question that, in response to the entreating gesture, he let himself be handed the beaker and drank: "Who are you?" he asked again, after he had put down the beaker, and the persistent questioning going on within and coming out of him astonished him anew. "Who are you? I have already met you . . . was it a long time ago?"—"Give me the name that you know," was the response. He mused perplexedly and he knew only that the boy had called himself Lysanias, yes, that much he just managed to remember, and then everything became dim; dimmer and dimmer, and he no longer remembered the name, nor any name, not even that by which his mother had called him long ago. And still it seemed as if his mother had just called him, as if she were calling from this vanishing undiscoverable place or time, as if she were summoning him to return to a namelessness which had its home in the maternal and beyond the maternal. Ah, the child seemed nameless to its mother, and more and more she endeavored to protect the child from the name, not alone from the false one, the evil-bearing chance-name, but also, and perhaps even more, from the true one, the chance-exempted name that was preserved in

186

the endless chain of ancestors, because he, who had raised him up and named him, was the same who had gone down into the depths, so that in the rudimental-sphere of all creaturekind he might be endowed with the consecration of paternal priestcraft, which was enshrined in all sacrifice and enshrined the sacrifice in itself; but the mother, bound to the creative sacrifice of birth that was her significance, shrank back from the offer of rebirth, she shunned it for the child she had born, she shunned another creation, she shunned the unmastered, the unmasterable, the unattainable, which she surmised might possibly lurk in the inaccessible truth that shone out from the depths of a name, she shunned the resurrection in the name as something unchaste, and she preferred to know the child unnamed. Existence became nameless, it became so when his mother called him, and shuddering from the namelessness of such fore-awakening and breathing out from some undefined fostering, he said: "I do not know of any name." — "You, my Father, you know them all, you gave a name to everything; they are all in your poem." Names and names—the names of people, the names of fields, the names of landscapes, of cities and of all creation, home names, consoling names in times of trouble, the name of the things created along with the things, created before the gods, the always resurrected name containing the holiness of the word, always to be found by the true watcher, by the arouser, by the divine founder! nevermore might the poet lay claim to this dignity, nay, not even were the sole and final task of poetry to be that of exalting the name of things, ah, even when its greatest moment sounds, were it to succeed in casting a glance into the creative fountain of speech, beneath the profound light of which the word for the thing is floating, the word untouched and chaste at the source of the world of matter, the poem though well able to duplicate the creation in words was never able to fuse the duplication into a unity, unable to do so because the seeming-reversion, the divination, the beauty, because all these things which determined, which became poetry, took place solely in the duplicated world; the world of speech and the world of

matter remained apart, twofold the home of the word, twofold
the home of the human being, twofold the abyss of the creaturely, but twofold also the purity of being, thus duplicated to
unchastity which, like a resurrection without birth, penetrated
all divination as well as all beauty, and carried the seed of
world-destruction in itself, the basic unchastity of existence
which came to be feared by the mother; unchaste the mantle of
poetry, and nevermore would poetry come to be fundamental,
nevermore would it awake from its game of divination, nevermore would poetry turn into prayer, into the sacrificially-valid
prayer of truth so surely inherent in the genuine name of things
that the supplicant, included in the supplication, closes off the
duplicated word so that for him and him alone word and thing
shall succeed in becoming one—oh, purity of prayer, unattainable by poetry and yet, oh yet attainable for it, insofar as it
offered itself, as it overcame and annihilated its very self. And
again as though wrenched out of him, a moan, a cry: "The
Aeneid to be burnt!"—"My Father!" He took the great fright
ringing through the outcry as rejection of this project, as well
he might; displeased he answered, "Do not call me father;
Augustus keeps watch, he is guarding Rome, call him father,
not me . . . not me . . . guarding is not the poet's office."—"You
stand for Rome."—"That dream of every boy was perhaps
once mine also . . . but I have only made use of Roman names."
The boy was silent; then, of all things, he did something quite
unexpected: with the somewhat awkward skill of a peasant boy,
he swung himself aloft on an arm of the candelabrum, as
though it were an elm-branch, broke off one of the burnt candle
stumps and lit it from the flame of the oil lamp—, what did he
want with it? but before an explanation could be found, the boy
had fastened the stump to a plate with the dripping wax, and
now he knelt before the chest: "Would you like to have the
poem? I will hand it to you . . ." Was it not the boy Virgil
who was kneeling there? Or the little brother Flaccus? thus
they had often knelt together on the floor, sometimes in the
garden under the elm, sometimes in front of the toy-box—,

who was this boy? Now the box-straps snapped back smartly, the leather lid sprang open with a soft airy sough, a whiff smelling, of paper and leather, a whiff of the past doings, of softly scratching writing-sounds rushed wanly-homelike out of the opened receptacle, in the interior of which, cleanly arranged, the ends of the manuscript-rolls were visible, — roll after roll, poem after poem piled one after another in neat rows—, the familiar, seductive and calming sight of work. Cautiously the boy lifted out a few pieces and laid them on the bed: "Read them," he pleaded and shoved the plate with the candle nearer to afford a better light. Was he not still in his father's house? was that not still the little brother? why did the mother no longer live if Flaccus was alive? why in her grief had she been obliged to follow him into death? was this not the identical candle that even then on the table had brightened the shadowy room, while outside lay the soft Mantuan meadows in-gathered by the Alps as the slow autumn rain fell grayly in the dark of evening? He was to read—ah, read! was this still possible? before all, was he fitted to do it? had he ever learned to read, or even to spell? hesitatingly, almost anxiously he opened one of the rolls, hesitatingly, almost anxiously he smoothed the opened end, shyly he felt of the paper, even more shyly of the dried written characters and, with all the timidity proper to a consecrated gift-offering, he let his fingers glide over them but not without twinges of conscience, because this was like a renewing of recognition, a brief re-acquaintance with the craft and the former pleasure of craftsmanship, but over and above that, it was like a great, inadmissible remembrance that reached back beyond all remembering and forgetting, back to where there was no question of learning or performance, only plan-ning, hoping and wishing: not his eyes, only his fingertips were reading, they read without letters or words a wordless speech, they read the unspeakable poem behind the poem of words, and what they read consisted no longer of lines, but of an endless immense space stretching out on all sides to infinity, a space in which the sentences did not follow one another in order, but covered each other in infinite crossings and were no longer sentences, they were rather a dome of the inexpressible, the dome of life, the creation's dome of the world, planned for in time unknown: he was deciphering the inexpressible, deciphering the undepictable landscapes and inexplicable occurrences, the uncreated world of fate in which the created world was imbedded as if by accident, deciphering the creation that he had wanted to re-create, that he had been compelled to re-create; yet whenever this had become manifest, unfolding to expression, at every spot where the sentence-waves and sentence-cycles crossed one another, there war, treachery and bloody sacrifice showed up also, there warfare, lifeless and callous, conducted by beings essentially dead, came to view, there the feud of the gods could be seen in its godlessness, there too was revealed the nameless murder in a nameless sphere, executed by phantoms that were merely names, executed at the behest of fate, holding the gods in bondage, executed by language, through language, for the sake of illimitable speech, in the god-governed inexpressibility of which fate has its cause and completion. It made him shudder. And although he had not read with his eyes, he averted them from the page as one who no longer wishes to read: "To destroy all language, to destroy all names, so that again there may be grace," he said to himself, "that was the way mother wished it to be . . . grace devoid of destiny and without speech" . . . "The gods have presented you with the names and you return them again . . . read the poem, read the names, do read them . . ." He was forced to smile at the urgency of the repeated request, and it diverted him somewhat that the boy did not grasp his meaning and perhaps was not even meant to grasp where all this was leading, and he remarked, "Read? does this go with the sleeping potion, little cup-bearer? . . . no, we have no more time, let us make a start, come and help me . . ." Yet the boy—and even this seemed curiously right—made no move to assist him, and when he continued to hold back it at once became clear that he had not the right to help; and even though time were to stand still, even though the cycle were to be closed, enkindling and extinguishment coming thus to be one and the same, and if in addition the child's acceptance of the maternal fostering be indistinguishable from the acceptance implied by submission, even if all completion remained only a perpetual planning, yes, even if he had never, oh never, learned to speak, leading and helpfulness do not go beyond the first turn of the cycle; the voice of the boy had become an echo that still answered back but comprehended nothing, it was a pale echo, a fore-echo prior to the awakening, it was the shining reflector in advance of the ultimate, great, unspeakable and awaited effacement, it was the advance annunciation of a voice that would be the word-in-wordlessness, uniting the not-yet-said to the no-longer-said, to the ineffable shining in the spacious abysses of all language. Such speech was not to be learned, not to be read, not to be heard. "Take the rolls away," he ordered, and this time the boy obeyed, though not quite willingly, rather with a childish, disappointed defiance and a little reluctance that showed by his letting the manuscripts lie on the table instead of in the chest. This was even slightly amusing. And when again as though for the last time he observed the boy's features, the clear eyes which had darkened still more although they still glanced up expectantly, the familiar face became unexpectedly, noticeably strange; and in faint yielding, as it were in farewell, he again said "Lysanias." He was not impatient. The candle-light on the table was flickering out in sputtering cobwebs, a light-echo and fore-echo of the gleaming thunder from the other world to come that waited beneath the stars, waiting for the sacrifice, waiting for the flame of abnegation, while here the drizzling of the wall-fountain was murmuring, soft as a shadow. And standing bent half over the table, in this wise half reading and half from memory, at first timidly then becoming louder, the little fist beating time on the table-top, the boy began—was it a last seduction?—to recite the verses, the verses with the Roman names, and they glided into the night and into the nocturnal murmur of the trickling water:

"Charmed is Aeneas, and letting his eyes rove in quick
        admiration,
Scans the whole region about him, notes all and lets
        nothing escape him,
Asks for and hears with delight the record of earlier
        heroes,
Told by Evander the king, the founder of Rome's early
        stronghold:

'Native-born satyrs and nymphs once ranged about this
        very woodland,
Likewise a genus of men who emerged from the hard grain
        of oak-trees;
Art they had none, neither wont, they knew naught of
        yoking the oxen,
Knew not to harvest or till, nor how to lay by of their
        plenty,
Living from fruit of the trees, from the rude, ruddy fare
        of the huntsman.
First from the heights of Olympus came Saturn who,
        hurried and headlong,
Fleeing the weapons of Jove, his own realms abandoned
        in forfeit,
Gathered this unruly folk, dispersed over mountain and
        hill-top,
Bound them together with laws and chose for this place
        the name Latium:
(Being the latent land which had sheltered and kept him
        in safety.)
Under his reign came to pass the fabulous age we call
        golden—
Such the perfection of peace in which he governed his
        people—
Till in a gradual decline there followed an age of dishonor,
Baser and wanting in light, an epoch of greed and of
        warfare.

Then the Ausonian hosts, the Sicanian hordes followed after,
Frequently lost to the land was the name it was given by
    Saturn.
New kings arose and then Thybris, a giant of turbulent
    power,
Thenceforth his name we Italians gave to our river, the
    Tiber,
Letting its true name of Albula fade in the dawn of
    tradition.
I was an exile from home, a wanderer over the waters,
Cast on these shores by the order of fate and by almighty
    fortune,
Forced to this land by the ominous words of my mother,
    Carmentis,
One of the nymphs; divinely enjoined by command of
    Apollo.'

Scarce was his speaking done when he walked further on to
    an altar,
Showing Aeneas the gate which the Romans have called
    Carmentalis,
Set up of old as a shrine to honor Carmentis the wood-
    nymph,
Destiny's seeress was she, the first to foretell the true
    greatness
Due to the Aenean line, the glory of proud Pallenteum.
Next he made pause at the grove where Romulus, wise and
    intrepid,
Made his Asylum known beneath cold Lupercal, the wolf-
    hill,
Named for Lycean Pan in accord with Arcadian custom;
Also the sacred grove, Argilentum, he showed to Aeneas,
Treacherous Argus he named, who died here of drinking
    the Lethe;
Thence to the rock of Tarpeia and on to the Capitol,
    golden,

Shining today where of yore lay a thorny, impassable
  thicket.
Yet, even now, a reverent awe moves the hearts of the
  peasants,
Bidding them pause and reflect as they pass by the rock
  and the forest.
'Deep in this grove,' he cried, 'its trees rising dense to
  the summit,
Lives, it is said, a god, but one whose divine name we
  know not:
Simple Arcadians think they have often beheld the dark
  Aegis
Shake in the right hand of Jove as he summons the clouds
  and the lightning.
Look now beyond to those forts, their ramparts and towers
  dismantled,
Relics of bygone days, memorials left by our fathers,
Janus the builder of one and Saturn who raised up the other,
This one Janiculum called and that with the name of
  Saturnia.'

Talking together in this way they came to the cot of
  Evander,
Cattle were lowing about, the very same field where they
  pastured
Bears now the Forum of Rome and houses the brilliant
  Carinae.
Reaching his humble door, 'Take heed,' he said, 'of the
  threshold
Hercules crossed in his pride: the god made his home in
  this dwelling.
Opulence dare to despise, Illustrious Guest, let thy spirit
Follow the path of the god, our poverty never disdaining.'
Thereupon said he no more, but ushered the noble Aeneas
Under the roof of his hut and offered a couch for his
  slumber,

Freshly bestrewed it with leaves and decked it with Libyan
bear-skin.
Night came apace, enwrapping the world in her shadowy
pinions."

Night came apace . . . the reading voice became softer and
softer, then it died away completely. Were the verses continuing to be enacted? Were they being enacted somewhere
outside of the voice? Or had they also vanished to protect what
seemed to be sleep? Perhaps he had actually slept and had
not even noticed that the boy had gone in the meantime: with
closed eyes as if he were not allowed to make sure, he waited,
a listening guest like Aeneas, waiting for the voice to be raised
once more, but it remained silent. Nonetheless, the last verses
rang on in his ear, they kept on resounding and in so doing
were being changed more and more, they altered—or, more
correctly—they re-composed themselves to something that was
like a material picture, a picture, to be sure, beyond any actual
possibility of being depicted, in the same way that the moon-
bright space in the window could even now be held as a picture
behind closed eye-lids, while yet transmuted in form and light
to something like sound; it was an after-sound in the ear, an
after-image in the eye, both of them sensed but unsensual,
weaving together into a unity that, already far beyond the visible
and audible, was only to be grasped by a kind of sensibility
in which, strangely a part of this very sensibility while strangely
apart from it, the boy's voice as well as his smile were merged.
Did Saturn want to take back the names he had given? The
landscape of the verses, the landscape of the earth, the landscape of the soul were becoming nameless, and the longer that
he, ensconced with closed eyes in the Saturnian fields, tried
to feel out and follow up this transcendental-figurative phenomenon, the more profoundly he felt and sensed it within himself,
yes, the more he longed for it to be changed back to complete
reality, the more he longed for the return of the reading boy,

yet the more he wished all the while that this would vanish; for not only had the sorrow-dispelling seduction emanating from the boy captivated him as the advance-knowledge, the fore-echo of ringing finality, but it had also stood in the way of the ultimate voice; it was not only the entering portal but also the closing slab of the unforeseeable view opening up behind it. Was not the great whispering, the soft booming, the commanding kindness of that far-near, inconceivably all-inclusive voice, which he had heard without being able to hear it, hidden there also? Deeper than anything earthly, but yet of earth, lay the hidden birth-grave of the voice, the tomb of the beginning, the enclosed source of the birth-giving end; deep below the audible and the visible lay the meeting-place of the voices, the place which contained them all, from which they issued and to which they returned, the place where they were inaudible, the place where they were most inaudibly united and in unison, the place of their complete accord, the accord a voice in itself, the most mighty and the only one which included in itself all voices, all voices with the one exception of its own. To include all life within oneself and yet to be excluded from all life—, was this the voice of death, was it here already? was this it? Or was that which was hidden still greater than this voice? He listened into the inaudible, he listened with all the force and fervor that his will could command, but over the seas of silence, over the veiled landscapes of primal sound, breathed out into the very beginning and very end under the brooding sound-dome of primal perception, there still floated a falling sigh, enclosed in forgetfulness, enclosing forgetfulness, a most delicate dew, breathed up from the color-less-ringing plains of transparency, from their mutely resonant fields, the image of the boy's voice, just barely visible, just barely revealed and revealing, but already veiling itself, an earthly resonance, no longer a word, no longer verse, no longer color or colorlessness, no longer transparency, but only a smile, an image of yore, the image of a smile. Names? Verses? Was there a poem, had there ever been an Aeneid? In vanishing was it flickering up a last time in the name—Aeneas?—as if this name contained an intimation of the great and good command which was lost forever, but nothing more was to be found; all that had been lived, all that had been created, the whole vast streaming-together of existence with all of its substance was being flooded off, wiped away; he found neither year nor day nor time in his searching recollections, he found nothing of anything that was known to him, he listened into his memory, although his listening perceived only a glassy confusion, terrestrial still, but already exempt from earth-bound time, exempt from earthly remembrance, a glassily-feverish singing confusion of shapes growing out of a no-time and extending into a no-time, and the more his memory reached toward the Aeneid, the quicker song after song vanished, leaving no trace, dissolved into the ringing intricacy of this glare: was this coming home to the sources of the poem? The memorable content of the poem was disappearing; whatever had been celebrated by the poem, —seafaring and sunny strands, war and the sound of arms, the lot of the gods and the orbits of the starry courses—this and more besides, written down or unwritten, fell quite away, all of it stripped off, the poem had discarded it like a useless garment and was returning back into the unveiled nakedness of its hidden being, into the vibrating invisible from which poetry stems, subsumed again by the pure form, finding itself there like its own echo, like the soul housed in its crystal shell, singing of itself. The superfluous had been discarded but was nevertheless preserved, having become durable in an indestructible form, the purity of which excludes forgetfulness and impresses even the perishable with the stamp of eternity. Poem and speech existed no longer, but the soul common to both was still in existence, surviving in its own crystal reflection; the human soul had died off into the profoundest depths of forgetfulness, but the language of the soul lived on, surviving in the singing clarity of its form; soul and speech, parted from each other yet implicated in and reflecting one another—, did they not receive this reflected light from that inaccessible abyss from which everything issues and to which it comes home? were they not, though each locked off in itself, communally included in that home-voice which bursts through all boundaries, because in vibrating beyond every limitation it gives promise of the goal, of encouragement, of help, and of comfort? Oh, voice of yore in your rising and falling, soft cradle-voice having once sounded, enveiling and unveiling the world, starry voice of the cradle-night, singing the sweet companion song of unity! "I am alone," he said, "no one has died for me, no one dies with me; I looked for support, I have striven to the utmost for it, I have implored it, but it has not been bestowed upon me."—"Not quite here, but yet at hand," came the response so dream-soft from his own breast that it was no longer the voice of the boy but far more that of night and of all nights, the voice of silvery space which is nocturnal solitude, the ever-seen but never-explored dome of the night, along the walls of which he had groped ever so often and which had now come to be only a voice. "Not quite here, but yet at hand," gracious and lordly, seductive and enjoining, night-lit and deep-hidden, the spontaneous sounding of the word and the spontaneous sounding of the soul, the unity of language and humanhood; and it was like taking leave of the ageless, erstwhile youth of all things earthly, and yet saluting the home-land, everlasting in hope, where even the stone had turned into transparency and the grave-slabs had become transparent as though they were composed of crystal and ether together. In this wise he stepped through, he didn't step, he stood suddenly in the midst of a dream-dome that was nothing but the beaming impression of voices, he stood in a bottomless radiance, in a radiance without walls or ceiling, amidst domes of radiant transparency and, seeing into the midst of the invisible, he was unable to see even himself, he too had become transparent. Without having taken a step, indeed without the least attempt to take a step or make any movement whatsoever, he had been moved forward, but still not moved across; it was still the fore-court of reality that surrounded him, he had not yet forsaken terrestrial things, it was still an earthbound dream, and he—

a dream within a dream—realized the dreamy nature of what was happening to him: it was a dream on the borders of dream. For although nothing in this steadily increasing clarity of streaming transparency recalled the former clash of realities, and although nothing concrete, nothing human, nothing animal was to be seen, moreover, although even the memory of them was no more to be traced, washed as they were in the radiantly booming, inaudible waves of muteness, he knew himself to be in the hopeless entanglement of clashing voices, now as before, only that now voices, things, creatures, plants, animals and men, one and all, had turned into most inconceivable beings, into an airy structure in which names still shimmered like stars, though by this very act of shimmering the names were cast off; he found himself in a region in which only the quantities, the arrangements and the correlations of earthly things were valid, likewise only the knowledge emanating from them and their erstwhile forms, and it was occurrence and knowledge, perception and exposition in one single, gleaming possession of truth, it was an unimaginable exposure of the creation's multiplicity, empty of content but complete, the integration of everything that had occurred or could occur, differentiated a myriadfold but indistinguishable, the suggestive meaninglessness changed to pure form, to the bare outlines of form which is nothing more than crystalline clarity, an impenetrable, sparkling transparency, inexistent even while existing, being without origin. He was in the realm of the infinite. The pathways of the millenniums revealed themselves as endless sheaves of light, straggling in any and all directions, they were carriers of the eternal and brought the finite into ultimate infinity, the thing done having the same weight as the thing undone, good and evil crossing each other with equal impressiveness and illuminative force, and there was no way out of the seeing-blindness, the hearing-deafness of the dream, no way out of the dream-dome, of the dream-dazzlement, the dream so estranged from discrimination that it opens up no path to the good, an unbounded, shoreless flood. And this silvery, coruscating, radiant dream-stuff—, did it touch the soul? did it touch the god? Oh, were the dream ever so earthly it was beyond the earthly affairs of men, and the dreamer was one who had lost his human birthright, his human productiveness, he was fatherless and motherless from his very inception; he was in the pre-maternal cave of fate itself, from which there was no escape. No one laughs while dreaming, no one laughs where there is no way out, the dream was not to be burst asunder. Oh, who dares to laugh where even mutiny is silenced! There was no possible defiance to oppose to the dream, there was only entanglement and acceptance, entanglement in the happenings of the dream. And involved in the dazzling thicket, caught into the ramifications within the dream and extending beyond it, identified with each single dream-point, with each separate crystal ray of the million-faceted transparency, he also transparent, he also homeless and rootless, a dream-orphan from the very start, he also occurrence and knowledge in one, enacting himself in a dream, aware of his own dreaming, himself a very dream, he spoke; and speaking from a breast that was no longer a breast, from a mouth that had ceased to be a mouth, with a breath that was less than a breath, speaking words that were scarcely words, he said:

"Fate, thou camest before all the gods,
Thou wast prepared in the mists long before any creation,
Nakedness thou of the clouded beginning, and true
To self alone, the cold, all-penetrating form.
Creation and Creator thou in one,
At once occurrence and knowledge and meaning,
The force of thy nakedness penetrates god and man
Commanding the Created.
Upon thy command the god delivered himself
From his inexistence and became Father,
Calling the name of light out of muteness,
From the womb of the primeval, darkness-enshrouded mother,
Calling to identity the unnamed,
Calling the unshaped into shape.
Primordial silence became speech and primal sound

Turned into singing, the spheres themselves singing thy word.
But in the dream, oh Fate, thou takest it back again,
Thou hushest it back into blankness,
Terrible, all-concealing, into thy denuded being,
And as a crystal flake the god himself sinks
Ray-melted into the empty dome of the dream."
Unmoved and gleaming the dream-dome absorbed the silent
words, reflecting them silently and carrying them off into the
echo-lack of the last light, and it seemed as if they themselves
had been that radiant echo. Then he spoke on:
"Dream-saturating, dream-chilled Fate, thou
Revealest thyself in dream, bringing the dream
To the grandeur of a time in which reality inheres, making the
    dream
The receptacle of the Creation, working through thee
And through thee timeless; for thou knowest neither before
    nor after,
Reality that thou art.—
Lavishly flows thine essence, oh arch-form, flows
Outspreading and fertile with life-stuff between the storm clouds
Mute-mighty in union, between the light and the night
Of Creation, created at thy behest; but thou
Transformest thyself from one into the other
With the looping current of thy flowing,
Wishing to flow lightward—ah, canst thou?—yet where
Thy currents converge, as at a goal, stream on stream dependent,
There in serenity thou revealest the name and object of worldly
    truth,
United one into the other, evoked into wholeness to mirror thee,
Fate-stamped, the archetype of being, the archetype of truth.
Dream-form emerges from dream-form, overlaid and unfolded,
In dream thou art I, thou art my perception,
Born with me as an unborn angel,
Beyond mischance, the shining omni-form
Of essence and order in which knowledge itself is born,
Shape of myself, my knowledge.

God-delivered, god-destroying Fate,
Eternal Reality, I am eternal with thee,
A mortal, god-destroying in dream where I,
Enacting myself in thee, dissolving in thy brightness,
Enclosed in childhood, am myself the habitation of the god."

Was this the last habitation? was this the final resting-place?
was not even this in movement? did he not have to move it
forward? he tried to take a step, he tried to lift his arms, he
tried to impart himself to this gleaming space which he already
was, he tried this with great will-power, with utmost effort, and
although the glassy transparency of his no longer apparent being
did not allow for any sort of movement, he succeeded: a trembling, dreamy and remote, ran through him; oh, it was scarcely
the intimation of a trembling, oh, it was scarcely an awareness
of such an intimation, however it was at the same time—how
could it have been otherwise—like a sympathetic vibration of
the dream-dome, flooding back and forth as though the quiver
were passing through the motionless, glinting paths of streaming
light, through their intersections, raying out in every or no
direction, passing through their effulgence of which it can
and cannot be spoken, like a first and final shudder, scarcely
noticeable yet somehow felt, the breath of a receding shadow,
unstirred by a breath but withal a recollection of earthly life.
Thereupon he spoke again:
"Unescapable! Have I mounted to thee or
Have I stumbled into thy depths?
Abyss of form,
Abyss of above and below, abyss of the dream!
In the dream no one is able to laugh, likewise
No one is able to die—, behold,
How over-near to laughter is death, and behold
How far from both is Fate, to whom, since he is merely form,
Death has taught nothing of laughter—
This Fate, thy self-betrayal.
But I, a mortal, I, familiar with death,

202

Compelled by death to laughter,
I revolt from thee, I trust in thee no longer.
Dream-blind and dream-enlightened, I comprehend thy death,
I know the limit set for thee,
The boundary of dream that thou deniest.
Art thou also aware of it? Dost thou will it so?
Does thy being halt at thy command? Or does something
    greater halt thee?
Does still another Fate stand behind thee, stronger than thou art,
More inevitable, less discernible, and beyond and beyond,
Fate upon Fate, blank form on blank form, row on row,
Waits there the unattainable Nothing, the birth-death,
The very twin of Chance?
All law is subject to chance, to the fall into the abyss,
And thou too, oh, Fate, for in thy realm, including thee in its
    havoc,
There rages the chance of finality.
Suddenly growth ceases and the branches of wisdom,
Bough from bough sprouted, die off and drift
Into nullified speech,
Isolated into the object, isolated into the word,
Order in ruins, truth in ruins, brotherhood and concord
Benumbed in incompletion, torpid in the underbrush
Of specious existence.
Thou bringest forth the incomplete, thou sufferest the mishap,
Thou must tolerate evil, imperfection, deception, and
Thyself unrealized, no longer eternal in thy frozen form,
Fate of Fate, thou diest of evil, while yet in the crystal with me."
It was not he speaking, it was the dream that spoke; it was not
he thinking, it was the dream that thought; it was not he dreaming, it was the dome of destiny radiating into the dream which
dreamed; it was the dreaming of the unattainable, the interminable domed fixation of light, transfixed by evil, transfixing
through evil, and there, motionlessly flooded in the cascades of
light, was the temple of his unattainable soul. The light was unstirred, unstirred the healing cycle of adversity, unstirred even

the breath. And lacking breath the dream spoke on:
"Form, even though arch-form, perishable for the mortal,
Perishable for the god, perishable in thy unreality,
Perishable in thy seething and specious wholeness,
Beyond redemption! though the part may pretend to be all,
Though it wish to hark back to the womb of the erstwhile
    maternal arch-night,
Though, usurping completeness, it even assume the summoning,
The office of the summoning Father,
Still nothing saves thee, Fate, from the reversion to nothingness;
Ravished with thine own fate, thou fallest back in empty
    reversion,
While worlds are wheeling,—interminable, inevitable their
    course
In the vacant orbit of beauty—drunken of thee
And drunken of death.
For creation is more than form, creation is resolution,
Is parting the bad from the good, oh only
This election is truly immortal.
Thou who art only form, hast thou called gods and men to truth
Only that they should take over thy determining mission, that
    they
Should establish the form of the world for all time?
Hast thou charged me therewith and ordained me in the
    creation?
Inadequate art thou, the tool of evil, thou didst make it,
Thyself art the evil, and thou canst not stem it,
The divine is exhausted, and the human indeed
Remains unfortified—, these thy works, enchanced with thee
    in the greater Destiny,
And the Evoked, only form like thyself and deprived of a name,
Is beyond reach, he never swerves,
He hears no call in the fading dream."
Yes, he was beyond call: muteness surrounded his own mute-
ness, nothing spoke to him any more and he was able to speak of
nothing; nothing called to him and he was unable to call to

anything. But the impression of dream-voices was spread about him, glistening and impenetrable, immobile and illimitable, glossy with the god-quelling evil, unescapable, all-encompassing, annulling the creation, the good and the evil blended together, the paths of light endless, their intersections without number, the light supernatural; yet for all that numbered, limited, earthly and destined to die away——, was the dream fading? and with the fading dream was the dreamer also fading away? Nothing was to be remembered, yet all was memory in the unhallowed desecration, in the shadowless, lovely light of the indiscriminate, in the light of the interminable enclosure, sunk memory-deep in fate's iridescent, stagnant game of limitations, the limits of which can and must be exceeded whenever the game has played itself out, plumbed to the uttermost depths of its diversifications, with its differentiations and cross-versions enumerated, the admixture of good and evil drained to the dregs, oh, evil itself drained to the dregs, fate's very form exhausted, died off in the dying memory, which no longer remembered to remember. Oh, memory, oh, extinction of light and the spheric singing of the world, oh the endless chain, the orbit of fateful consequences of extinguishment and re-lighting on earth, experiment after experiment of the creation, ever repeated, ever forced to be repeated until the evil is cast out of the light, until the ghostly-uncreated is removed from the self-creative in order that——the re-arched heaven being a certainty——the confirmation will again be manifested, will again shine out, the human countenance lifted up unto the borders of the spheres, unto the unseen linear play of the stars, lifted up to the stone-cool, starry face of the sky. And as if the constellations of the inner and outer worlds, vanishing to shining muteness from the excess of splendor, had preserved just a shred of breath, as if though beyond call they possessed just a remnant of darkest power wherewith to shine, as if the heart's lyre and that of heaven could resound once more, as if existence were not yet completely transformed into crystal, as if his own equilibrium were not completely restored, the scales of the universe not having come to a complete standstill, so that he still had some awareness, so that he was still permitted some awareness, the crystal's awareness of itself, the dream's awareness of itself, the awareness of the future and of consummation, the awareness of the ever-existent and the never-attained, revealing itself in a silvery tone from the most hidden self-recollection of the universe in which the crystal speech of dream is latent, the fore-echo of a future sound, this now spoke out in a last muteness:

"When, oh when?
When was there Creation delivered from form,
Creation, oh, when without fate? Oh it existed,
And without dream it was, neither a waking nor a sleep,
Only a moment, a song, once only
The voice unique, a smiling call, unevocable,
Once there was a boy;
Once there was the Creation, once again it will come to be,
The miracle, chance-delivered!"

Would the bowl of heaven shimmer up there again within the dream-dome, bearing the beaming cross of the middle carried by the starry shield? Would it shine out in the real splendor of a newly performed act of creation? It had announced itself as an expectation, it was really here in the form of expectation, yet it had not actually appeared. For a still deeper silence had settled over the silenced light-voices of the dream, and this silence turned into waiting, was the essence of waiting, silent and almost miraculous, that imposed itself like a second and richer form upon the immobile, continuing luminescence which was the form of fate's nakedness, lying upon it like a second irradiation of light, as if the waiting were already an increase of riches, even though one expected and was entitled to expect a still further enrichment, a still stronger irradiation, perhaps even a second and more pervading immensity, in order that from this one the divine might stream out freshly again, abolishing evil forever. It was an undirected waiting, as undirected as the radiation, but for all that directed to the waiter, the dreamer;

it was a sort of invitation to him to make a final attempt, a last creative effort to get outside of the dream, outside of fate, outside of chance, outside of form, outside of himself. Whence came this expectant challenge? from what beyond, from what undefinable region had this dimensionless omnipresence sunk itself into the entity of the dream-dome? Although it was strong with the strength of dream, it was really no summons, it was just nothing, coming from anywhere and somehow reaching him; it had suddenly filled and fulfilled him, just as it had the dream, splendor sunk in splendor, transparency in transparency; it did not order the dream back to reality, nor the multiplicity of directions into a single plan of direction; it was certainly not reversion, not a loss of creativeness, not re-constriction, no, it remained within the dream while vanquishing the dream and challenging to conquest, it charged the remaining within the dream as a challenge to achieve new knowledge by the knowledge gained from dreams; it was there in mute streaming recollection, never seen but nevertheless recognized, nevertheless understood in its dream-decree. And he, his own transparency involved with that of the dream, contained in the dream and containing the dream, he lifted himself in the enormous, god-like effort required of him and with a final piercing through of the dream's border, with a final shattering of every sort of image and every sort of revelation, with a last shattering of memory, the dream grew beyond itself, he growing with it: his thinking had become greater than any form of thinking, and in achieving this it became a knowledge of the spheres which is greater than destiny, greater than chance; it turned into a second immensity, including the first and being included by it, it became the law which caused the crystal to grow, the law of music, stated in the crystal, stated through music, but over and above that, expressing the music of the crystal. It was a secondary memory, the memory of aeons and universal experience which, though lost to recollection, aghast at the world, aghast at form, had dissolved itself to a secondary form; it was a secondary human language predestined for eternity, if not yet eternal in itself, yet holding the irretrievable in recollection, and in the newly disclosed and re-arched heaven, in the law of its being, perishable even in imperishability, the stars were circling again as an ever-enduring wonder, exempted from chance; immortally cool came the music of night, gently stroked by the unrelenting-soft breath of the moon, carried in it immobile, drenched by the motionless tide of the Milky Way, the ringing silver space encompassed by the incomprehensible, but still encompassing in itself the incomprehensibility of all things human, the homecoming, the second homecoming of dream—,

—, oh homecoming! oh homecoming of him who must no longer be a lodger! irretrievable is that smile in which we were once imbedded, irretrievable the smiling embrace, that fullness of being on awakening or just before awakening, day-brightened but still obscure; oh irretrievable is that tranquility into which we were wont to bury our face, to assure ourselves that what we had seen should not prove to be mere chance; oh everything was ours in being bestowed upon us again, nothing came accidentally to us, nothing was perishable because universal time is imperishable, without continuity; oh universal time, in which nothing was mute to the mute eyes of the child, and everything was a new creation—,

—, oh homecoming, oh music within and about us! submerged in us it has remained with us as a knowledge of yore; submerged in us, we shall be lifted through it into its greater being, and submerged in us, greater than ourselves, it is ours beyond all chance; oh music within and about us! only that which the self harbors is greater than we are, it is immortal for us and exempted from chance, singing along with the word of the spheres, but that which we do not carry within us, that is chance and remains chance, it is mortal for us, neither now nor ever is it greater than we are, it never confines us—,

—, oh homecoming! everything is taken in by a child, everything is music to him, everything is immortal, everything has the greatness of allness, being always there to protect and fulfill him with its smile, since he may fly to its embrace, eye sunk

208

into eye; the universe in all things! Oh, it is irretrievable for us, irretrievable because of our very growth! And should we wax ever so greatly, so that our arms branch out like rivers, our body spread out over continents and oceans unto the utmost limits of the worlds, the moon in our hair, we filling all of space, we ourselves the starry pinnacle of night, the glittering dome of dream, endless, endless in sheer radiation, yet we remain outside of ourselves, we are still expulsed, no night embraces us and no morning welcomes us, because we are bound and dazed, without flight or goal for flight, unsurrendered even to ourselves, because our arms have drawn nothing to our hearts—,

—, oh homecoming, homecoming into the utterly-incomprehensible that will be granted to us when we shall have become prepared to fly to it again; oh, the utterly-incomprehensible that we seek for even in dreams because in dreams fate, our fate, becomes dreamily comprehensible for us; mortal is dream, mortal is fate, both such things of chance that we, bound and dazed even in dream, dazed because of our mortality, bound by chance, dazed by death, seeking escape, fearing escape through flight into dream, shudder back from it, dismayed by the impossible; oh mortal is that chance which is not contained in ourselves and in which we are not contained; all that we comprehend of it is death, for death reveals itself to us in the phenomenon of chance, verily only in chance, but we, neither containing ourselves nor contained in ourselves, bearing death within us, are only accompanied by it, it stands at our side, as it were by chance—

—, oh homecoming, homecoming into the divine, homecoming into the human! mortal to us, indeed, our fellowman whose fate we have not taken upon ourselves, on whom we have bestowed no help, the unloved human being, whom we have not included in our own life and whom we have thereby rendered unable to embrace us inclusively in his own being, oh he seems undivine to us, we seem undivine to him, so enchanced in chance that we hardly know if he, who appears before us as living, who passes by us, who staggers by us and turns the next corner, whether he, creature of fate like any other, like ourselves, has not long since died or perhaps has not even yet been born—

—, oh homecoming! oh, Plotia!—

—, oh homecoming! irretrievable homecoming; mortal are we along with all that is mortal, mortal in ourselves are we who have taken no fate upon us, having in this way made ourselves one with chance, our occurrence and being and knowledge inescapably arrested in the blank form of fate, mortal are we in the midst of immortality, mortal under the music of the stars, mortal through guilt, strayed into a thicket of voices, girded round by the mute-pressing light of the indiscriminate, forfeited to dream-death, forfeited to a death of growing cruelty that no longer holds aught of immortality—

—, oh homecoming! resting and hearkening in the infinite stretch of the Saturnian meadows, in the Saturnian landscape of the earth and the soul, in the golden, homelike peace of eternal earthliness, shielded from Janus, although this is a twofold hearkening, directed upwards and downwards, an intent listening into the depths of heaven and earth for the name of the thing bestowed on it by Saturn, shielded from the deadly cruelty of dissension and war, shielded from destruction, even though the hearkening is at the same time a forgetting, a forgetting of the names that are forgotten by virtue of their association with home—

—, oh homecoming! he who is allowed to come home comes back to creation, he comes there where, behind the fluid boundaries of beginning and ending, behind the comprehensible and incomprehensible, he divines the ultimate statute, he escapes the indiscrimination in which good and evil are benumbed to blank fate-forms, he buries his face in the utterly-incomprehensible from whose relentless-mild voice, fate-bidden and predestined, issues the judgment that existence be loosed from its form and be sundered to right and to left—

—, oh homecoming! oh sorrow redeemed by suffering, the miracle of immortality! Oh, we may be allowed to touch it, we may perhaps obtain an intuitive grasp of the incomprehensible if only for a moment's length, yet—the heart receiving the miracle—forever, if our including and included destiny take on itself that other, grown higher and wider in surrender, fleeing into yet giving cover to the other one until, with the miracle of the second self which we have borne through the flames, we are granted a second childhood, transformed and belonging to the father, knowledge beyond knowledge, perceiving and perceived, chance come to be miracle, having embraced all knowledge, all occurrence, all existence, fate overcome, not quite here but yet at hand, oh, miracle, oh, the music awakened once more so poignantly, within us and about us, the opened countenance of the spheres, oh, love—

—, oh homecoming! for love is resolution! oh homecoming forevermore! for love is the readiness for creation—

—, and resolution was that perception which, born from dreaming yet giving birth of itself, was flooded to him like an occurrence and yet passively from out the invisible, now become visible; it was a perception in the realm of the speechless and the wordless, a final effort of the dream that awakes of itself and recognizes its own borders, the dream constantly coming home in its own birth, encased in birth's darkness which, for all that, was still held within the full radiance of the dream. The perception was not in himself, it came out clearly from the invisible crystal of the structure, it was the crystal of dreams. Was this the perception of genii or angels, when they, the listening messengers inherent to the Creation, floating unborn with it, perceived the divine command? Was he floating with them outside of the dream-border? in dream? in recollection? The enormous effort to shatter dream, to shatter fate, did not relax; no, it increased, it became more pressing, directed more to the goal, more toward perception, and the more it grew the more perfect became the visibility of the dream, the more its boundless radiation was interwoven with the recollected or intuitive knowledge of all past earthly happenings, which, the content recognizable despite all change of form, was arising like a second dream within the dome of the first one, overlaying and enriching it, yielding image after image, storing landscape on landscape, in evidence here as of yore,—the dream-existence in the morning of childhood, transparent in its depth of memory, twined about by waters and wreaths, the arch of the unseen heaven above it sparkling with layer upon layer of stars, muteness and music coalesced into crystal, ever experienced yet never remembered, ever perceived yet never understood. And there, surrendering to the succession of images, there he listened to the heart of the dream, and softly at first, then more and more distinctly, he heard the beating at the heart of the dream. For in the memory which mounted up to him or into which he sank—the direction being indeterminable in the quiescence of the occurrence—in this upsurging and absorbing radiation, in this fluid meeting where things merged without movement, there was contained, not less immobile, not less symbolic, that which he had always sought for in language and in poetry and which was again evaporated to nothingness for the sake of understanding; here all speech was annulled, all poetry was annulled, so that only the deepest recesses of the dream-abyss might shine through, as if it were the final form of fate within the unavoidable multi-formity, the form which is the pattern of all forms within the radiantly inevitable, knotted and looped, flowing and fixed, but within every form, in every figuration, stretched endlessly and invisibly over the light-plains of dream, dream opened up unto its root-depth to give birth to the dream: oh this, this very depth it was that floated up to the heart, oh in it the heart was floating, radiating up from and into it, interradiated to a knowledge utterly ungraspable through speech; it was the heart of dream entering, enpulsing and suffusing the human heart to a crystal-line wholeness and consummation, and he deemed that fate was on the point of being transformed again in the vibration of light-surf into which he sank or which surged up to him as if here, in this last abyss of roots, the new reconciliation of form to its eternal content were about to succeed: the awakening! Oh, the rousing torment of a dreamed awakening, fate-conditioned this too, enclosed in borders within the dream, which presents

212

itself even in the midst of perception although the boundary of dream has already been overstepped, already sundered, because the heart, once having started to beat, constantly pleading for admittance and ready for reality, palpitates even unto its borders and knocks on its portal—

—, for love is abiding readiness, containing every prospect and all peace, for love is creative readiness: not quite here but yet at hand, this is the threshold on which love stands in the forecourt of reality, there where the portals shall swing back to allow the borders of reality to be crossed, opened to awakening, opened to rebirth, opened to the resurrected, the re-animated, the never-heard, the forever-yearned-for language of a new life in ultimately redeemed consummation, opened to the final word of judgment which shall ring beyond any dream-life whatsoever, beyond the world, beyond space, beyond time; oh it is before such a renewal of creation that love stands, still enveloped in twilight and merely hearkening, yet itself the awakening help, the incipient awakening—

—, and the brightness of the dream-dome quivered up and away from itself like the beating of a heart, the dome itself quivering, vibrating in the infinite and voluminous voices of its radiant completeness, in the diffusion, the concentration and refraction of its boundless beam-tracks and light-paths; and the starry pinnacle trembled also, the dream as a whole inhaling and exhaling itself, the breath waiting, the dream waiting, waiting in the recesses of his heart, the receptacle of the spheres waiting. Would the new speech, the new word, the new voice be wrung out of such a breath? Would the voice-source of time's beginning and ending open of itself, disclosing the cross-road common to all paths in the infinite abyss of dream? Would there, oh, would there be intoned from the dream that spontaneous echo-accord of world-unity, world-order, world-comprehension which would, which must be the final resolution of the earthly task, comprised in the totality of voices and comprising them? Merely an intimation, it was no more than that, an intimate trembling up from the roots of dream, but trembling on and on to the furthest reaches of dream, shutting off the voices and releasing the voices in the wavering light-breath of the occurrence; earthbound still the heart's beating, but transcending earth in its waiting, still earthbound as the dream-instrument of that fatal force which, unsevered from evil, malice and chance, carried death in itself, but already transcendent in its readiness to hear the command, supernal in its vigilant readiness. Verily, nearer to the unearthly than anything else was this willingness to awaken, nearer than the readiness for death, which was bound up with dying to mundane things, saturated with self-seeking and fame-seeking, with intoxication and hatred; verily, it was nearer to the revelations of death, nearer to it than his own readiness for death, under whose relentlessly unavoidable regency he had placed his life, fancying to force a homecoming through the offering of himself, breaking through the boundaries and listening for the voice as if he could imitate it through his own dying, and win it over by virtue of this imitation. It had remained inimitable, for this was a voice that could not be won over. For this voice of all voices was beyond any speech whatsoever, more compelling than any, even more compelling than music, than any poem; this was the heart's beat, and must be in its single beat, since only thus was it able to embrace the perceived unity of existence in the instant of the heart's beat, the eye's glance; this, the very voice of the incomprehensible which expresses the incomprehensible, was in itself incomprehensible, unattainable through human speech, unattainable through earthly symbols, the arch-image of all voices and all symbols, thanks to a most incredible immediacy, and it was only able to fulfill its inconceivably sublime mission, only empowered to do so, when it passed beyond all things earthly, yet this would become impossible for it, aye, inconceivable, did it not resemble the earthly voice; and even should it cease to have anything in common with the earthly voice, the earthly word, the earthly language, having almost ceased to symbolize them, it could serve to disclose the arch-image to whose unearthly immediacy it pointed, only when it reflected it in an earthly immediacy: image strung to image, every chain of images led into the terrestrial, to an earthly immediacy, to an earthly happening, yet despite this—in obedience to a supreme human compulsion—must be led further and further, must find a higher expression of earthly immediacy in the beyond, must lift the earthly happening over and beyond its this-sidedness to a still higher symbol; and even though the symbolic chain threatened to be severed at the boundary, to fall apart on the border of the celestial, evaporating on the resistance offered by the unattainable, forever discontinued, forever severed, the danger is warded off, warded off again and again, the chain of symbols closed when the unattainable deigns to transform itself into the attainable by descending to earth, by becoming an earthly event, solidified to an earthly deed, so that the chain of expression in ascending and descending could close to a cycle, to a cycle of truth, to a cycle of eternal symbols, true in each of its images, true because of the cyclic balance in play around the opened borders, true in the constant interchange of the divine and the human act, true in their common symbolic quality and in the symbol of their mutual resemblance, true because the creation renewed itself in them forever, entering into the law, into that law of constant rebirth which was charged with the overcoming of chance, of fixation, of death; no earthly preparation for death, were it ever so intuitive an imitation of the divine sacrifice, was able to summon the earthly enactment of the subliminal; only the contemplative preparation for the awakening was really valid, and the dreamer, bound like fate to the dream, unredeemed and averse to death though death-enclosed, harbors in his dream only the preparation for the awakening, made susceptible to it alone by his knowledge, unbetrayable in his dream-knowledge, in his unerring knowledge of the awakening and its universal validity, for the sake of which the dream has revealed itself, opened up in the singing abysses of its unsearchable depths, in the darkly radiating root-abyss of its shimmering shafts, with its heart, even more conscious, opening still more, trembling to a voice that was no longer a voice, far rather a deed, the deed for which it descended to retrieve the name, fate-bidden to turn around, to return for the summons to homecoming—

—, oh homecoming in that deed which signifies love, for only the serving helpful deed, in that it bestows the name and fulfills the empty form of fate, is stronger than fate itself—

—, not quite here but yet at hand! And it was knowledge at the heart of an inconceivable loving distance that was buried in the innermost heart of the dream, it was awareness of the similarity in that tidal flood, the heart of this side and the heart of the beyond pulsing and beating within each other, the divine symbol kindled in the human being to a common language, the language of the divine-human pledge of allegiance, the language of everlasting creation in prayer and more prayer, mounting and subsiding in creative images; and it was the knowledge of this language of the redeeming deed, of this language of loving sacrifice, which floated as far above every human offering as the envoiced other-worldliness of the one voice floated over the babble of voices on earth, as the loving other-worldliness floated above every love that operates from man to man, the divine-human heart contained in divinity and humanity, containing both god and man; but it was likewise an awareness of him who—because the voice to be credible on earth must have an announcer—was destined to be the bearer of the creative deed, the deed and the doer born into earthly life from an unearthly conception, for only he who in his very origin is already exempt from chance is able to reunite chance with the miracle of that ultimate lawfulness to which fate itself is subjected; for only he who originates from a destiny beyond fate and who, despite this, drains the destined calamity to the last drop, only he is given grace to turn calamity into salvation again and to become the bearer of salvation; oh to him and only to him, the divinely-conceived figure in heroic human form, is it permitted to carry the father across the fires of iniquity, and he alone is entrusted with the rescue of the father, he is allowed to carry the one who conceived him, taking him on his shoulders and bearing him off to the ship and to the homecoming flight into a new country, into the land of promise that has always been the homeland of the father. Not quite here, but yet at hand! That land lay before him in the knowledge of the enjoining, name-giving father-summons which embodies the divine in the human and inspirits the human into the divine; it lay before him in radiation and counter-radiation, it lay before him in the knowledge of the salvation-bearer and in the salvation-bearer's knowledge, full of humanity, full of divinity, the brands of iniquity changed to pure sacrificial flames, the rigidity shattered, the gravestone of the middle lifted, good and evil parted and purified, god and man enlarged to a resurrected creation, the prophecy reclaimed in a future in the name of the father, forever sanctified in the name of the son, forever affianced in the spirit, not quite here but yet at hand, the promised one. Was that which he perceived already recognition? was it only the recognition in dream? was it already the awakening? Oh, it was still this side of the boundary, but even though the dream palpitated against it, it had not broken through the border; the vision was not to be grasped, it was not recognition, it was only awareness, a dream-awareness, a dream-recollection, a distant memory of the never-heard, ever-resounding voice of a Once, the furthest recollection of the never-encountered land beyond the border, through which he had always wandered, a land enlarged by distance, reduced by distance, the source, the estuary; it was the memory-strengthened approach to the border, but it was still a spellbound quivering, a throbbing, expectant illumination. And just for that reason, even in this peering knowledge, in this extremely transparent blindness, that without being recognition was a form of recognition, a transparent bandage over his eyes, yes, for that reason, although sunk into the dream-meadows and overgrown by their bracken, he found himself placed abruptly on the peak of a very high mountain, as if he had been ordered there so that he might look beyond the border, he a beholder, but still not an announcer, placed there and held there by a gentle-unyielding hand, held into a future yet always existent actuality, beat upon

by the throbbing of a heart that though enshrined in him yet
enshrined him by being greater than himself; breathing with
reality and animated by this throbbing, he was enabled to release his arms from the crystalline transparency and to stretch
them upward, upward toward the luminous dome wherein the
stars were shining and great suns were beginning to revolve, a
single star above them all: he gazed out over the fields of dream,
over the fields of those countries predestined to be the theater
of the deed, the theater of his vision, beyond touch, beyond
tread, yet his own from the very start; he gazed out, spellbound,
dreambound here as he was, unable to part from or to be removed from his dream, gazing out over the landscape in which,
though it was beyond his touch and tread, he was stretched out
with his own dream radiation and his own dream illumination
and, surveying both the landscape and the dream, he saw that
they were reciprocally merged, he saw amidst the landscape
all the crystalline formations, the light-cubes, the light-circles,
the light-pyramids, the light-clusters of the dream; he saw,
stretched out and imbedded in the dreamy confluence and
boundless radiation of its light-paths, the landscape, made rich,
transparent and magical through memory; indeed, it was imbedded in the dream with all its night-times and day-times, va-
cillating between light and darkness, inflating and deflating under
the twofold dusk of morning and evening, filled with every possible kind of earthly shape, filled with a motley crowd of all
creaturehood, filled with the roaring medley of all earthly voices,
filled with intoxication, with torment, with yearning, filled with
the created and the developing creation, filled with the silence of
beaches, of undulating meadows and of fading mountain summits,—the heights bearing loneliness and the plains bearing
cities,—filled with the peaceful glow of human life and living
but also filled by the rustling and crackling of the evil flames,
endless, endless, endless; everything there was to be wandered
through, nothing could be trodden, dream and landscape imbedded one into the other, shining into and shading out into
each other, joined in expectation, joined in yearning, joined

in a readiness for awakening, waiting to receive him who would stride through them, bringing the voice of the awakening. And he too was waiting; with uplifted arms he waited with dream and landscape, he gazed over the still pastures on which the cattle were grazing without motion, he perceived the muteness of the motionlessly burning brands, and no bird-flight moved across the pavilion of the air; the flames rose higher into the immobility, the confusion of the manifold voices increased in the unbreakable silence, the yearning became deeper and deeper, the suns stood still and the throbbing of the heart beat more and more heavily against the walls of the boundlessness within and without—, oh when was the end to be? where was the end to be found? when would the desecration be quaffed to the last drop? Was there a nethermost stage to this deepening silence? And then it seemed to him that just such an ultimate silence had now been achieved. For he saw the mouths of men gaping at each other full of terror, no sound wrenched itself from the dry clefts and no one understood the other. It was the last step of silence on earth, it was the ultimate silencing of men; and beholding this his mouth also yearned to open in a last mute cry of horror. Still while seeing it, almost before he had really seen it, he no longer saw anything. For the visible had vanished into most abrupt darkness, the light of dream quenched, the landscape disappeared, the flames quelled, the people evaporated, the mouths abolished, this was night, timeless, spaceless, wordless, toneless, the most empty blackness, an empty night without form and without content; empty and black became the waiting, even the throbbing died down, sucked up by emptiness. The bottom of existence had been reached. He stood at the boundary, he stood at the edge of destiny, at the border of chance, he stood at the boundary with blank expectation, with blank listening, with blank looking, with blank wisdom, yet drained as he was and in this blankness he knew that the border-line would be opened. This began to happen very softly as if not to alarm him. It began as a whisper that he had heard once before, it began in his innermost ear, in his innermost soul, in his innermost heart, yet simultaneously surrounding him and penetrating him, stemming from the uttermost darkness, streaming in and out of the night; it was the same quietly great power of the tone to which once before he had had to submit in repentance, swelling out now as then, fulfilling him, enwrapping him, although it was no longer the accord of many voices; it was not the accord of the voice-herds, it was not the accord of any voice-multiplicity, instead it was far rather a single voice, making itself more and more solitary, a voice of such great loneliness that it glowed like a single star in the darkness, nevertheless an invisible one shining in the invisible, for as the summons grew greater and more distinct, it was subsumed not less greatly into the infinite and inscrutable, which is inaudible because it is mute: what took place here was beyond the visible and the audible, it was beyond the reach of every sense-perception, it happened obscurely and for all that it was of a most compelling, perceptible clarity; it happened in a realm of shadows, yet included the forms of every essence, oh, it occurred as equilibrium, it was manifested as an infinite, inconceivably balanced order, giving meaning, content and name, comprised of all being and all memory, including the iron booming of seas as well as the silver susurrus of autumn, the celesta-stroke of the stars as well as the warm breathing of flocks, the flutetone of the moon even as the dew on the sunny hedges of childhood; it was a beholding of the unbeholdable, a listening into the inaudible, and he flooded in darkness, the world's diversity and entity likewise held in balance within the flood of darkness, in this last command to equilibrium which is the only reality and which annuls chance, he heard, no he did not hear, he saw the voice which brought this to pass; and it was not one of those voices which, belonging to the world, insert themselves into the structure of world-facts in order to turn them into a symbol, symbolizing one thing by another but also symbolizing the word by the word, this was not the voice of worldly truth, neither one of them nor the summation of all such truths, no, it was unterrestrially, inaudibly, invisibly beyond the world; it was the

extra-worldly agent of truth, the extra-worldly agent of equilibrium, it was the essence of the outside, bringing near all the
strength and all the amplitude of the outside as it brought itself
nearer, comprehending all that is within in order to be comprehended by it, the all-embracing receptacle of the spheres; and
thus he realized it, hearing by seeing, seeing by hearing the
voice in the shadow of whose word peace and homeland are
ever to be found, the voice of timelessness and of the everlasting
creation, the judgment-voice of the beginning and the end, the
equilibrating voice outside the dream, the voice of safe-keeping;
its tone was brazen and crystal and flute-like in one; it was
thunder and the preponderance of silence, and it was all sounds
and yet a single sound, commanding and gentle, forgiving and
discerning, a single lightning-flash, oh, an unspeakably gentle
blinding, quiet because consummate; oh, thus it disclosed itself,
grace fused with the pledge, disclosing itself not as word, not
as speech, far rather as symbol of a word, as symbol of all
speech, as symbol of every voice, as the arch-image of them all,
overcoming fate in the form of the holy father-summons; it
revealed itself as the tone-picture of the annunciating deed:
"Open your eyes to Love!"

S OMETHING was being done, and it was being done for him.
He did not have to open his eyes, the beneficence opened them
for him. He did not have to breathe, it breathed him. This
had been a symbolization in the allegory of which the night
was restored to itself, and, in the symbolization of the voice,
muteness came home to silence as if silence were the first
content with which the empty form must again be filled in order
to be revived. And, by virtue of the fulfillment, the diverse directions of the dream were streaming back to the earthly spaces;
they streamed back from an undimension into a dimension,
turned into the flow of night, constituting a space that was flooded

by the tides of night. Nothing was audible except the silence, nothing within, nothing outside of him; he was flooded in a saturation of night, the silence surrounded by night. Even the little oil flame of the hanging lamp had burned itself out, as though sucked up by the darkness in order that the all-fulfilling silence should not be interrupted or disturbed by the small hard point of light. In a like manner the great throbbing of the dream had quieted down, had ebbed and was ebbing further, lulling itself into a silvery drizzle that welling up from a nowhere and flowing off into a nowhere yet issued from the wall-fountain. Rinsed by the surrounding silence, the elusive had come to rest again between the past and the future in the vividly present now; softly the scale of time was swaying, softly tinkling were the silver chains of its saucers, which in their gradual rise and fall met and released symbol after symbol, weighing their truth, symbol after symbol given significance by the test of weighing; and the linking of this chain merged softly and silverly into the gentle stream of existence, newly fulfilled. Fulfilled by an imageless silence yet image-fraught. And the silence-bearing night, its bell-tone quiet and gentle, recreated itself there before his eyes, his eyes unfolded, he himself once more unfolded, the night again unfolded, mysteriously blind with silence, pregnant with shadows, liberal and loving in recovered naturalness, the night which was being swept along, carrying him onward in her branches, in her plumage, in her arms, in her breath, on her breast. He lay. He lay, he rested, he was allowed to rest on. But, even as he rested, he also knew that the silence of the night's happenings was only a prelude, that they must come to an end. For not only had the un-space flowed into the limits of space, but his body had been flooded back from there, he lay bodily in his bed, his feelings became more and more bodily, his was a bodily peace, and in the fullness of his peace he perceived that the fever had waned—beneficent and buoyant, the cool still waves of every night-ending as far back as he could remember. And just as the hour of lessening fever came back to the physical-earthly, so also the night came to the diurnal hour, hurried toward its rim, toward the hour of earth's recurrent fulfillment, of earth's recurrent efformation, toward earthly night. Still nothing happened, the night-darkness held, only the silence became deflated, lost its fullness, creased with scarcely perceptible tracings, very uncertain and perceptible only to the keenest listening, the silence seemed to ruffle itself back from its uttermost borders, to loosen up; darkness-enflooded creation coming softly into being was being engraved into the uneventfulness of silence by a loving gentle hand. Name after name arose at the soft night-summons, formed itself to an entity with remembrance, became firm by memory, becoming through memory a participant in the creation. Did a cock crow in the distance? Were there dogs barking out there?—the footsteps of the guards, as if they too had been surrendered from un-space, were making their rounds of the palace as before, the wall-fountain drizzled more distinctly as if having gained in water-supply, and the window-sash framed anew the abundance of stars, the head of the snake conjurer flickering brightly in their midst. Breath-quickened the silence, breath-filled the night, and growing out of the night and the silence was that which was always at hand, the breathing world-sleep. The darkness was breathing again, becoming more and more formed, more and more creaturely, more and more earthly, richer and richer in shadows. At first shapelessly, scarcely recognizable, in a certain sense like a point of noise, in scraps of tone and in separate tones, then condensing and collecting into audible form, the creaturely was approaching; it was a creaking and rattling moan, and it came hither from the peasant-carts that were traveling along in ever-narrowing rows bringing victuals to the morning market; sleepy-slow they moved onward, with a rumbling of wheels in the pavement ruts, the creaking of axles, the gritty stroke of the wheel-rims on the curbstones, the click of chains and of harnesses, sometimes with the snorting groan of an ox, sometimes with the sound of a sleepy call, and often the soft, heavy pulling-gait of the animals came into an evenness of step that was like the march of the breath. Breathing creatures

223

wandered through the breath of the night, fields and gardens and nourishment wandered with them, they too breathing, and the breath of all life was opened to receive the creature, opened to world-unity which includes love and form. For love begins in breathing and with breathing mounts to immortality. Down there the peasants were driving, sleepy-headed, heads nodding they traveled on vegetable-carts piled high with cabbage-heads and lettuce-heads, and when one of them let his chin drop as far down as his chest he grunted just as a beast does in its sleep. Some elements of the plant and the animal are contributed to human sleep, and in death the countenance of a peasant seems like stiffened clay. Coming out of the fateless, leading into the fateless, with hardly anything assigned to chance, the peasant's path runs on the very brink of destiny and on the brink of sleep. Should his prayer, delivered from chance, be answered, then earth, plant and beast are without fate for him; and though he sees the stars only when he goes to market or when he must attend a cow, calving by night, and though he immediately falls back into the dreamless-light sleepy progress of his nights and days, he remains lovingly bound to that nature which is beyond fate, a nature that he lets run through his fingers as smooth, golden wheat, that he touches with softly stroking hand on the hide of an animal, that he tests, crumbling it through his fingers as fertile ground, so very lovingly, so very knowingly — oh ground, beast and fruit so well grasped—that he himself shall be grasped, held and hidden in the knowing-loving hand, peacefully held in it, the hand that shuts and opens itself around him in the passing of the years and days, he mingled with them, mingled in their tides, mingled with their restful warmth, mingled with the knowledge of their future chill, from which he will one day glide crumblingly into the fateless, sleepy womb of his beginning, the farmer dying into the earth; only his breath, the unearthly having become free and rid of its fetters, mounting into that which is beyond, into the invisible with its voices, into the divine: down there the peasants were driving, driving past and away, one cart after the other, on each of which crouched someone, sleeping, head-wagging, snoring, with hardly a fate, hardly a chance, every one in his creaturely cycle of night; so they traveled, old or young, full-bearded, stubble-cheeked, smooth-faced; so they drove on as their fathers, grandfathers, and great-grandfathers had driven, embodied in the vast repose of their security, peacefully embodied in the vast tides holding them, driving on in the tranquility of their fate-quelling patience, driving asleep, unmindful of the voice that floated above them, the voice of their obscure yearning, yes even, it may be, of their conviction, but which for all that they scarcely heeded, because in the timeless span from generation to generation there is no set time, and it is irrelevant whether the fulfillment be granted to the father, or grandchild, or great-grandchild; confined in activity greater than themselves, and one that they confined in themselves with a careful sort of love, they drove on deliberately through the darkness toward the brink of night, and they dared to sleep. But he, even though once belonging to them, even though once having been likewise a peasant, he lay here cut off from them, cut off from the soil, cut off from plant and beast, still in the grip of fate he lay here, a night-seer: oh, submerged in every human soul there is some function, sheerly unreachable, a function that is greater than himself, greater than his soul, and only he who achieves himself in this final preparation for death discharges his special function, he it is who watches vigilantly over the sleep of the mortal world. Oh homecoming, oh vigilance! Where was it? who kept watch over the world, who guarded those who drove on through the darkness, sleeping? Did the voice do it? was he doing it in having been found worthy of the grace to perceive the voice? Was he now placed on guard? Never! never would he be fit for it, he who was incapable of any help, unwilling for any service, he the mere word-maker who must needs destroy his work because the humane, the round of human action and the human need for help, had meant so little to him that every-thing which he should have retained and depicted in love was never written down, but simply and uselessly transfigured and magnified to beauty; what presumption to think that under such circumstances he could be ordered to watch, while the veritable watcher, the announcer of the voice had still to come! Was it all nothing but an empty dream? Had the voice in all its reality been actually bestowed upon him? Why then had it been silenced? Where was it? Where was it? He asked, he asked; he called on high for it, and yet as he asked—he asked no more! He kept on seeking for it and yet as he sought—it was no longer a search! For the revelation that he meant not to believe was present everywhere, he perceived it everywhere, perceived it in the groaning of the wagons, in the sluggish pulling-gait of the beasts, in the sleep-creased peasant faces, in their breathing, in the breathing of the darkness, in the breath of the night, and everything—the fateless as well as the fateful, the earthly and the human—had entered into him, had already become part of his own functioning, was his fate also, so much so that whether it remained unwritten, forevermore uncomposed, the promise of not-being-lost had come to be granted, the promise of an infinite further-bestowal in an infinitely further-bestowing love which would remain there through pure beneficence always and forevermore; the night as it vanished was listening, heavy as if with tears. Sleeping or not sleeping, it was all one, beginning and ending the same, fountain and source, root and crown, the flowing tree of the spheres, in the branching of which, fate-assigned and fate-delivered, humanity continues to rest. It existed, it was already in the world, and still it had not come to pass. And bound in with the whole, enslaved by its destiny, and bearing it in his own, he too rested, happily feeling the alliance, feeling it physically with all the fibers of his fever-freed being, happily feeling the coolness that forced him to wrap himself more thoroughly in his coverlet, happily aware of time gliding through the re-opened world of night and bringing coolness as it came, happily aware of the relaxed breathing assimilated into the drizzling breath of darkness issuing from all the fountains of the world, feeling the murmur of the world, feeling the naturalness, while the drizzling sounded cooler and cooler, the stars became cooler, their space became cooler, and cooler that which was audible therein. The wagon-train down there had gradually thinned out, the oncoming and outgoing teams differentiated by their sounds, the distance between them had increased, and finally only a few stragglers were left. And as the pauses between their journey-noises became greater, these were filled more and more distinctly by something like a susurrus that ran widely and silver-clear in and out of the great darkness; it was expected and full of expectation, it was the sea with its drizzling waves, surging in the darkness, although already called out to by the approaching morning. Maybe, oh it may be that he deceived himself—this nearly dismayed him—perhaps his hearing deceived him, perhaps he was ready only for another self-deception, perhaps it was only yearning, an empty yearning of the heart, a yearning for the sea, a yearning for the voice of salvation to surge within the sea-surge, so that he might be able to hold converse with it, a yearning for the voice to become irrefutable by the very strength of the surging, its annunciation irrefutable in the power of the natural—but no, oh no, it was the sea, the sea in its tritonic-immeasurable reality, the revealed activity of the inexpressible and inaudible voice was interwoven with the moon-swept silver rumbling, woven into the endless stour of the billows, woven into the unshackling below and the liberation above, woven into the darkness and into the light-veil with which the darkness had started to extinguish itself, woven into the paling stars, no, still more, more still: filled with the voice, the waters listened, the sea listened, the stars too, the darkness listened and everything that was human listened, the sleeping as well as the wakeful, the universe listened, all listening to themselves in that which fulfilled them. The natural conformed to the natural and there in this mutual conforming love was abiding. Did evil exist? had it been judged? had it been cast out already? The voice woven into the universe did not answer and it was almost as if the answer were not to be brought until daybreak, as if everything had come to be merely a waiting for the day-star, as if beside this nothing more were permissible. Night gathered itself in to its goal, intent on the goal, its blackness stripped of softness; the starry flickering out there played itself out into a greenishness. The color of air stood motionlessly in the darkness, picking object after object out of the shadows, and inch by inch, starting from the window, the room became a room again, the walls again became walls. Shone upon by the last star in the window, the candelabrum in front of it rose up black as a tree without foliage, its branches still hung with the shreds of night. And in the alcove, indistinct but recognizable, the boy rested in the armchair, asleep; he had drawn his legs under the seat, his face was supported in his hand, his dark hair was like shadow, the clear eyes invisible, hidden under the shadow of the closed lids, but his listening could be observed, a listening to that which he had announced to himself in his sleep, suffering and dissolving suffering, without help and yet helping, desiring and desireless, love without greed of lust, the unborn angel in the earthborn man: the sleeper. Oh, vanishing night, that bears away the sleeper unto the last drawing of his breath, on and on, eternal in your branching, bearing him in your arms, upon your breast! Once more the great bow of night was stretched out before him, starting with the reddish fumes of hell and with the clamor of voices outside the windows, mounting to the craters of all death, accompanied by all the grimaces and discordances of death, hurtling into the void of most abased nothingness, but taken up again by the commanding, gentle, name-calling voice of annunciation in order to filter —a fading bell-tone—into the first seeping of light, emptied into the light and merging with it into dawn. Could it be possible that all of it had happened before this same window, that something was still happening here? What was transient had sounded up and sounded off, had been unrolled and rolled up, and had come to be enduring, the day rising before him was transient, and for a long time he had given up glancing toward it; his eyes were veiled although they remained open, tear-veiled without tears, but through the veil he saw with estranged glance the coming of day; he saw the dawn, observing wistfully how softly it laid its colorless color, layer after layer, on the roofs outside; he saw it yet he no longer saw it, his seeing had come to be a sensing, and in this sensing, by means of this sensing, the day was born for him, becoming his own with its new light: the early morning grew apace; it was wafted to him in the increasing cleanliness of its smell, in its very distinct, very light-gray clarity, across which, without mingling with it, the thinly acrid threads of smoke from the first hearth fires were drifting; it was wafted to him with the morning-fresh sharpness of the silver, salt breath of the sea, quicksilverly arising from the silver surf, soft in the distance, arising from the first shimmering of the cool, damp shore which, with its clean sand and pebbles rinsed by the silver waves of dawn, had been made ready to receive the morning sacrifice; it was wafted toward him, unfolded and unfolding as the natural beginning of a new creation, and in receiving the unfoldment and being received by it he felt that he himself was being flooded on by its drizzling action, carried on in surge upon surge, enfolded in its heaving breath, as though on wings that were cool to the touch, as though in a vast breath, and yet securely on earth as if, resting in the shadowy fragrance of a laurel bush after an hour of rain, he were breathing it in, rain-dark and dew-clear and refreshed. Thus he was borne along, on and on, and yonder where the flight settled, landing lightly among the blond harvest-billows of the fields, yonder where the sheaves were tossing, grapes hanging on the thorn-bush and the ox lying side by side with the lion, there stood an angel before him, not exactly an angel, more like a boy, but for all that an angel, wrapped in the cool wings of the September morning, dark-tressed and clear-eyed, one whose voice was not that of the deed, the symbolic annunciation of which filled the universe, no, it was much more the quite distant echo of the symbolic arch-image hovering in the empyrean, very soft as he spoke, but nevertheless the bronzen shadow of the aeons: "Enter into the Creation that once existed and again exists, but let you be called Virgil, your time has come!" This is what the angel said, terrible in its gentleness, comforting in its sadness, unreachable in its yearning, this is what he understood from the lips of the angel, this he had heard as the language within language, in all its earthly simplicity; and hearing it, called and assigned to the name, he saw again the waving fields spread out from shore to shore, infinite the waves of grain, infinite the waves of waters, both stroked by the cool, slanting light of earliest morning, coolly glistening the near at hand, coolly glistening the far away, he saw it, and then there followed the sweetness of perceiving everything and perceiving nothing, of knowing everything and knowing nothing, of sensing everything and sensing nothing, there followed the sweetness of complete forgetfulness, sleep without dream.—

EARTH—THE EXPECTATION

THE AWAKENING OCCURRED WITH THE FEELING OF REMISS-
ness: this too was a mere impression like his falling asleep,
however it came abruptly, and feeling that someone was near
his bed, he also felt that this would spell frustration for him;
with the second prod of this sensation he crossed the sill of awareness, knowing that he should have rushed to the seashore at dawn
to destroy the Aeneid, and that it had become too late to do
this. And he fled back into sleep again to find the angel who
had vanished, perhaps even hoping that the strange glance
which he felt still resting on him might be his. He was certain
it was not; all too surely he sensed the strangeness that stood
next to him, and actually to frighten it away, even though still
with a last spark of hope for the angel's presence, he asked out
of sleep: "Are you Lysanias?"

The answer was something unintelligible, uttered by a quite
unfamiliar voice.

Something sighed in him. "You are not Lysanias . . . go
away."

"Master . . . ," came hesitantly, almost pleadingly.

"Later . . ."; the night must not end, he did not wish to see
the light.

"Master, your friends have arrived . . . they are
waiting . . ."

There was no help. And the light hurt. The cough was in
his breast ready to break out and there was a risk involved in
speaking.

"My friends? . . . which ones . . . ?"

"Plotius Tucca and Lucius Varius have come from Rome just to greet you ... they would like to see you before they are called before Caesar ..."

The light hurt. Slanting from southward, the rays of the September sun cut sharply through the corner alcove, filling it with warmth, the light and warmth of a September morning, and the room although beyond reach of the sunrays was affected by them, having become sober-looking in the light, ugly in the heat: the dark floor of relucent mosaic was soiled, the tall candelabrum with its faded flowers and its burnt-down candles looked shoddy. Over there in the corner of the room stood the commode, a necessity and a temptation. Everything that could hurt began to hurt. The friends would have to wait. "First of all I must cleanse myself ... help me."

Dragging his legs over the edge of the bed, he sat there, his crooked back quite bent over, struggling with the urge to cough, the painful impulse having again assaulted him; likewise the mawkish lassitude of fever made itself felt again, firstly in the drooping legs, thence creeping upwards streakily, it spread in soft wavelike thuds over the whole body, finally invading his head; and seized by weariness, his glance fastened itself with slow, tired, long-lasting concentration on his naked toes, unable to bring their mechanical half-gripping movements to a standstill, peering as if something important might be discovered there, perhaps even the origin of the fever—, ah, need the engrossing life of organs and senses begin again? And though one could not ask any intimate question of a slave, his glance wandered up to the one here, seeking enlightenment, almost involuntarily, almost against his will in its questioning, only to be immediately disappointed, because in the oriental, slightly thick-nosed, impenetrable, mask-like and ageless servant's face there was nothing to be seen that could qualify as an answer, nothing but a stern subjection and a subjected sternness, that although unapproachable was prepared to take orders, waiting without impatience for the guest to make them known and to decide to rise. But just this seemed impossible, because a discord was everywhere observable, and not only in his body; it was a universal discord, and until it had been resolved not a limb could be moved: he who wished to arise, to hasten to the sacrificial deed on the shore, might not do so in discord and division; the officiant must needs be faultless, faultless the offering, if the dignity of complete validity were to be attained for the sacrifice; and it could not even be ascertained whether all the rolls were in the chest, so that the work in its entirety could be offered for destruction, or whether some of the rolls had gone astray in the course of the night—who could answer? To be sure the top of the chest was so neatly and stoutly fastened that one might actually think it had never been opened—, but who would dare touch the offering and loosen the straps? Discordant the body and its limbs, discordant the world—, could integration again be hoped for? He waited and the slave waited with him, both without impatience. But in the midst of all this the door was opened rather unceremoniously and Plotius Tucca as well as Lucius Varius, irritated by the waiting, doubtless having heard from outside that he was awake, entered the room in short order. He withdrew his legs into bed again.

And Plotius was scarcely inside the room before he broke out as usual into an expansive, noisy heartiness. "We were told that you were lying here sick and we spent the whole long night rattling out here, and now one catches you trying secretly to slip out of bed; but it is just as well that we have caught you, this is the way you always behave . . . but how do you really feel? The gods be thanked, you look all right; no different than ten years ago; you are a tough bit of leather . . . naturally, you are again the prey of your cough and your fever: we know all about that . . . if you had consulted your friends they certainly wouldn't have allowed you to go on this craziest of all journeys! We were told of it afterwards by Horace; you could tell him because you knew he would not try to hinder you, all that's important to him are his own verses! What in Hades did you have to do in Athens? Naturally you had to keep it a secret, and it was just your luck that Caesar dragged you out and brought you back in time ... Augustus, wise as usual, and you, yes, you just as inconsiderate as ever ... for we, your friends, are now put to it to get you well again!" He let his heavy body drop creaking into the arm-chair, elbows bent, fists doubled up; he sat there now like a rower or a coachman, and his ruddy, fleshy, liver-spotted, double-chinned face shone with cheerfulness.

Lucius Varius, on the other hand, who took care never to sit down at all, because he had to be mindful of the elegant, well-pressed folds of his toga, remained standing, dignified and spare in his usual posture, one arm resting on his hip, the other raised admonishingly at right angles: "We have been much troubled on your account, Vergilius."

Despite all the preparation for death, the anxiety of the sick, which nobody can escape, was being aroused: "What have they been telling you about me?" And as if to anticipate the answer the expected and feared fit of coughing shook him suddenly.

"Just let yourself cough," said Plotius, soothing him, and wiped his own eyes inflamed by a night's travel. "People are bound to cough in the morning."

The reassurance that Lucius tendered sounded more correct: "The last news that we had of you is more than a week old ... Augustus wrote to Maecenas that he had found you ill and had insisted that you return, and the Senate being in session today because of the birthday, Maecenas was unable to come on to receive you, so we gladly took over his commissions for Augustus in order to have the opportunity of seeing you at the same time ... that is all."

It sounded correct and plausible, and yet the "Let yourself cough" of Plotius had been more of a comfort. "Ugh," said Plotius at this point, "rumbling along the whole night; that's no way to sleep, being waked up with every change of horses ... in our procession there were at least forty carriages, and at that

236

we were not the only ones. I guess that more than a hundred have arrived here since yesterday. . . ."

Had Plotius come on one of the peasant-carts? He had the good strong face of an old peasant, and that was just how one might, nay, how one must imagine him, sitting on a peasant's cart, with his head nodding, his chin sunk onto his breast, resting there, snoring merrily . . . "Yes, I heard you driving . . ."

"And now we are here," said Plotius, again resembling a rower.

"Many were driving . . . very many . . ."

"Don't speak while you are coughing," observed Lucius, busy with the folds of his toga, wrinkled from the night's journey. "You mustn't speak . . . Don't you remember that this has always been forbidden by the doctors!"

Ah yes, he remembered, and this was certainly well meant of Lucius despite his elegant posture, but it was this that as always roused him to contradiction: "It is nothing; had not Caesar taken me along to Megara I wouldn't have been sick at all . . . this is only the after-effect of the sun's heat during the festival . . ." A fresh coughing spell rewarded this longish statement and he tasted blood in his mouth.

"Keep still," said Plotius.

But he did not want to keep still; less than ever now that he perceived that Plotius was sitting in the very chair in which the boy had slept, and immediately he was compelled to ask: "Where is Lysanias?"

"A Greek name," said Lucius thoughtfully, "who is that? —Do you mean him?" And he pointed toward the slave, who had retired to the doorway and was waiting there now with the same unmoved expression on his face as before.

"No . . . not him . . . the boy . . ."

Plotius became attentive: "So you have brought a Greek boy back with you . . . then you are not in such a bad way after all . . . Just think of him with a Grecian boy!"

The boy—, the boy had disappeared. But the beaker was still standing there on the table, a carved ivory bowl with silver mountings, and even a sip of wine remained in it: "The boy . . . he was here."

"Then let him return . . . call him in, show him to us."

How could he call him in when he had vanished? And besides he had no wish to exhibit him: "I must go down to the beach with him . . ."

"Lying down on the dry sea-sand wearily we care for the body, and sleep trickles through our members," recited Lucius freely, only to add, "but you will not do that today, my Virgil, you will postpone those indulgences until you have recovered . . ."

"Quite so," agreed Plotius from the alcove.

What were these two speaking of? it was all incongruous; he hardly heard them: "Where is Lysanias?"

Turning to the slave, Plotius ordered: "Fetch the boy."

"Sir, there is no boy anywhere about here."

Yonder from the door the boy's voice had spoken to him, had whispered to him by night, now the slave stood there, and in gratitude for his having helped to deny the far-near voice, he beckoned him nearer: "Come, I want to get up."

"Let that wait," advised Plotius. "The doctor may now be on his way to you, and he will treat you in bed: You only ruin your health with such trifling . . . It is senseless for you to trump up some business just to withhold your boy from us."

Was the slave perhaps a substitute for the boy? had the latter sent here a stronger comrade who would convey the sacrificial gift to the shore? "Take the chest," he heard himself say, startled at the same moment to have heard it, simultaneously blinking in the direction of his friends to ascertain whether or not this made an impression on them.

And sure enough, Plotius, for all his ponderousness, was on his feet at once, while Lucius, nearer to the bed, moved over to it, searching for the invalid's pulse like a doctor: "You have fever, Virgil, be quiet."

Plotius, however, was dispatching the slave: "Inquire about the doctor . . . hurry."

"I need no doctor." This too was said against his will.

"That is not for you to decide."

"I am dying."

There was a pause. He knew he had spoken the truth, and he was curiously little affected by it. He knew he would hardly live out the evening, and yet even this was a respite to him, offering no end of time. He felt relieved that it had been uttered.

It seemed as if the other two were aware how grave things were; that was to be sensed, and for that very reason it took quite a while for Plotius to find words: "Do not blaspheme, Virgil, you are as far from death as we two . . . what should I say, who am ten years older than you and apoplectic besides . . ."

Lucius said nothing. He had let himself down on the chair next to the bed and was silent. And it was touching that he had omitted to put the folds of his toga to rights as he sat down.

"I am going to die, perhaps even today . . . but before that I am going to burn the Aeneid . . ."

"What iniquity!" It was a real outcry, and it was Lucius who had uttered it.

Again silence followed. The room was Septemberishly still and clear. Outside a rider trotted past on his horse, most likely one of the Imperial messengers. The hoof-beats clattered sharply on the pavement, then the four-four rhythm ebbed off into the distant city noises. A woman called something from somewhere; it sounded like the name of a child.

Suddenly, with long and measured steps, Plotius began to pace the room, backward and forward, trailing a lap of his toga behind him, and suddenly he shouted: "If you want to die, well, that's your own affair, we will not prevent you from doing it, but for a long time now the Aeneid has not been your affair, so get that out of your head . . ." And something savage gleamed in his small, fat-sunken eyes.

It was significant that Plotius bore himself so wildly, for

there had existed with him for years a silent convention, even though mutually not quite accredited, that their hour-long conversations on the harvest and the cattle were far more important than all the discourses on artistic and scientific themes that had been carried on in the presence of Lucius and Maecenas and the many others comprising their circle. And it was a refutation of that convention for Plotius to attach so much importance to the existence or non-existence of the Aeneid; it was a refutation of that bit of good conscience, embodied for him in the person of the country-nobleman, Plotius Tucca, and was therefore not to be tolerated: "The world is neither richer nor poorer for a few verses, on that we were always agreed, Plotius."

Lucius shook his head earnestly: "You must not call the Aeneid a few verses!"

"What else is it?"

At that Plotius laughed, actually it was a forced laughter, but nonetheless, it was laughter: "Obtaining praise through modesty is an old vice of poets, Virgil, and as long as a person pursues old vices, there is nothing to fear for him."

And Lucius added: "Do you really want to hear it again? Do you not know better than any other that the greatness of Rome and the greatness of your poem can no longer be divorced from each other?"

A kind of dismay arose in him and became apparent: these two did not want to understand what a boy had grasped, but the finality of his decision, once taken, was not to be disturbed, and this had to be brought home to them: "Nothing unreal is allowed to survive."

It had been formally, firmly and sententiously said, and now Lucius seemed to comprehend what it was leading to: "So in your opinion, both the Iliad and the Odyssey should also be called unreal—oh, divine Homer! And how does it stand with Aeschylus and Euripides? Are these not reality? how many names, how many works shall I still quote you, all of them of immortal reality?"

"For instance Thyestes or the Caesar-epic of a certain Lucius Varius," Plotius could not refrain from adding, and his laughter was again that of a kind, fat man.

Lucius, touched on his most sensitive spot, smiled a little sourly. "The seventeen performances of the Thyestes are certainly no proof of its eternal validity, but . . ."

". . . but it will outlive the Trojan Women . . . don't you think so too, Virgil? . . . now, you are laughing, I am glad that you can laugh again."

Yes, he was laughing; but he was not able to laugh properly; his chest gave him too much pain and he was even ashamed of this laughter that fed itself on Lucius' embarrassment, unconcerned that it was really he who had wanted to defend the immortal worth of the Aeneid, and so for this reason it was imperative to return to seriousness: "Homer was the proclaimer of the gods, he lives on in their reality."

Without bitterness for the laughter directed against him, Lucius answered: "And you are the proclaimer of Rome, you survive in Rome's reality, you will live as long as Rome endures —forever."

Forever? He felt the ring on his finger, he felt his body, he felt the past. "No," he said. "Nothing earthly is eternal, nor Rome either."

"You yourself have exalted Rome into the divine."

This was true and not true. What was Lucius talking about? Was this not like the table-talk at Maecenas's, gliding over the surface, scarcely touching on reality? Darkness was about him as he said: "Within the earthbound, nothing becomes divine; I have adorned Rome, and what I have done has no more worth than the statues in the gardens of Maecenas. Rome does not live by the grace of the artists . . . the statuary will be torn down, the Aeneid will be burnt . . ."

Plotius, who would gladly have gone on laughing, stopped in his tracks. "When one considers what these master-artists have patched together recently, you have reserved a nice bit of sanitation for the years to come . . . what a lot there will be to be burned and cast down . . . a lifework for a Hercules, that's what you've been planning for yourself . . ."

The conception of this great work of disposal reacted on Lucius with surprising exhilaration; his dignified author's face started to fold into merry wrinkles, and he was unable even to continue with the conversation, so much did the picture of a general book-burning amuse him. "The two Sossii have acquired the publishing rights for the Carmen Saeculare from Horace and they will lose a good bit of money on that if you intend to burn his writings as well . . . and, of course, Horace may not be excluded."

"Horace sent me some farewell verses to the boat when I left for Athens."

"That's the sort of thing," Plotius supported Lucius so boisterously that one might think they wanted in this way to drown out the sound of death. "That's just it, and just that is his sin, and that is why his iambics and his odes, in fact everything that he has perpetrated, must perish . . ."

Actually, why had Horace sent these lovely verses of congratulation to the boat? Had he wished in this way to soothe his own jealousy of the Aeneid? A jealous friend, but still a friend?

But Lucius considered: "One ought to leave the choice to me; Horace I would spare, he is really gifted . . . but I would clear out all the mediocrity, all this mediocrity that has come up and is constantly on the increase . . . what decay, what degeneration! No more eloquence, no more theater, no more art . . . in truth we are the last, and nothing will come after us . . . that is why there must be a clean sweep, and it is going to be terrific!" Again he was possessed by laughter.

"Laughing in the dome of death as, turned into stone, he descended into the shimmering sea!"

Lucius stopped short. "A wonderful verse, Virgil, say on, or better still, write it down."

From what unfathomable depth had this line of verse emerged? whence had it come? yet now it pleased him too, and the appreciation of Lucius did him good, although it was not the beauty of the verses that should be praised; no, beauty in itself was never the important thing, but something of a different nature, something greater, something in truth was deserving of praise, and of praise desirous. Oh, now he knew it, now, for the first time, he knew what it was! True esteem could only be an acknowledgment of the verse's meaning, an acknowledgment of that which rose beyond it, the unachievable full reality, which disclosed its preciousness when a word penetrated to it without rebounding from its stony, smooth surface: he who praised a verse as such, without troubling about the reality of its meaning, confused the thing created with that which creates, became consciously or unconsciously guilty of the perjury which denies or destroys reality, became the accomplice of all perjurers. Oh, the enormous mountain-crag of reality, impervious and opposed to all invasion, permitting at most the outward touch; oh, the enormous crags of reality, over their pathless surface man could only creep along, clinging to the surface, constantly falling, constantly in threat of the fall. Lucius knew nothing of falling; to him surface and reality were one. Oh, craggy mountains of reality, rearing enormous, although rooted in the very depths, impenetrable, with sheer smooth sides; yet creatively opened, and the stumbler dashes into the opened shaft.

Plotius shifted his arms like a rower, resting himself: "Agreed, so let Horace be spared and go on writing . . . and you, you will do the same, even if you should burn everything; for of course you would continue to write . . ."

Horace! Yes, he had fought as a soldier for Rome, he had offered himself as a sacrifice that Rome might exist, and that was also the reason for the surprising and repeated outbreaks of reality in his poetry. Not even Plotius realized it, not even he realized how irreplaceable to the poet was the serving deed. "Oh Plotius, the serving deed in its reality . . . without it there is no poetry."

"Aeneas," affirmed Lucius, while Plotius only nodded.

Aeschylus fought as an infantryman at Marathon and Salamis, Publius Vergilius Maro had never fought for anything.

Yet, warmly encouraging him, Plotius spun out his musing: "Besides you have to keep on writing, because before you burn it, the Aeneid must be finished . . . one does not burn something unfinished, and in a few months, even weeks, you will have got this little piece of work behind you . . . so even though you may be in haste to die, you must still hold out that little bit longer."

To finish? To have finished? verily he had finished nothing. What significance had the Aeneid in comparison with a truthful history of Rome like the one Sallustus had written, or even in comparison with the grand scale of that work on which Livy was now engaged? what were the Georgics compared to the real knowledge which that most learned of all scholars, the most honorable Terentius Varro, had dedicated to Roman agriculture?! Compared to such achievements there was nothing that could be finished; whatever he may have written, whatever was left to be written, all this had to remain as unfinished. For, of a surety, Terentius Varro, like Gaius Sallustus, had actually served the Roman State in sober reality whereas Publius Vergilius Maro had never served anyone.

And as if to settle the question, Plotius affirmed: "Oh Virgil, you have only been able to write the Aeneid, just so far have your faculties sufficed, but don't flatter yourself that you are able to comprehend it. Nor do you know anything of its reality or that of the man Virgil; you know them both only from hearsay." And folding his hands over his abdomen, he seated himself again in the easy chair near the window.

The man Virgil! Certainly, he lay here, and this was his reality, nothing else. And the reality was that he had been endowed, fed, and kept by Asinius Pollio and by Augustus—they who had fought for Rome, who served Rome, they who had established and maintained the existence of Rome by what they were and what they did. They were the ones who paid him for the shallow enhancement of their works, and they did not even realize what trash they had paid for. That is what the reality of Publius Vergilius Maro looked like. And he said: "I shall not finish the Aeneid."

Then Lucius smiled: "Do you want someone else to finish it for you?"

"No!" he burst forth, full of apprehension that Lucius would offer himself for the job.

Lucius smiled now quite broadly: "That's what I thought . . . and so you must really know that you are still in arrears to us, and to art . . ."

In arrears? To be sure! He had been in arrears, he was still in arrears—already there below in Misery Street they had known of his arrears—, aye, in himself he was in arrears to existence; however, nothing more could be collected from him. Beyond reach of the glance, he saw the sea before him, spread out to the horizon like liquid quartz, carrying the sun in its azure shimmer, seeming in its luminous, gigantic depths like a yawning mountain summit which, ready to take on and to bear, swallowed all reality in itself and gave it forth again day and night in a brazen booming; and as this brazen surf rose up and subsided he heard the symbol of the voice issue from it, the voice swelling and fading, the symbol of all reality: "What I have written must be consumed by the fire of reality," he said.

"Since when do you draw a line between reality and truth?" interposed Lucius, ready as always for a discussion, moving up a little pretentiously to begin new arguments: "Epicurus says that . . ."

Plotius cut short his words: "Epicurus may say what he wants, we two will see to it that the Aeneid is not consumed by any touch of reality."

But Lucius was not so easily halted: "Beauty and truth are one with reality . . ."

"Even so," admitted Plotius peacefully.

Sharper grew the morning light, more azure the sky in the window frame, blacker the root-like branching of the candelabrum in front of it. Without rising, Plotius with a few shoves pushed himself with his chair out of the sunny region of the alcove into the cooler shadows of the room. Why were these two determined not to grasp the true reality? Why did they, who for thirty long years had been his devout familiars, need to come here only to become unfamiliar and strange to him? It was as if a sharper light were penetrating the spheres of existence ever more acutely, as if the surfaces of existence and the reality of existence took on more perceptible distinctness, and it was incomprehensible that everyone should not crave the veritable reality. Plotius should have had an answer, Plotius, whose worldly-trained, worldly-efficient, worldly-important maturity had always emanated so much of good intimidation that it gave one courage to recover, a never-ending courage beginning in childhood, that was like a refuge in its earthly, irresistibly-gentle warmth, which held one unhesitatingly on this side and brooked no resistance; indeed, Plotius should have given an answer, but this seemed not to have struck him: a little troubled, he sat there heavily, thumb joined to thumb, sometimes sending over worried glances, and as always it was almost impossible to discover the once youthful features in his good, maturity-padded countenance.

Lucius, however, was in fine form: "Lucretius, whom you, oh Virgil, do not honor less than all of us, Lucretius, no less great than you, Virgil, although no greater, he was granted the comprehension of the law of reality, and the song into which he composed it came to be one of truth and beauty; no longer is beauty shattered on reality, no longer consumed by it, but the reverse takes place: that which perishes at the touch of reality falls away from it as soon as its law is perceived and demonstrated in beauty, only the beautiful remaining, remaining as the one and only reality."

Alas, he knew this language, this twilight speech of literature and philosophy, the language of the benumbed, unborn word, dead before it was born; it had once been familiar to him also, and certainly he had believed then in what it expressed, believed or thought that he believed; now, however, it sounded alien, almost incomprehensible. Law? There was only one law, the law of the heart! Reality? There was only one reality, the reality of love! Should he not, must he not, shout this aloud? should he not, and must he not, tell this to them so that they should comprehend it?! Alas, they could not comprehend it, they had no wish to comprehend it, and so he said simply: "Beauty cannot live without approval, truth locks itself off from applause."

"The approval of centuries and millenniums is not the approval of the present, it is not the shoddy applause of the cheaply charmed masses . . . in becoming immortal, the immortalized work of art comes to be a recognition of truth." Thus ran the agile answers of Lucius and he wound up with: "In immortality truth and beauty are united, and this holds good for you too, Vergilius!"

This immortality which Lucius was erecting was an earthly one and therefore not timeless, being at most of eternal duration on earth, and not even that! For only the Saturnian meadows endure eternally, stretched out in the divine forgetfulness of their infinite renewals, while here the concern was only for glory. Did not this imply the ghastly possibility that the immortals were unable to die? Did not this portend damnation?! He who equates truth with everlasting beauty abolishes the life-giving timelessness, abolishes salvation and the grace of the voice! Then Homer and Aeschylus, Sophocles and Euripides, those sovereign elders, as well as Lucretius, gone early to his rest, would live on in the ghastliness of their eternal earthly death, a death that must endure until the last line of their writings be tilled out of human memory, until there was no human mouth to recite their verses, until there was no stage that would show their works; a thousandfold death would be their portion, called ever and again from the underworld, evoked into the ghostly, absurd interrealm of earthly immortality. If this were so—and it was not impossible that it was so—should not these immortals, they before, and like all others, should not they also have destroyed their creations, for the sake of more blessed fields in which to abide? Oh, Eurydice! Oh, Plotia!

aye, so it was: "Deadly the wound of Apollo's arrow e'en though it fails to kill."

"How true," said Plotius. "If I did not have my monthly bleedings I would long since have been under the ground with my forefathers."

Lucius nodded assent. "By Apollo eternally wounded . . . and the fastidious dignity of his attitude is the only choice left to him wounded by immortality, if he wants to live according to the exalted example of Epicurus." And he himself was the purest example of this attitude as, with one leg thrown over the other, resting his elbow on it, the palm of his hand turned upward, he offered this explanation. "For what could well be put in the place of beauty and the harmony of its pure and noble form, since human life reaches no further than seeing and hearing and the other senses? The seeing and hearing of beauty is the ultimate that Apollo has to bestow, and the artist selected by him to receive such divine gifts must accept his lot . . ."

"Is it so hard for you, Lucius?" asked Plotius.

"I do not speak of myself. But this applies to every artist, and before all to our Virgil . . . and he will admit that these conclusions must of necessity be drawn from the principles of Epicurus, but also that they lie close to Plato's views on the beautiful, perhaps even going beyond them and certainly never to be refuted by them . . ."

"I admit it willingly, it may be so." Possibly Lucius was right, but it was of no moment.

And yet, and yet: even though human life did not reach beyond seeing and hearing, and though the heart could not sound any further than it beat, and even though, in consequence of this, harmony was set up before men as something of final dignity and worth, fate-destined to be form and only form, yet, despite this, everything that happened merely for the sake of beauty remained prepossessed by empty nothingness and greatly exposed to damnation; for even in the moderation of harmony it remained in bondage to intoxication, a reversion of the path, it was simply a subterfuge and did not aim toward that perception in which alone divinity was at rest. Oh, woe to the seeing of the gold-glinting universe that looks on beauty; it remains, in spite of that, imprisoned in leaden blindness! Oh, beauty-bedecked world, decked out for beauty! This was the world in which Rome was erected, rich in gardens, rich in palaces, that picture of a city, a rising image that moved nearer and nearer, transported in itself, yet near at hand and filling the azure sky: the house of Augustus and that of Maecenas were there, and not far off his own house on the Esquilin, the pathways adorned with columns, the quadrangles and gardens with statues; he saw the Circus and the amphitheater in a turmoil with the furious playing of organs; he saw the gladiators wrestling to death for beauty's sake, the beasts set upon men; he saw the masses jubilant with lust, crowding about a cross on which, roaring and whimpering with pain, an insubordinate slave was being nailed—the intoxication of blood, the intoxication of death, and withal the intoxication of beauty—, and he saw more and more of these crosses, saw them multiplying, lapped by the torches, licked by the flames, the flames mounting from the crackling wood and from the uproar of the crowds, a flaming ocean that closed over the city of Rome and ebbed away, leaving nothing but blackened ruins, wrecked pediments, tumbled statues, and a land grown over by weeds. He saw, and he knew it would come to pass, because the true law of reality revenged itself irresistibly on mankind, and must so revenge itself, when, being greater than any manifestation of beauty, it was bartered for beauty—plainly affronted by this, despised by being overlooked: high above the law of beauty, high above the law of the artist, which was only greedy for corroboration, there was the law of reality, there was—divine wisdom of Plato—the Eros in the urge of existence, there was the law of the heart, and woe to a world which had forgotten this last reality. Why had he been singled out to know this? Were the others still blinder than he? Why did they not see, not grasp it? Why not, at least, his friends? Or did his blindness make him incapable of showing them? Why was he too paralyzed, too weak, too inarticulate to make them understand? Blood was what he saw before him, blood was what he tasted in his mouth; a rattling moan tore through his chest, rattling through his throat, and he was obliged to let his head sink back on the pillows!

Oh, truth alone is immortal, immortal in truth is death. Only he who closes his eyes has a sense of the seeing blindness, a sense of overcoming fate.

For even though the law could be perceived only in the eternal and unchangeable form assigned it by fate, and even though this form, and with it fate itself, lay in the cold unchanging imprisonment of the Saturnian realm, yet the Promethean endeavor was aimed toward the fire in the conjoined depths above and below, and shattering the prison of mere form, thrust forward to the first ancestor enthroned there, in whose hands lay the truth of inner reality.

And therefore: terrible on the outmost edge of reality hung laughter, the very sister of death, terrible beyond all darkness and every abyss, hung in a perilous balance, a floating border between greed for life and self-destruction, tilted toward this side in its earth-splitting, volcanic yelling, and toward the other in its sea of smiles which confronted the night, embraced the world and burst it asunder. But there was no longer a trace of laughter, no longer the hint of a smile. Plotius said gravely: "The doctor should have been here a long time ago . . . we'll look for him ourselves as we go to call on Augustus." And both of them stood.

However, he wanted and was compelled to detain them; their blind blindness had to be banished: overpowering was the compulsion to make them understand, so that they should not be estranged from him, overpowering the compulsion to tell them what they had not grasped, and had not even wished to grasp. And although he himself hardly knew what it meant, a phrase presented itself: "Love is the reality."

So it became audible and suddenly it was no longer enigmatic. For the gods had blessed man with love to ease the pang of his lusts, and he who has partaken of this blessing perceives reality; he is no longer a mere lodger in the realm of personal consciousness in which he is caught. And again he heard: "Love is the reality."

"Quite so," affirmed Lucius, seeming neither shocked nor surprised, "that is what you taught us, and when I observe Tibullus or Propertius or even young Ovid who is so full of poor taste, I want only to maintain that you have taught this a little too fervently, because their immaturity, which proposes to follow in your footsteps and even perhaps to surpass you, you, the unsurpassable, has no longer any other theme than love, and I must confess that I am quite glutted with it, as little as I am inclined to turn against love as such . . . where, by the way, is the Greek boy whom you mentioned before?"

It had failed. It had again glided into the trivial and the literary, gliding over the surface of the real within existence, as if to show that he deserved no better, that he was in a literary no-man's-land, which did not touch even the surface, that encompassed nothing, neither the depths of heaven nor of earth, at most only the empty province of beauty. And it oppressed him anew. For he who had trodden the unholy path of reversion, he who had always intoxicated and inflamed himself on beauty alone, he who possessed by mania wanted to deafen the weakness within him by the vastness outside of him, he who had not been able to search for the immutable in the human heart but had been compelled to gather together into one company the stars, the primal-ages and all the doings of the gods, he had never loved; and what he had held to be love had been only yearning, nostalgia for that lost landscape, in which once, oh once, lost long ago, childhood forgotten, the beyond forgotten, love had existed even for him; only this landscape had sufficed for his poetry; never had a song for Plotia escaped his lips, and even then, when gripped by the beauty of Alexis, made his by the favor of Asinius, he had thought to sing for the boy, it had not come to be a love-song but an Eclogue of thanks for Asinius Pollio, dealing but in a most negligible way with love in a longed-for landscape. No, it was an error to assume that he, who had never loved and who therefore had never succeeded in writing a genuine love-poem, had brought any influence to bear upon these young poets of love, or even that he could qualify as their spiritual ancestor; they did not stem from him, they were more honorable than he: "Oh, Lucius, they have a better progenitor than I, he is called Catullus; they have not been my followers, nor should they ever have been."

"You will not be able to shake them off, even if you dismiss them from your charge, despite the fact that this is so beautifully expressed in your Eclogue; nevermore shall I sing songs, and no longer am I your guardian! No, Virgil, you are and you will remain the progenitor, verily the one whose force they will never equal."

"I am very weak, Lucius, and have always been so, and, considering my lack of force, it is possible to call me their progenitor, for truly they share this with me . . . all that we have in common is that we are both short-lived . . ."

"All I know is that Catullus and Tibullus died at thirty, and you are already in your fifties," stated Plotius firmly.

Ah, even though the littérateur in his weakness has the fancy that the landscape of his childhood for which he may be yearning is the infinity of the Saturnian fields, and that, were he there, he would hearken to the depths of heaven and of earth, the landscape proper to him is that of sheer platitude, and he listens to nothing, least of all to death: "When was it that Tibullus was snatched away, Plotius? Scarcely a few weeks past . . . and Propertius lies sick unto death, even as I do . . . our weakness is apparently unpleasing to the gods, and now they mean to root us out thoroughly . . ."

"Our friendly, calm Propertius is still alive, alive for his own and for our benefit, and so are you and never more than now . . . and in twenty years the two of you, he at fifty and you at seventy, despite your everlasting sickness, will be striving as you now strive with all the youngsters, should they be called Ovid or some other name . . ."

"And just as today they would be unimaginable without your

Eclogues and Georgics," stressed Lucius, who was more concerned with correct literary definitions, "just as now you have pointed out the way, the way to the idyllic, the way to the bucolic, the way to Theocritus, just so will you precede them on new paths . . ."

"I am not in the line of Theocritus, this is truer of Catullus, even though this might be argued . . ."

Reluctantly, Lucius narrowed his prophetic literary forecasts: "Still, Catullus was your compatriot, Virgil, and a common homeland often leads to common aims and common inclinations . . ."

"Catullus or no Catullus," grumbled Plotius, "Theocritus or no Theocritus, and with them all their followers, you are Virgil, you are you, and even in twenty years, should I live so long, you will be my preference, essentially more to be preferred than all of them together; in my opinion you should have no truck with them."

It was a sharp line that Plotius had drawn, overestimating him and underestimating the young, and it felt good to be counted among the grown-ups, among the forceful who need not die before their time. Nevertheless, one had to rectify these false evaluations: "Be not unjust to the young, Plotius; they are honest in their way, more honest, it may be, than I have ever been."

Again Lucius cut in: "To speak of honesty in art is always somewhat beside the point. One can say of an artist that he is honest if he keeps close to the traditional, eternal rules of art, but on the other hand that just this constitutes his dishonesty, because he hides his own ego behind tradition. Are we dishonorable in making the Homeric world our own? Are the young dishonorable in emulating a Virgil? Or are they even more honorable when committing some lapse of taste?"

"Lucius, the question of honesty and dishonesty is no longer an artistic question: the aim is toward the essential in human life before which art is almost negligible, since it is able to express only the human element."

"What are you talking about?" asked Plotius. "That is just rhetorical bilge and I decline, as you well know, to take part in it."

"Virgil maintains that the young are more honest than he, and we cannot possibly be expected to stand for that."

"That's a matter of indifference to me," persisted Plotius in his staunch, friendly blindness, "Virgil is honest enough for me."

"Thank you, Plotius."

"It is just that I am fond of you, Virgil . . . however, you may nevertheless oblige Lucius; admit that you are more honest than the young."

"That would be downright dishonesty . . . I find that the young in their love-poetry have struggled through to an original-ity which I am unable to approach . . . Lucius does not want to admit that all reality rests on love, and that behind the love-poetry, for which he may not care, this great original reality is to be found . . . reality is honesty . . ."

Lucius seemed to be slightly nauseated; his finger moved to and fro in refutation: "Such cheap honesty suffices in no way for art, Virgil; only exalted love, as depicted by you, and exem-plified for all time in that which was between Dido and Aeneas, only such love is entitled to a place in art, in contrast to the petty love affairs with which the young gentlemen like to fill out their poetry."

Then Plotius grinned: "They mean nothing to me, but they are rather pleasantly readable."

"Once again you are over-critical, Lucius; no one will doubt that Catullus was a real poet . . . and need I assure you that we have to recognize such a one even in Ovid?"

"A genuine poet?"—Lucius took fire, but with dignity— "What does it mean to be a genuine poet? It does not mean talent alone, many are talented, talent is cheap, and if possible love is even cheaper, and turns for the most part to the cheapest possible stammering, even though the gentlemen grind out their verses to the best of their ability . . . naturally, I should be guarded in giving these judgments public utterance for, good or bad, we writers belong together, but here in our limited circle, nothing should restrain us from defining things plainly . . . in short, I am able to see nothing of honesty in a lascivious stripping, and even less of true art or true poetry . . ."

Was Lucius right? He could not be right; what he said was comprehensible, as comprehensible as everything that a craftsman has to say, but precisely for that reason it remained arrested in the professional realm, unperceptive of strivings which were aimed at shattering this very realm. Catullus had been well aware of this, he was the first to point out the new way, and for the sake of justice this had to be acknowledged: "Genuine art bursts through boundaries, bursts through and treads new and hitherto unknown realms of the soul, of conception, of expression, bursting through into the original, into the immediate, into the real . . ."

"Fine!—and you actually want to perceive all this in that allegedly so honest love-poetry . . . as if in every single verse of the Aeneid there were not more true reality!"

"I do not want to wrangle over this with you, Lucius; in a certain sense you defend your own poetry also when praising mine . . . for my part, I admit myself more easily beaten than you, and so you may lay it only on me and the Aeneid if I maintain that the new art could no longer travel on in our grooves, that it is bound to find something more immediate and more original, bound to do so by a command that points to the primal cause of reality . . . indeed, this is how it is, whoever yields to that command has to go back to the primal cause of reality, and he must begin again with love . . ."

Now Plotius took sides with Lucius: "Well, to be just, I rather like to read this stuff, but for all this originality of which you speak, these fellows are still too weak; only a real man can love in reality, and all that comes along with it is negligible in comparison . . ."

"Weakness? Which needs more growing power, the juicy blade in good pasturage, or the poor leaf which has to force

255

itself between stones? The latter is of a weak aspect, nevertheless it has power to sprout, nevertheless it is grass . . . Rome is stony, our cities are stone, and it could almost be called a miracle that despite this something original has grown out of them, certainly weak in appearance, but still original, still real . . ."

Plotius laughed: "As far as I know, no grass has yet succeeded in picking out its growing-place, and even if it should prefer to be munched by a cow on a lovely meadow, it still remains in bondage to its stones, while these lads are quite free to seek the original wherever it is growing, and where men cause it to grow; verily nothing forces them to remain among the stones of the city, nothing more than their own lusts and inclinations, for the indulgence of which it is more convenient to stroll about in Rome, to sleep about in Rome, and to turn small kisses into small verses. First of all, they should once learn how to milk a cow, to curry a horse, and to handle a sickle."

The urbane existence of Lucius felt itself attacked and offended: "The born artist, no matter whether he be great or mediocre, is not born to be a farmer; you cannot treat them all alike, Plotius."

"I merely protest against the immediacy of such grass-love as advanced by Virgil . . . I have a certain understanding of these things. Weakness remains weakness."

"And I protest in turn against the injustice shown by you two toward the young."

Lucius had accompanied the statements of Plotius with an approving nod: "That's it! They are weak and that is why they never succeed in getting beyond the imitative stage . . . how then can one talk of injustice! They are imitators of Theocritus, pupils of Catullus, and whatever they can take from our Virgil, that they take."

Alas, they both remained inconvincible, each one captive in the circle of his own thoughts and words, half asleep and unable to shatter and burst through them, unable to escape the old habit of speech. The one called it grass-love, called it weakness, the other called it imitation, both with justice, yet both did not notice, did not want to notice, that even such a weak, urban love, pining between the walls and stones of a city, that even such a miserably-narrow, earthly-personal and often lasciviously disclosed love—a love such as this—was still touched by the miraculous lawfulness of human existence, touched by the shadow of the divine, whenever it succeeded in extending the one self toward the other self, feeling its way toward the beloved, feeling its way into the other, both imperishable in their union with love. Yes, just this could be sensed in the verse of the young, this was the new reality of truth in its human aspect which occasionally rang out from their poetry, and which they never would have found had they been his pupils. For this reality of love, which by including death annulled and transmuted it into the truly immortal, just this had been denied him, the over-prized poet Virgil, once and forever; hollow his poems, hollow even the Aeneid, and, like the poem, he too had shrunk into his own cold circle and had nothing to teach; and to Cebes, to the one who most tenderly and devotedly had wished to become his pupil, he had inclined only because he had loved himself in the mirror of this youthful soul, in order—alas, it had so happened as though under the order of demons—to shape him in his own image into a cold, beauty-possessed writing man. Catullus, Tibullus, Propertius, they had been able to love, and from love they had derived a premonition of reality which was stronger than any harmony and passed earthly things. Only what proceeds from such a premonition permits the clouded heart of man to ring out, to prepare for the coming annunciation of the voice, ready as a harp is ready to sing under the wind; and, as if in a renewed challenge to Plotius to recognize the true reality, and in appreciation for his blindly-staunch friendship, the breath, exhausted by speaking, found strength for further speech: "Only the purity of the heart is immortal."

With no comprehension, but with benevolent kindness Plotius confirmed what he heard: "In this I agree with you, my Virgil, for it is your purity which is immortal."

"Were that not so," added Lucius, "they would not emulate you as they do. The original, the immediate, the new which you project has always been that pure harmony of truth, and it is that which you have shown to the present as well as to future generations; whoever strives in that direction seeks your companionship. Now there arises a new line, one of a loftier order; these are the words in which you proclaimed it, and of this new generation you are guardian."

The reality of love, the reality of death, one and the same; the young were aware of it, and these two never once perceived that death was already near them in the room—, was it still possible to arouse them to real knowledge of this sort? They had to be waked, to become aware, and it seemed almost impossible to do; one could merely answer: "Lucius, that was something I once happened to write . . . but believe me, I have proclaimed nothing, I have only felt of the crag . . . perhaps I have been hurled from it . . . I am not sure."

"You torment yourself, and you want to hide this torment behind riddles; this sort of thing is not good for men," said Plotius, "the darkness is not good." And he drew his toga tighter about him as if he were chilly.

"It is difficult to express, Plotius, and maybe not only because of my weakness, maybe there are altogether no words for ultimate reality . . . I have made my poems, abortive words . . . I thought them to be real, and they are only beautiful . . . poetry arises from the twilight . . . all that we do or make stems from this same obscurity . . . but the voice of reality has need of a deeper blindness than that of the cold realm of shades . . . deeper and higher, aye it goes deeper and for all that it is brighter."

Whereupon Lucius said: "It is not merely a matter of truth; even a simpleton speaks truth, is able to enunciate the naked truth . . . truth in order to be effective must be tamed, and therein lies its real harmony. How many a one speaks of the madness of the poet,"—and he looked over at Plotius, who by chance was nodding—, "but the poet is the very man who possesses the gift of taming his own madness and guiding it."

"Truth . . . its terrible madness . . . the calamitous within truth." The voices of the women had been naked, naked as the truth that they were compelled to announce—nevertheless evil.

"I disagree," insisted Lucius, "truth when tamed is no madness, much less a calamity."

The truth in blindness, the flat truth, without good or evil, without height or depth, the naked truth of the eternal return into the realm of Saturn; nevertheless lacking in reality: "Oh, Lucius, to be sure . . . but it is not poetry which is able to enunciate this purest form of reality . . . poetry does not possess the discrimination . . . nor I . . . I have merely groped, merely stammered . . ."—the fever crept on, now it was in his chest, and his voice failed, stifled by a rattle—, "not the first step taken . . . stammering, groping, even less than this . . . no purity . . ."

"You may call it stammering or groping if you like"— Lucius spoke very softly and with unwonted warmth—"it was always harmonious, and therefore annunciation at its purest."

"In spite of all this—now you need the doctor," decided Plotius, "it is more than high time; so we are leaving; later we shall return to you."

Dark, heavy, soundless, it rushed through him. The dismay was there again. They would leave without having understood. They meant to come back—would it not have become too late by that time? First they must be convinced, they must realize it at last—oh, unable to be awakened from its twilight state, the human soul lay encompassed by evil—, and wrestling with his cough, he brought out hoarsely in an almost inaudible cry: "You are my friends . . . I must have clean hands . . . from beginning to end there must be purity . . . the Aeneid is unworthy . . . without truth . . . only lovely . . . you are my friends . . . you will burn it . . . you will burn the Aeneid for me . . . promise . . ."

Plotius' face into which he was staring remained heavy and mute. It became filled with love and scorn. This was distinctly seen in the ruddy, liver-spotted flesh, stippled by the blue-black beard; love could be seen in the eyes and gave him hope. But the lips remained silent.

"Plotius . . . promise . . ."

Plotius had begun to pace the room again. He walked back and forth steadily with long steps, his abdomen expanding the folds of his toga, a wreath of gray hair bristling around the bald spot at the back of his head, and, as many fleshy persons are wont to do, he held his arms slightly bent and his fists doubled up: yet, in spite of his sixty years, he was the very picture of ebullient life.

As though to demonstrate the needlessness of a hasty answer, the walking continued for quite a time before Plotius terminated it, and condescended to reply: "Listen, Virgil," he said with all the adult firmness that his voice was careful to assume when giving an order, "listen, you have plenty of time . . . I see no hurry . . ."

The firmness with which this assurance of no hurry was tendered could not be gainsaid; it promised protection by its very intimidation, just as it had always done, and the command to recover his courage was as incontrovertible as ever; he bowed before this command and he enjoyed doing it, although he could scarcely have done otherwise, and with the restored relief his speaking had again become calmer and easier: "It is my last request, Plotius, that you and Lucius burn the Aeneid immediately . . . you cannot refuse me this . . ."

"Oh my Virgil, how often must I assure you that there is plenty of time ahead for you and for us? Therefore you have time and to spare for a ripe deliberation of your project . . . but watch yourself while you are about it"—yet, in contrast to his admonition to be deliberate, his hand in its impatience was already on the door-knob—, "a farmer who wastes or destroys seed-corn isn't worth much."

And then, together with Lucius who, venturing neither opposition nor interruption, seemed no less intimidated, he disappeared from the room; there followed a somewhat rude closing of the door.

ENRICHED yet robbed, yes, so had they left him, left him alone; the scornful and well-meaning friend had bestowed calmness upon him and taken away his anxiety, but beyond the anxiety something more had been taken away, a piece of himself as it were, and it seemed to him that Plotius had expelled him from adulthood and had turned him again into a child, thrown him back into the plan-forging callowness with which they had both been seized as youths in Milan, and from which Plotius alone had had the wit to extricate himself; oh, he felt himself plunged back so completely into the unfinished that it would have seemed quite natural to him if his friend had taken the Aeneid upon his strong shoulders and born it away together with the anxiety. Was the chest still standing there untouched and well-locked, or was this merely a delusion? It almost seemed wiser not to make sure; this was a state of defenselessness and of felicity; but it was also shame. And it was all the more shame because this strange belittlement of himself had just happened in front of Lysanias, for, most amazingly though not surprisingly, the boy was sitting exactly as he had sat there in the night, and in the self-same easy chair. Was is possible that the chair could suddenly offer room for a second occupant? Just a moment ago Plotius had been sitting there too. Truly, it would have been more desirable and even more fitting had Plotius never set foot in the room. The boy reclined there, gracious in forgetfulness, sorrow-freed and sorrow-freeing, and sounding afar was the sunny sea; if one peered at it closely one could see that the face was that of a hobbledehoy and nimble peasant lad, and on looking still more closely it appeared full of dreaminess and quite lovely. On the boy's knees lay the rolls of manuscript from which he had read aloud during the night.

And as if he had only been waiting for an invitation, the boy began to read:

"Twofold the portals of sleep, and twofold 'tis said in their
    nature;
One of them fashioned from horn releases the true visions
    skyward;
Carven from elephants' tusks the other is gleaming and
    candid,
Through this, however, the spirits are sending up false
    apparitions.
Sage in his discourse and counsel, Anchises his son and the
    Sybil
Leads to this place, and releases them both through the ivory
    portal.
Straightway Aeneas repairs to the ships and meets there his
    comrades,
Skimming the shore in an even course to the bourne of
    Cajeta.
Anchor is dropped from the prow, the sterns lie at rest on
    the sea-shore."

This was what he had composed in honor of Cajeta; he recognized the section: "Cajeta is soon to be buried, Cajeta the nurse . . . now that Aeneas is back from below, matured, resurrected . . ." The speech proceeded with surprising ease, as if the air had become more fluid.

"Was it not your path, oh, Virgil, that which was trod by Aeneas? You too pressed on in the darkness, pressed on for the homecoming journey, there where the moonbeams quivered in light on the ebbing sea . . ."

"Yea, I was driven toward darkness, yet it was not of my willing, pressing on ever within it, I pierced at last to its womb, yet I did not dive under; stony the cave that I found, no river ran through it, beyond all my search was the lake in the cavern of night's staring eye . . . Plotia I saw, but I found not my father, and she also vanished . . . no one was waiting to guide me, I foundered without resurrection; then came the voice, then I heard it, and now there is light . . ."

". . . and now it is you who are leader."

"Driven by self and by fate, there was no question of leading, scarcely a guide for myself, and still less a guide for the others."

"Wherever you may have been driven, that was the path that you showed us."

"Was it then I who discovered the way through the night's howling alleys? Was it not rather you?"

"You alone constantly led us, you shall remain as our leader; linked to your side forever, it seemed that I ran on before you, and though oft from your sight I have vanished, I return into you again, called back by you to the timeless lapse of that era whose tranquil leader you are."

At this he had to smile: leader of men—to be general, priest or a sovereign, once was the wish of a boy, and this boy now put it in words. Had Plotius not actually turned him into a boy again?

Lysanias, however, spoke on: "Henceforth no general shall lead us, no monarch shall lead us henceforth, even the verse cannot lead us in times when great issues are stirring: ranging freely within them, leading us onward and onward, the purposeful deed shall rule us, the deed bent on purity."

More light came into the room, the air was floating more freely, serener the godly breath. Likewise as if they were closer, close as the sought-for fulfillment, far strands were gleaming in sunlight, and inaccessible copses resounded in songs that were sun-filled, songs from a mouth always singing, the shimmering daughter of Sol.

"See you, Lysanias, that eye, gold-streaking the violet heaven? Noon it is, waking and peering, and in his innermost glances, there are the traces of night."

"Pathway and goal was Apollo, he led you on earth as the sunlight, behold even now he is with you under the guise of the day."

"Golden the glance of Apollo, his threatening bow shines in silver, knowledge of him comes like radiance, radiant the death it evokes: one are they both in radiance, his word and his arrow celestial, winging by virtue of oneness back to their source divine. Oh, even to him is hidden the well-spring of the glance, Night, as she reposes in the glance of the god himself: he alone struck by the arrow, he alone pierced by the light, may see the dark veils tear asunder, so that with failing eye, still peering, already in blindness, he may see in a single glance the primal-dome of oneness, the dome from which he sprang, as he fathoms beginning and ending, this being of night and of light."

"Unconquerable sun," a murmur sounded and he saw that the slave was again in the room.

"Unconquerable, though still obeying the father, the rams-horned father of day, Jupiter, who holds fast the fate of the gods in his mighty hands which scatter the lightnings, Jupiter, fate-bidding and fate-bidden in one, the Chronide who bound by his own kingship never escapes Cronus. Yet the curse of shifting mastery, yielded or filched one from another, expends itself at last,"—thus spoke the slave—, "if in the chain of divine generation there appears one whom a virgin has borne: as the first one not in rebellion, he enters into the father and the father into him; they are united in spirit, eternally three in one."

"Are you Syrian, are you Persian?"

"They brought me here from Asia as a child."

It was a drily polite answer, and the man's face which but a moment since had been opened to the sun was impenetrably transformed into that of the servant. How was that possible? The occurrence seemed in this way to be cut off; Lysanias seemed no longer to be present, and it was becoming harder to breathe: "Who are you?"

"I am a room-slave in the exalted house of Augustus, may the gods protect him."

264

"Who taught you your religion?"

"The slave honors the gods of his master."

"And the religion of your ancestors?"

"My father suffered a slave's death on the cross, and I have been separated from my mother."

This was grim torment rising in tears: oh, these were tears clouding the sight, painfully compressing the chest, tears from an immeasurable sea out of which humanity is constantly resurrected. But the face of the slave remained unmoved; blank and shut it lay above the abyss.

A few minutes passed: "Can I be of help to you?"

"Sir, let not your kindness so condescend: I glory in my lot, I need nothing."

"Still you came."

"I was ordered to do so."

Was the slave actually just a tool? Had he been ordered to keep silent before the guest, because guests must find out nothing. Impenetrable was the attitude of a human being when cast down to being an orphan; a cold mantle was flung around his soul, hiding layer after layer of horror, and a slave was a being terribly lonely and orphaned. Had this one been sent here to rob him of the Aeneid as well as the boy? And in so doing to turn Lysanias too into an orphan? The chair in the alcove was empty, and the hand that stretched out after the vanished one encountered nothing, was unable to rescue him from an orphan's fate! Thereupon his cry became one of horror: "You have frightened him away!"

"If I have erred, Sir, condemn or condone it, for the fault was not intentional. I was pledged by my task to help you and to be at your command."

Still his mistrust was not allayed: "Are you his substitute? have you been ordered to relieve him? have you taken over his name?"

"Oh, Sir, a slave owns nothing, he has no name; he bears his fetters nakedly. Whatever you choose to call me, that is my name."

"Lysanias?"

It was a question. But, conjured by his name, Lysanias was again in his place; he reclined in the alcove-seat, and instead of the slave it was he who answered quickly: "Always yourself you were seeking, but 'twas I whom you discovered, and as you found yourself, then have you sought for me."

Sought for, oh, sought for—, oh, source,—oh, again the lostness asserted itself, well-spring after well-spring opened up, the place of memory, the unbordered abyss of the past, wreathed about by the world-snake, redolent of happenings never beheld. And from the shuddersome snaky coils, never lost yet ever remembered, Cronus, the earliest Titan, extricated himself, the first to stamp upon the earth with thundering feet.—

—, and in the turmoil of memory the answer of the slave was to be heard: "He who chooses a name for himself rebels against fate . . ."

—, sought for, oh, sought for—the Titan had been overthrown, and tribes of heroes, tribes of men, serving the gods, generation after generation in endless succession, were trained for duty, were trained for death; they forgot the blood of the Titans, until suddenly it welled up anew, and the tardy descendant, born large and terrible to be a Titan, stamped through the fields of creation, as his ancestor had done, crying out to heaven in sudden recollection of the once-committed crime, so stricken by memory that he chose to wreak a horrible revenge for the murder of his ancestor whom he felt within himself; he clambers upward to blind the light-god, to overthrow the reigning father-god, and, just as he is about to succeed in tearing the spark of fire from the eye of the god, Jove again proves victorious, hurling back the Titan, stretching him out upon the stony ground; thereupon duty continues to reign and, guided by Sol's own hands, the fire-wagon rolls onward, bearing the shining Archer defended by his bow, on through the heavenly pavilion, day after day in the zenith—,

—, and surrounded by light the slave spoke on: "Though you intended to call me, yet I have never been summoned; imposed though I was upon you, yet you are bound to accept me because of my service to you . . ."

—, sought for, oh, sought for,—the Titan had fled, but left behind in the futile flight, a spark from the snatched fire flared up into spheres of unnumbered stars, and even though the Titan had not succeeded in obtaining the divine bow, even though he had not been able to turn it against the father, making himself thereby into his own ancestor and bringing time to a standstill, so that coming generations might be delivered from force, and one's own name become immortal, acquitted of duty as he who bears it, oh, though it had not succeeded, yet henceforth the spheres remained reconciled within the starry spaces, reconciled to the stellar mandates, as were duty and force and death . . .

—, and now the boy spoke again: "I am Lysanias, Virgil, and as your life began, sorrow-freed and guarded in childhood, your mother, dispelling sorrow, took you naked and smiling into her arms . . ."

—, and the slave continued: "I remain nameless, Virgil, however you choose to call me, vast is that which is nameless, ever naked about you hovering, so that it may enfold you nakedly at the end . . ."

—, sought for, oh, sought for—, oh homecoming—, end joined to beginning, beginning to end, the gods were reigning, the gods reign on, apportioning duty. And thus it was commanded by the light-lavishing god: comprehend death while still in life so that it may illumine your life; only for him who presses on to the sources,—oh, exploring is remembering the gods—, remembering and more than remembering the region of roots before the beginning, only for him who so remembers will the end be turned into the beginning; and he bethought him of every future buried in the depths of the past, only he who retains what is fleeting restrains death in what has passed. Unbounded the abyss of yore, unbounded and nameless. The Muses serve death, they serve it like vestals guarding the holy fire, Apollo's golden light.

And something in the countenance of the boy and that of the slave brought up the long-lost past, life, the magnificent, entombing death; and with it came a realization of truth, and he knew the love within love, its meaning stripped of madness, its truth the ultimate protection from madness, love retrieved from the nothing, transformed but still love, great in its reality, the miracle. Oh, homecoming!

Was it the slave, was it the boy? The former was again declaring: "Even if now I approach you, you who have always contained me, know it is only to aid you, but never again to compel you."

Then quoth the boy once more, but in a higher voice: "Something invisible led you, transforming its own to your service, yet, having now come so far, you are set free of its guidance. Searching, you came upon that which likewise was searching for you."

Sterner came the answer, yet it was also a comfort: "Nothing of earth can remain for him who is destined for service, possessing himself he owns nothing, no name for his own, no desire; back, oh forced back into childship, fate is beyond his possession. Yet with each fresh denudation, he comes closer to all that is living; he only, who bears his chains naked, is given this simple assurance: grace will descend upon him who is humble and ready to take it; then if he weeps in contrition, the miracle holds back no longer, reduced to the state of a child, he is first to behold the light."

Like the sound of a single voice the voices were interwoven, weaving a double-toned cadence, the voice of the boy ringing clearer: "One and the same are they, coming hence and then going hither, childship of the beginning, childship of the end, childship fled into love."

Yet, like an echo of tears from a sphere-surrounding sorrow, followed the words of the slave: "Drudging in vilest enslavement, having no father to name us, lacking the care of a mother, claiming no past in our history, lacking a zeal for the future, orphan to orphan in fetters, we form the band of all bondsmen, forged in a chain, never-ending; stripped of a fate though we be, yet chosen by fate for the blessing of knowing in brother the brother."

"Humanity is naked whenever it emerges, naked its beginning and naked is its end, naked the bonds of duty rasp on the bruised flesh; yet even the Titan is naked and naked is his courage, and when he opposes the father, it is done without weapon or shield, nakedly-burning the hands which grasp at the stolen fire, bearing it naked to earth."

Oddly in tune with the boy as if each one were answering the other, both having one thing to say and both of them speaking, the slave added: " 'Twas with the aid of arms that the first of the line was slaughtered, murder is always repeated with the clattering might of arms, suppressing men to be slaves, man roots himself out of the earth, himself the slave of the weapon, he lets creation be shattered, letting the glowing embers die down and grow torpid and cold. He shall be first of all heroes who lets himself be disarmed."

"Weapons ring out through your song, yet not grim Achilles finally wins your love but rather the pious Aeneas."

"Weaponless are we, we slaves, brought low without arms to defend us, but as we bide without weapons our tomb opens up of itself, torpor relaxes for our sake, the stone itself yields to our hand."

"Weaponless shall be the end, the beginning-anew without weapons, when from the nocturnal stone the god mildly mounts toward the zenith, creation transformed into childhood."

"For you have beheld us, Virgil, and in looking you saw the fetters, weeping the while you looked, you saw the new time arising, saw the beginning-anew that is destined to spring from our tears." Thus spoke the other and—impenetrably—became again the servant who stands ready for service.

"Virgil, you saw the beginning, but you are not the beginning; Virgil, you heard the voice, but you are not yet that voice; the heart of creation beating you felt, yet that heart is not you, you are the eternal guide who himself does not reach the goal. Immortal shall you be, immortally the leader, *not quite here but yet at hand, your immortal lot withstanding every turn of time.*"

"You bear the chain with us, but from you, oh Virgil, it is already softly lifted."

Then it became still and they listened all together. They listened, the three of them, to the unfolded light. And the light was like a rustling, a rustling that seemed to come from cornfields, the golden rustling of sunny rain, gentle and strong, unspeakably proclaiming the unlost, the unlosable, the voice of annunciation. The day-song was floating brightly above the darkness.

Then said the boy, lifting his hand: "Behold the star, behold the guiding star."

There stood the night-star in the midst of the violet, sunny sky, and glowing softly the star moved eastward.

Prostrated for prayer, his face pressed to the ground, remaining motionless at first, then rising to a kneeling posture with arms upraised, swaying gently back and forth upon his knees, the slave began his prayer:

"Thou, most unknown, most inconceivable, most inexpressible, Thou who reignest infinitely, Thou proclaimest Thyself through Thine eye, glancing down blindingly, overpowering in its brightness though but a shadow of Thy hidden being, a gleam from Thy obscurity, the reflection of a reflection. And my eye, my glance, a further shadow thrown by the reflection of Thy reflection, this further reflection dares to lift itself to that of Thine, not that it may rest in Thee, but only that painfully it may return to expectation. Lion and bull are ranged at Thy feet, and the eagle soars unto Thee. Thine eye is Thy voice and Thy brow lowers with thunder. None can compel Thee, neither he who bears off the fire nor he who masters the bull, nor he who makes himself into an ancestor, none can compel Thee. For Thou sendest out to salvation him who does not oppose Thee. And in the glow of the mission, childlike the star releases itself from Thy brightness and, at Thy bidding, wanders back there where Thou hast tarried and will tarry again with the breaking of day. Thou hast created me for death and I am cast in death's shape. But when Thou created me, Thou, most invisible in utter invisibility, Thou created along with me the homecoming; and when the star lowers itself, then Thou, most nameless in utter namelessness, callest out the name which Thou takest on to wander as mortal, to die as mortal, visible to the earthbound in Thy second shape, in which Thou wilt again arise to Thyself, transformed back into Thine own light, the star once more sun-enfolded to a single eye; then permit me, the least shadow of Thy namelessness, the slave of slaves, then permit me to share in Thy name, in Thy countenance, in Thy radiance, oh Most Unknown, Most Invisible, Most Inexpressible, to whom I belong and whom I praise today and forevermore."

And now there arose the noon-wind, the fervent breath-kiss of life; scarcely perceptible, it came drifting from the south, a soft flooding undulation, the breath-sea of the world which daily floods its banks, a waft of the self-completing never completed cycles of time above which the constellations circle: breath of the ripening earth, of the olive trees, of the grape-vine, of the wheat-fields, breath of care and simplicity, breath of the stables and the pressed fruit, breath of communion and of peace, breath of country after country, of field after field, breath of loving, serving, labor. Breath of mid-day, oh, mighty noon, sacredly brooding over the world and the universe, as though the wheels of the sun-wagon were standing still, at holy rest in the zenith. The hanging lamp swayed lightly in the breeze, its chains clinking silverly.

One human life does not suffice. It suffices for nothing. Oh, memory, oh, homecoming.

And in the most unknown, the most invisible, in the most unutterable, in remotest divinity, there ruled one whose shadow was the light, always sensed, never known, the most unnamable, the utterly hidden. Was it not he whom the peasants shudderingly honored, believing that he dwelt in the primal woods of the Capitoline? No statue was erected to him, none could be erected, symbol of himself was he, although he had announced himself in the symbol of the voice. Oh, open your eyes to love! And high above the breath of the noonday song which kept flooding in, warm and full of the anxious love of men for the earth, full of the fearful love of earth for men, the star of night took its wandering course, it also a symbol, a symbol of the unnamable love that longed to descend, in order to lift the earthbound into likeness with the sun. Thus the midday rested in the breath from above and below; the span of the fiery wagon rested; the wheels were at rest, and Sol was resting.

WAS this happiness that he felt? he did not know and he scarcely wanted to know; surely it was hope, a hope so exceedingly strong that, like a strong light or a strong tone, it became sheerly unbearable, so that when the motionless occurrence came suddenly to an end it appeared to him as a solace. Nor did he know how long it had actually lasted. Yet as it ceased, as the noontide was again set in motion and the glittering wheel started turning again, as the span again resumed its course and the wandering star was suddenly no longer in the sky, the door into the room opened, as if to give passage to the fleet-footed boy escaping at that very moment, but, in reality, opening because it had been clicked open by a somewhat portly, full-bearded man who now stood in the doorway with a friendly smile as though presenting himself as a cause for rejoicing, his arm raised in greeting, paying no heed to the boy scurrying past: it was not difficult to recognize this man as the expected physician; his demeanor, his looks, his whole effect made that clear, particularly his full, short-cropped, well groomed scholar's beard, its blondness spun through with silver threads as though artificially inserted to inspire confidence, like the silver threads of age; and had any doubt existed, it would have been entirely dispelled by the attendants armed with instruments who followed after him with more pomp, if that were possible; and every qualm would have been silenced by the worldling's professionally delighted welcome which came readily and smoothly from the ringleader's smiling lips:

"I counted on a recovering patient but I find one who has recovered."

"Yes, that you do." It was said more quickly and with more conviction than he could have expected of himself.

"Nothing can be more pleasing to a physician than to find his diagnosis confirmed, and the more so when this comes from such a great poet . . . however, if you declare yourself well only to evade the physician . . . now, what does your Menalcas say? 'Thou shalt not escape me today, whither thou callest, there shall I appear!' "

The blandness of the court physician was not agreeable, even though no patient is able to draw back from the secret charm of the medico; but a real country leech would have been preferable—, one could have talked to him of all sorts of things. Now the thing to do was, willy nilly, to come to terms with the one who was here: "I am not escaping from you . . . but, for the rest, forget the poem."

"Forget the poem? if your appearance didn't contradict it, I should believe that it was the fever speaking out of you, Virgil! No, neither shall you escape me, nor shall I ever forget your poem; our ancestors are much too closely related for that: Hippocrates and Theocritus both came from Kos, and so I flatter myself that I am somewhat related to you . . ."

"I greet you as a relative."

"I am Charondas from Kos." This was said with an emphasis that befitted a famous name.

"Oh, you are Charondas . . . so you are not teaching there any more; there will be many to deplore that."

It was not a reproach, at most it was the astonishment of one for whom teaching had always been a high goal impossible of attainment; however, he had touched a sore spot in the conscience of the court physician who started to defend himself: "It was not at all for the revenues that I obeyed the summons of Augustus; had I been keen on riches I needed only to continue treating my wealthy patients, of whom there were certainly enough; but who thinks of riches when it comes to serving directly the sacred person of Augustus! And it seems to me that by being in the center of state affairs, in which I can participate, I can accomplish something beneficial for science and for the welfare of the people, perhaps even more than I could as teacher . . . we shall be building cities in Asia and Africa; that is where a clinical adviser is indispensable, to give one instance out of many . . . of course this did not, and does not prevent me from feeling real pain at giving up my vocation as teacher; all in all, there have been years in which I have trained more than four hundred students . . ." and while he was holding forth about himself with this sort of chatter, half in candor half in vanity, in the attempt to establish a friendly intimacy, he had seated himself on the bed so that, by the help of a sandglass reached to him at his signal by one of the assistants, he could count the pulse . . . "but now keep quiet, we shall be through in a moment . . ."

The sand in the glass trickled thinly, smoothly, inaudibly, uncannily, as it were with swift slowness.

"The pulse means nothing."

"Wait, you may speak in just a moment . . ."—the sandglass spent itself—"now, it does not seem quite so unimportant to me, after all . . ."

"Of course, we have been taught the importance of the pulse by Herophilus."

"The great Alexandrine—how much more he would have been able to accomplish had he joined the school at Kos; well, that's a long time ago . . . but as to your pulse, far be it from me to insist that it is bad, but taken as a whole it could be much better."

"That signifies nothing . . . I am a little weak from the fever, and that always affects the pulse . . . I am quite easy on

274

that score; I still know a few things from my medical studies, I haven't quite forgotten them . . ."

"Professional comrades make the worst patients, there I really prefer poets, and not only on the sick-bed . . . and how about your cough? and your sputum?"

"The mucus is bloody . . . but that is bound to be; the secretions are getting back into balance."

"With all respect for Hippocrates . . . how would it be if you forgot to mix the art of medicine and the art of poetry for a while?"

"Yes, the art of poetry deserves to be forgotten; I should have become a physician."

"I am quite ready to change places with you as soon as you are well."

"I am well. I shall get up at once." Again it was as if someone else spoke out of him, one who was really well.

In no time the physician had lost his man-of-the-world expression, the impartial proficiency which had been so disagreeable; the eyes in the smoothly cushioned smiling face. dark eyes with a golden glint in them, became sharp and observant, yes, almost worried, and the almost jolly conversation was incompatible with the look that accompanied it: "I am really and truly glad that you consider yourself in perfect health, but 'make haste slowly' cautions Augustus in cases such as these . . . also in convalescence there are gradations, and it is for your physician to decide how far you have climbed the ladder of convalescence . . ."

The searching glance, the jolly talk, all this was disquieting: "You really mean that my convalescence may already have gone too far . . . what you really mean is that what I felt was an all-too-complete convalescence . . . you mean it is euphoria, do you not?"

"Ah, Virgil, if that were so, I should wish you a very long-lasting and prolific euphoria."

"This is no euphoric condition. I am well. I want to go down to the beach."

"Well, I am not going to send you directly to the beach, but very soon to the mountains instead . . . had I been with the Augustus in Athens, I should have had you go at once to Epidaurus for the cure; be assured I should have insisted on that . . . now we must make the best of it here, as far as possible . . . but nothing is impossible when both patient and physician have set their minds on getting well . . . how about your morning meal? Do you feel any hunger?"

"I wish to remain abstemious."

"That's all that is needed . . . who is the house-slave here? We shall begin with some hot milk . . . let the house-slave be off to the kitchen . . ."

The slave, who had remained at the rear of the attendants, his face blank, made ready to carry out the order.

"Not he . . . he is not to leave here . . . he is to prepare my bath."

"Today there will be no bathing . . . even though we may be glad to try out the baths later; what Cleophantes taught two hundred years ago as to the effect of bathing is still valid today . . . the nature of human beings does not change, and a truth once found remains a truth, notwithstanding the new remedies that we are now blessed with . . ."

"In these things, as far as I know, old Asklipiades was also a follower of Cleophantes."

This interpolation called out the expected and even hoped for resentment, although it sounded quite restrained: "Yes, that old fox from Bythinia, who acts as if he had taken over water, air and sun as his own exclusive domains . . . whereas I as a young doctor, when the reputation of Asklipiades had barely started, had already achieved marked success with my bath and rest cures . . . of course, I respect him, and though it is not entirely improbable that even then he had got wind of my successful healings, I stand by my view that we physicians are here to cure our patients, and that arguments as to who was first to succeed ought to be strictly forbidden as undignified displays of professional jealousy . . . a physician needs only let his experiences mature; he has no need of noisily affirming the priority of his discoveries, which, alas, is the custom of so many people . . . twenty years ago I could have written a treatise on the effect of baths and I did not do it . . . how much harm has been done, for instance, by just this old Asklipiades with his writings on the effect of wine! one might be bold enough to say that he needs his 'bath-cures' only to rectify the harm that originated from his 'wine-cures' . . ." The speech ended in clear, smooth laughter; it was as if the surface of one laughter struck with mirror-like smoothness on the surface of another, in order to filch and retain a bit of it.

"May one infer from that, you would never prescribe wine?"

"In sensible quantities? Why not? Only I have no intention of turning my patients into tipplers . . . that is where Asklipiades is essentially wrong . . . well, let us skip that, for you are to have neither wine, nor a bath, but just some hot milk . . ."

"Milk? as a medicine?"

"It makes no difference whether you call it breakfast or medicine, unless you desire something else."

Milk was to be poured into him as if he were a child; even the physician wanted to reduce him to a child. One must rebel against this, it was imperative: "The night was not a good one, it was very hot . . ." The fever-dried fingers moved themselves almost automatically, in order to demonstrate visibly their craving for water—, "I have need of a bath."

But the rebellion came to nothing. The slave had hurried off without noticing the suggestion. Was he a traitor? Oh, the beaker had disappeared from the table and the boy had certainly been frightened off. The fingers continued their automatic, unbridled play and the ring was pressing as though it were suddenly too small. Why did this have to happen? why had they not let him alone with those two? why did they constantly hurl him back into this people-filled loneliness? Even the commode had been moved away.

"I have to cleanse myself and I need a bath."

"Certainly you have to be cleansed, and not only you but

this room as well, for the Augustus, as he ordered me to tell you, intends to greet you here in his own person, and very soon at that . . . my assistants will wash you presently with tepid vinegar . . ."

This meant giving up all resistance: "The Augustus will be welcome . . . let them get everything in readiness."

"We are already at it, my Virgil; but first take this medicine." And a glass with a transparent liquid was handed to him by the doctor.

The liquid appeared unsafe: "What is it?"

"A decoction of pomegranate seeds."

"That is harmless."

"Absolutely harmless. It is used only to make the stomach capable of absorbing food again. After a strenuous night, such as you have behind you, this seems to me an urgent necessity."

The drink had a cleanly bitter taste: "The guest must conform to the customs of the house, and I too must subordinate myself; whoever has erred must subordinate himself."

"Whoever is ill must accustom himself to subordination; that is the first request that a doctor must make."

"Every illness is an error."

"Of nature."

"Of the patient . . . Nature doesn't make mistakes."

"Lucky that you do not think it an error of the physician."

"Just the same he becomes a co-sinner by his help; he is a false bearer of salvation."

"Truly I shall take that upon myself, Virgil, all the more as you yourself are thinking of becoming a doctor."

"Did I say that?"

"That is what you said."

"I have always been ill; the false bearer of salvation has always been in me . . . I have always erred."

"You may really have studied the writings of our honored friend, Asklipiades, all too closely, my Virgil."

"Why?"

"Well, his doctrine that it is possible to avoid every sort of

illness by a proper conduct of life has an unmistakable resemblance to your theory that errors materialize as illnesses
. . . with all due reverence, I dare to call this nonsense and
absurdity that comes close to a belief in the medicine of magic
. . . and that is no wonder, in the face of the moving atoms that,
according to Asklipiades, are thought to be wandering about
in the human body . . ."

"Are you so opposed to magic, Charondas? Is there any
healing at all without magic? I almost believe that we have
only lost the veritable magic."

"I believe in the love-conjurations of your Enchantress, those
that bring back Daphnis, oh, Virgil."

How wonderfully forgotten things emerged. Daphnis! The
Eclogue of the Enchantress! Had he not sensed even then that
any magic was preceded by love? that all evil, all error, could
be identified as a lack of love? Whoever did not love was
stricken by illness, and only he who was reawakened to love
was able to recover: "Oh, Charondas, every doctor who possesses real healing magic frees his patients from their errors,
and even you do this, though you are often unaware of it."

"I want to know nothing of it, because I cannot see illness
as error . . . even animals and children fall sick, and surely
these do not commit errors . . . this also, without wishing to
detract from his importance in other matters, is something that
Asklipiades has not gone into thoroughly."

Reduced to a child, reduced to an animal, brought low by
illness, and because of illness retreating deep into a region the
borders of which lay even deeper than those of the animal
kingdom or those of childhood: "Oh, Charondas, the animal in
particular is ashamed of its illness and hides itself."

"It is true that I am no veterinarian, Virgil, but insofar as
I know my patients, most of them are quite proud of their illnesses." This was said a little aside, because the business of
combing his beard would not permit interruption, since a
court physician must be in fine form for Caesar's expected visit,
and therefore he had taken out a hand mirror with comb from

the folds of his toga, and had posted himself diagonally facing the window to catch the light more advantageously in the mirror, completely devoted to beautifying his scholar's beard. And without interrupting this occupation, with his lower lip shoved upward to tense the skin and causing him to mumble, he continued aloud: "The sickness-pride of the patients is only surpassed by the healing-vanity of the doctors."

This was certainly true; there is no shame of illness so great that it leaves no room for the vanity of illness, an arrogant, sacrificial vanity which thinks to have rounded off an accomplishment because illness annuls the sexual drives, because all desiring and all that is desirable is expunged from the face of the sick—the vanity of self-destruction. And for this reason, or in spite of it: "Give me the mirror."

"Later, when we have tidied you up a bit; now you still look somewhat neglected."

"Permit me my illness-vanity; give me the mirror."

And when it had been handed to him, it gave him back the long-familiar yet strange image of his own face, very repellent and yet commanding, many-layered under the olive-brown, unshaven skin, with the ambiguous, dark eyes undershadowed in black, with the taciturn, shrunken, kiss-weaned mouth; and as he looked into this peering cave-countenance, which, as it were, submissively contained all the faces of life, this face-abyss of the past, into which one face after another had been flung, taken in and taken for eternity, the face of the mother mirrored in that of the child, even though her light-colored eyes had not been bestowed upon him, oh, as he glanced into this chain of faces, he saw the last face which was still to follow and was already outlining itself: the face of his hope, the face to which he had wished to transform himself by the force of illness, and it was the death-face of his father, the face of the dying potter, who had laid his forming hand on the head of the boy, the face that had called out his name; a wonderful assurance emanated from it, the other faces paled beside it, and whether it had been won by one means or another, whether illness had been the right way to achieve it, now that it was attained, seemed almost irrelevant: "Doctor that you are, heal me so that I can die."

"No one is omnipotent, you wrote that yourself, Virgil; I am only able to heal you back to life, and I shall do it too, with the help of Aesculapius."

"I shall have a cock kept in readiness for him."

"With which he can awake you to immortality? Oh, Virgil, you no longer need death to give you immortality; and now we should do better to start washing and shaving so that the Caesar doesn't catch us at it; we are already pressed for time."

"My hair needs shortening too."

"Give me back the mirror, Virgil, lest the requests of your vanity increase beyond measure; it is true that your hair has not been treated by a court barber, but for my taste it seems unnecessary to cut it now."

"The forelocks have to be shorn for the sacrifice; those are the regulations."

"Is your fever mounting? or do you say this only as a concession to magic-medicine? if it helps, I am in agreement, for my treatments are not one-sided; I flatter myself that this is one of their assets . . . so you are welcome to have your hair cut for the so-called sacrifice, but in that case it is advisable to hurry a little."

It was the tone with which one seems to comply to a child's wishes, to coax it into obedience. However, it was all one, whether the idea of the sacrifice was absurd or not, there was nothing else left but to submit himself. And resistlessly he let them treat him according to the doctor's orders. He was being lifted by skilled hands and carried to the commode and the doctor was watching over the process as if he were caring for a little child. "Now," he heard them say, "now we would like to move you into the sun for a little while so that you can take your milk in complete relaxation."

Thus, wrapped in blankets and sunshine, he sat there in the easy chair near the window and drank the warm milk in sips that ran into the darkness of his body in small waves of heat.

The slave stood next to him, in readiness to relieve him of the bowl. But the slave's eyes looked out of the window, stern, rejecting, yet submissive.

"Do you see the limping man?"

"No, Sir, I see no limping man."

The room was now filled with activity; the flowers which had hung on the candelabrum limp and smelling sweetly of decay were cleared away, the candles renewed, the floor washed, the bed-sheets removed. The doctor, again armed with mirror and comb, drew nearer: "Which limping man?"

"The night-limper."

Full of apprehension, searching for something palpable, came a further question: "Oh, do you mean Vulcan, do you mean him for whom your Aetna-song was intended?"

The apprehension was quite touching, the effort to understand almost comical: "Oh, forget the poem, Charondas; do not burden your memory with any of my poems, least of all with this early and unfinished product which, by rights, I should do over again."

"You want to revise the Aetna-song and burn the Aeneid?" The apprehensive lack of understanding with which this was uttered became more and more comical. And yet it might prove worth while to take up the theme of the Aetna-song again in order that now, having more knowledge, more earnestness, more perception than formerly, one could spy on the limping smith in the demon-infested, iron depths of his smithy, blind from the glare of the underworld, nevertheless able, by virtue of this blindness—oh, the blindness of the singer—to see the splendor of the ultimate heights: Prometheus embodied in Vulcan—redemption in the form of calamity.

"No, Charondas, I only suggest that you forget both verses, the one as well as the other."

Then it was again touching to see how the features of the physician lightened, because it had been possible to construct a bridge of understanding: "Oh, Virgil, though it may be the prerogative of the poet to demand the impossible, memory is not so easily stilled on order . . . oh, Virgil, all that Apollo once sang and Eurotas heard enraptured, all of this was sung by that one . . ."

"And the mountains bore the echo unto heaven" added a soft voice from an echoing distance, itself an echo, mirroring the vanished voice of the boy.

The sounds rose upward toward the echoing heaven and they were the sounds of the day, the sounds of diligence, the bustle of a thousand work-shops, a thousand households, a thousand stores, the fusing, swelling city-noises, merged and rife with all the smells of the city, rising from it to heaven, the floating rubble of day which harbored as little anxiety as did the cooing of doves or the chirping of sparrows with which it was mingled. The tile roofs, black striped or entirely black, were filmed in a thin, quivering layer of smoke, glints of copper and lead, glints of iron were to be seen here and there, shining under the rays of the now paler day-star, and in the glare of noon the heaven had become faded; without a cloud, its paler azure spread out over the flickering mid-day world.

Should he worry the doctor once again by asking after the star which had vanished into the invisible transparency? Unlosable, even if not to be espied the star drew on toward the east; it traveled the width of the sky, yet at the same time passing through a region beyond the sky's last dome, submerged in that oceanic mirror in whose abysmal depths the echo of skies and more skies were assembled forever. A drifting star binding the spheres together. Undiscoverable, light's radiant roots were reaching down through every language, undiscoverable, the branchings of vision were groping up through every language, yet with this piercing ray penetrating man more and more infinitely, he must return with his eyes and more than his eyes, to his profoundest depths in order to reach the oceanic abyss of echo from which his image will be flashed back to heaven, aye, farther than to heaven, to the eye of the god. Was his labor, which he pursued bent toward the ground, and which he must pursue in humility, already an espial of the depths, was it that searching care which willed to find the higher image? did man with his earth-bent labors reach unto the endless depths lying beneath those of the underworld, which are at once those of the highest heaven? or must he wait until the god pierce him mortally with light's ultimate ray, the death-dealing ultimate, the god himself entering him, so that with his echo in man, man might be taken back into his divine being, sinking upward over the majestic steps of the aeons, sinking upward to the opened spaces? Oh, where had the star wandered, the star which showed the way?

Tucked into the arm-chair he blinked up into the colorless flicker, he did it cautiously as though it were something forbidden. And in this blinking, painful yet compelling, in this blinking, at once passive and active, there emerged, strangely distorted and yet sharply contoured,—was it here? was it there? —an image such as had appeared in the mirror, repelling, many-layered, a palimpsest of a face, despite that not a completed face, the refraction of a reflection, rising like a shadow on the deepest surface of the mirror, on the remotest depths of its abyss. Verily, it had not been carried thither over the steps of the aeons, far rather it seemed to have slunk in through the smallest, meanest door in the background, squinting up like a bad conscience, ah, truly not beaming up.

Then the slave, having relieved him of the bowl and disposed of it, remarked: "Sir, protect your eyes, the sun is strong."

"Leave that to me," he was reproved by the doctor who turned thereupon to the group of his assistants: "Has the vinegar-water been warmed yet?"

"Certainly, Master," came the reply from the darkness of the chamber.

And so at a nod from the master he was being carried back again into the shadows and put to bed on the couch. But his glance remained fixed on the patch of sky in the window-frame, so irresistibly attracted by the brightness that the accompanying words came to him without effort: "He who gazes aloft toward the heaven of day from the depths of a well-pit sees it as dark, and he is able to see the stars in it."

Immediately the doctor was at his side: "Have you some trouble with your eye-sight, Virgil? you need not be uneasy about it, that is not unusual . . ."

"No, I have no difficulty in seeing." How blind this court-physician must be not to know that one who is in blindness, awaiting a superior blindness, can have no eye trouble.

"You said something about stars."

"Stars? oh yes . . . I should like to see them once more."

"You shall see them still many times . . . I vouch for that, I, Charondas from Kos."

"Ah, really, Charondas? the desire of a patient could hardly go beyond that."

"Oh, do not be so very modest, I can promise you still more than that with an easy conscience . . . as, for instance, that in a few days, yes, I might almost say in a few hours, you will feel entirely well, for after a crisis such as you seem to have passed through last night, and evidently in a most violent fashion, it is customary for a most tempestuous recovery to set in . . . actually we doctors cannot ask for anything better than such a crisis, and in my judgment—which however is not shared by the whole profession, and which, though I am not annoyed by it, has earned me the reputation of an outsider—it is absolutely advisable under certain circumstances to bring about such a crisis by artificial means . . ."

"I already feel entirely well."

"So much the better, so much the better, my Virgil."

Yes, he felt perfectly well; stretched out naked on the bed, his back supported by a few pillows which had been placed under him to retard his coughing, he was first being carefully washed with tepid vinegar and then gently dried with heated towels, and the longer this mild alternating game lasted the more he felt the fevered weariness vanishing from his body; he let his head fall backward over the edge of the pillow to present his chin and throat to the razors of the barbers working about his head, and this letting go came to be a gentle alleviation, became so as much with the soft, sure gliding of the razor over his stretched skin, as with the removal of the heating stubble of his beard, and with the rapid succession of hot and cold compresses which were applied afterwards to his clean-shaven face, this being more than an alleviation, even a pleasant stimulation. However, when this was done, and the barber wanted to attend to his hair he interrupted him: "First shorten the hair on my forehead."

"Just as you please, Sir."

The scissors clicked coolly about his forehead, they passed coolly with short, clicking cuts toward the temples, and besides this they clicked in mid air, because the hairdresser let them open and close with the tremolo of a virtuoso after each snap, and, as the aesthetic sense of the hair artist demanded symmetry, the crown and back of the head had to be trimmed before they could begin washing with an emulsion of oil and alkalines, culminating in oft-repeated rinsings with cool water, for which purpose a suitably shaped wash-basin had been slipped under his neck. And while this careful sequence was being followed out, the medical assistant busied himself with a careful and skillful massaging of his limbs, beginning with his toes.

The head-washing was at an end, and the hairdresser asked: "Lily, rose or mignonette-scented pomade, Sir, or do you prefer amber?"

"None of them; comb my hair, but do not use any pomade."

" 'That woman smells good who smells of nothing,' said Cicero," remarked the Doctor, "although he said many blasphemous things in which he himself did not believe, and mignonette would be quite wholesome for you; mignonette has a soothing effect."

"Just the same, Charondas, I should rather not have it."

Outside the sparrows twittered, and a blue-gray, swelling dove walked along the window-sill, cooing and nodding in the

286

radiance of the light-shedding heaven, opening up from the very core to the opened heavenly light.

The doctor laughed: "If I had forbidden you to have cream you would certainly have demanded it; patients of your kind are no novelty for us, one has to know how to cope with you, and to speak frankly, I have had plenty and more than plenty of opportunity to learn how . . . you see I am a person who explains his tricks in advance so as to win in the end; incidentally you may have your way this time, for what you need fundamentally is not a soothing but rather a reviving of your animal spirits; and I am wondering whether to let you drink **a good** strong aphrodisiac—yes, joking aside, I would almost recommend it in your case, considering that our courage to live, our desire to live, our animal spirits are animated, if not entirely, still very strongly and, I may say, more strongly than we wish or know, from the lower centers of our organism, from these often quite enjoyable lower centers, to which we doctors must assign a rather important role in the urge to recovery . . . but you probably know this as well as I, and I only wanted to say that a little more of the will to live and be healthy would do you no harm . . ."

"I have no need of an aphrodisiac to strengthen my will to live, it is, I believe, quite strong enough in itself . . . I love life intensely . . ."

"Do you lack for reciprocal love? if so, you do not quite love enough!"

"I am not complaining, Charondas."

No, the will to live was in no need of an aphrodisiac; he who lies down to love closes his eyes, they are closed for him, even as for one who lies down to die, by a strange, familiar hand, but he who would live, standing up to life, holds his eyes wide open to the sky, to the opened light of heaven from which all desire and will to live is born: oh, to be allowed to see azure sky again and yet again, to see it tomorrow, the day after tomorrow, for many a year, and not have to lie here with broken-closed eyes, laid out with a clay-brown, stiffened countenance, while outside stretched the bright arc of the azure sky that could no longer be seen, filled with the cooing of doves that had become inaudible. So had that day been, bright and blue, so had that day been on which his father had lain on his bier. Oh, to be allowed to live!

The hairdresser came equipped with a mirror to let his finished handiwork be admired: "Are you satisfied with the cut, Sir?"

"Entirely so . . . I have confidence in you without further examination."

"You look splendid now," commended the physician, Charondas, evidently highly pleased, tapping his fleshy left palm with three fingers of his right hand by way of applause, "most splendid, and I hope you feel much refreshed as well: for there is no better means of revitalizing the secretions and the pulse than by such a thoroughly careful and workmanlike kneading of the entire body; by rights you should already feel the wholesome effects, indeed I can already discern it!"

Outside the starless, opened brightness of heavenly blue was extending; oh, to be allowed to see it forever! even at the cost of enduring illness and fatigue! Oh, to be allowed to see! How was it that the garrulous physician, Charondas, could still expect an answer? All the same he had told the truth, for there really was some refreshment to be felt, even if it was only a kind of refreshed fatigue. It was like a release from fear. The tired limbs were refreshed, fear-freed of their separate existence, even though under the kneading grips they had become more aware, if that were possible; they had dropped off their ancient fear, as if it were no longer an experience, rather only the knowledge of one, something that had happened only in a spectacle, but was no longer in his own body. Withal this spectacle was again none other than the body itself, yes, the body was spectacle and mirror simultaneously, taking in not only the occurrence but the knowledge of it as well, so that it could be delivered of fear and yet remain in immediate physical prox-

imity, unbroken, as a new, a physical awareness, unbroken, no
matter how he, the one no longer aware, might lose or be losing
himself in any un-nearness whatsoever; all was becoming soft,
the world pulsed softly, inside and outside pulsing, the tides
of day and night pulsing, as well as the great, gently-impetuous
harmonic order of life, upon whose foundation even the tides
flow into one another and are silenced; the bell-tone of night
merged with the sunny storm of day, softly the breathing
pulsed, and softly-quietly the breath passed into the rising and
falling breast, relaxed and helped by the kneading strokes of
a strange, invisible, soft hand; from suffering delivered, with
suffering endowed, from awareness delivered, with awareness
endowed, this was a re-experiencing of the physical being,
enmeshed in a noiselessness which made it seem that of a
spectacle seen in reflection—smooth and mute, as though trans-
piring in a mirror; the bustling went on everywhere in the room,
directed by the now noiseless voice of the physician; noiselessly
the slaves scurried in and out, strangely featherlight; a basket
filled with linen had been brought in, and fresh bedclothes lay
suddenly under the weightless, uplifted body, a fresh tunic
enwrapped him; fresh flowers wreathed the candelabrum, and
their scent mingled with the scent of vinegar, skimming along
moist and serene, a trickling fragrance borne from the moist
drizzle of the wall-fountain, the murmuring, falling drops of
the soul. Strange that there was security, strange the way it
unfolded. To be sure, his body on which such care had been
lavished was the body of disintegration, but some knowledge
of himself as a mirrored spectacle allowed him to preserve his
contour, a loose and floating figure sheltered and floating between past and future, peacefully at one with both, itself a
mirror, itself peace, airily identified with the present, held
arrested on the breath, gazing at the open sky. And, moreover,
it was as if all of this, everything that was happening here, all
this fostering that was going on so noiselessly and swiftly, consisted only of an empty transparency, as though by this means
alone a bright, airy, and trumpery structure of supports had

been set up, a framework that no longer had to support anything except lightness itself, yes, it seemed as if there had been an exaggerated and almost ghostly expenditure that aimed only at producing a shelter for something which could no longer be sheltered, nothing that such sheltering could enfold, for what at most might be something very indistinct, very evanescent, perhaps the reflected image of a nonentity; but beyond that it seemed as if this mirrored blur and dissolution, as if this almost intangible, abandoned thing were, in spite of abandoning itself, still to be saved from disintegration and retained in itself at the last moment, saved, as though by a miracle, just as it strove to become separate; and it almost seemed as if it had received form and stature out of an awareness which, though it was only a reflected awareness, was still possessed of enough earthly strength to take the most transparent elusiveness into its sheltering care and, by virtue of this very sheltering, to transform it once more to reality; for even in its furthest reflection the deed of loving service had the power to establish reality; and even when, as in this case, it was manifested as a playful reflection, as a pretense of healing that was no longer healing, playfully approaching the portal of death, it was still the invisible substance of the world which creatively transformed knowing to knowledge, the sheltering into the sheltered, creating the enfolded by the strength of the enfolding; oh, so transformed, so brought back to earthly creation that this created world— permeated by a strange sort of accuracy, determined as much by the extraordinary as by the commonplace—became a reflection of this very self, that was at the same time a reflection of the human being, a reflection of the inner and outer selves. Was this still his own body that he felt? or was it rather the reflection of his body, or perhaps merely the reflection of his sensibility? In what lay the reality of this peaceful existence which surrounded him and which was himself? There was no answer to be imparted and none was imparted; but even the not-imparted answer was a constituent of this concord, as was everything that surrounded him, corporeal and incorporeal in a single breath, in a single pulse-beat, floating between original and semblance, touching neither one nor the other, but rather a symbol of both; floating between things remembered and things that could be seen, their common mirror, and peacefully reconciled to both, the ethereal present; and in the depth of the mirror, in the depth of the peace, deeply sunk into the present and into reality, shimmered the star on the far-dark ground of day's brightness.

WHY should all this not remain forever? why should such effortless felicity change? And no change occurred. Indeed, one could have imagined that even the proceedings inside the room, though taking their course, were not subject to change. Nevertheless they became more significant, more and more extensive. Pregnant with the scent of flowers lifted on the odor of vinegar, the peaceful breath of being lingered on, yet at the same time it was growing, and the harmonious order of the world came to be a whisper charged with warm freshness; this was consummation, and the wonder of it was only that it had ever been otherwise. Now everything was given its proper place, one that might well be retained forever. Impetuously though gently, room and landscape united, the flowers pushed up impetuously in the field, they grew higher than any house, piercing the tree-tops and embraced by their branches; human beings swarmed diminutively among the plants, camping in their shade, reclining against their stems, and were just as ineffably transparent, just as serene as they. The physician, Charondas, who was still standing in front of the window, he too could be seen yonder in the circle of the frolicking nymphs, as with a courteous, critical manner he continued to comb the blond beard of his obese face, keeping the mirror at hand to reflect everything: mossy springs that rose from an even softer sleep, the greening arbutus, which tremulously tinged the mossy moisture, glowing and drying in the noonday sun, all this was mirrored; the juniper as well as the chestnut tree heavy with shaggy fruit, and the tiny mirrors on the taut grapes that hung from the ripening wine-shoot, these too were mirrored—, oh, mirrored nearness, mirrored buoyance, oh, how easy it seemed in this reflecting reflection to become one of them, to be one of those yonder, helping to guard the herds, helping to tread the juice-filled grapes in the vaulted stone arbor. Oh, the transparent was becoming transparency, keeping withal its own existence; the skin and clothing of the people were indistinguishable, and the souls of the people participated in the outermost surface as well as in the most invisible, yet somehow visible home-depth of the human heart looking out from the pulsing infinity. Somewhere there was meeting, meeting without end, alluring by its tender, trepidant longing. The odors of laurel and of blossoms arched across the rivers and floated from grove to grove, carrying with them the gentle salutes of those who communed happily together; and the towns dimming in the distance of light had shed their names so that they were only softly palpitating air. Did the slave still have the milk at hand so that, as was proper, a cup of it might be sacrificed to the golden image of Priapus? Red-glowing gold dipped in milk, thus it appeared in reflection, surrounded by the river-hemming poplars dedicated to Alcides, by the bacchanalian vine, by the laurel of Apollo, and by the myrtle which is dear to Venus; but elms were bending over the stream and moistening the tips of their leaves, and from out one of their tree-trunks stepped Plotia and advanced across the bridge made by the bending boughs; she sauntered nearer with a light step amid a cloud of butterflies and noiselessly twittering birds; she strode through the surface of the hand-mirror, through the gold-gleaming arch of the rainbow, striding through its smoothness which opened and closed itself behind her, stepping along the ivory paths of milk, and stopped a short way off from him, who leaned against the elm-branches of the candelabrum.—"Plotia Hieria" he said with fitting courtesy as if he had not met her before. She held her head bent as if to greet him, in the dusk her hair shimmered bestrewn with stars, and despite the considerable distance which lay between them they clasped hands so closely and fervently that the stream of their joint lives flooded back and forth between them. However it might still be a delusion and it was essential to make sure: "Have you come this way by accident?" "No," she replied, "our destinies were united from the beginning." Their hands were joined, his laid in hers, hers in his, oh it could not be distinguished which were his and which were hers, but as he seemed to be as many-branched as the elm, being also able to clasp with playful fingers the flowers and the fruit which were sprouting from the tree, the answer was not quite satisfying and he had to question further: "But you were born from another tree and you had to come a very long way to reach this one."—"I went through the mirror," said she, and with this explanation he had to be content; yes, she had come through the mirror, she came through the mirror which doubled the light, and with double strength the beaming roots pierced down to the source of the destined unity, so that it might pulse up again from the source to a new and united diversity, to a new and manifold unity, to new creation. Oh, lovely surface of the earth! Yonder noon and evening seemed to hover simultaneously, the herds wandered with slow ambling tread; yonder stood the cattle with deeply sunken heads, muzzles and tongues dripping near the trickling water-hole, there under the lush willows, there among the rolling meadows, there in the region of cool springs, there would they wander, hand in hand: "Did you come, Plotia, to hear the poem again?" Now Plotia smiled a long slow smile, beginning in the eyes, gliding to the softly shining skin on her temples, as though the tender veins which showed beneath it must also share in smiling, and slowly, quite imperceptibly, it melted to the lips which trembled as if under a kiss before they opened to smile, disclosing the edge of the teeth, the edge of the skull-bone, the ivory-colored, rocky border of human existence. The smile hovered on, remaining in the countenance, the border-smile of the earth-bound, the border-smile of eternity, and the shimmering, silvery expanse of sunlit sea came by smiling to be the spoken word: "I want to stay with you always, world without end."—"Stay with me, Plotia, I shall never desert you, I shall always take care of you." It was a plea, a vow of the heart, and, at the same time, fulfillment, for Plotia without having taken a single step had come a little nearer, and the outermost branches of the broad elm-tree were touching her shoulders. "Stay and rest, Plotia, rest in my shade,"—it is true this had formed in his mouth, had been uttered by him, and yet seemed to have been spoken from out the branches, conjured out of the branches which seemed to have been endowed with the gift of speech through contact with the woman. And so it was only right that she nestled her face in the leafy branches and murmured her answer to them: "You are home to me, and home your shadows, folding me in to rest."—"You are home to me, Plotia, and when I feel your repose, I feel I could rest in you eternally." She had sunk down on the manuscript-chest and, notwithstanding her fluid lightness under which the leather cover of the chest did not bend the fraction of an inch, her hands were so closely and physically linked with his that his fingers were blissfully able to feel her soft features, for she held her face buried in her hands, just as the boy had done. Thus she sat, shrouded in shadows, and a living communion was being bestowed on them, growing out of their hands, growing into something unalterable, though as yet only a sensing breath, anticipatory and rich. But although this communion was so physical, blood and breath melting together, their mutual existence melting into one, nevertheless the slave was able to walk through it, as if he himself, as if both their arms were nothing more than so much air—, did he want to part them from each other? a vain attempt; their hands remained placed one into the other, linked into one another, grown into one another, become one for evermore, and even the ring which was on Plotia's finger was the common property of the inseparable hand-unity. So it was necessary to rebuke the slave, and Plotia, again covered by his form, undertook to do it: "Take yourself off," said she, "go away from us, no death has the power to part us." However, the slave paid no attention to her and did not get out of the way, but instead stooped to the listening ear: "It is forbidden you to turn back; beware of the animals!" Which animals? Might it be the herds there near the springs? might it be the snowy bull, the luckless Pasiphae, who lingered there beside the cows? Or the bucks stirring about and mounting the she-goats? Pan's midday quiet lay soundlessly over the flowering groves and yet it was already evening, for the fauns had begun their gambols, stamping their hooves, their heavy phalluses stiffly erect. The distant sky over the dance-clearing was full of the clarity of evening, and the coolness of evening was wafted hither; stonily cool the moss-grown moisture trickled within the grottoes, the bushes at their entrance filled with nocturnal shadows and the cooing of doves, and over them fell the larger shadow from the mountains, larger and darker; evening, lovely and poignant in its sweetly-fatuous, sweetly-exalted simplicity; was this the reversion? was this the return? And again Plotia took over the answer: "I can never be a memory-image to you, Virgil, and though you recognize me, you are seeing me, even now, for the first time. Oh you are homecoming, turning home without turning back." "You will find homecoming only at the goal which you have still to reach," interrupted the slave, handing him the well-gnarled copper-studded traveler's staff, "it is not fitting for you to halt, and you are no longer permitted to remember; take your staff, grasp it in your fist and wander on!" This was a vigorous challenge, and had he taken it up he must have reached, staff in hand, the dark valley in the wilderness of which the golden bough was growing; it was a command of such force that it would have compelled obedience forthwith had not the staff remained most miraculously in the light hands of Plotia, out of reach of the slave, and this also was like the delight of a first memoryless recognition, it was like the first recognition by woman: "Oh Plotia, your destiny is mine, since you recognize me in it." "Falsehood," said the slave, sternly making a shadowy effort to wrest the staff from her, "it is falsehood; the fate of the woman lies in the past, but that of you, Virgil, lies in the future, and no one who is the prisoner of the past can ease it for you." The warning sounded serious, directed as it was against the caressing, flowerlike serenity of the incident, and it struck him to the depth of his heart: destiny of the future that was man's, destiny of the past that was woman's—, they had always been incompatible for him, notwithstanding all his yearning for happiness, and again this incompatibility threatened to rise up as a barrier between Plotia and himself. Where lay reality? Was it with the slave, was it with Plotia? And Plotia said: "Take my destiny, Virgil, shape my past within you so that it may become our future." "Falsehood," repeated the slave, "you are a woman and you have followed after many a man limping on his staff." "Alas," sighed Plotia, overcome by such cruel severity, and this short relapse into gentle submissiveness was taken advantage of by the slave to seize the staff and to divide the tree-top with it so that the sunlight came in with the painful, hard glare of noon. To be sure by this means he also frightened off the monkeys, who up there in the foliage were carrying on their lewd game of self-satisfaction, and who now scurried away with shrill screams, which reestablished the day's good humor; everyone in the room laughed up at the monkeys, taken unawares, and the physician turned the hand-mirror towards them as if to catch again, or at least jeer at, those who had been frightened off by the light, for as the beasts made off through the air, he quoted: "Henceforth let it be the wolf who flees the sheep, let the rugged oak bear golden apples, let the narcissus blossom beamingly from the alder, amber ooze from the bark of the marshy thicket, and Tityrus be like Orpheus singing through the woods, be like Arion among the dolphins." By this time Plotia had also overcome her discouragement; she pressed herself more fervently into his hands, and her eyes turned upward toward the open light: "Along with the light I can hear your poem, Virgil."—"My poem? This also is a thing of the past."—"I hear the poem yet unsung."— "Oh Plotia, are you able to hear despair? Despairing is that which is unsung and undone, a mere searching without hope or goal, and its song is nothing but vanity."—"You search into your own darkness whose light is forming you, and hope such as this will never abandon you, it will always be fulfilled when you are near me." Instantly, fleetingly, the everlasting future was manifest there, instantly mirror's light dipped into mirror's light. His hands lay upon her breasts, the points of which became harder under his touch—had she guided his hands?—and captured by the soft texture of her body, he heard her say: "Beyond any poem is the unsung within you, greater than what is formed is that which forms; it forms you also, unattainably far from you, since it is your very self; yet when you draw near to me, you come near to this self and attain it." Not only her face, not only her breasts took shape in his hands, nay, also her unseen heart nestling into the caressing embrace did so, and he asked: "Are you the shape that I have become, the shape of my becoming?"—"I am in you and yet you penetrate within me; your destiny is growing in me and therefore I recognize you in the unsung future."—"Oh Plotia, you are the goal, unattainable."—"I am the darkness, I am the cave that receives you into the light."—"Homeland, that is what you are, undiscoverable homeland."—"My knowledge of your being awaits you; come, you are discovering me."—"In your knowledge reposes the undiscoverable, reposes the future."—"Tranquilly I carry your destiny, in my knowledge lies your goal."—"Then entrust me also with your future destiny, so that I may bear it with you."—"I have none."—"Tell me also your goal so that I may seek it with you."—"I have none."—"Plotia, oh Plotia, how shall I find you? Where, in the undiscoverable, shall I look for you?"— "Look not for my future, take my beginning upon yourself, know only that, and the reality of our present will come to be an ever-enduring future." Oh voice, oh speech! Were they still speaking? still whispering? or had the dialogue already become mute, more comprehensible to them in the transparency of their bodies, spellbound one into the other, their souls become one under the spell of transparency? Oh soul, living only for the sake of the undone and unsung, for the sake of that future form in which fate shall stamp you! Oh soul, shaping to immortality and to this end yearning for a mate in whom to recognize the goal! Oh, eternal timelessness of shared existence, enclosed within the linked hands! Softer became the drizzling waters, softer the fountain, and very softly there whispered in his soul, in his heart, in his breath, very softly there whispered within him and out of him, "I love you." "I love you," came back so inaudibly that it seemed only a mute pressure of their hands. And their hands clasped, their souls clasped, he reclining in the branches of the tree, she sitting on the chest; neither of them moved, neither moved the breadth of a finger from their places, and yet, for all that, they were being brought nearer to each other because a floating force was at work to diminish the distance between them, drawing together the elm-branches garlanded with the half-cut grapes to a narrowly closed leafy arbor, to a gold-green cave filled with light, and with barely enough space for anyone else: this was like a leafy semblance of the abysmal cave which had been prepared for the brief, oh, so brief, bliss of Dido and Aeneas. Ah, did it follow that the gold-green foliage was likewise an illusion? Was it to betray him? It shimmered golden, but naught could be seen of the golden bough, naught heard of a golden sound coming from the bush. Oh, only a moment of actual happiness had been bestowed on this heroic couple, only a single moment in which Dido's past destiny and Aeneas' future destiny had been allowed to coincide —faded the image of the past, the love of her youth, Sychaeus untimely dead, and faded too the image of the future, the mastery of Italy commanded by the fateful verdict of the gods —both of them re-formed and conformed to one another, to the immortal, momentary present of their union, their reality, that lasted only for the single moment, this moment, however, already overcast by the many-eyed, many-tongued, many-mouthed, many-winged, gigantic figure of Fama soaring across the night, the terrible figure which frightened lovers apart, and drove them into shame. Oh, would the same lot overtake them here? would this be allowed to happen? Were they not already too closely united, conformed to a last reality, for this to be possible? Ineffable was the smile of Plotia extending across the landscape, almost sad in its serene immobility, and the landscape, having become transparent through smiling, disclosed itself in its maturing, profound with its past, pregnant with its future, becoming ready for procreation, being born and giving birth. Foliage and blossom, fruit, bark and earth were touching his fingers, and it was always Plotia whom he touched, it was always Plotia's soul that smiled to him across the endless planes of the landscape. But from the treetops the voice of Lysanias was audible: "Return home into the smile of the beginning, return home into the smiling embrace where you found shelter of yore!"—"Do not turn back," came the slave's voice again in warning, and it was answered in an undertone by the physician, commanding quiet: "Hush, he is no longer able to turn around." And thereafter the landscape became somewhat darker though it lost little of its transparent serenity, and, not at all troubled by the slight gloom, Plotia's smile remained, infusing a tinge of sibylline smiling into her voice that came out of the landscape as its own speech: "From the beginning I signified the goal to you, never the reversion; and you are nameless to me because I love you, nameless like a child are you to me, soul, about to be." —"Oh Plotia, you came to me by your name, and in loving you your existence became my resolution."—"Flee," warned the slave in a last, almost frightened importunity. But the branches had been so densely entwined with grapes, had closed to such a dark, shadowed grotto, that flight seemed utterly impossible, and indeed he had no wish to flee; indeed he would not have plucked the golden bough if the slave had shown it to him: it was satisfying to love Plotia, assuaging the nearness of her womanly nakedness, peaceful to send one's glance out across the branches there to the wood-bounded fields and flowery groves where no wolf lurks in wait for the herds, no trap is set for the deer, where Pan and the shepherds, where nymphs and dryads, are fulfilled in lilting joy, and where the heifer, fearful yet longing for the bull, sinks down beside the trickling brook, exhausted by longing. Nothing fearful, nothing fear-inspiring could be seen; even the head of the snake, coiled in green, shimmering rings about the tree trunk was gentle, and its golden glance, accompanied by the delicate darting of its tongue, was familiar and invited confidence. The life about one was sweet and drowsy —who would wish to flee! No, he did not want to escape, no, he had taken his resolve and it was the resolve called love, which was greater than the beloved creature, for it embraced and comprehended in her not only what was visible but what was invisible as well: "Never again shall I flee, never again shall I flee you, Plotia; nevermore shall I leave you." Now Plotia was nearer, and her breath was cool: "You are near me, you are the resolution, I await you." Yes, it was the resolution, and of a sudden Plotia's ring could be felt quite distinctly around his finger, perhaps it had been transferred to him automatically, perhaps put on secretly by her as a tie, a union of a sweetness which would never end. For past and future came together in the ring, to an unending present, to a constantly self-renewing knowledge of destiny, to a constantly self-renewing rebirth: "You are my reason for homecoming, Plotia, you came and made our present into an eternal homeland."—"Are you coming home to me, beloved?"—"You are home to me, the home to which I come back and enter."—"Yes,"—and it was like a sigh—"Yes, it is right for you to desire me." And though at first it seemed amazing that she should say this so baldly, it was still right that she did so, it had to be right, because in desire and its immediacy past and future counterbalanced each other,—the face itself extinguished in the great smile of love—because in this almost rigid immobility the transparent clarity of the unchangeable lapse was established, and because just this brought about a compulsion, aye, a decidedly sweet compulsion, to call things by their real names; the circumstance was defined by the extraordinary as well as by the commonplace; both were to be called from a veiled to an unveiled expression, and this applied to him as well: "The stream of your being flows to me, Plotia, timeless and eternal, and I desire you intensely." Like a veil she moved a little away from him, or rather she was wafted away. "Then send Alexis away." Alexis? in truth! : amidst the landscape, pranced about by the stiff-phallused satyrs, Alexis with his blond locks and white throat was standing near the window, he was standing there in a short tunic and dreaming out into the shimmer, dreaming across to the distant mountains, their peaks sailing about the sun-fog of the horizon, and a pink and white blossoming bough arched over his head. "Send him away," pleaded Plotia, "send him away, do not look in his direction, you are holding him with your eyes." Send him away? Could he send away anyone whose destiny, oh, whose future fate he had taken upon himself, and whom, for that reason, he loved? If so, he should also have to send away the amorous Cebes who had meant to be a poet—was such a thing permissible? did it not portend the degradation of human destiny to the level of accident? was it not a transforming of the future into the past? Certainly in the immediate naked reality of the occurrence there could be no halting deliberation and, with the same nakedly transparent immediacy, Plotia was urging: "Are not my breasts more desirable than yonder boy's buttocks?" Alexis, whose sentence was being passed upon him in this way, made no sort of movement, not even when he was softly twitted by the voice of the doctor: "Charming youth, rely not too much on your rosy coloring," even then he gave no indication that he had heard and understood; on the contrary, he gazed still further into the landscape, dreaming toward the flowery groves and the valley, shady in the mid-day heat, where a blessed shadow was cast by the branches of the holm-oaks, softening the air as with the cool of evening; the youth dreamed on into the serene and unmoving transparency, but when Plotia, as if in deep, tender affright, called to the beloved of her body and soul, when she cried "Virgil!"—a cry which despite its softness was one of terror and also of triumph—the form of the youth vanished as if absorbed by the sun, dissolved, transformed into ether, and Plotia with a smiling sigh of relief looked up: "Tarry

no longer, my beloved."—"Oh, Plotia, oh, my love." As if at
her behest, the branches had closed to an impenetrable, opaque
thicket, and he, drawn by her hands, sank to his knees; he knelt,
his hands in hers, kissing the points of her breasts. And floating
together, lifted by a floating force, floating on those strong
waves of light streaming from the eyes of one into the eyes of
the other, they were carried away, lifted up and placed lightly
upon the bed, and without having disrobed they were lying
there, naked flesh to flesh, naked soul to soul, cleaving together
along their quivering whole length, yet motionless with desire,
while about them, soundless amidst the heaviness of stars although felt ever more strongly, the thunder of light rolled in,
filling the world. Extinguished now the memory of the past and
the future, sweetly extinguished to a chastity devoid of memory.
Thus they lay there without stirring, mouth pressed to mouth,
and her tongue wagged stiffly, like a tree-top in the wind; thus
they lay until her lips, trembling within his, murmured: "We
cannot; the doctor is observing us." So the denseness of the
shrubbery did not protect them! How was it possible? How
could a glance penetrate this thick shade?! And yet it was so!
Without the green-dark foliage having cleared in the slightest,
the bed was exposed on all sides and at the mercy of all glances;
the glances were not to be warded off, nor were the scornfully
outstretched fingers, most of them adorned with rings, pointing
from all sides toward the couch; neither were the monkeys,
grinning in wild glee and throwing down nuts upon them, nor the
bleating goats eyeing them askance with looks merry and lewd,
while over them floated the enormous shadow of a mocking
bat; oh, not to be warded off this shadow of Fama, the shadow of
her gigantic and terrible form who announced with malice and
blinding contempt the things which had never happened as well
as those which had: "They dare not fuck, they dare not, only
Caesar may do so!" Oh, not to be warded off the noise, the
blare of the many blinding planes of light; and before an explanation could be found for all this, aye, even before he could
seek Plotia's glance or loosen his mouth from hers, she too had

changed into laughter, gliding along him as stone-cool laughter, smooth as ivory, floating up like a leaf carried on a gust of light—and seated herself once more on the chest. Did she think by this to cancel the threat which was announced by the uproar? If so, she did not succeed—renunciation is not sacrifice enough —the uproar of light was not quelled, the thunder did not subside, on the contrary, it became more and more distinct, stormier and stormier, it filled the visible world, it filled grove and mountain, it filled the room and the waters, becoming so overpowering, so violent, that people interrupted their occupations, standing as though benumbed, even more, ranging themselves in rows as if it were impermissible for one to stand out from another in the face of this thunderous, approaching power—oh, terrible and overpowering the strain of its approach—and at last, oh, at last, the door to the landscape was pushed open, servants stood on guard at the two wings, and between them, awe-inspiring and yet human, dapper and at the same time majestic, the consecrated person of the Augustus stepped quickly into the room.

Silence greeted the sacred one; only the birds twittered in the hushed landscape, only the doves on the window-sill, puffed up and pecking, cooed on unconcerned; yonder where the fauns had been dancing, one of them still piped his lay as though uncaring that his companions had left him, but his flute had a broken sound. The storm had passed but the world had not won back its color, because the two-toned cloud of dusk hung in a blanching silence over it and its muteness, like a relic of the storm caught into immobility; and even though the draught, caused by the abrupt opening of the door, came in from the stone-cool corridor for a moment, setting the lamp in quivering motion, it too came to rest and everything waited for the word of Augustus.

"Leave us alone."

Stepping backward before the majesty of the ruler, but as before the majesty of death as well, one after another of those present left the chamber, bowing reverently, and even the landscape, as though participating in this act of reverence, dismissed all the creatures from its domain, indeed, it faded also to such an extent that, although its main features remained, it was progressively losing all assurance and finally it was just an intimation, like a pen and ink sketch drawn into the universe, the groves, the grottoes, simplified to mere pen strokes, the thinly drawn bridge swinging between shores no longer to be seen, denuded of color, shadow, and light; for even the cloud of dusk had changed to a papery pulp of scarcely contoured whiteness, and the wide-open, colorless eye of heaven was empty, was nothing but the empty sorrow of dream. The room, however, had become quite palpable, for walls and furnishing, floor, candelabrum, raftered ceiling, and hanging lamp had entirely recovered their firmness of color and dimension, and Plotia had vanished before this heavy palpability: crushed under the weight of reality, her lightness had fled, and although she who had come to stay forever did not belong with the others, and therefore had not gone with them and was certainly somewhere in the room, she had become invisible.

But Augustus was visible, standing palpably before him, a familiar sight with his slightly undersized figure, which although almost foppish succeeded in being majestic, with his face still boyish beneath the already graying shortcut hair, and he said: "As you did not feel like taking the trouble to come to me, I had to seek you out; I greet you on Italian soil."

It was strange that from now on speech and reply should have to alternate, yet the surrounding tangibility which, however, was already giving rise again to the feeling of illness, made speech seem easier: "By means of your doctors, Octavianus Augustus, you have forced me to this bad state of grace, but at the same time you have rewarded me by coming here."

"This is my first moment of leisure since landing, and I am happy to be able to devote it to you. Brundisium has always brought luck to me and mine."

"In Brundisium, as a youth of nineteen coming from Apollonia, you stepped into the inheritance from your divine father, in Brundisium you closed the treaty with your adversaries which cleared the way for your blessed reign; there were only five years intervening, I remember that."

"They were the same five lying between your Culex and Bucolics; you dedicated the one to me, the other to Asinius Pollio, who came off far better than I, though he may have deserved it, just as much as Maecenas deserved the dedication of the Georgics, for without these two the Treaty of Brundisium could hardly have been so favorably concluded."

What was the meaning of the gentle smile accompanying these words of the Caesar? Why did he speak of the dedications? Caesar's words were never without significance and intention; it might be better to lead him away from the poems: "From Brundisium you marched against Antonius in Greece; had we returned but two weeks earlier you would have been able to celebrate the anniversary of the Attic victory here at its starting point."

"Actium's strand shall also be honored by contests at Ilium. This is about the way you put it in the Aeneid. Isn't that correct?"

"Yes, your memory is admirable." The Caesar was not to be diverted from the poems.

"There are few things that memory holds so dear. Was it not soon after my return from Egypt that you submitted the first draft of the work to me?"

"You are right."

"And in the middle of the poem, truly its crux and high-point, on the shield of the gods which you presented to Aeneas, at its center, you placed a picture of the Attic slaughter."

"Yes, that I did. For that day at Actium marked the victory of the Roman spirit and its customs over the evil forces of the East, to whose dark secrets it had almost succumbed. This was your triumph, Augustus."

"Do you know the passage by heart?"

"How should I? My memory is not as good as yours."

Oh, no evasion was possible: Augustus had turned his eyes unmistakably to the manuscript-chest, and kept them fixed there, oh, there was no evading it, he had come to take the poem away!

And the Augustus smilingly gloated over his terror: "How is it that you know your own work so little?"

"I do not remember that part."

"Then for the second time I shall have to tax my memory; I hope I shall succeed."

"I am convinced of that."

"Well then, we shall see: 'But there stood Caesar Augustus in the middle of the shield directing the naval engagement of the Italian people who . . .'."

"Pardon me, Caesar, that is not how it goes; the verse begins with the armored ships."

"With the armored ships of Agrippa?"—Caesar was evidently annoyed—"just the same the armoring was a clever invention of Agrippa, in a certain sense a master-stroke, one with which he turned the tide of the battle . . . so my memory has not failed after all; now I remember . . ."

"Since you are depicted at the center of the battle and of the shield, your person is placed in the center of the verses; that is as it should be."

"Read the verses to me."

To read aloud? To take out the manuscripts and unroll them? Caesar was after the manuscripts and it was a cruel game that he was playing. How was it possible to defend one's manuscripts against such designs? Would Plotia do this? In no case should the chest be opened: "I shall try to recite the part."

And as though Caesar had guessed his thoughts the smile did not disappear from the beautiful face, only it was hardly a smile but rather something malicious and cruel. However he still stood in his characteristic gracefully-free attitude near the bed, he did not sit down, and it was so hard to guess what his next move would be, that suddenly the suspicion arose that he wanted to frighten Plotia away from the manuscript-chest. Perhaps this was a figment of the imagination, such as a high temperature sometimes produces, it was most certainly just a figment of fancy, for here everything was firmly real and strongly colored; one need take scarcely any notice at all of the limned landscape out yonder, but if one looked at it a little more closely, one became aware that the papery white light, though somewhat grayly shadowed, came even into the palpability of the room and penetrated into all things that were there, lending them an ever so strange note of unreality; the evil was engraved in the things, it could be seen even in the colors of the flower wreath, as finely-drawn as a lovely temptation; and finely-drawn it stood in the wrinkle between the eyes of Augustus; but now he only said: "Begin, my Virgil, I am listening."

"Will you not sit over here near me; I must recite lying down since your doctors have forbidden me to get up."

Fortunately Augustus showed himself willing to comply to the request, not choosing to sit on the chest, he took instead a chair near the bed, and it almost seemed that he had only waited to be asked; reaching between his outstretched legs with a most un-Caesarly gesture, he pulled the chair under his buttocks and sat down with a small, comfortable sigh of relief and with no thought of his great ancestor, Aeneas, whose custom it must have been to seat himself in a more dignified fashion; this first sigh of relaxation in the grandson of Aeneas, this gentle weariness which was like the first sign of approaching age, was rather touching and conciliating, and also conciliating was the way he leaned back his head and crossed his arms, preparing himself to listen: "Well, let me hear you."

And the verse took sound:

"There on the shield was the bronze-armored fleet in the
    Attic encounter;
Strewn with the trappings of warfare were also the shores
    of Leucate;
Blazing with gold were the waters, and there stood the
    Caesar Augustus,

High on the poop with his chieftains to lead the Italians to
battle;
There midst the spirits of gods and Penates he stood, and
his temples
Burst into flames at each side, his father's star shone on
his forehead.
Yonder Agrippa departs, by winds and the gods too well-
favored,
Leading the squadron to war; and see on the brow of the
hero,
Glittering, a sign of his combats at sea, the crown etched
with ship-prows.
Here, with barbarian might, and laden with all sorts of
armor,
Full of his triumph, Antonius brings from Aurora's red
beaches
Tribes out of Egypt, the men of the east from as far off
as Bactra,
All in his train; and there follows—oh horror—his consort
from Egypt."

The Caesar was silent, as though continuing to listen. It was
some time before he said: "Tomorrow is my birthday."

"A blessed day for the world, the blessed day for the Roman
Empire. May the gods give you eternal youth and preserve
you."

"I can reciprocate with the same wish for you, my friend,
since you will celebrate your fifty-first birthday in exactly three
weeks, and therefore you are my senior by only seven years.
I only wish I had found you more fit to travel, I have to leave
very soon in order to be in Rome tomorrow, at least for the
evening celebration, and I should have liked to take you with
me."

"This is farewell, Octavian, and you know it."

A somewhat demurring gesture was the answer: "Farewell,
yes, for at most three weeks; you will be in Rome for your
birthday at the latest, but it would have been pleasanter if you

could have read the Aeneid aloud for mine, much pleasanter than the state celebrations to which I am committed. I have ordered great games to take place again the day after tomorrow."

The Caesar had come to take his farewell, yet it was more important for him to take the Aeneid with him, and he wanted to hide both intentions behind a wall of words; even Caesar lived in the midst of unreality, and the light—was the sun so far along its course?—had become paler; "Your life is one of duty, Caesar, but the love that awaits you in Rome is your compensation."

Caesar's habitually so reticent glance became quite candid: "Livia is waiting for me, and it will do me good to see my friends again."

"Happy you, to love your wife—" floated hither from a soft nowhere in the voice of Plotia.

"And to have you missing from our circle during just these very days, Virgil, will be very painful for all of us."

He who truly loves a woman is able to be a friend and a help to others, and no doubt this was also true of Augustus: "He is a happy man, Octavian, who has the solicitude of your friendship."

"Friendship makes one happy, my Virgil."

Again this was said so frankly and warmly that one could almost hope that the design upon the manuscripts had been abandoned: "I am grateful to you, Octavian."

"That is both too much and too little, Virgil, for friendship does not consist of gratitude."

"As you have always taken the role of giver there is no other response left for your friends than that of gratitude."

"The gods have granted me the grace of being able to be useful to my friends, but their grace in letting me find friends was even greater."

"These are all the more in duty bound to be grateful to you."

"You are obliged simply to make some return on your own terms, and such you have tendered, generously and more than generously, by your existence and through your works—, why have you changed your mind, why speak of an empty gratitude which is apparently not inclined to acknowledge any obligations?"

"My mind is unchanged, oh, Caesar, even though I cannot admit that my accomplishments have ever offered a sufficient return."

"It is true that you have always been too modest, Virgil, though not a person of false modesty; it is clear to me that you are intentionally minimizing your gifts so that you can withdraw them behind our backs."

Now it had been uttered, oh, now it had been uttered—, unerringly and stubbornly Caesar was pursuing his goal and nothing would hinder him from appropriating the manuscripts: "Octavian, let me keep the poem!"

"Yes, Virgil, that's it . . . Lucius Varius and Plotius Tucca have informed me of your terrifying plan, and I did not want to believe it any more than they did . . . are you actually planning to destroy your work?"

Silence spread over the room, a severe silence, pale and finely-contoured, that centered itself in the thoughtfully stern face of the Caesar. Something was lamenting very softly from a nowhere and this also was as fine-drawn as the crease between the eyes of Augustus, their glance resting upon him.

"You say nothing," said the Caesar, "and this probably means that you actually wish to take back your gift—, consider, Virgil, it is the Aeneid! your friends are greatly pained, and I, as you know, reckon myself one of them."

Plotia's gentle plaint became more audible; thinly strung together, the words came without stress: "Destroy the poem, let me have your destiny; we have need to love each other."

To destroy the poem, to love Plotia, to be a friend to his friends; strangely convincing, temptation followed upon temptation, and yet it was not Plotia who was allowed to participate in it: "Oh, Augustus, it is being done for the sake of our friendship; do not press me."

310

"Friendship?—, you act as though we, your friends, were unworthy to keep your gift."

Caesar's lips, barely moving, guided speech and reply, although he had the power and no doubt also the will simply to have the manuscripts taken away, and Plotia was silenced, as if awaiting the outcome of the conversation: unshatterable, stubborn, fixed, and stern in its shape was the moment that rose up and encompassed them, and though all that occurred at this moment took place in conformity to the will of Augustus, he too was included in its order.

"Oh Augustus, it is rather I, or my poem, that is not worthy of my friends: yet do not again accuse me of false modesty; I realize that it is a great poem, though little compared to the Homeric cantos."

"Since you admit so much, you cannot deny that your plan of destruction is criminal."

"That which happens by the command of the gods cannot be criminal."

"You are evasive, Virgil; when one is in the wrong he takes refuge in the will of the gods; I for my part have never yet heard of them ordering the destruction of public property."

"It is an honor to me, oh, Caesar, that you exalt my work to the level of public property, but I make bold to say that I wrote it not only for the reader but primarily for myself, that this innermost necessity brought it to pass, that it is my work and that, therefore, I must and may dispose of it as I deem necessary, just as it has been determined for me by the gods."

"Can I, on my side, set Egypt free? Can I strip Germania of troops? Can I surrender the frontiers to the Parthians? Or renounce the Peace of Rome? Are these things permitted me? No, they are not; and even though I were given the order by the gods, I should not dare obey it, even though it is my peace, my work, and I have fought for it . . ."

The comparison was lame, because the victories had been those of Caesar and all the Roman people, backed by their legions, whereas he had finished his poem by himself; but it did not matter whether the comparison was contradictory or not, the mere presence of Caesar made it free of contradiction and incontrovertible.

"Your work will be measured by standards relevant to the state, mine by those of artistic perfection."

Artistic perfection, that gracious compulsion of work which permitted of no choice and reached beyond all that was human and earthly.

"I fail to see the difference; even the work of art has to serve the needs of the people and, in so doing, of the state . . . the state itself is a work of art in the hands of one who has to build it up."

A certain aggrieved weariness became noticeable, making Caesar's manner which with all his worldliness was always very reserved, even more so; dissertations on works of art were not important to him, and it was a little unwise to stress the point: "Even though the state may be considered as a work of art, it is one which has to remain in movement, allowing for greater perfection; poetry, on the other hand, must be in seclusion, reposing to a certain extent in itself, and until it has reached its consummation its creator is not free to take his hand away from it; he is compelled to alter, to strike out the inadequate, he is charged to do this, he must do it even at the risk of ruining his entire work; there is but one standard, and that is the aim of the work; one can judge what may remain and what must be destroyed only if one knows at what the work is aiming; this goal is the one concern, not the work which has been done, and not the artist . . ."

Impatiently Augustus cut short this discourse: "Nobody will begrudge the artist the improvement of inadequacies or even the elimination of them, but nobody will believe you when you declare your entire work to be inadequate . . ."

"It is inadequate."

"Listen, Virgil, you have long since renounced your right to such a verdict. More than ten years ago you revealed to me the plan of your Aeneid, and you may recall with what intense pleasure we, who were able to share in it, agreed with you and your project. During the ensuing years you read the work aloud to us, bit by bit, and when you became discouraged by the magnitude of your project and the power of your design—and yet how often this happened—then you gained new strength from our admiration, or rather from the admiration of the whole Roman populace; consider, that already substantial portions of the work are generally known, that the Roman people are aware of the existence of the poem, a poem that glorifies them to an extent never yet achieved, and that they are entitled, absolutely entitled, to be given the entire work. It is no longer your work, it is the work of all of us, indeed in one sense we have all labored at it, and finally it is the creation of the Roman people and their greatness."

The light became more livid; one might almost imagine an eclipse of the sun to be in progress.

"It was a weakness in me to show unfinished work, the groping vanity of the artist. But it was also my fondness for you, Octavian, which made me do it."

There was a familiar twinkle in Caesar's eye; it was boyish, almost crafty: "Incomplete? is that how you speak of your work, unfinished, eh? So you could have done it better, or should have?"

"It is just as you say."

"A while ago I had to be ashamed of my poor memory, now let me redeem my honor . . . I shall let you hear a few of your own verses."

Small and friendly, malicious, yet very boyishly came the wish that Caesar might fail again, although at the same time— oh, the vanity of the poet—a praise-avid curiosity asserted itself immodestly: "Which verses, Octavian?"

And beating time with lifted finger, accompanied by a soft tapping of his sandal, the ruler of Rome, the sovereign of the world, recited the lines:

"Others I doubt not will hammer the flexible bronze to soft
    features;

Skilfully draw from the marble a latent and livelier
  resemblance;
Plead with a craftier tongue, each his cause; in tracing the
  sky-way,
Measure with rods, thus truly foretelling the course of the
  planets.
Thou, though, O, Roman, consider as thy task the ruling
  of nations,
This be thine art: to found and to foster a law that is
  peaceful,
Sparing the vanquished and vanquishing any who dare to
  oppose thee."

The time-beating finger remained uplifted as though pointing out the lesson that was to be drawn from the verses, and
to be heeded: "Well, Virgil, are you caught in your own net?"

This was, of course, an allusion, a very transparent allusion,
to the insignificance of the pure work of art, which was negligible compared to the real concerns of Rome, but it was too
gratuitous; one need not go into that: "Yes, Augustus, that is
how it goes, you have rendered the verses with absolute fidelity;
those are the words of Anchises."

"Is that any reason for their not being yours also?"

"I have nothing to say against them."

"They are flawless."

"And even if they were, they do not constitute the entire
poem."

"That is irrelevant. Just the same I do not know by what
shortcomings the rest of the poem could be considered marred;
you yourself admit that the Roman spirit is above small deficiencies of form and there can be no question of anything
else . . . your poem emanates the spirit of Rome, is not at
all artificial, and that is the important thing . . . , indeed, your
poem is the very spirit of Rome, and it is magnificent."

What intimations had Augustus of the real inadequacies?
what did he know of the deep incongruity which stamps all life,
the arts before all? how could he judge of artificiality? what

did he really understand of such matters? and even though he called the poem magnificent, thus flattering the author—alas, that no one is able to resist this sort of praise—, the praise was impaired because a person who fails to take note of its evident deficiencies cannot understand the poem's hidden grandeur! "The imperfections, Augustus, go deeper than anyone suspects."

Caesar paid no attention to this interruption: "You have interpreted Rome and therefore your work belongs to the Roman people and the Roman state which you serve, even as we all must serve it . . . , only what is unfinished remains our possession, perhaps also the failures and those deeds which were unsuccessful; but what has actually been accomplished belongs to everyone, and to the whole world."

"Caesar, my work remains undone, terrifyingly undone, and nobody wants to believe me in this!"

Again the familiar intimate twinkle appeared in the reserved countenance, this time with a touch of superiority: "All of us are acquainted with your fits of doubt and despondency, and it is understandable that you are more subject to them now that you are confined to bed by illness; but you want to make a sly use of them for your own hidden purposes, and these still seem dark, to me at least . . ."

"This is not the sort of despondency you think it is and from which, it is true, you have rescued me often enough, Octavian; it is no depression over the unmastered or unmasterable . . . no, I am surveying my life and I perceive all that remains undone in it."

"To this you must resign yourself . . . in the life and work of every man lurks some undone remnant; this is the lot that we all must bear." It was said sadly.

"Your work will continue to fulfill itself; it will be carried on by your followers just as you wish it to be, but for me there is no successor."

"I would entrust my succession to Agrippa . . . but he is too old; otherwise he would be the best one." And apparently seized by a sudden worry, Caesar stood and went to the window as if he could gain solace by scanning the far reaches of the landscape.

Men relieve one another, their mortal bodies follow, one after the other; perception alone flows on as an entity, flowing into an uttermost distance and into an inexpressible encounter.

"Agrippa will arrive soon," said Augustus, looking down toward the street which Agrippa was bound to take.

Marcus Vipsanius Agrippa with his morosely intelligent soldier's face, his simple frame, ponderous with power; it rose up in a sudden awareness that was prompted by some voice, perhaps that of the slave, suggesting that the consuming quality of this life dedicated to force would soon consume itself, snuffed out prior to that of Augustus. However, the latter certainly wished to hear something else: "You yourself are young, Octavian, and you have sons, perhaps even some yet unborn; your line will endure."

A weary gesture was the response.

Then all became calm and silent. Augustus stood there at the window, narrow and quite slender, a mortal with a mortal body divided into members, wrapped in a toga, thus he stood there against the light from the window, a narrow human back, covered in the draped folds of a toga, and suddenly one no longer noticed whether a front view existed, even less if there was a countenance, graced with the power to see and therefore radiant, least of all whither its glances strayed. Was it not Alexis who had stood there not long since on the selfsame spot? But yes, it had been Alexis, childishly slim and with an almost touching beauty, almost like a son, the son whose future fate and unfolding he had intended to take upon himself, nursing him not only like a father, no, also as a mother nurses her child, but whom, in spite of this, he had formed with parental strength after his own image: he had stood there with averted face as if he still resented this misguidance and this fateful hold upon him, but still he had been dreaming out into the dreaming landscape, into the flower-woven dream-sun, into the

316

laurel-scented dream-peace, and for him, the beautiful boy, the fauns, inebriate of the fields, intoxicated by the lute, had danced their measures; for him the landscape, moved to its very core by the dance, had opened out, even the oaks keeping time by the mighty swaying of their leafy tops; all this transpired for the boy, the whole creation unto its final borders moving in the dance of desire, the invisible had become visible, the averted had turned into view, woven into one great aspect by virtue of an incessant in-and-outflowing desire which was full of recognition, enveloping the seen as well as the unseen and unseeable in its trembling flow, so that in this wise it might be moulded to a recognizable shape: ah, indeed, enveloped in perceptive desire, himself desiring, Alexis had stood there, and since he had become moulded into shape everything surrounding him took shape also, becoming a recognizable unity, so that mid-day and evening might flow together simply as a single manifestation of light; however, nothing of all this was now to be seen; even the ranging mountains of the night had faded away to emptiness, absorbed by the emptiness of the surrounding landscape which was only a mutely sparse tangle of lines, almost severe in its sharpness, engraved into the declining, brownish, nebular light of the sun's growing eclipse; alas, duller and duller became the colors of the blossoms, Caesar's purple toga turned a black-violet in this light which was as dry as scorched paper, but it was utterly severed, without relevance or counter-view, cut off because of the stubborn one-sidedness that emanated from the narrow figure over there near the window, cut off by severity, by obduracy, by sharpness, sheerly unreal despite its palpable, superficial efficacy, and even the humane, ah, even the human relationship seemed to be subjected to the one-sidedness of a secretive, free-flowing surface that covered nothing; for strangely unsensual, strangely desireless, a curious, sober, almost disapproving attachment was stretching across to the lean figure which stood there motionless, was a bond with it, a bond irrelevant and strange in that it could not be dissolved. Nothing stirred any more, even the twittering of the birds had died away in the darkened shadows, alas, the dream would never return. For all that, Plotia, bending down from the dream to such immediate nearness that one could almost feel her breathing, whispered as though in secret promise: "I recognize you in the unsung future, you are not bound to anything that has been; return to me, my beloved"—, thus she whispered as if she were whispering into the gentle exhilaration of the dream-peace, too fine to be heard, out into the palpable world that had become heavy and dim, whispering thus into a benumbed world and then dying off into speechlessness as if the task were too great for her waning strength. The silence lasted for a long time, unmoved the man at the window peered out, he who ruled the world in the name of the gods, he, the meagre-mortal vessel of divinity, peered unmoved into the landscape of roofs and lines becoming more and more shadowy; all remained quiet and peaceful, but it was no longer the peace of the dream, the buoyancy of which had previously surrounded him, it was the stern and inflexible peace of Augustus, and only the scent of the laurel lingered, pervading the room with dreams now as before, lingered as a reminder of the delicate flower-like animation, although the laurel, almost affected by the inflexibility, standing now as it stood then, served as a boundary.

Augustus turned around impulsively with an unusually vehement gesture: "Stick to the point, Virgil, . . . why is it that you want to destroy the Aeneid?"

This came as such a surprise that for a moment he did not know what to answer.

"You have talked of inadequacies; I grant them to you although I do not believe in them, but there are no artistic inadequacies that Virgil should be unable to cope with . . . that was only quibbling."

"I have not achieved my goals . . . I have not reached them."

"This is another explanation that means nothing to me . . . what goal is it that you seek?"

This was said quite sharply and directly; Augustus had again come nearer the bed, he seemed like a stern, questioning father, and the intimidation that he inspired was strange in the extreme, not only because of the actual difference in their ages, but still more because everyone who knew Augustus had to be, and was, far too familiar with this habitual sort of cross-questioning to regard it as frightening. Perhaps the intimidation lay in the unavoidable justness of the question; he who does not know how to answer is intimidated; where did his goals lie? they were not to be found, they had evaporated under the palpable weight of the moment! "Alas, where are they? Oh, Plotia, oh, sibylline voice, which goals?!"

And Plotia said, and it sounded like recollection: "I bear your destiny; in my knowledge lies your goal."

Again Augustus—and this was something he liked to do in a cross-examination if he was trying to gain a certain point—changed his tone and shifted to the winning amiability which was so much his: "There are many aims, Virgil; I myself have a goodly number of them, and among them your friendship is truly not to be reckoned as least, indeed, it will yet be part of my future fame that I was the friend of Virgil . . . but now confess to me what dreadful goal is that which lures you on, permitting you to harbor such an inconceivable resolution . . ."

The fever was mounting again, he could feel it between his hot fingers, the ring hurt; nevertheless he must answer: "My aims? . . . knowledge . . . truth . . . the end of all searching . . . perception . . ."

"And this is the goal you believe you have not attained?"

"No one has attained it."

"Well . . . as you confute yourself, it is inconceivable that you continue to have qualms; . . . mortals are not meant to achieve everything."

"But I have never even taken the first step toward perception, nor once made an attempt to take the first step . . . it is incongruous, everything has been incongruous."

"What do you mean? you do not even believe that yourself; no more of that." The voice of Augustus had become annoyed; he was displeased.

"It is true."

"My Virgil . . ."

"Yes, Octavian . . ."

The lamp swung softly, although there was not a breath of air stirring, the silver chains tinkled softly: Was an earthquake coming along with the eclipse? He felt no fear; like a lightly swaying bark was his body, like a bark making ready to sail, and from the shore Augustus reached a friendly hand, while outside the mirror-like sea, smooth and unruffled, reflected the livid light in its unbroken surface as it moved up and down.

And Augustus, also giving no heed to the earthquake, said pleasantly: "Listen Virgil, listen to me as your friend and also as a connoisseur of your work: your poem is filled with the most exalted knowledge; Rome is proclaimed in it throughout, and you comprehend Rome, comprehending it in its gods, its warriors, as well as in its peasants, you encompass its glory and its piety, you encompass the whole extent of Rome and the time of Rome as far back as its powerful Trojan ancestors, for you have retained everything . . . isn't this perception enough, even for you?"

"Retained, retained . . . yes, . . . yes, I thought to hold fast to everything, everything that was happening, everything that had happened, and that was why nothing could succeed."

"You have succeeded, my Virgil."

"I was impatient for perception . . . and that is why I wanted to write down everything . . . for this, alas, is what poetry is, the craving for truth; this is its desire and it is unable to penetrate beyond it . . ."

"I agree with you, Virgil, that poetry is just this, it encompasses all of life, and therefore it is divine."

Caesar did not comprehend, no one grasped the truth, no one knew that the divinity of beauty was only a sham-divinity, the shadow cast by the coming of the gods.

"There is no need of poetry, oh, Caesar, to understand life . . . Sallust and Livy are more competent with regard to the extent and time of Rome, as you call it, than are my songs, and though I may be a peasant, or rather I might have been one, a work such as the admirable Varro's is far more valuable for the understanding of agriculture than my Georgics . . . how insignificant are we poets compared with them! I have no wish to disparage any of my colleagues, but nothing is achieved by mere glorification, least of all for perception."

"Everyone contributes his share to the store of knowledge, every creation does this, and mine likewise; but the greatness of poetic perception, and therefore also your greatness, Virgil, lies in being able to grasp all of life—as I said before—in a single survey, in a single work, in a single glance."

Writing down, writing down everything that happened within and without, and yet it had led to nothing: "Ah, Augustus, I too once thought this, just this, to be the perceptive task of the poet . . . and so my work became a search for perception, without becoming, without really being perception . . ."

"Then I must ask you again, Virgil, toward which goal have you been striving with your poetry since it seems it was not toward an understanding of life."

"The understanding of death."—It was like a re-found, a re-recognized, a homecoming enlightenment and had been said quickly as if springing from a state of illumination.

A pause ensued; the soft seismic swaying of existence kept on, although Caesar still did not heed it, seeming to be far more struck by what he had just heard, and it took quite a while before he answered: "Death is a part of life, he who under-stands life, understands death as well."

Was this true? it sounded like truth, and still it was not true, or rather it was no longer true: "There has never been a moment of my life, Octavian, that I did not wish to hold onto, but also not one in which I did not feel that I wanted to die."

Caesar's perplexity was struggling back to pleasantness: "It is just your good fortune, Virgil, that your wish to die has so far come to nothing; this time also it has only sufficed to make you ill. With the help of the gods, your will to live will prove itself the stronger."

"Yes, . . . yes, certainly I cling to life, yes, I have to admit it; I am insatiable for life just because of my great hunger for death . . . yet I know nothing of death . . ."

"Death has no meaning; it is futile even to talk of it."

"You have seen a great deal of death, Octavian; perhaps that is why you know more about life than most people."

"Possibly I was shown just a little too much of death, because, really, my friend, life means as little as death; life leads to death and both amount to nothing."

Had this not been so casually and wearily said, it would have been astonishing, because it was quite in contradiction to Augustus' general views; but spoken thus it was surely not meant to be taken seriously: "This does not quite fit in with the teachings of the Stoics, whose disciple you have often called yourself."

"If the obligation to be good continues to hold, it will somehow be able to be brought into conformity with Stoicism. But actually that is hardly important for us, and certainly not very essential."

Augustus seated himself, and again with a somewhat tired and not altogether heroic gesture. For a short time he closed his eyes, his hands sought support and found it on the wreathed candelabrum, his fingers, playing about, rubbed a laurel-leaf into tatters. And when he opened his eyes again his glance was languid and a bit empty.

Oh, this also one should retain and be able to set down, one ought to write it down just like all else that had flowed past throughout these many years without having been written down, like all other human traits that now were scarcely a memory, an indistinct multitude of heads and face-shapes, peasant-faces, city-faces, all of them hairy and covered with skin, wrinkled and smooth and often quite mottled, an indistinct multitude of figures that had been drifting past, slinking past; an eternally

322

invariable, multifarious circle of men to which even Augustus, the earthly vessel of divinity, irrefutably belonged, he quite as forgotten as this whole impenetrable, innumerable, undepictable multitude of living creatures, just as unremembered as any of them, as unnoted as the basic carnality that was inherent in them all, feeding and sleeping, filled with fluids and semi-solids, unrecollected the bony frame under the fleshy covering, the erected framework of bone that helped them to move, unrecollected the human being, oh, the human being in whose smile divinity dwelt in spite of everything, this smile in which man divinely recognized the fellow-man, the fellow-soul—the essence of human compatability, the birthplace of human language: the smile. Nothing of all this had been retained, and in its stead a moderately successful imitation of the Homeric model had been erected, an empty nothing filled with gods and heroes of an Homeric cast, compared to whose unreality even the weariness of the grandson who sat here was still an indication of strength: for even the weariest smile flickering in Caesar's countenance was still divine, whereas in the poem the hero of Actium possessed neither a countenance nor a smile, he possessed nothing but his armor and a helmet; the poem was without truth, his hero, Aeneas, was far from reality, and also the grandson of Aeneas as therein depicted; it was a poem lacking any depth of perception, incapable of it because light and shadow are sundered by perception only for the sake of form—, the poem remained leaden and shadowless. However, a voice was speaking and it was not that of Plotia, but a stranger's, no, oddly enough it was the voice of the slave, who had no business to be here, and the voice was saying: "You need no longer retain anything."—"Why is it you who counsels me, why not Plotia?" And now it was really Plotia who answered with the same airy gentleness as before: "Obey him, it is not for you to write down things any more." In this way it became binding, although he surmised that possibly Plotia herself was afraid of being reckoned among the forgotten, and that was her reason for reinforcing the slave's advice with her own; yet it was nonetheless binding. Yet, why this binding command? why? For even now, yes, even now, he might succeed in catching up with his neglected task so that the poem could still be saved, and even though it was in a manner of speaking the last moment, already too late for further effort, one must succeed if only one could retain this very moment, this unique moment of the here and now, perpetuating the palpability of the surrounding existence, the stony permanence of the walls, the floors, the houses, the town, all so firmly grounded yet afloat and flowing off into immobility, if one could take note of the seismic swaying over which one rode as if in a boat on a mirror-smooth surface, reflected in the light of noon now gone leaden; oh, if one could perpetuate it, retaining the earthly weariness beneath the surface of the hard, yet gentle, Caesarly countenance, actually retaining just a tiny fragment of the conversation which like an invisible chain had reached from one to the other, retaining this give and take between two creatures who had arisen from the dank multitude, incomprehensible their communion, as incomprehensible as the divinely streaming glance of their meeting eyes; oh, if one could hold fast to this, if one were permitted to do so, if this could actually be accomplished, it would be like a first and final shedding of light, a real perception of life. Would this come to pass? "Whatever you may yet accomplish on this earth will no longer satisfy you," said the slave, and this was so comprehensible that it seemed unnecessary for Plotia to confirm it: for though the perceptive spirit should penetrate existence ever so profoundly, though he even dissect the primal elements, separating the passive from the active, earth and water on one side, fire and air on the other, though he should dissect it into ever so many of its living parts, even groping into the secret of the atomic vortex, and though, going further, he might uncover the motives of men, these creatures subdivided into members, though he might scrutinize fragment after fragment of this divine life, the self-betraying actions, the self-betraying speech, though he might strip all this down to its deep and final nakedness, peeling off the flesh, blowing out the very marrow

324

of the bones, pulverizing the thoughts, so that nothing remained save the winnowed, the divinely contrite, the incomprehensible ego, though the perceiving spirit might accomplish all this, exploring it step by step, retaining it and able to describe it, no further step would have been taken; perception remained a thing of this world, bound to terrestrial things, it was still only a perception of life and not the perception of death; the flashes of truth were joined to one another in an endless chain, casting light on fragment after fragment of the nocturnal chaos of the beginning, a chain as endless as life itself and just as meaningless, so long as the light of undying death did not deliver to all of them, who know and are known by death, the simple truth of their existence: the unity of the creation. For the perception of life, earthily bound to the earth, never possessed the power to lift itself above the thing known and to endow it with unity, the unity of an enduring meaning, a meaning by which life was and is maintained as creation, eternally to be remembered as such.

For only he who through his knowledge of death became conscious of the infinite was able to retain the creation, to retain the single part within the whole creation and the whole creation in every single part. For the part could not be retained by itself; it could be retained only in its connotations, only through its lawful context, and it was the infinite which bore all the connotations within existence, bearing the law, bearing the form of the law, and precisely for this reason bearing faith itself; the infinite forever hidden, but for all that the soul of man.

Augustus sat there as before, he was rubbing a laurel leaf between his fingers and seemed to wait for some agreement or at least for an answer.

"Oh, Augustus, you spoke of what is essential . . . you would not be you, should you not realize that neither life nor death can or may be considered as nothing, or if you failed to realize that just the reverse of what it pleased you to say is applicable to perception . . . in truth, only he who is able to perceive death is also able to perceive life . . ."

A somewhat absent smile indicated an indifferent, casual assent: "It may be . . ."

"But surely, that is how it is, and life's immeasurable meaning can come only from the fullness of meaning revealed by death."

"So that is what you mean by the goal of your poetry, that is where you have placed it."

"Insofar as my performance was really poetry, this was its goal, for it is the goal of all genuine poetry; were this not so, were it not so utterly compelling to grope one's way toward death, and to do so with every thought, with each act of the imagination, were not this enormous compulsion always at hand, this compulsion to draw nearer to death, there would have been no tragic poets, no Aeschylus."

"The people may have other ideas about the ends of poetry. They look for the beauty and wisdom to be found in it."

"These are adjuncts, effortless and even cheap; the people think it is for these they are searching, and yet they sense what lies beneath them, the real end which is essential, because it is the goal of life itself."

"And this goal you have not attained?"

"I have not attained it."

Stroking his brow and hair, as though just waking and trying to collect his thoughts, Augustus said: "I am familiar with the Aeneid and for that reason you ought not to misrepresent it; the poem contains every metamorphosis of death, you have pursued death into the shadows of the underworld."

Never, never was this man to be persuaded that the sacrifice of the poem was an unavoidable necessity; he had not even once noticed the darkening of the sun and the Poseidonian heaving of the ground, he had no intimation of the calamitous conflagration of the earth which had been in evidence and continued to be, he divined nothing of the coming overthrow of the creation, and never would he admit that sacrifices—and not only that of the Aeneid—must be consummated, so that the sun and stars should not halt in their day and night courses, and that no darkening should ensue, so that the creation might endure and death be transformed to rebirth, the creation resurrected.

Aeneas pursued death to the shadows of the underworld and returned thence with empty hands, himself an empty symbol, without salvation, without truth, without the truth of reality; oh, his undertaking was no less futile than that of Orpheus, although he had not descended like the latter for the sake of the beloved, but for the sake of the ancestor who had established the law—; the force to send him deeper had been lacking and now it was necessary to consummate the sacrifice; it was necessary that he himself reach the nothingness along with his poem, in order that death appear and shatter the empty metaphor: "I have only hemmed in death by metaphor, Augustus, but death is craftier than the symbols of poetry, and knows how to escape them . . . metaphor is not the same as perception, metaphor follows perception though sometimes it precedes it, rather like an inadmissible and incomplete forecast brought into being by words alone, in which case metaphor becomes nothing but a dark screen standing in front of truth and concealing it instead of shining out from its midst."

"I deem the metaphor proper to all art, even that of Aeschylus; all art is symbolic . . . is that not true, Virgil?"

Surely this was a sound argument: "We have no other means by which to express ourselves. All that art has is the metaphor . . ."

"And death eludes the metaphor, or so you said."

"Of course . . . all language is just metaphor, all art of any kind, and even the deed is a metaphor . . . a metaphor of perception, or that is how it should be, what it strives to be . . ."

"Good, then that goes for me as well as for Aeschylus"— Augustus smiled—"we agreed on this, ruling is a kind of art, it is the art of the Romans."

It was not easy to keep pace with the quick-witted slyness of Augustus; it was easier to comprehend the fact that he was sitting here at the bedside than to comprehend the things he said, and if they concerned the Roman state, the work of state which he had created and over which he ruled with such skill—where was it? finely-drawn, it was being built up outside there in the landscape, between landscapes, within men, between men, barriers there as here, correlation here as there, invisible and yet present, and it cost some effort to project oneself into all these spaces in order to find it: "Your work, Augustus . . . indeed, it is a metaphor . . . the state is yours . . . and it is the symbol of the Roman spirit."

"And in the profusion of all these symbols, in the profusion of all the metaphors that round out our life, are just those you have created so bad that they must be destroyed? Is it only you who have not reached your aim by their means? For myself, I ask that what I have done shall remain . . . in this too I want to be like Aeschylus, who most assuredly did not destroy his work . . . do you want to be the sole exception? or is it that you have still not garnered enough glory and wish to add the title, Herostratus, to your name?"

The Caesar was greedy for glory, he kept on speaking of glory, he pursued glory, and therefore one could not tell him that glory, even if it outlasted death, could never annul death, that the path of glory was an earthly one, worldly and without perception, a false-path, one of reversion, of intoxication, a path of evil: "Glory is the gift of the gods, but it is not the goal of poetry; only minor poets regard it as a goal."

"At any rate you are not one of these . . . why, then, are just your symbols not to remain in existence? Your poem is comparable to the Homeric songs, and it would be absurd to maintain that your images have less power than those of Aeschylus. You, on the contrary, have been contending that you have only clothed perception instead of revealing it, and that in this way you have failed to get nearer it; were this the case, one should have to make a similar statement in regard to Aeschylus."

It was impatience, no doubt, which drove Caesar to such insistent, almost oppressive perseverance, and nevertheless the

328

sharp, clear answer he expected could not be given him: "In the case of Aeschylus the perception preceded the poetry from the very beginning, whereas I meant to search for it through my poetry . . . his symbols, born from an innermost perception, are one in inner and outer meaning, and thus, like all great examples of the Greek art, they have passed into permanence; born from perception they have become a lasting truth."

"The same homage is due to you."

"Not to me . . . images which have been derived simply from externals are earthbound, and consequently they must of necessity be weaker than a primary vision of reality; they are too weak for the task of perception, unfit for the task of truth, they are not the same in their inner and outer meanings, but merely superficial . . . and the same thing holds true of me."

"Virgil,"—and now Caesar with his sudden and again very youthful movement was again on his feet—, "Virgil, you are beginning to repeat yourself, even though with new and very persuasive words. I can only gather from this that I have also repeated myself, that the mysterious objections to your work which you express, at one time saying you have missed your aim, at another calling it lack of perception, have to do basically only with formal shortcomings; no one except you will be able to feel your images as inconclusive, and the doubts that every artist harbors about the success of his work, in your case have almost degenerated to a mania; perhaps because you are the greatest of poets."

"That doesn't hit the mark, Augustus."

"No, what then?"

"You are in a hurry and I must not detain you with long-winded perorations, and such would be necessary to persuade you that the Aeneid, while possessing all the qualities of a finished work of art, is nevertheless unjustified."

"You are playing with words, Virgil, and if ever you moved only upon the surface of things, it is now."

"Oh, Octavian, do believe me." Caesar stood there, at an

incalculable distance; it seemed as if no word could reach him any more.

"Long-winded arguments are always meant to conceal something, especially when, as is evidently the case now, they try to establish themselves on time-wasting philological arrangements."

"This is no philology, Octavian."

"But it sounds like a commentary that you should add to the Aeneid."

"Yes, it might be so described."

"A commentary by Virgil on his own work! Who would want to miss that! But we can't exclude Maecenas from this, Maecenas who takes such a passionate interest in questions of this sort. Well, you shall give us a lecture on the subject in Rome and we shall order a slave-scribe for the occasion to take down your words . . ."

"In Rome . . . ?" —How strange it was that he was never to see Rome again! Still, where was Rome? Where was he himself? And this place where he was lying? Was it Brundisium? where were the streets of the town? did they not run off into a nowhere, tangled together, this way and that, tangled into those of Rome and Athens, and into the streets of all the other cities of the globe? doors, windows, walls, all were changing their locations, everything was involved in this series of permutations, outlook and way-out led into uncertainty, and the whole world seemed to be a single gigantic landscape, a single town-scape, devoid of shadows, the four points of the heavens lost; no one knew where the east lay.

"Certainly, my Virgil, Rome is expecting us," said the Caesar, "it is getting time for me to depart, and in a few days you are sure to follow me, and in the best of health . . . but until then, you are not to worry either about your recovery or your manuscript; no harm must come either to you or to it, we need you both, and it will not be hard for you to make me the promise if I ask it of you: to be responsible for yourself and your manuscript . . . where have you put it? very likely in there?" And, as if incidentally, but actually with deliberate intention, Caesar, making ready to depart, pointed to the manuscript-chest.

Oh, it was extortion, sheer extortion, leaving no other choice open to him: "I am to promise you that?"

"There are many portions of the poem of which no copies have yet been made . . . I have to save you as well as the poem from the rash step you think of taking. It may be that you will convince me and all of us of the rightness of your intentions; here too 'make haste slowly' is valid, and first of all we want to hear your commentary. If you think you cannot keep your promise, I am perfectly willing to take it into my own custody so that you will find it on your arrival."

"Octavian . . . I cannot part with the manuscript."

"It is painful to me, my Virgil, to see you disturbed in this fashion and yet I can assure you it is just a mania of yours; there is no reason for this perturbation, and there is no reason to justify the destruction of your work . . ." Now he was standing close to the bed, gentle in his encouragement.

"Oh, Octavian . . . I am dying, and I know nothing of death."

Plotia spoke from afar: "The knowledge of death is closed to one who goes alone, it is open only to two who travel united."

The hand of Augustus stretched out and grasped his: "These are gloomy and unnecessary thoughts, my Virgil."

"I am not able to chase them away, nor am I allowed to do so."

"There is still time enough before you, in which, with the help of the gods, your knowledge of death may increase."

Much there was that fluctuated about them, many things changing into each other; five-fingered, the hand of Augustus lay in his own, one self inclined to the other self, and yet it was not Plotia's hand; at death's portal there was no such thing as a long or short time, the last moment, if it brought illumination, should endure longer than all of the preceding life, and Plotia said: "Our union is timeless, timeless our knowledge."

"The poem . . ."

"Well, my Virgil . . ." it was still the same gentle tone of encouragement.

"The poem . . . I must attain perception . . . the poem stands there like an obstruction to perception; it is in my way."

Augustus drew back his hand, his manner became hard: "That is of no consequence."

Nothing remained of the hand's pressure; only the ring could be felt again, and the high fever, and Caesar's words were becoming distantly unintelligible: "You yourself spoke of the essential, Augustus . . . and it is death . . . it is the perception of death . . ."

"All of this is unessential compared with duty . . . even though in your poetry you may have surrounded death with metaphors, as you said before . . ."

Everything was fluttering away, one must try to call it back once more: "Yes . . . to retain life in order to find in it the resemblance to death . . ."

"So be it, yes, so be it . . . no one asks the soldier in battle whether or not he has already found the symbol of his death or some knowledge of it; if the arrow strikes, he must die; regardless of knowing or not knowing he has to fulfill his duty . . . may the gods protect you from death, my Virgil, and they will do so, but what I cannot tolerate is your playing it out like the trick move in a game, for there is not the least connection between death, your knowledge or ignorance of it, and your duty toward humanity . . . if you do not change your mind you really force me to protect your work against yourself."

Caesar was impatient and angry; the thing hung on a thread: "Perception is not just a matter for the individual, oh, Caesar; perception is the concern of humanity."

His own perception had reached no depth, it had remained arrested on the surface, on the stony surface over which the mob clambered; his perception of death did not extend beyond the earth-realm, knowing only the stony earth-bound skeleton of death and therefore knowing nothing, a poor state of helplessness, and incapable of all help. But one could not come with such reflections to Caesar; he would have refused them in advance, with fury and without understanding.

"And so you want to help humanity by destroying your work? are you in earnest? what has become of your duty, what of your consciousness of duty? I beg you, I earnestly beg you, not to start fencing with words again."

Something in the eyes of the angry man betrayed that his irritation was not very serious, that his benevolence was to be counted on now as before; if one succeeded in arousing it all could still be saved: "I am not evading my duty and responsibility, Augustus, and that you know; but I shall be able really to serve humanity and the state only when I first shall have pressed on to my own perception, for what is at stake is the task of helpfulness, and just this is impossible to perform without perception."

As a matter of fact Caesar's anger was subsiding: "Then for the moment we are going to preserve the Aeneid as a kind of provisional perception . . . if not quite as a symbol of death, since you deny it this attribute, yet still as a symbol of the Roman spirit and the Roman people whose property it is, all the more, since despite what you call the unrightness of your symbols, by means of them you have been the best helper of your people, and will always remain so."

"Caesar, your work, your state, is the definitive symbol of the Roman spirit, the Aeneid is not; and that is why your work will remain, whereas the Aeneid is doomed to be forgotten and to be destroyed."

"Has not the world room enough for two valid symbols side by side? Has it not? And even though the Roman state may be a more valid one—I admit that much—is it not more than ever your reasonable duty and service to fit your own work into this more comprehensive one?" — Again wrath became apparent in the strained countenance, now it was a wrathful mistrust—, "but you, however, give it no heed, your pride is not satisfied that art, that is to say your art, be assigned to a

333

role of service in the state, and rather than suffer it to serve, you would destroy art in its entirety . . ."

"Octavian, do you know me as an arrogant man?"

"Until now, no; but you seem to have become one."

"Well, Augustus, I know that man must be humble, and I hope I have learned how to be; but as for art, there I am arrogant, if you want to call it that. As a man I acknowledge every duty, for man alone is the bearer of duty, but I know that one cannot impose any duty on art, neither duties of state nor any other kind; for by so doing one makes art into a sham-art, and should the duties of men go beyond the realm of art, as they do today, men have no other choice than to drop art, though not from disrespect . . . just our time demands the utmost modesty from the individual, and in utter modesty, aye, more, in self-effacement, he has to serve as one of the state's many nameless servants, either as a soldier or in some other capacity, but not with works of poetry which have no enduring substance and are nothing but arrogant examples of a sham-art, compelled to be sham-art as long as they presume to serve the state by virtue of their superfluous existence . . ."

"Aeschylus built his superfluous poetic work into the state-craft of Cleisthenes, and by so doing outlasted the Athenian state. I only wish that my work may endure as long as the Aeneid."

This was said quite frankly, only one had to discount the sweetness with which Caesar was wont to trick out his friendships.

"What was true of Aeschylus, Caesar, does not apply to me; those were different times."

"Indubitably, Virgil, five hundred years have elapsed since then and no one will deny this, but that is all it amounts to."

"You spoke of duties, Augustus, and certainly the duty of helpfulness remains unchanged throughout time, but the means of helping change, and today art is not the means . . . duty remains, but the object of duty is altered by time . . . only in a realm without duty is time without significance."

334

"Art is not dependent upon time, and those five hundred years are a sign of the poem's eternal merit."

"They testify to the eternal effect of a genuine art-work but not further, Octavian . . . Aeschylus was able to produce works valid for eternity because by means of them he fulfilled the task of his era, and therefore his art was the equivalent of perception . . . the time determines the direction in which the task lies, and he who goes contrary to it must collapse . . . an art that is consummated outside these limits, evading the real task, is neither perception nor help—in short it is not art and cannot endure."

Caesar paced back and forth over the swaying floor; with every dip of the wave he turned round so that he was always walking up-hill; but now he must have reached the top for he stopped—yet maybe he did feel the Poseidonian movement—and held on to the candelabrum: "Again you speak of things that cannot be proved."

"In art we are everywhere imitating the Greek forms, in the conduct of the state you are forging a new path. You are fulfilling the task of your time, not I."

"That proves nothing; the newness of my path may be argued, but eternal form remains eternal form."

"Aye, Augustus, you simply do not want to see, you do not want it to be true, that the poetical task no longer exists."

"No longer exists? No longer? You sound as though we were standing at the end of something . . ."

"Perhaps it would be better to say, not yet! for we may assume that a time for artistic tasks will dawn again."

"No longer and not yet,"—Caesar, much dismayed, was weighing these words—"and between them yawns an empty space."

Yes, no longer and not yet; that is how it sounded, how it had to sound, lost in nothingness, the lost, passed-away inter-realm of dream—, but had it not sounded different before, similar, but different? and already the boy's voice was announcing itself, the voice of the boy, Lysanias. And it said: "Not quite here, but yet at hand"; that is how it had sounded and how it would sound.

"The empty spaces between the epochs"—Caesar's words continued, as if they were speaking by themselves, as if they were unfolding without his help, as if the words and not Caesar were soliloquizing: "the empty nothingness that yawns wide, the nothingness for which everything comes too late and too early, the empty abyss of nothingness beneath time and the aeons, which time tries to bridge over cautiously and on a hairline by stringing moment to moment in order to conceal the stony petrified crevice, oh, the abyss of unformed time must not become visible, must not be allowed to gape open; no interruption must occur, time must flow on incessantly, each moment simultaneously enclosing the end and the beginning, the moulded time . . ."

Was it actually Caesar who had said this? Or had the words of his most secret fear been speaking? Time flowed past mysteriously, the empty, shoreless stream that led to death, always cut into by the present, the present that constantly and elusively was being washed away: "We stand between two epochs, Augustus; so call it expectancy, not emptiness."

"What happens between epochs is empty and without chronology, impervious to moulding, impervious to poetry; you yourself have maintained this, and at the same time, almost in the same breath, you have praised this time of ours, this time that I have been at pains to mould, as the culmination of human existence as well as of poetry, as a veritable time of burgeoning. I remind you of your Eclogue in which you declared that the glory of the ages had been fulfilled by our time."

"Fulfillment on the way is almost fulfillment. The tension lies in waiting, in expecting the fulfillment, and we who are blessed to wait and to watch embody that tension; we also ready for fulfillment."

Waiting between epochs while yet between the shores of time, these invisible shores; waiting between the unattainable shores of life! We stand on the bridge that is spanned between

336

invisibility and invisibility, and nevertheless we are caught in the stream; Plotia had longed to check the mysteriously incessant flow, and perhaps she would have been able to check it, perhaps she would still do it. Oh, Plotia—

Caesar shook his head: "Fulfillment implies form, not merely tension."

"Behind us, oh, Augustus, lies the drop into amorphousness, the drop into nothingness; you are the bridge-builder, you have lifted this time out of its depths of rottenness."

Now the recipient of this praise nodded in approval: "Yes, it is true, the times had become completely rotten."

"They were marked by loss of perception, loss of the gods, death was their password; for decades the barest, bloodiest, most raw lust for power was in the saddle, it was civil war, and devastation followed upon devastation."

"Yes, that is how it was; but I have re-established order."

"And so it follows that this order, which is your work, has become the one commensurate approximation of the Roman spirit . . . we had to drain the goblet of horror to its dregs before you came and saved us; the times were sunk deeply in wretchedness, more filled with death than ever before, and now that you have silenced the powers of evil, it must not be allowed to have been done in vain, oh, it must not have been in vain, the new truth must arise radiantly from the blackest falsehoods, from the wildest raging of death the redemption will come to pass, the annulment of death . . ."

"And from this do you conclude that art now has no task to fulfill?"

"Yes, that is my opinion."

"Then remember that the war between Sparta and Athens dragged out much longer than our civil war, that it was broken off only by a still greater calamity, and that nevertheless this could not be warded off, for just in the time of Aeschylus the Attic country was laid waste by the Persian hordes, just then the poet's homeland, Eleusis, and Athens were burnt to ashes; and remind yourself that at that very time, disregarding such horror, the poet achieved his first dramatic triumph, as if announcing through it the early transcendence of Greece . . . nothing has changed since then. At that time poetry existed and it can exist today as well."

"I know that death on earth is not to be exterminated, I know that man is separated from men by the struggle for power wherever people dwell side by side."

"Pray keep on remembering that this happened before Salamis and Plataea . . ."

"I do remember."

"Actium, which you lauded, became our Salamis, and Alexandria our Plataea . . . led by the same Olympian gods, and in their name, we have again been victorious over the dark powers of the East, even while paradoxically forfeiting the gods and still aping Greece."

The powers of the East—discredited through worldliness, ground down until they should have purged themselves in order to ascend from the stream of time, redeemed and redeeming—, the star outbeaming all stars, the heaven without eclipse.

"Nothing was changed. The great example remained and all art was divinely unfolded as Athens, led by the wisdom of one admirable man, was presented with the peace of Pericles."

"It is as you say, Augustus."

"Annulment of death? There is no such thing; glory alone outlasts death on earth; and even the glory that comes from war and terror, which certainly I do not wish to be mine; I strive for the glory of peace."

Glory and again glory, whether it be the ruler or the literati, the only concern was with glory, with the absurd annulment of death by glory; yes, they lived for the sake of glory, it was all that was essential to them, their sole value, and the only comfort to be derived from it, curious though it might be, was that all which was done under its auspices could come to be more essential than glory itself.

"Peace is the earthly symbol of an unearthly annulment of death; you have bidden the earthly death and devastation to

338

cease, you have set your peaceful order in its place."

"Is that the way you think of it?"—Augustus, who had been emphasizing his speech by pompous gestures as if addressing the Senate, stopped short for a moment and let his hand fall to the back of the chair near him—, "so that is how you think of it? you mean to say that the Athenians rose up against Pericles because in spite of peace he did not ward off death? because the plague broke into the symbol? you mean to say that the people desire such a symbol?"

"The people are acquainted with symbols."

Augustus disregarded this: "Well, we haven't had the plague so far, and it has been granted me to rule unarmed over a united Italy. And if the gods will only continue to send me their help, this peace will hold not only within our country but will spread, it will be completed, and very soon at that, by the pacification of the whole empire up to its borders."

"The gods will not deny you their help, Caesar."

Caesar became thoughtfully silent, and then his smile appeared, almost boyish, sly: "Then, just for the sake of the gods and in homage to them, my state must not be lacking in art; the peace that I am establishing is in need of art as much as that of Pericles, who gloriously crowned his by building the sky-towering Acropolis."

So Caesar had succeeded in returning to the Aeneid: "Really, Augustus, you are not making life easy for me, really you have . . . " Life? should it not rightly be called death? something gray opened up somewhere, elusive, bridgeless, halted in itself; mysteriously time was flowing on, and yet reluctant to flow longer—

"What do you want to say, my Virgil?"

The voice of the slave took over the answer: "There is no time left and none to talk about art; art can do nothing any more, it is not able to annul time. For my power is greater." And almost at once Plotia added: "Exempt from every transmutation of its mutable course, time will come to stand still in the immutable as you let yourself be converted to me . . . in holding me you will hold time." She had spoken silently and coolly from out the coolness of time, invisibly her hand emerged from the invisible, feather-light, to clasp his.

Caesar glanced toward him, glancing at the seal-ring, no, it was upon Plotia's invisible finger, delicate as a breeze, that he looked, and still he smiled: "Is the time that I formed by virtue of my peace worth less than that of Pericles? It is my peace, it is our time, our era of peace."

"Ah, Augustus, you really do not make it easy for one, and besides the Acropolis substantiates you as do the buildings with which you have adorned Rome . . ."

"A city of bricks was transformed to one of marble."

"Certainly, Augustus, architecture flourishes, for much like the state which you have made, it has established a similitude of order in space, and is itself order."

"So you concede something to the art of building."

"Order is latent in the mutability of time, in all things terrestrial, oh, Augustus, and whenever one has been successful in creating order on earth, the real order of human existence, there follows also the wish to erect a counterpart of that order in space . . . there is the Acropolis, there are the Pyramids . . . as well as the Temple of Jerusalem . . . bearing witness to the striving for the annulment of death by order within space . . ."

"Well, now . . . this is indeed a concession, even though it is the first I have been able to wrest from you, and it is even a delightful and important one, especially in regard to Vitruvius, who otherwise might ask me at any time to demolish his buildings . . . but, seriously, I should not like to weigh architecture against poetry, nor Vitruvius against Virgil, even though Vitruvius, if I am not in error, dedicated his book on architecture to me, while Virgil intends to take back from me the Aeneid; however, and in all seriousness, I want you to consider that the concession which you have decided to make to architecture implies a similar one for all other arts as well; the wholeness of art is not to be torn to tatters, the right to exist which you grant architecture necessarily brings poetry in its train, and as proof let me go further and say, with no reference to Pericles, that there has never yet been a flourishing civil community which at the same time did not help every single art, including poetry, to a full unfolding."

"Of course, Augustus, art is an exalted unity."

"Your all too swift agreement is dangerous, Virgil; the more quickly it comes the more likely are you to follow it with a denial."

"On the contrary, I extend the agreement . . . whether art expresses itself in this way or that, in all its branches, yes, even in architecture and music, it serves perception everywhere and gives it expression; the unity of perception and that of art are sisters, and one like the other stems from Apollo."

"Which perception? that of life or of death?"

"Both; each existing only by virtue of the other, and therefore united in a single shape."

"So, yet again this perception of death?! Admit that you are heading toward a retraction of your concession."

"Nowhere, however, is this perceptive duty of art so compelling, so binding, and so sharply prescribed, as in the realm of poetry; for poetry connotes speech and speech connotes perception."

"And the conclusion to all this?"

"You honored me before by citing the words of Anchises . . ."

"I do honor you, Virgil, though a little less so for the moment, because you are again trying to slip in a distraction; that quotation was only to make you aware that you yourself have thought such zeal over small inadequacies of form, and the playful tendency to polish your verses to a flawless perfection, incommensurate with a serious purpose and with the dignity of Roman art . . ."

"I agree, Caesar, the ravishing game of constant polishing and correcting . . ." How alluring it would be to be able to start it all over again: yonder stood the chest with all the cleanly written rolls of manuscript which one could have scanned line after line for grammar, metrics, melody, and for meaning, oh, how alluring, how very, how very alluring! But the slave spoke, now very near, yes, from the very edge of the bed: "Do not dream of doing this; disgust would overcome you if you did." And Plotia's hands had again been wafted away.

Caesar, however, standing amidst the silent-lurid emanations of the sun's eclipse said: "Those were the words of Anchises, and it profits you nothing to characterize as ravishing this sort of playing about with art; you can neither dispose of your own pronouncement nor make it weaker."

"The words of Anchises..." Anchises was among the shades, only words remained; not only the light was leaden, nay, shadowy and leaden were the times as well.

"The words of Anchises are your own, Virgil."

"Now that they press up from the realm of shades, I realize that I meant far more by them..."

"In what way?"

"You have given them too weak an interpretation by far, Augustus."

"If my interpretation is too feeble, then you must rectify it; I deplore my feebleness." Caesar had let go of the candelabrum, he supported himself by both hands against the back of the chair, the sharp crease of anger appeared once more between his eyes, and his foot beat upon the tiled floor in quick hard taps; so had it always been, the slightest contradiction sufficed to provoke this sort of sudden and unexpected irritation.

"Your interpretation is not feeble, it merely leaves room for some intensification ... many things that at first are mere presentiments gain their inner meaning only by time."

"Divulge it."

"Compared to the art of ruling, compared to the art of state-regulation and peace, compared to this essentially Roman art and task, all other arts, not only the alas so ravishing one of artistic dalliance, are pale, aye, even this exaltation, bearing and born of felicity, pales also, this exaltation in which eternal

342

art is embodied and was bound to be embodied, insofar as it presumes to be more than a mere sham-artistic, decorative adornment of life . . . aye, even it pales in comparison; this is what I intended to express with the words of Anchises, and it was this very opinion that I repeated when I estimated your work, your state, your expression of the Roman spirit, as the sole validity, superior to the influence of every art . . ."

"And I have refuted you . . . art lasts longer, negated by no time whatever."

Mysteriously, an empty stream, time flowed on.

"Permit me, Augustus, to draw the most provoking conclusion yet about the things into which you are enquiring."

"Speak up."

"Just the greatest art, that one most conscious of its task of perception, is also aware of the loss of perception and the godlessness through which we have passed; it is constantly confronted by the terror of death's devastations . . ."

"I have already reminded you of the Persian wars."

". . . and therefore there are indications in this art that, along with the new order created by you, a new perception must also come to flower, growing up from the depth of our lost perception, growing as high as our loss was deep, for else the new order would be purposeless, the salvation that we have received at your hands would have been in vain . . ."

"Is that all?"—the Caesar seemed quite satisfied—, "is this your final conclusion?"

"Yes . . . the more that any art, and before all the art of poetry, shows signs of conscious perception, the clearer one sees that it does not suffice for the new perception, despite all its power of metaphor; it harbors reflections of the coming perception, for this very reason it must withdraw before the stronger metaphor."

"Very well, I have no objections to the new perception, but it seems to me you are making too great a display of art's perceptive task for your own purposes . . ."

"It is the very core of the artistic spirit."

"And you deliberately overlook the fact that the oneness of spirit extends even beyond art . . ."

"The counterpart of the new perception lies outside of art; that is the essential thing about it."

"You deliberately overlook the fact that every era that is fruitful for the state is also fruitful for perception, you deliberately overlook the fact that in Athens' greatest period philosophy flowered along with the other arts, and you overlook it, must overlook it, because philosophy fits as little into the queer picture of your unattainable or death-annulling goal of perception as all the other genuinely true facts of life; may you come to see how wrong you are, while I, for the moment, shall rely on philosophy to find the new perception that you demand."

"Philosophy is no longer capable of finding it"—the words came of their own accord, it had not been necessary to think them through or think them over, they had come, so to speak, immediately from eyes to tongue, for back of them—was it here in the palely-shadowed room? was it outside in the pallid pen-sketched landscape? no, still further, much further off, strangely lifted out of time,—the city of Athens was arising, the longed-for city, the city of Plato, the city in which shelter had been denied him, denied by fate, fate which still hung over the city like a cloud of death, hovering there, yet casting no shadow by its leaden light.

"No longer capable . . . ," repeated Augustus, "no longer, no longer! First art, and now philosophy, Virgil! is this another case of too late and too early, and does this 'no-longer' apply to philosophy as well?"

There in the spaceless space of the words the city was arising, it was nothing but a shadowless word-picture, it was just empty twaddle, unstable and evanescent, it was without a symbol, and having forfeited its symbol it had lost its substance; truly, fate had been kind to him when it had not allowed him to remain there: "Time is unrelenting, Augustus, thinking has reached its limits."

"Men are able to carry thinking as far as the gods, and should be content with this."

"Yes, the human mind is limitless, but when it touches on immensity it is thrown back . . . becoming devoid of perception . . . then death's devastations begin on earth, then come the great floods, the din of arms, the disgraceful rivers of gushing blood . . ."

"Philosophy has nothing in common with civil war."

"The time is ripe . . . now the plow must again be turned round in the furrow."

"With every day time becomes ripe for something or other."

"Without a common ground of perception, without common principles, there is no understanding, no elucidation, no proof, no persuasion; the commonly shared vision of the infinite is the basis of all communication, and without it even the simplest things are incommunicable."

"Well, after all, Virgil, you manage to convey a number of things to me, even now, so our fundamental agreement cannot be said to be in such a bad way; for me, anyway, it suffices."

Ah, Caesar was right—, what sense was there in all this? how did it concern Caesar? it was taxing but nevertheless like a compulsion, happening, it seemed, for the fate of the Aeneid: "Philosophy is a science, it is the truth of the mind, it must be able to prove the need for a ground of perception, and percept . . ." —somewhere there was laughter, mute, and boisterous, and complacent.

Was it the slave? or was it the demons, announcing their return by laughter?

"Why do you not continue, Virgil?"

Again Athens appeared, again there was the singular disappointment that Athens had proved to be. Where did the laughter come from? from Athens?

"The ground of perception precedes all things intellectual,

all philosophy . . . it is the first assumption linking inner and outer things simultaneously . . . you really did bring me back from Athens, Octavian? Isn't that true?"

Mother-of-pearl, the shell of heaven opened over the Adriatic Sea, the boat rocked, the white horses of Poseidon showed their heads, there was laughing and noise in the guest-room, at the stern in the graying light a slave musician began to sing in the voice of a boy.

"It was salutary and proper for me to bring you back from Athens, my Virgil . . . or do you imply that now philosophy is exempted from its task, since you were not left uncared-for in the city of philosophers?"

Caesar should rightly be on the other boat and not here: "Philosophy has come to have no base for its perception, it having dropped away . . . deep, deep down into the ocean . . . and having been obliged to grow upward to touch infinity, philosophy's roots do not reach down far enough, even though they also grow into infinity . . . else I should not have traveled home with you, Octavian . . . where the roots fail to grip, there is the shadowless void . . . the ground of perception has dropped away, and there is a great deal of empty chatter on the ship; perhaps you do not notice it as acutely as I, because you have not become clear-sighted through seasickness . . . formerly philosophy still had a ground of perception on which it could establish itself . . . like you, I refused to see it had been lost . . . I went to Athens, yes, I really went there . . . but today that creatively potent ground in which philosophy was once rooted is definitely lost . . . thinking has become unmasculine."

Indeed, so it was, and it was no laughing matter. Even the god, who recognized the nothingness and wished for it, dared not laugh. And actually, the unwarrantable laughter was silenced. In its stead Plotia spoke: "Acquiescence is silent, needing no confirmation. Return home into the open shell of silence." And this was so soothing to hear that even the progress of the ship slowed down and the water became very smooth, the down-beat of the rowers was now scarcely noticeable, there

346

was scarcely any creaking in the yards, only now and then the clink of a chain was to be heard.

Leaning against the mast of the candelabrum, one hand grasping among the laurel-sails, stood Caesar, the loving husband, traveling as a male to his mate, to Livia who awaited him, and since time traveled with the ship, there was no calculating how long it took before he began to speak; at last he said: "If philosophy has lost its ground of perception its present duty is to regain it."

Caesar must really have been on the other ship, or was still there, since he had not heard that the roots did not reach down far enough; perhaps it was possible to make him comprehend it by other words: "The wood of elms is not suitable for shipmasts; firm and yet flexible, these must stand and grow . . ."

"Do you feel tired, Virgil? would you like to have the doctor again?" Octavian had pushed the chair hastily aside and was bending over the couch, his face very near.

The face was very near, almost as near as Plotia's face had been. And then the fog tore apart: "I feel quite well, Octavian, . . . very well in fact . . . but it may be that I was dizzy for a moment . . ."

"Your words sounded rather obscure . . . though that happens often with you; if one reflects on them afterward they seem to have become wisdom."

"Wisdom? no, never . . . and now it seems to me that I was seeking a suitable example with which to answer you, without being able to find one . . . but you, and of that I am certain, were speaking of the perceptive ground of philosophy."

"That is correct, Virgil, and I feel relieved."

"And that philosophy was not in position to produce its own ground of perception . . ."

"That has not yet been made clear . . ." Augustus' mind was not entirely on the matter—, ". . . besides this question is of no importance to us, Virgil."

The seismic swaying still persisted but everything else was clear and without strangeness, clear and natural was the fading

347

of the softly pen-sketched landscape outside, clear and natural the elm-candelabrum; and the bed was no longer a large ship, instead it had shrunk clearly and naturally to a simple skiff in which it was comfortable to journey onward; only Caesar's presence, despite his utterly familiar behavior, seemed neither wholly clear nor natural, at least as long as he must continue these efforts to convince him, to bring him back to reality: "The intellect is incapable of creating its own assumptions, and consequently philosophy is also unable to do so; no one is so generatively efficient that he can make himself into his own ancestor,"—that laughter! had it not sprung a while back from his own throat, from his own breast? that is where he felt it now, and it was mysteriously painful—"forefather and fore-fore-father cannot be generated, nor can assumptions; nothing and nobody has ever possessed the Promethean power to surpass the limits proper to each, and no one will ever do so . . . Untrue!"

Untrue, untrue—, the word had been suggested, whispered out of a nowhere by the slave or by Plotia, he did not know which, more likely by Plotia, for it was she who spoke on: "Love constantly breaks through its own boundaries."—"Oh, yours too, Plotia, yours too?"—"It did and still does; in loving anything one transcends oneself."—"Oh, Plotia!" "Do you feel me? In loving you I feel you intensely."—"Plotia, I feel you near, I realize you."—"Yes, Virgil, yes."—and the borders of their bodies were interlocked, the boundaries of their souls were flowing one into the other, growing and overgrowing their limits, perceiving and perceived.

Astonished, Augustus questioned: "What is untrue, Virgil?"

"One can overstep one's own borders."

"That is pleasant for me to hear; so your concession still holds good?"

"Overstepping the boundaries . . ."

"Philosophy? poetry? what is overstepping the boundaries?"

"Wherever Plato succeeded in doing that, philosophy became poetry . . . and at its highest peak, poetry was capable of transporting across the boundaries . . ."

348

Though somewhat absent and hasty, a friendly affirmative nod was the response: "In any case your artistic modesty is great enough to question your own wisdom, but your artistic ambition wants to take account of it, at least for art as such . . ."

"It is not wisdom, Octavian . . . the wise man does not become a poet, at all events not a man with a calling for wisdom . . . no, it is a sort of divining love that is sometimes allowed to burst the boundaries . . ."

"I am satisfied that at least you feel yourself called to wisdom . . . and so we shall no longer debate the question of philosophy, rather, should it actually prove incapable of pressing on to its own assumptions, let us send it on toward poetry; and we shall challenge philosophy to draw its ground of perception from art, in whose beauty, as you have admitted, all wisdom is gathered."

"I should concede this to very few and indubitable works of art, and all of them are those of a very distant past."

"And your Aeneid, my Virgil?"

Again it was time which announced itself, mysteriously opposing the past to the present, mysterious in its effect, mysterious in its motive, fateful in both: "Once more I must disappoint you, Augustus, by repeating, stubbornly repeating, that the artist's power of metaphor is strictly conditioned by time, and no longer suffices for the new perception; the ground of perception may be divined from art, but its creation, its re-creation lies beyond the power of art."

"There is no such thing as a new creation; one can only recreate what has always existed independent of time, and therefore still exists, even though, as today, it may remain hidden for a period . . . man remains the same creature that he has always been, and no doubt his ground of perception, about which you are constantly speaking, remains the same also, so much the same that it may easily, and for your pleasure, precede all perception. Basically nothing changes, nothing can change, nothing has changed."

"Oh, Augustus, perceiving and perceived, the gods of yore surrounded the mortal."

"Do you refer to the time of Aeschylus?"

"Yes, to that time also."

"The gods have not vanished, and your reference is the best confirmation of what I have been maintaining, yes, my friend, that it is; just because the Olympians once reigned, undoubted and unopposed by man, just for this reason we have to return to the faith of the fathers, so that art and philosophy may find the same ground of perception which was that of our people and, consequently, is the only right one for us."

The constant necessity to speak and to answer was becoming too much of a strain: "The faith of the fathers . . . in those days there had been no fall into the loss of perception."

"That has been overcome."

"Certainly, but for that you had first to come; at that time, however, it was not first necessary to re-awaken faith, for it was still alive; it was one with human life, the inward and outward life together."

"It is no less alive now than it was then, and the gods pass through your poem in their most lively form, Virgil."

"They entered it from outside; I had to search further and further into the past for them."

"You traced them to their origin, to the source where they are fundamentally perceived, and in so doing you have once and for all presented the people with the reality of the gods, with the reality that is the truest perception of divinity; Virgil, your depictions are of the liveliest reality, they are the reality of your people."

This had a seductive and gratifying sound, and withal it was Caesar's honest conviction. Nevertheless these were only hollow words; perhaps because now Caesar was contending scarcely at all for the Aeneid but primarily for his own work; but perhaps for that very reason he would relinquish the Aeneid: "No, Caesar, I have already said that mine are only superficial images."

350

"They do not satisfy you because you demand from them a perception of, and an annulment of death, which no one on earth is capable of giving . . . you have even placed my work under this exaggerated challenge."

"My images are inadequate because . . ."

"You are stuck . . . Virgil, you know you are wrong."

"Time, Augustus . . . in a mysterious way we are captives of time, it flows on mysteriously . . . an empty stream . . . a stream on the surface, and we know neither its course nor its depth . . . and yet it must close to a ring."

"How can you maintain that art does not lie in the trend of this era and its task? Which priestly inspector of vitals has divulged this to you? No, Virgil, this is not right; there is nothing mysterious in time, and nothing which needs a liver-gazer."

What was the mystery which lay in time? emptily the empty stream flowed toward death, and if its goal were removed, then stream and time disappeared. Why would time be annulled if death were? Things fitted together dreamily and it was a dream-voice which spoke: "The serpent-ring of time . . . the heavenly viscera."

"And you call this the basis of your perception? it is that of a haruspex . . . What are you hiding, Virgil?"

"We are captives of time, all of us; and this is even true of perception."

Caesar was noticeably disquieted: "You make time responsible for the actions of men, you make it responsible even for the loss of perception . . . by this you release men, and naturally yourself also, from every responsibility; that is dangerous . . . I prefer to make men responsible for the time they live in."

What was time? was it, after all, a stream that flowed on without hindrance? was it not rather in spurting movement, sometimes like the almost still water of a lake, yes, even of a swamp lying under the two-toned cloud of dusk, and again like a roaring cataract throwing out a spray of seven-colored glittering spume, a flood that inundated everything and rushed on?

"Caesar, there is always scope enough for human responsibility; man performs his duty well or ill, and even though it be time that prescribes the sphere of his task, even though he may be unable to exert an influence upon it, his responsibility to his duty remains unchanged and independent of the modifications in the realm of the task: his duty is to duty."

"And I cannot admit that the course of duty is altered through time . . . man bears the responsibility for the duties and tasks which he has set as the goal of his actions; at all times he has to adjust these to the community and to the state, and when he fails to do so, then the time is formless. Man, however, has to shape time, and he shapes it within the state; this constitutes his highest duty."

Mystery of time, mystery of its emptiness; why was the human course of duty altered within it? Endlessly the Saturnian fields spread out over time, never changing throughout time, and the human soul was in bondage to time; but beyond the surface, in the depths of heaven and earth, lay perception, the goal of humanity.

"Perception continues to be a duty, it continues to be the divine task of men."

"And perception realizes itself in the state." Augustus glanced toward him in direct challenge, without losing his expression of apprehensive uneasiness.

What was time? what were the changes in the sphere of human duty which developed under its command? what was the variable element in time? mysteriously it evolved of itself—, what was it that with time closed to a circle?

Whither was the journey leading? the boat rocked: "The perceptive man . . . held into time . . ."

"No, Virgil, it is he who holds time in his hands."

Oh, it was perception itself which altered, often hesitating, often bogged down to a standstill, only to be hurled forward again like a cataract, the perception of existence extending over all that existed, the perception-web of the world that circumscribed men in what they could and must believe, the great web of perception in the flowing meshes of which men were caught and at which they must, despite this, work on unceasingly, so that it should come to be the web of the universe and not rend asunder: mysteriously united to existence, enlarged and transformed along with it, existence mysteriously transformed to perception itself—in this wise perception went forward, thus it must go forward for the sake of creation, for the sake of time, in which creation becomes reality, for the flow of time was nothing else than a change of perception.

"Man is held into creation and he holds creation in his hands . . . oh, Augustus, it is time and yet not time; time is shaped by man through perception."

"I will never admit time to be stronger than man . . ."

Stronger than time was fate, in which the final secret of time lay hidden. For fate's commandment to die was binding even on creation, even on the gods, yet constantly held in balance by its charge to be reborn, this charge on both the gods and men, not to allow the web of perception to be rent, constantly to reknot the thread, to preserve in such wise and forever, knowing and known, the creative work of the gods and the gods themselves; gods and men bound to each other by the pledge of truth.

"A change in perception connotes time and nothing else, Augustus, and he who brings about a renewal of perception shapes the further course of time."

Augustus ignored that: "And never will I admit that our times are less than those of Aeschylus, no, on the contrary, in many respects they are incomparably greater, and I may even assert that I have contributed something to them; in most matters we have outstripped the Greeks, and even so our knowledge is constantly on the increase . . ."

"Oh, Augustus, it seems we are speaking of opposites . . . superficial perception may be increasing, while the kernel of perception may be shrinking . . ."

"Then is my work nothing but a fleeting and surface metaphor, too?"—the solicitude of Augustus had become an unmistakably hurt protest—"is that what you are implying?"

Mystery of time! Saturnian mystery of perception! Mystery of fate's commands! Mystery of the pledge! Light and darkness, united in the two-toned dusk unfold of themselves to the seven colors of the earthly creation, but when the transformation in being will have reached to universal perception, having become unalterable by virtue of being whole, only then will time come to a standstill, not immobile, not like a lake, but like an all-embracing moment, an unending sea of light, lasting through all eternity, so that over the reality of its day of judgment and rebirth, the seven colors will be merged to final oneness, to the ivory shimmer of pristine daylight, compared to which every earthly light is leaden, every earthly reality shaded off to a suggestion, to a mere play of lines.

"Your work is carried by time, Caesar, fulfilling time's task, and it aims toward the fate-commanded renewal of perception in which creation with its divine attributes shall once again stand firm."

Disappointment was mixed with disdain in the gesture of rejection: "Merely to aim at perception is not the same thing as reaching it."

"Your work is peace."

"Ah, but if I am to believe you, it is only metaphorically that peace annuls death, and even when I shall close the door of the Janus temple, as I certainly hope to do in a very short time, to you it will be only a metaphor, and far from a real annulment of death."

"Rome is the emblem, Rome is the symbol which you have created, Caesar."

"Rome is the deed of our ancestors, Virgil, and the reality established by them extends very far beyond the merely symbolic."

"And Rome has come again to be your deed, Augustus, the Roman order in the Roman state."

"Yes, my emblematic state as you called it; yet the Roman state has to be more than perception's emblem, empty of content." The disdainful rejection had grown into outright repug-

354

nance; Caesar stood ready to depart, and it seemed as if he had forgotten the matter of the Aeneid.

"You have re-established order in earthly affairs, given it body, and it stands as your perception."

"Then why call it a metaphor, why do you adhere to this?"

Metaphor, perception, reality—, how could one ask that Caesar's pride be reconciled to the concept of metaphor, since he had never accepted the humility of perception? since he had never been willing to perceive the abyss? since for him reality was only that of the surface? But perception emerged out of the abyss, it was the humble emerging from the depths of contrition to a new humility, was the bringing home of reality from the nothingness into which it had necessarily been cast so that it might be born: perception, born out of darkness, born to return into metaphor, the rebirth of reality changed in the abyss, yet in itself unchangeable.

"You have recognized the divinely-lawful order in celestial things, and recognizing it again in the Roman spirit you have integrated them both, embodying them as an earthly entity in and through your work of state, giving them visible shape as the commensurate symbol of the Roman spirit, the commensurate symbol of a celestial order of perception."

"Why, the same thing can be said of the Aeneid."

"Never!"

"Never?"—Curiously this time the contradiction did not increase Augustus' anger, in fact he seemed to be somewhat mollified—, "Really! how is that?"

"The deed is the task of time; not the word, not art; time asks only for the perceptive deed."

"Then I ask you again: why only as a metaphor?"

Speaking was becoming a great strain, oh, and thinking even a greater one: "Oh, Augustus, to recognize the celestial in the terrestrial and by virtue of that recognition to bring it to earthly shape as a formed work or a formed word, or even as a formed deed, this is the essence of the true symbol; it stamps the primal image within and without, containing it and being contained by it, just as your state, filled by the Roman spirit, lies embedded in that very spirit; and born by the celestial which it represents, nay more, which has entered into it, the symbol itself comes to outlast time, growing as time endures, growing to death-annulling truth, of which it has been the symbol from the very beginning . . ."

"So that is what the genuine metaphor is like . . ."—Caesar seemed to consider this, although with the look of one who is unable to grasp something—"The symbol which has more than a superficial meaning . . ."

"Yes, the genuine metaphor, which is the lasting one, the genuine work of art, the genuine state . . . the enduring truth within the metaphor."

"I cannot test the validity of these conditions . . . they are very complicated."

Caesar did not have to verify anything. There was no use in checking upon what one did not grasp, one had merely to accept it, even though one were Caesar: "You have founded peace and order; on the ground prepared by your deed, every perceptive deed of the future will unfold to an annulment of death, and your work, already a symbol, is growing out to meet it . . . is that not enough for you, Caesar Augustus?"

At this Caesar smiled thoughtfully, meanwhile preparing to leave: "This is all very long-winded . . . doesn't it belong to the commentary that we wanted to keep for Maecenas?"

"Perhaps . . . I do not know . . . yes . . ."—Why did Caesar not go away, since he wished already to be gone? yes, all of this was extremely long-winded, extremely tiring, extremely strenuous, and really one should put it off to some future meeting with Maecenas, or perhaps altogether. Defer it for a long time. Softly the wall-fountain trickled, and its trickling echo was trickling everywhere, trickling deeply down toward the sea, trickling on to the nocturnal waves of the sea and turning into a wave itself, a white-crested wave in the darkness, it held a trickling conversation with the voice of Plotia which floated mutely inaudible above the trickling sound gleaming silverly

356

through the night, waiting for Caesar to be gone, waiting for the loneliness of the night. Was this the night? oh, how hard it was to open one's eyes again. Oh, to put off both day and night.

But notwithstanding his initial leavetaking, Caesar suddenly was no longer in a hurry; he seemed to be considering some other request and abruptly sat down again; he sat there like someone who meant neither to stay long nor to leave immediately, veering a little toward the edge of the chair, his arm hanging over the back, and after remaining silent for a while he said: "Possibly so . . . possibly all that you say is right . . . but one cannot live in a chaos of symbols."

"To live . . . ?" was this still the question? was there still a concern for life? round about was the soft and enticing trickling—, to live, oh, to live on, so that one would be able to die.

Who had to decide that? whose voice was the decisive one? Plotia's silence held.

But Augustus said: "Let us not forget that there is a reality, even though we are limited to metaphor in expressing it and giving it shape . . . we are alive . . . and that is reality, simple reality."

Life was to be grasped only in metaphor, and metaphor could express itself only in metaphor; the chain of metaphor was endless and death alone was without metaphor, death to which this chain reached, as though death, even though lying outside it, were its last link, and as though all metaphors had been shaped simply for the sake of death, in order to grasp its lack of metaphor despite all, aye, as if language could regain its native simplicity from death alone, as if there lay the birthplace of earth's simple language, the most earthly and yet the most divine of symbols: in all human language death smiled. And now Plotia spoke: "Reality is mute, and we shall live in its muteness; go forward into reality, I shall follow you."

"To go forward through the chain of metaphors, to move into increasing timelessness . . . metaphor turning to metaphor, which in turn becomes reality . . . dying without death . . ."

Now Caesar smiled: "Yes, that is a very circumstantial kind

of reality . . . are you serious in thinking that reality is subject to such involved conditions? I see scarcely any difference between them and those you have imposed on metaphor . . ."

Though Cæsar was sitting so near, his voice broke through from a strangely immeasurable distance, but not less strangely and from a distance still greater, if possible, came his own words although from an opposite direction: "The metaphor of reality and the reality of metaphor . . . oh, only at the very end does the one merge into the other . . ."

"I believe in a simpler reality, my Virgil; for instance, I believe in the homely and robust reality of our everyday life . . . yes, Virgil, in just the simple reality of everyday life."

"In every day's simple reality . . ." Even in their simplest meaning the words of men stemmed from death, but further than that, from the cavern of nothingness which gave birth to reality, they stemmed from the enormous cave behind the two-fold portal of death, they stemmed from immensity, and therefore the listener who received them was no longer himself; he had become another person, removed from himself because he participated in immensity.

"The simplicity of the fathers and forefathers, Virgil, the simplicity of your Aeneas; it was in the simplicity of their everyday life that they set up the Roman state . . ."

There were sun-eclipses in the sky, the lightlessness was lion-colored, the horses of Poseidon, trampling the waves, stamped on, and the lion of Phoebus was not to be seen—, had the heavenly span, forgetful of the divine taming, already broken free of the reins and gone back to the horse-herds of the waters? Oh, it was Lucifer rising, and washed by the waves of the ocean, he who was followed by Venus, chosen by her as the light-star, lifting his holy head eastward, his glances were likewise up-lifted, dawn was released by his glances—, had this been the reality of Aeneas? had he been permitted to leave earth's sim-plicity so far behind him? had he really pushed on so far? was this how he saw it? "Oh, Augustus, everything was simple reality to Homer . . . that was his perception."

"To be sure; you are merely confirming my statement. Whatever meant reality to our ancestors persists, and is hidden in every kind of art . . ."

"Oh, Augustus, the ground is shaking . . . nothing shook for Homer or his heroes . . . however, for Aeneas . . ."

"Are you speaking about reality or art?"

"About both."

"Well then, about both; so you must realize at last that Rome and your poem are one, and that Rome's plain reality is contained in your poem . . . nothing shakes in it, its reality is as well founded as the Italic soil . . ."

Even the moon's shining orb, even the sun's very fire, spirit was feeding them both, mind reached through all the world's members, uniting as into one body the whole of existence by essence—, perceiving and perceived, does the star travel eastward? "Oh, Augustus, all reality is but the growth of perception."

"Rome sprang from the perception of our forefathers: Rome was the perception of Aeneas, and there is no one who knows this better than yourself, Virgil."

It was above an earth in repose, not above states that the star would wander; however, of this Augustus wanted to know nothing. And yet it must not be held back in silence: "The ancestors planted the seed of perception when they created the Roman order . . ."

"I do not wish to hear again that the reality of Rome, the reality of what has been created and is yet to be created, has been merely a symbol . . . the reality of my work must be more than a mere metaphor . . ."

"Rome was founded in the likeness of perception; it carries truth in itself, evolving more and more into reality . . . there is no reality save that of growth and development."

"So the present counts for nothing?"

"Born from perception, the Roman state will grow beyond itself; its order will come to be the kingdom of perception."

"The Empire does not need to grow any further; with the

help of the gods we shall succeed in pushing the German frontiers as far as the Elbe, so as to establish the shortest possible line of defense between the Ocean and the Euxinian Sea, and the Empire having reached its natural limits, to safeguard it in the north from Britannia to Dacia . . ."

"Your domain, oh, Caesar, will come to be even greater . . ."

"It ought not to be greater; were it to be, the Italic progeny would not suffice to support Roman order and customs throughout the whole territory."

"The realm of reality which you are helping into existence will be more than an expansion of government over militarily protected territory."

"Verily, what has been accomplished counts for nothing with you, and since it counts for nothing you reduce it to a metaphor that has no claim on reality."

Breathing was wearisome, speaking was weariness, and wearisome the struggle against Caesar's increasing distrust and his sensitive assertiveness: "Swordless is the peace which you have founded within the empire, oh, Caesar, and it shall embrace the whole world without the aid of the sword."

"True . . ."—the explanation seemed to have been satisfactory—"indeed, it has been my care to ensure peace through treaties and not through the sword; however, the power of the sword must stand behind the treaties in order that they shall not be broken."

"In the kingdom of perception the sword will come to be superfluous."

Almost startled, Caesar looked up: "How will you protect yourself against broken treaties and perjury, how will you do this without a legion? The golden age has not yet arrived."

The golden age in which iron should be transmuted to gold again, the age of Saturn who was immune from observation in the changelessness of his interminable change—, but he who hearkened into the depths, both of heaven and of earth, surmised —possibly beyond the Saturnian realm—the future reunion of the human with the divine: "Only the true perception can uphold the pledge."

Augustus smiled: "That may be, but it will be better able to do so if supported at the same time by one or two legions."

"You no longer need troops for the inner peace of Italy."

"That is true, Virgil, and I have good reasons for not keeping garrisons here . . ."—a sort of a sly candor was discernible in Caesar's countenance, a twinkle in the eye, understandable for the friend alone—, "troops within range of the Senate and its agents seem to me a somewhat too solid reality."

"You are mistrustful of the Senate."

"Men do not change, either in their good or bad aspects, and the garrulous malice that wrought the downfall of Julius Caesar, blessed be his paternal name and memory, operates in the conclave of the Senate, just as it did twenty-five years ago; even were I to exert a still greater influence over the senatorial nominations, these gentlemen are to be relied upon only so long as they know that I can throw Gallic and Illyrian legions into Italy at any time, and I take care that they do know it."

"The people support your sovereignty, Augustus, not the Senate."

"That is so . . . and being the Tribune of the people is the most important of all my offices." Again the features disclosed a cunning candor, this time indicating that it was not for the sake of the people, but because of the right to veto the decisions of the Senate, that being the people's tribune was of such prime importance.

"You are the symbol of peace to the people and that is why they love you . . . the golden age has not come, yet it is promised by your peace."

"Peace? War?"—The cunning in Caesar's countenance was tinged with pain—"the people accept the one like the other . . . I was in conflict with Antonius, I formed an alliance with him, I destroyed him, and the people scarcely took any notice of these changes; they do not know what they really want, and we have

361

only to see to it that no other Antonius appears . . . the people cheer any victor; they love the victory, not the man."

"This may hold good for the huddled masses lured into cities, but not for the peasants; the peasant loves peace and him who brings peace. The peasants love you for the man you are, and peasants are the real people."

For a moment, for a heartbeat, oh, for a painful breathing-space, the sun's eclipse faded, the livid light and sketched land-scape, as well as the wavering stability, faded without actually fading out, as if to give place to the picture of the Mantuan plain, the mountain-shadowed region of fields whispering of childhood, spread out in sunshine, in rain, spread throughout all seasons and all stages of life.

As though there were no more need to hurry, Caesar settled back properly in the chair: "I cannot root out the cities from the surface of the earth, Virgil, on the contrary I have to erect cities because they are supporting points of the Roman order, as much today as ever before . . . we are a city-building people and first and foremost came the city of Rome . . ."

"Not as the city of merchants and money-lenders. Their golden age is coined and stamped."

"You are unjust; the merchant is the Roman soldier of peace, and if I want him to exist I have to tolerate banking . . . this is all part of the state's welfare."

"I am not unjust, I see the avaricious swarms in the streets, I perceive the impiety; the peasant is the only one who retains the piety of the Roman people, although he too is in danger of succumbing to the greed for money."

"Insofar as you are right, it is only an urgent reminder for us to take up our educational task without delay; we must see to it that the city masses become what they should be by virtue of their civil rights: a united Roman people."

"They will become so by virtue of the perception for which they are avid."

"They are even more avid for the circus . . . which certainly does not lessen our task, or its urgency."

"Yes, they hanker for games . . . the path of reversion . . ."

"Whose path?"

"Whoever is without perception must dull his sense of emptiness by intoxication, consequently also by the intoxication of victory, if only as a spectator."

"I have to reckon with established facts and I must not overlook anything that may be relevant to a unification of the masses. They are welded into a people by the sense of victory; feeling themselves victorious they are ready to band together for their country."

"The peasants do so for the sake of their country's peace," —oh, Mantuan meadows that lie spread out yonder—"the peasant always lives in that community which is called 'the people'; within it when he plows his fields, when he drives to market, on every one of his feast-days . . ."

"I have always made a point of promoting the peasantry; I have reduced their taxes, I have divided the vast areas of the crown estates for the benefit of small tenants, and regulated the terms of cultivation. However, our unpleasant experiences with the colonization of the veterans was an unmistakable sign of changed circumstances in our national economy . . . Rome has grown beyond its peasantry and we are more concerned with the corn of Egypt than with that of Italy and Sicily; we may no longer support ourselves exclusively on our peasantry, we may hope even less to bring our masses back to peasantry; in either case we should be condemning the state-economy and the state itself to destruction . . ."

"Yet the Roman freedom which you have taken under your protection was, and is supported by the peasants."

"Freedom? Certainly, certainly, I am responsible for the freedom of the Roman people; no one shall disturb it, neither Antonius nor any other. This is the task of the Roman state, and for this it must be made firm. By letting the people participate in the state's momentum, we give them the feeling of freedom for which men strive, since this aspiration is intrinsic to human nature and must be satisfied. The one and only place to shelter this feeling for freedom is in the commonwealth of the state: here it is accessible to everyone, even to the slave, and it is more than the freedom of the soil, of which you speak; it is the freedom of a divine order! Indeed, Virgil, that it is. All else is dream, without reality, nothing but a dream of the golden age, in which there was neither order nor duty. It must suffice for our pleasure to play at this dream-freedom during the Saturnalia. Were we to celebrate the Saturnalia the whole year round, the state could not exist. The Saturnalia are symbols but the state is the reality. I am not able, nor am I called upon, to usher in the golden age, but the age that I am called upon to prepare and that I am preparing shall be mine and that of my state."

Now the slave spoke: "Freedom inheres in us; the state is ludicrous and earthly."

However, Caesar gave no heed to this. He had risen, and strangely undisturbed, strangely motionless, yet seeming to be moved from within, and curiously exalted, he continued his speech: "Insofar as it is part of the state's welfare, even freedom must be a reality and dare not be a sham reality, for it too must be more than an empty symbol; all too often has it been reduced to one, and in particular by the Senate itself. By just such means the gentlemen in the purple togas succeeded in betraying the people again and again, and incited them to civil war! Miserable trickery! Certainly the doors of the Curial stood open, and everyone who wanted to could listen to the Senatorial sessions; but this was the only freedom granted to the people, the most insidious of all popular freedoms, the permission to listen while laws were being passed by the utterly unscrupulous, to suppress and to fleece them! Symbols or no symbols, institutions which are obsolete turn reality into a farce of reality, freedom to a farce of freedom, and provide the best soil for all kinds of criminality; that's the sort of thing I had to clear away. Aye, in the old peasant-state that you have in mind they were still possessed of sound judgment, there the citizens could survey matters of public concern, there a people's assembly could exercise its will. Today, however, we have to deal with four million Roman citizens, today we have before us blind, gigantic masses without judgment, and these follow anyone who is clever enough to wrap himself in the glittering and seductive mantle of freedom, trickily disposing its folds so as to conceal how it is patched and pieced together with scraps of meaningless and outworn form. That, and that only, is what freedom for the masses is like, and verily they know it themselves! They are aware of the profound insecurity in which they live, both of body and soul; they are aware of their lack of judgment; they know, without being fully conscious of it, that they are surrounded by a new sort of reality, which they are neither able to grasp nor direct; they know only that they are exposed to incalculable forces, forces of an unimaginable dimension, forces that they are often able to name as famine or pestilence, as a failure of crops or a barbaric invasion, but which are nevertheless the expression for them of the far greater threat that stands behind these things, deeper, more unaccountable, more inconceivable than these; assuredly the masses know something of the dangers of their freedom, they know it for a sham freedom whereby they are turned into a frightened, veering, leaderless herd. And just in view of this insecurity, in view of this inner and outer threat to which such masses of people are exposed, I repeat, and must repeat, that the only real freedom is that which is found in the Roman order, in the well-being for everybody, in short—in the state. No other freedom exists. The state that my idolized father, blessed be his memory, wished for, the state that I am at pains to build up as his legacy, this state in itself constitutes freedom, immortal and real; it represents freedom in the reality of the Roman spirit."

"The reality of the state you have created will be completed in the kingdom of the spirit."

"The kingdom of the spirit is already at hand; it is the state, the Roman state, the Roman Empire unto its last frontiers. State and spirit are one and the same."

The answer took shape from afar, even though shaped in his own mouth: "The kingdom is freedom . . . the kingdom of man and his humanity . . ."

"The kingdom of the Roman, Virgil! For the Hellenic freedom, the Hellenic spirit, has appeared again in Rome. No one has contributed more to it than you, yourself! Hellas was the promise, the Roman state is the fulfillment."

And the voice of the slave said: "Eternal will be the kingdom, without death."

Did Caesar take up the discussion anew? One could not decide this, for he spoke and yet did not speak. The words stood motionless in space as if they were Caesar's innermost thoughts: "The state must again provide the masses with that physical and mental security which they have lost, it has to guarantee them a lasting peace, it has to protect their gods, and it has to dispense freedom in accord with the needs of the common welfare. This, and only this, is the humanity of the state, perhaps the only possible humanity, in any case, certainly the best one, even though it often tends toward being quite inhuman, inconsiderate of the individual or separate group when the common welfare is at stake, for the sake of which the individual on his side should and must bow to the rights of the whole, the individual freedom to the collective freedom of Rome, the peace of the neighboring states to the Roman peace; verily, it is a hard humanity which the state has to offer, all the harder as the state, serving the commonwealth and, in so doing, personifying it, demands service in return from the individual, and his full subjugation to the power of the state, aye, going even further, it demands the right to requisition the life which has been protected by the state's power whenever that life is needed for the protection and safety of the community. A disciplined humanity is what the state strives for, and what we, along with the state, must also strive for, a humanity within the bounds of reality, controlled by discipline and devoid of coddling, subsumed in the law of reality, the hard reality of Rome through which Rome has become great . . ."

Oh, Mantuan landscape, landscape of childhood, the sweet landscape of childhood, the landscape of the fathers which could not be lost—nothing more of it could be seen outside; it had faded into immobility. Existence was motionless, motionless the one who stood there at the window, no longer Octavian, but a gentle and stern and strangely rigid picture, almost beyond anything human, while on every side the state expanded in far-reaching, spectral lines.

"Even though now you may still have to protect the boundaries of the state, oh, Caesar, the kingdom will be unbounded; even though now you still feel you must separate major rights from minor ones, justice will become indivisible, the community will be vulnerable in the individual, and the right of the individual will be protected by the community; and even though today you may still feel forced to mete out freedom so parsimoniously as to leave none to the slave and very little to the Roman, in order to guard the freedom of the whole, in the kingdom of perception the freedom of men will exist without restrictions, a freedom on which the all-embracing freedom of the world will be erected. For the kingdom of freedom into which your state will blossom, the kingdom of true reality, will not be a kingdom of popular crowds, not even a kingdom of the people, but rather a kingdom that is a community supported by men of awareness, supported by the individual human soul, by its dignity and freedom, upheld by its power to reflect the divine likeness."

"Ours, however, will be the perception," concluded the voice of the slave, "we shall find it in the utter humility of our extinction."

Augustus seemed to have heard nothing; unmoved, he continued: "The reality of Rome is earthly, its humanity is earthly, sober and mild for the submissive, sober and hard for those who seditiously attempt to disturb its order. It is not only in Italy that I have protected the peasant against dispossession, no, I have adhered to this principle throughout the whole empire; I have minimized the pressure of taxes in the provinces, I have restored to the people their rights and special privileges, I have put a stop to the mismanagement of the so-called Republican administration, which by calling itself Republican cast shame on the name of the Republic. My critics may reproach me by calling these achievements very sober ones, not at all brilliant. Well, with these sober achievements of mine I have brought the disreputable name of the Republic to honor again, and despite the ravages of civil war I have restored well-being to the whole empire. Sobriety is the splendor of Rome, and sober is Rome's humanity; this sobriety takes care of the community's well-being and it competes for nobody's favor, indeed it often seems to cut short the development toward a better humanity, or at least to postpone it till later. I have, to be sure, been active in ameliorating the lot of the slaves, but the welfare of the Empire demands slaves, and they have to accommodate themselves to this fact, disregarding the rights due to the oppressed for which they might clamor; truly it was most unwillingly and against all my desire for clemency, that I have had to accustom myself to limit by law their widespread emancipation, and should they rebel against this, should another Spartacus arise as their leader, like Crassus I should have to let thousands of them be slain on the cross, as much as a warning to the people as to divert them, and in order to make them, who are always ready for cruelty and fear, realize with fear and trembling, how impotent the individual is in comparison to the all-commanding state."

"No," said the slave, "no, we shall be resurrected in spirit. For every imprisonment is a new liberation for us."

Without granting him the slightest attention, the speech of the ruler continued: "Ourselves a part of the people, we are the property of the all-commanding state, we are owned by it with all that we are and have, and in belonging to the state we belong to the people; for just as the state personifies the people, so must the people personify the state, and if the state has unrestricted rights of ownership on us and our achievements, the same rights come in turn to the people. Be our achievement great or small, be it called the Aeneid or anything else, the people are entitled and duty-bound to exercise their rights of ownership; each of us is the slave of the people, the slave of immature and tyrannical children who resist any kind of guidance, but for all that are in need of it."

"This people calls you father, and it is the perception of a father that they expect from you, Augustus."

"The people are as uncertain as children, fearful and ready for flight when left in the lurch, dangerous in their uncertainty, inaccessible to consolation or to advice of any sort, far from being humane, without conscience, unstable, fitful, unreliable and cruel, yet also generous and magnanimous, ready for sacrifice and full of courage when they become secure in themselves, full of the utter assurance of a child who senses in himself the dawning of the right path and makes for his goal like a somnambulist. Oh, my friends, it is a great and magnificent people we have been born into, and we have to be grateful for the duty of serving them with all our works, more grateful even for the leadership which has been bestowed upon us, most grateful for the divine command to put this leadership into action. In our concern for this great childlike quality which has been entrusted to us, we have to discipline it without robbing it of anything, we have to let it retain all its valuable qualities as well as its childish intoxication with play and cruelty, by which it protects itself from weakening, but, along with all this, we must take heed that all this is held within certain limits to prevent injury or self-injury, or running amok, for nothing is so terrible and dangerous as the bewildered madness of this child, which is called the people; theirs is the madness of a deserted child, and therefore it must be our care that the people never feel abandoned. Oh, my friends, we have to nurse the childlike qualities of the people, we have to provide them with the security of a child in his father's house, and he who knows how to guide the people in this paternally mild and firm manner, who by this means creates security for their livelihood, their souls, and their faith, he who brings this to pass, he and he only is the one

chosen to summon the people to the state, not only to life in
the state's security, but still more, to death for it in the hour
of danger, in the hour when the state must be defended; oh,
my friends, only a people thus guided and controlled will be
able to defend itself, as well as its state, with enough endurance
to keep both of them immune for all time and eternity from an
otherwise inevitable downfall. This is the goal, eternal in its
validity, eternal for the state, eternal for the people."

Who gave the answer? Was one to be found? And yet it
came: "Eternal alone is truth, the madness-freed, madness-pre-
venting truth of reality, retrieved from the depths above and
below, for it alone is immutable reality; and summoned to
truth, summoned to affirmation, summoned to the deed of truth,
the folk, and beyond all folkhood, men as men, will participate
in the kingdom forever, participating in its boundless bounty.
Only through the deed of truth can death be annulled, death that
has been, death that is to come; only thus is the somnolent soul
to be fully awakened to the perception of the whole, which grace
is inherent in everyone bearing a human face. It is toward
truth and into truth that the state is growing, seeking therein
its inner growth, finding therein its ultimate reality, reaching
back to its divinely-supernatural source, so that the glory of
the ages may fulfill itself in this time, fulfill itself as the kingdom of mankind, as the divine realm of humanity, as the kingdom that stands above all nations and embraces them all. The
goal of the state is the realm of truth, extending over all lands
yet growing like a tree from the depths of earth to those of
heaven, for it is the growing piety out of which will unfold the
kingdom, the peace of the kingdom, and reality as the revelation
of truth."

Again Augustus did not let himself be turned aside, and
again it seemed as if they had not heard one another. Again
their speeches, unmoved in the immobility, glided past each
other: "The gods have no care for the individual, they are indifferent to him and they take no note of his death; the gods
turn toward the people, their own imperishability turns toward

the imperishability of the people, which they wish to maintain, perhaps because they realize that their own would vanish with that of the people; and yet, should they set their mark on a single mortal, it is done only to lend him power to build up for the state a way of life in which the eternally destined and imperishable continuity of the people shall be organized and secured. The earthly power is a reflection of the divine power, and framed between the reality of the gods and the reality of the people, between an eternal order of the gods and an eternal order of the people, both realized in the state, the earthly power itself comes to have eternal existence, comes with the gods and the people to be greater than death and life, greater by virtue of its twofold reality. And framed between godhood and folkhood, a reflection of one and a likeness of the other, earthly power does not turn toward the individual, nor the state toward the multiplicity of mankind, but always toward the people as a whole, in order to preserve in them the reality of its eternal existence. No sovereignty supported by men alone can maintain itself; it perishes as these perish, indeed, be it ever so richly blessed, it will be brushed aside by the first breath of human fickleness; it was thus with Pericles' work of peace, Pericles who was driven out because he could not ward off pestilence from the city, and it might have been the same with me when famine threatened Rome three years ago. To be sure, the gods who contributed daily bread also laid on me, their surrogate, the task of keeping up the Senatorial distributions of grain to the people; yes, at that time the gods granted me their greatest protection, allowing me to set up the Alexandrine corn-fleet, sending favorable winds that shortened the journey, and letting the worst misery be prevented, but their help would have come to nothing, and the unrest springing up everywhere would without doubt have been my undoing, had not my power been founded on the totality of the gods and the totality of the people. And I would continue to expose myself and the entire Roman state to every chance in the game of public opinion were I to permit the exercise of power to be dissipated by dealing with groups, or with a single individual. The state is the supreme reality, invisibly spread over the landscape, but so much the highest reality that nothing mortal or perishable may be tolerated in the sphere of its validity; I stand here a mortal and perishable, but in the state's sphere of validity, in the sphere of my power, I must strip off the perishable and become the symbol of the imperishable, for only as a symbol may a mortal fit himself into imperishability, into an imperishability which, like the Roman state, stands by virtue of its own reality above any symbol whatsoever . . . The state, in its twofold reality, has not only to symbolize the gods; it is not enough for it to have built the Acropolis for the glorification of the gods, it has also to set up a symbol for the people who constitute the second half of its reality, a strong symbol that the people will see and comprehend, a strong symbol in which they in turn will recognize themselves, the likeness of their own power to which they may and will bow, sensing that power within the earthbound always inclines toward the criminal—Antonius was an example of this—and that only a bearer of earthly power who is at the same time a symbol of eternity precludes this kind of danger. And therefore I, who have been given the power to maintain Roman order as a vassal of the gods and as a heritage from my blessed father, only to be able to pass it on, in the future to the last grandchild in an uninterrupted chain of generation, I have been permitted, nay, more, commanded to set up my images in the temples apart from those of the gods on whom the various peoples of this empire otherwise depend, as a symbol of the empire's unity, of its growth into a common order extending from the ocean to the borders of the Euphrates. We force no one to accept our institutions, we do not need to disturb anything, we have time and can wait till the people of themselves take advantage of our justice, our weights and measures, our coinage, and indeed there are already some indications that they have begun to do so, but we have inexorably taken over the task of accelerating as much as possible this inauguration into a Roman way of thinking. This we must do at once, without delay we must awake the consciousness of the empire in the various people belonging to it, we must do it for the sake of the gods who represent the summit of Roman thought, and we can do it, but only by means of a symbol and its image; the Roman people realized this when they demanded that statues of me be set up, not to pray to me superstitiously as to a god, which I am not, but rather to pay that pious respect to my god-appointed office which the alien peoples within the empire's borders are also obliged to do, because in the symbol of my office the true inner growth of the state is shown forth, the necessity for its growth to a total empire, organized in the security of Roman peace, and for all time."

For all time! The Caesar had ended his speech, his gaze was fixed into the distance, into spacelessness and timelessness, there where the Roman State extended in invisible lines over the landscape of the earth, still unlighted though filled with light, and waiting for the light to come. Mysteriously time flowed on, echoing despite all its emptiness with hoof-beats heard in the Poseidonian quaking, flowed on like a heavy stream, without water, without shores, and the wall-fountain trickled, also in need of water. Waiting pervaded the world.

"Time, oh, Augustus, unfolds in the growing piety of mankind, in piety the kingdom is growing, unswayed and unswayable by earthly might and earthly institutions, which remain together still within the realm of the symbolic. But this symbol will be realized in the kingdom as a mirror of the creation, will come to be the reality into which your work will unfold by the growth of that very piety to which you have pointed the way."

Caesar's gaze, lost in the distance, came back again into the room: "I have resumed the Auguries and the priestly Order of Titus and am about to reform the Lucullian festivals; on all occasions I remind the people of the venerable forms of religion and take pains with the pious and solemn festivals with which our progenitors surrounded their faith. This suffices for the gods, this suffices for the people, and this constituted the true piety of your Aeneas, faithful and strong in the memory of

Anchises, his father. In memory of my blessed father, to whom I have proved faithful, the people appointed me to sovereignty, recognizing in my zeal the ancestral beliefs toward which they yearned, and they have chosen me to embody them as the embodiment of the people's power, not only by making me Tribune, but also by entrusting me with the highest priestly power, with the symbol-filled office of Protector of the Faith. There is no need for Roman piety to grow, it has always been there from the very beginning, like the Roman gods which it served, and it is merely a question of winning it back."

"Oh, Augustus, you who have achieved the piety of human existence primarily by surrendering yourself to your father's will, you who in his holy name protect the forms of religion so powerfully that the people obey you through love, that no transgressor would dare lay hands again on the order set up by the gods and re-established by you, oh, Augustus, the traditional piety of the people, and yours also, reaches beyond the circles of the manifold gods, it extends beyond the glorious chain of the fathers, for piety turns toward the prime ancestor, devotedly waiting for him to announce himself, to entrust his mission and his creation to the son, steadfast in piety."

"Apollo was the protecting divinity of my line, and he, sun-god and earth-god in one, he the founder of order, the averter of all evil, he is the son of Zeus, the heavenly father whom we all serve. All lucidity springs from him."

And now the slave could again be heard; from a great distance his voice came hither, like pen-strokes thin and dry: "Even Zeus himself is piously serving fate, but beyond Zeus, yonder where unsearchable light veils every thought, there fate itself is serving, aye, more than serving the primal unknown whose name is forbidden."

Over in the alcove Caesar leaned back, thinking, and all was quiet. Everything remained immobile, but the lividness of the light receded, the light resumed shape as if wanting to become the sun-lion which guarded the border, the powerfully-pawed lion who was to come and to lie down with soft paws at the feet of the pious subduer. The heaving of earth subsided, Poseidon was calming down, the sun-eclipse on the point of vanishing.

"All lucidity gives birth to new piety, Augustus."

"But our piety must lead to lucidity."

"He who is pious, Augustus, is already in awareness; he lives in the memory of the law given by the forefathers and therefore his memory is able to speak with him who is to come, although his step has not yet been heard: he serves him in serving love, although the command to do so has not yet been received; thus he summons the unsummonable one, and by invoking him, he creates him . . . piety is that knowledge by which men escape their inescapable loneliness; piety is seeing to the blind and hearing to the deaf, piety is the perception of the simple . . . the gods arose from the piety of men, and in serving them, piety will come to be the death-annulling perception of love beyond the gods . . . the return from the depths . . . error and rage annulled . . . the perception-bearing truth . . . yes, that is piety."

"What next, Virgil! Where are you heading! All this leads far beyond the earthly realm and has nothing more to do with the earthly task. But I have been placed in the sphere of earth and I have to acquiesce in that. The Roman people have made their own laws in accordance with the will of the gods, thereby curbing their own liberty; they have transmuted it into the state, and thus pointed out to themselves the way to Apollonian lucidity and order; this course must be adhered to . . . I must take care of that . . . and though the path has been opened through the influence of human piety, piety may not be allowed to go beyond this path and its goal; it may not go beyond the state which, in that case, would have to be abandoned, the reality of the state shattered, and with it the reality of the gods and the people. Piety and the state are one, to be pious is to serve the state and to coordinate oneself with it; the pious person is one who serves the Roman state with his whole being and the whole of his works . . . I want no other kind of piety; but this one is a duty from which neither you, nor I, nor anyone is excluded."

All this that Augustus had just expressed sounded curiously implausible, implausible and at the same time painful in its masked way; and the reaction that it created was painful, as of a loss, of disappointment, of aversion, perhaps even shame, maybe, because in spite of all one felt caught by it, caught either by the inescapability of friendship, or it may be by the inescapability of death. Actually was it not Augustus who must die? His words sounded like a legacy for the future leader of the Roman Empire, yet the words themselves were dead, reaching neither to the gods nor to men. It seemed that Augustus had become tired, for he sat down again; isolated, self-absorbed, he sat there bent slightly forward, and his handsome, boyish face did not look over, but his hand lay on the lion's head. Whatever the earthly realm contained, Caesar had participated in it to its utmost limits, and he had remained imprisoned in its earthliness; now he was tired. But withal, a monarch.

And even so, yes, just for this reason one had to speak, to speak out: "Beyond the piety of the gods there is the piety of the individual soul, it is beyond the piety of the state, beyond that of the people; though the gods may restrict themselves to the people as a whole, wishing to know nothing of the individual, the soul is scarcely in need of the gods whom she has created, she has need of them no longer, neither this god nor that one, as soon as she finds herself in converse with the inscrutable . . ."

The converse with the inscrutable! Oh, as long as the invisible cloudy cover stretched between above and below was not pierced, the prayer brought back only its own echo; the god remained unreachable, he vouchsafed no answer.

But Caesar said: "If by way of such pious conversations, which nobody, not even you, can verify, you want to exempt yourself from your duties to the state and the people to whom you owe your work, I can understand your motive although I cannot approve of it; if, however, your remarks are intended to minimize the hereditary faith and to put Roman piety on an equality with that of the barbarians, then I must remind you that you yourself have characterized the Egyptian gods as monsters . . ."

"There is but one kind of piety, and the barbarian whose piety betokens growth is better than the Roman whose soul shuts itself against growing."

A little bored, with a sort of bored attentiveness as if to settle the matter, came the answer: "A piety that produces monsters is no piety, a state which worships monsters is no state; piety without the gods is unimaginable, it is unimaginable without the state or the people and can only be exercised within the whole community, for men can be united to their gods only within the whole Roman fatherland which is one with its gods."

"The organization into a whole would never have taken place had not the individual soul found its immediate connection to the supernatural; only the work intended for direct service to the supernatural serves all earth-bound humanity as well."

"These are extremely dangerous and novel ideas, Virgil: they are derogatory to the state."

"Through them the state will perfect itself into a kingdom; from a state of citizens it will become a kingdom of men."

"You are shattering the structure of the state, you shatter it to a shapeless uniformity, you split up its ordinances, you destroy the firm texture of the people." All fatigue had disappeared from Caesar's manner; these were things that concerned him and the thing had come to a point of vehemence.

"The order will be a human one . . . the order of human law."

"Laws? As if we were not more than blessed with them! In nothing is the Senate so fruitful as in the enactment of bad laws . . . the people wish for order but certainly not for insidious laws by which they and their state are endangered . . . you speak of things you do not understand."

"The kingdom increasing in piety does not destroy the

state, but surpasses it; it does not annul its folkhood, but surpasses it . . . the people, indeed they are entitled to order in the state, but man is entitled to truth; it is this that he serves by his piety, and when he shall achieve perception then the new kingdom will be created, the kingdom within the law of perception, the kingdom graced by its power to ensure creation."

"You speak of the universal work of creation as though it could be influenced by measures of state. Luckily the Senate would not know what to do with your law of perception . . . if it did, the creation would not endure for long."

"When men are empty of perception, when they have forfeited the truth, they must go on lacking creation as well; the state can not provide for the creation but when creation is endangered so is the state."

"I will not wrangle with you over this . . . it is a problem the solution of which we shall leave with the gods. On the other hand you must agree that I have done my part; I have ministered to the knowledge of the people as far as lay in my power, and I shall continue to do so. The number of public schools has been increased, not only in Italy but in the provinces, and I am turning my whole attention to that higher education which will procure for us capable physicians, architects and expert canal-builders; furthermore, as you well know, I have founded the Apollonian and Octavian library, and I have not neglected to promote the already existing libraries by donations. Yet this kind of solicitude means little to the people; the masses have no desire to be given perception, they want to see strong images whose unequivocal meaning they are able to grasp."

"Above all knowledge stands perception itself and the people await it in the great image of the perceptive deed."

A kind of melancholy flippancy came into Caesar's expression: "The world is full of deeds yet empty of perception."

"The deed of perception is that of the pledge, Octavian."

"Well then, I made my pledge when I accepted my office, and whatever I swore to that I have kept. I think that covers your perceptive deed as well . . . what else do you want?"

Why not answer this vain man as he desired! It would be so simple and rational. And yet something compelled him to controversy and explanation: "Certainly, your work lies in doing the deed you have sworn to, and therefore it will be followed by the perceptive deed, the formative deed of perception, the deed of truth; but, Augustus, this concerns the soul of man and demands patience."—Oh, in spite of the irked protest in Caesar's manner it had to be said, because it was the human soul that was at stake, the human soul and its awakening to the annulment of death—, "yes, your work has extended the peace of Rome over the earth, has founded the unity of the state in symbolic grandeur, and now if actually there be added the deed of truth, bestowing on men a divine perception, shared by all, gathering the citizens into a human community, then, oh, Augustus, the state will have turned into an eternal reality of creation . . . then and only then will come . . . the miracle . . ."

"So you still insist that the state in its present form is nothing but a windy metaphor . . ."

"A genuine metaphor."

"Well then, a genuine metaphor . . . but you insist that it is to win its real stature only in the future . . ."

"Thus it is, Caesar."

"And when will your miracle take place? when is this transformation to genuine reality to occur? when?" Insistent and angry, yes, completely aggressive, the handsome face turned toward him.

When, oh, ye gods! when, oh, when? oh, when would it come to be, the form-freed creation without chance? Only the unknown, the pledge-protecting god, knew when. The ground heaved no longer, the bark glided on quietly, and even though breathing had become most painful in lungs, throat, and nose, the heart was breathing, and the heart knew within itself the enduring breath of the soul, a breath, merely a breath, but one so strong that one might think it would blow out over the world and sweep away crags. When, oh, when? somewhere there breathed that one who would bring it to pass, somewhere he was already living, still unborn, yet breathing; once there was creation, and there will be creation again, the miracle—chance-delivered! And surrounded by the receding lividness in the utmost distance, the star reappeared, heading toward the east.

"Some day there will come one who will again live in perception; in his being the world will be redeemed to truth."

"I wish you would confine yourself to earthly duties; this also is a superhuman task and one for which the time remaining to me is too brief."

"It is a task for a savior."

"But you have intended it for me . . . or have you not?"

"The savior conquers death, and you have appeared as death-conquering, in that you have brought peace."

"That is no answer, for the peace founded and ordained by me was and is earthly in its nature . . . or is that your way of saying that you entrust to me only the accomplishment of earthly tasks?"

"In the son of the idolized one men already see the redeemer who shall deliver them from evil."

"People are saying that, and so says the populace . . . but what do you say, Virgil?"

"Even twenty years ago when I began the Georgics and you were still a boy, even then I saw your image in the circle of the zodiac. For you signify the turning of the times."

"What were your words?"

"To thee, thou new star, as thou joinest the slow months in their passing, where Erigone leads on the Scorpion, a new space now opens, the fiery scourger himself yields a space in the heavens, withdrawing his claws from thy place in the serving sky."

"That was written twenty years ago . . . and now?"

"You were conceived and born in the image of Capricorn, the Ram, who dashes up the rocky fastnesses to the highest peaks on earth, and you have chosen him as your sign."

"The earthly peaks . . . and the supernal are denied me, eh?"

380

"Think of the verses that Horace composed for you, Augustus."

"Which ones?"

"In heaven the thunderer, Zeus, is reigning, but on earth you are the visible god, oh, Augustus."

"You are evasive, Virgil: You cite a time-worn quotation and you quote other people; but you conceal your own opinion."

"My own opinion?" Augustus was so remote; the words glided hither and thither, their flight was curious but they no longer formed a bridge.

The slave said: "This should no longer concern you."

"My own opinion?"

"Yes, that is what I want to hear and without digression."

"You are a mortal being, Augustus, though foremost among the living."

A scornful, malicious glance made it clear that the opinion Caesar had wanted to hear was a different one: "I realize that I am neither a god nor a new constellation, and it is unnecessary to remind me of that fact; I am a citizen of Rome and have never considered myself anything else, so I find you have still not answered my question."

"Salvation will always come to pass on earth, Augustus, the bringer of salvation is always earthly and mortal, and must be so; only his voice comes from the supernal, thanks to which he is able to call out the eternal in men who wish to be saved. You with your deed, however, have levelled the ground for the divine renewal of the world, and it is your world which will hear the voice."

"On what grounds do you dispute my fitness for the last step that is yet to be taken? Why do you protest that my work, for all that you concede it of preparatory value, should not be called on to consummate the salvation of the world? why do you claim that the symbol which you constantly see in my work may not already bear in itself the reality? why do you deny that I, who was still the first to posit the deed by my work, may not also be fit for the deed of perception?"

"I do not deny any of it, Octavian, you are the symbol of the gods and the symbol of the Roman people. You would never have been chosen to be this had not the symbol which you embody borne some traits of the primal image as well. The deed of perception may develop in your person rather than in that of another. Until now even the time for it has not come."

"Virgil, you are a little too generous with time, but only as it concerns me; you grant much less delay for yourself and your own purposes . . . rather say without more ado that I am not to assume this salvation-business." It was meant to sound cheerful but the grudgingly continuous indignation was unmistakable.

"Even the bringer of salvation and revelation, even he, is bound in the perceptive web of time; he will come when the time has become ripe."

Caesar sprang up: "You want to reserve this office for yourself."

Oh, was Caesar right in this? alas, was he right to an extent he himself could not realize? Was not the wish to be the redeemer a more compelling dream of grandeur in the poet than in other men? Did not Orpheus also wish to rise to that dream even as he tried to draw the animals into his spell in order to to redeem them to humanity? But no, and again no: art remained unsuitable for this purpose, as even Orpheus learned to his grief. The sibylline voice that was heard by the poet was that of a Eurydice, of a Plotia; and that he never found the golden bough of redemption was the will of the gods, the will of fate.

"Oh, Augustus, the writer is not really alive; the redeemer, on the contrary, lives more vigorously than all others, for his whole life is one single deed of perception; his life, and his death."

In the midst of his indignation Augustus smiled, and it was really a good-natured smile: "You will live, Virgil, you will regain your strength and finish your work."

"Even should I again recover . . . the more perfect the poem would become the further it would be from any deed of redemption, and the more unsuited to it."

"Well then, we shall not be able to accomplish the redeeming act, neither you nor I, instead we shall leave it to the savior you have in mind but in whom I can scarcely believe. And until his coming we must go on fulfilling our duty, you, yours, and I, mine . . ."

"We must prepare ourselves for his coming."

"Good, my work signifies preparation for him, anyhow. But yours is also that, and you will have to finish the Aeneid for the sake of your people . . ."

"I cannot and I dare not finish it . . . I cannot do it because this would be just the wrong sort of preparation."

"And how would you accomplish the right one?"

"Through sacrifice."

"Sacrifice?"

"Just so."

"To what end will you sacrifice? To whom?"

"To the gods."

"The gods have stipulated the sacrifices which are acceptable to them, they have given them over to the care of the state, and I see to it that they are punctiliously carried out in the whole empire. There are no sacrifices outside the state's sovereignty."

Augustus remained stubborn, he knew nothing of the pledge commanded by the unknown god; it was futile to try to convince him: "The forms of religion that you guard are untouchable, but to say they are untouchable is not to say that they are complete."

"How shall they be completed?"

"Everyone may be commanded by the gods to sacrifice, and everyone must be ready to be chosen as the sacrifice should it so please the gods."

"If I understand you, Virgil, you want to exclude the mass of the people from the sacrificial regulations and to have them replaced by the individual who is in some way concerned with the supernal; without doubt this is inadmissible and more than inadmissible. And besides, you refer this to the will of the gods in order to give yourself a semblance of justification and responsibility. Nevertheless, all of this remains vastly irresponsible, and the gods will be the last ones to take over the responsibility for your intentions, because the time-honored cult-forms and the sacrifices proper to them suffice for the gods, as for the people. They should not be exceeded by even half a step."

"They are being terribly exceeded, Augustus! the people dully sense that a new truth is in preparation, that the old forms will soon broaden out, they sense dully that the ancient rites of sacrifice suffice for no one; and driven by a confused longing toward the new, driven also by a confused longing to sacrifice, they crowd to the places of execution, and to the games which you organize, crowd to the impious sham-sacrifice that is bloodily offered them in death that grows in cruelty, so that in the end only the intoxication with blood and death is satisfied . . ."

"I have turned brutalization into discipline, unbridled cruelty into games. All this implies just the necessary hardness of the Roman people and has nothing to do with forebodings about the sacrifice."

"The people have forebodings, more so than the individual. For their total feeling is duller and more ponderous than the meditation of the individual soul, duller and weightier, wilder and more confused is their urge toward a world-redeemer. And faced with the blood-horror at the places of execution and on the sands of the arena they have a shuddering realization that from these the true sacrificial deed will arise, the real sacrifice, which will be the ultimate and decisive form of perception on earth."

"The profundity of your work often seems like a riddle, and now you are talking in riddles."

"The bringer of salvation will bring himself to the sacrifice out of love for men and mankind, transforming himself by his own death into the deed of truth, the deed which he casts to the universe, so that from this supreme and symbolic reality of helpful service creation may again unfold."

The Caesar wrapped himself in his toga: "I have placed my life at the service of my work, at the service of public welfare, at the service of the state. In doing so my sacrificial need found satisfaction enough. I recommend the same to you."

What passed back and forth between them now amounted to nothing, just empty words, or not even words any more, racing across an empty space that was no longer even space. Everything was an unbelievable nothingness, cut off and bridgeless.

"Your life has been one of deeds, Caesar, deeds done for the people and public welfare, and you have given yourself without stint. The gods chose you for this sacrificial deed and commanded you to it, and through it you have been nearer to them than any other mortal, as your life shows."

"What sort of sacrifice do you still want? Any work that is actually accomplished demands the whole man and his entire life; the same has been true in your case as far as I can judge, and you are just as much entitled to call it sacrifice."

The many layers of existence had faded to an amorphousness beyond that of any emptiness; no lines were to be seen any more, not the faintest shadow of a line—, where could one still find the means of recognition? "All I have done was egotism, it was hardly action, to say nothing of sacrifice."

"Then follow my example, pay off your obligations, give the people that to which they are entitled, give them your work."

"Like every work, it was born out of blindness . . . out of worldly blindness . . . whatever we are doing . . . nothing but blind work . . . we are not humble enough for the true, for the seeing-blindness . . ."

"And I also? . . . my work also?"

"No more layers of existence . . ."

"What?"

It was not worth while talking; one could only repeat oneself: "Your actions took place among the people and became a deed through the people; mine had to be taken to the people, not serving as a deed serves but in order to win recognition and applause."

"Enough, Virgil,"—Caesar's attitude expressed the utmost impatience now—"if you deem it egotistical to publish the Aeneid, have it published after your death. That is my last suggestion."

"The poet's search for fame reaches beyond his death."

"And then, what?"

"The work must not outlast me."

"By Jupiter! Why? At last I should like to know why. Give me your real reasons now!"

"Since I could not consecrate my whole life to sacrifice, as you have done yours, I must designate my work for this purpose . . . It must sink out of memory, and I with it."

"That is not reasoning, that is utter lunacy."

"The unchastity of remembering . . . I want to forget . . . to forget everything . . . and I want to be forgotten . . ."

"What a charming message for your friends . . . truly, Virgil, your memories would be more chaste if you clung to something friendlier instead of to empty and malicious wishes, which in fact are only empty and malicious evasions."

"The redemptive deed of perception is imminent; I must sacrifice in order to fulfill the pledge . . . salvation lies only in fulfilling the pledge . . . for everyone . . . for me . . ."

"Oh, your salvation, always your salvation . . . well, your savior will not arrive a day sooner because of your sacrifice, but you are robbing the people, your people, and this is what you call your salvation. Lunacy, just lunacy, that's what it is!"

"Only truth without perception is lunacy, this has to do with the truth of perception . . . in such reality there is no lunacy."

"So—there are two kinds of truth, are there, one full of perception for you and another without perception for me, who in your opinion talks like a lunatic, eh? Is that what you mean to say? Well then, say it bluntly!"

"I must destroy what is without perception . . . it constitutes

the evil . . . it is imprisonment . . . unliberated . . . redemption
will come through the sacrifice . . . it is the highest duty . . .
the imperceptive must yield to perception . . . only by doing
this can I serve the people's truth and further their salvation
. . . this is the law of truth . . . this the awakening from the
encircling twilight."

A sharp and hasty step—, Augustus stood close to his bed:
"Virgil . . ."

"Yes, Augustus?"

"You hate me."

"Octavian!"

"Call me not Octavian since you hate me."

"I . . . I hate you?"

"And how you hate me." Caesar's voice was shrill with
bitterness.

"Oh, Octavian . . ."

"Keep still . . . you hate me more than every other person
on earth, and more than all other men because you envy no one
so much as me."

"That is not true . . . that is not true."

"Do not lie; it is true . . ."

"Oh, it is not."

"It is true . . ."—furiously the hand of the scornful man
tore the laurel leaves from the wreaths of the chandelier—,
"indeed, it is true . . . indeed, it is true, for you have filled
yourself with thoughts of being a king but you were too weak
to make the slighest effort to become one; you hate me because
you had no other choice than to put your cravings into your
poem, by which you could show yourself, here at least, as
mightier than your kings; you hate me because I was able to
work for all that you desired for yourself and which, nevertheless, I have so despised that I could allow myself to refuse the
crown of empire; you hate me because you hold me responsible
for your own impotence . . . this is the source of your hatred,
your envy . . ."

"Octavian, listen to me . . ."

"I do not want to listen to you . . ."

The Caesar was shouting, and strange, ah, most strange; the louder he shouted the richer became the world; the visible with its many layers of existence appeared once more, and the leaden apathy came back to life, and again there was something like hope.

"Octavian, listen while I speak . . ."

"To what end, tell me, to what end? . . . first, with false modesty you hypocritically slander your own work so as to be able to disparage mine more easily, and then you want to reduce it to a windy semblance of a sham-image, and a blind one at that, thus abusing the Roman people and the faith of their fathers, which, as the expression of my work, does not please you and which, for that reason, you find necessary to have reformed, knowing quite well that all this is futile, knowing quite well it must continue to be futile for you, knowing quite well that I remain more powerful than you and must continue to remain so, knowing quite well that you cannot get the better of me, you now take refuge at last in the supernatural, yonder where no one, not even I, is able to pass, and you want to saddle me with a savior who doesn't exist and never will exist, but who is to subdue me in your stead . . . I know you, Virgil; you seem to be gentle, and you love to be worshipped by the people for your purity and your virtue, but in reality your allegedly pure soul trembles constantly with hatred and malice, yes, I repeat it, it trembles with a most abject malice . . ."

Without doubt the consecrated one was hollering his complaints; and yet it was so strangely good that it should be so, it was so strangely good, oh, so good, that this could still be possible, and it seemed as if there were an invisible firm ground showing within the invisible realm, that firm invisible ground from which invisible bridges could be flung again, human bridges to humanity, chaining one word to another, one glance to another, so that word, like glance, should again become full of meaning, human bridges of meeting; oh, that he would speak on!

388

Well, the Augustus did speak on, and not only did he speak, nay, rather he shouted, laying no restraint on himself: "Pure and virtuous and modest are you in manner, but just a little too pure, too virtuous, and too modest not to arouse suspicion . . . never would your so-called modesty have permitted you to accept an office that I could have tendered you, never would I have dared offer you one, because in reality none could be thought of that appeared good enough for you, you would have found objections to each one of them had it been that of senator, of pro-consul or any other of high rank, and the last thing that would have been possible for you would have been to accept any office from my hands, because you hate me too deeply and too thoroughly for that! Yes, sheer hatred of me compelled you to write poetry and build up your independence as a poet, for what you really wanted of me was to stand back and let you have my place, and in this I was, and still am, unable to oblige you, not to mention that you would decline my office also, because, being unable to hold it and conscious of your inability, you would have been forced to despise it . . . all of this proceeds from hatred and because of it your hatred is being repeatedly enkindled . . ."

"Never have I esteemed my poetry above any office you could have offered me."

"Keep still, and do not continue to steal my time by your hypocrisy . . . all that concerned you was that I resign my office, perhaps only that you might be able to spurn it, and this gave rise to your fuss about perception, your sophistries concerning sacrifice, and now to your proposed destruction of the Aeneid, so that I might learn from it how to give up and destroy one's own work . . . yes, you would rather have the Aeneid vanish from the earth than have to go on enduring or suffering the sight of my work any more . . ."

Layer on layer of existence piled up under these scoldings, and the room which Caesar was furiously pacing was an ordinary earthly room once more, part of an earthly house and furnished with earthly furniture, an earthly thing in the light of late noon.

And now one could even feel one's way across the invisible bridge: "Octavian, you do me wrong, a bitter wrong . . ."

"So, I do you wrong, do I? but you want to destroy the Aeneid so that you will not have to dedicate it to me! You dedicated the Georgics to Maecenas and the Eclogues to Asinius Pollio right gladly! On me, to the contrary, on me whom you hate, you wanted to foist the Culex, for me the Culex was good enough and still is, according to you, seemingly to prove that it was good enough for me twenty-five years ago, that I could claim nothing better at that time, nor can I today, . . . but that in these twenty-five years I have accomplished my work, and that this work fully entitles me to the Aeneid, well-grounded as it is in my achievement, in the reality of Rome and its spirit, and without which it could never have come into being, that is too much for you, you cannot bear it, and you would rather destroy the poem than dedicate it to me . . ."

"Octavian . . . !"

"It is immaterial to you whether a work, be it yours or mine, is greater than life or death, immaterial because of your hatred . . ."

"Octavian, accept the poem!" All the paperish pulp, the dull paper-like whiteness had disappeared from the atmosphere outside; the light shimmered over the landscape, almost ivory in color.

"I do not want to hear anything more of your bungling work . . . do what you please with it; I do not want it."

"It is not a bungling work."

Caesar remained standing and looked askance at the chest: "It has become a bungling work to me; you have reduced it to that yourself."

"You know that it was meant for you when I wrote it, that you were constantly in my thoughts, that you entered into the work and that you are, as you were, in the poem which is yours . . ."

"That is what you made believe to yourself and by the same token to me. Truly, you are right to call me blind, blind as a new-born kitten, for it was flagrantly blind to believe in you, flagrant for me to have had confidence so long in you and your trickery!"

"There was no trickery."

"If there was not, you hate your own work now just because it bears traces of me."

"I will finish it for your sake."

"And I am still supposed to believe that?" Again the Caesar looked askance at the box and this was unpleasant; but now there was nothing else to be done.

"You must believe me, Octavian."

Oh, even the tiniest whirling second released from a human soul into the abyss of time, only to vanish there, is greater in its incomprehensibility than any work, and now from Caesar's soul such a second released itself, a second of friendship, a second of affection, a second of love, distinctly felt although he said only: "We will reconsider it."

And now came the hardest part: "Take the manuscript with you to Rome, Octavian . . . with the help of the gods I shall find it there again."

The Caesar nodded and for the length of this nod a vast peace reigned, the peace of an affinity that reached out like a breath from the human heart, passing through all invisibilities ever and again toward the human heart, the great power of quietude: the brown-timbered ceiling was again becoming the forest from which it had been taken, the laurel scent of the wreaths turned back into the most hidden shadows resting deep in the sun-covered leafy vales, misty with the trickle of the fountains, misty and soft like the tone of a mossy reed and yet firm-fast, yet oaken-heavy, and the breath of the inexplicable heart was that of mutual intuition. Was it still on this breath that the lamp, as though for the last time, started to swing on its silver-sounding chains? nothing stirred around them, the waters were smooth as though holding their breath; the voyage halted. And Augustus standing under the laurel-elm, his hand in the laurel-leafage, said: "Do you remember, Virgil?"—

"Yes, I remember many things, but they are always too few."—
"Do you remember the horses and dogs that we picked out
together?"—"Of course, I remember: I predicted their speed
and their fitness as you were buying them."—"They were Crotonian mares and stallions and Iberian dogs."—"I advised you
against one of the stallions, but you bought him nevertheless,
Octavian."—"Yes, you knew all about it, the stallion proved
to be really no good."—"You paid dearly for him and you
might have saved the money, for my advice was sound."—"Sometimes it is well not to follow your advice, Virgil."—"Why? but
that was long ago."—"Very long ago. The stallion had a
pleasing appearance, a black stallion with a small head. Too
bad."—"Yes, too bad. A black stallion, he had white fetlocks
and his hind-quarters were too weak, although that was scarcely
noticeable."—"Quite so, his hind-quarters were too weak but
he had no white marks whatsoever."—"But no, Augustus, the
fetlocks were white."—"An animal that I have seen once stays
in my memory, I assure you the horse was without markings."—
"We raised so many horses in Andes that my memory for them
is keen; here I feel sure of my ground and no one can talk me
out of it, not even you, Octavian."—"And you are nothing but
a pig-headed peasant."—"I am a peasant and the son of horse-
breeders; as a child I galloped over the meadows clinging to
the horse's mane."—"If the nags you mounted at that time
were no better than your memory you need not be too proud of
them."—"They were not nags."—"And your memory is no
memory; mine is the better."—"It is all one whether or not
you are the Augustus, you may be that a thousand times, the
fetlocks were still white, white as snow."—"Fume as much as
you like, it is useless, they were not white."—"I say white and
that is final."—"No, say I."—"Really, Octavian, do not contradict me; I am ready to die on the spot should the fetlocks
not have been white!" Augustus who until now had stood there
with lowered brow, musing as if wishing to hold fast not only
to memory but to peace as well, now lifted his head: "We won't
gamble with such stakes, I forbid it, for that would be too high

a price for me, in that case I should much rather the fetlocks had been white." And thereupon they both had to laugh, overcome by a wave of soundless laughter, by a soundless, fluttering laughter that was a little painful, probably also for Augustus, for his saddened features—or were there even tears shimmering in his distant eyes?—let one infer that he too was feeling the anguish in his throat and chest, painful, like dream-laughter, sore at heart and choking because, alas, no one laughs in the dream and, alas, because the bliss-giving stillness that had enthralled them was being painfully dispelled since Augustus had raised his head, wakened out of the stillness that now was gone.

Was the sun-eclipse once more threatening? or the heaving of earth and ocean, shaken by the steeds of Poseidon? was there now a new threat of these? was this why the stillness had passed? no, there was no fear of these; gentle and earthly and peaceful the cooing doves walked along the window-sill, the song remained gentle, the gentle light held to its ivory hue, and even the voyage was again progressing, there was nothing to fear as long as the barks glided on so slowly and steadily. Nevertheless the hoof-beats of a horse became audible and it did not take long for it to appear, galloping hither across the air, carrying a boy in high spirits who held onto the rippling mane, tearing at it gaily. It was not a black horse but one that was snow-white, with black fetlocks however, and after the boy had dismounted in mid-gallop before Caesar, the horse continued on its way and sped through the window. But the boy stepped up to Caesar like a herald of yore, his head wreathed like a gift-bearer, and as such he was received.

"I greet you," said the Augustus, still leaning against the candelabrum with his hands among the laurel-leaves, "you want to present me with a poem and I accept it at your hands because you are Lysanias; I recognize you although I have never been in Andes, and you recognize me also."

"You are Caesar Augustus, the holy one."

"How did you find your way to me?"

And the boy recited:

"... Behold Caesar there and his issue,
All of the Julian line that is destined to mount to the heavens,
This is the man, this is he whom so often you heard the fates
   promise,
Caesar Augustus, the son of a god who shall give back to
   Latium,
Back to those fields where once Saturn was reigning a new
   age, a golden;
His is an empire shall stretch past the Indian and Gara-
   mantian,
On to a realm beyond stars where the sun and the year take
   their courses;
Heav'n-bearing Atlas is there and revolves the bright orb on
   his shoulders;
Aye, even now, the Caspian realms are aghast at his coming,
Scythians cower there too in fear of the gods' divinations,
Meanwhile the mouths of the sevenfold Nile are in tumult
   with terror . . ."

Thus declaimed the boy, and the picture that, disquieting
and almost breath-taking, arose along with the verses did not
have its origin in memory, neither in that of the boy nor his
own, but instead emerged from the strangeness of that which
was ever at hand, livid and mute though indicated by scarcely
a line, yet full of terror, thunderous as a brewing storm.

But there was no time left to reconsider because Augustus
who had listened to the verses with an assenting countenance
now said: "Yes, that is how you wrote it, that is how you wrote
it for me . . . or have you changed your mind again, my Virgil?"

"No, Octavian, my mind is unchanged, the poem is
yours . . ."

Now Augustus clapped his hands twice and almost at once
the chamber began to fill with people, with very many people

who no doubt had been waiting behind the door for this very signal. Plotius Tucca and Lucius Varius were among them, but so were the doctor and his assistants, the slave too was now visible in the flesh, standing in a row with the other slaves. Only Plotia was missing, although she had certainly not gone away. Possibly, she was only frightened by the mass of people, and remained in hiding.

But it was Caesar who said: "Were I speaking before an assemblage of the people I should strike a higher and stronger note; but as I stand before friends whom I love and who are of one mind with me, I can only ask them to share in my joy that our poet has resolved to continue his work on the Aeneid as soon as he shall have recovered, that is to say, very soon . . ."

Did Augustus really love these friends? He imagined that he spoke differently to them than to the people whom he guided but by no means loved, yet the address did not vary in any way from the beginning of a people's address and now he paused cannily to let his words ripen and take effect.

Lucius Varius promptly filled the gap: "We knew that you would succeed, oh, Augustus; you are blessed in everything."

"I am only the mouthpiece of the Roman people of whom all of us are a part; in their service and that of the gods I have presented their claims to the Aeneid, and Virgil, who loves the people, has recognized their proprietory right, the irrevocable and eternal right of possession."

But the slave standing there among the others with his stern unmoved lackey's face, unnoticed and certainly unheard, added: "The way toward true freedom has been opened, the people will take it; eternal alone is the way."

"I am the people's advocate," continued the Augustus, in a voice of dissembling sweetness that vibrated with a warmth difficult to evade, "a mere advocate here as everywhere, and Virgil too has acknowledged this, making me proud by that acknowledgment, happy that, because of it, the poem has been entrusted to me for safe-keeping . . ."

"The poem is yours, Octavian."

"Only insofar as I am the advocate of the Roman people; others possess private property, not I, as you know."

Holding a small laurel branch plucked from the wreaths in his ever restless fingers, there stood Augustus beside the candelabrum, as though among the shadows of a murmuring laurel; he stood there dapper and majestic, and what he said was pure falsehood, although he believed in it himself; for he took great pains and was quite successful in increasing the holdings of the Julian family to gigantic proportions, as every-one knew. And the slave said properly, though luckily without being heard: "You are lying, Caesar." And yet, had the one so addressed not heard him? For now, casting his eyes on the manuscript-chest, he smiled as though in answer.

"In whatever character you accept it, Octavian, I have given the poem to you, but I must ask a favor in return."

"Conditions, Virgil? . . . I thought it was a birthday present."

"It is an unconditional present; it rests with you whether you will grant the favor I ask, or not . . ."

"Then let me hear these conditions; I submit to them be-forehand, but call to mind your own words, Virgil,"—a sly, friendly twinkle appeared in Caesar's eyes—, "be lenient to the conquered and temper your arrogance to that end."

"The future!" exclaimed the slave in the midst of the crowd.

Yes, the future; that is how the words were meant; the infinite, unplumbed future of man and man's virtue, the future of humility—, yet how slyly Octavian had made use of them for his temporary and superficial ends, but nevertheless the Aeneid should and must belong to him: "You have limited the emancipation of slaves, Augustus; permit mine to go free."

"What? At once?"

What a curious question! at once or not at once—, was it not all the same? "Not at once, Augustus, but immediately after my death; that is how I shall designate it in my will and on your side I beg you to sanction this bequest."

"Of course, I shall do so . . . but consider, Virgil, will your step-brother, who, as far as I remember, takes care of your property in Andes, be in agreement with this bequest? you will create difficulties for him if you take away all of his slaves at one stroke . . ."

"My step-brother, Proculus, will know how to help himself. Besides which he is a kind man and the servants will be likely to stay with him even as free men."

"Good, that is not my affair; I have simply to give my signature . . . in truth, Virgil, if this was the only condition you had to make we could have been spared our long arguments!"

"Perhaps it was good to have had them, Octavian."

"It was good,"—the Augustus smiled—"in spite of the time you made me lose by them."

"But there is still the will, Octavian."

"Unless I am mistaken you deposited one a long time ago with my archivist."

"Certainly, but I must add to it . . ."

"Because of the slaves? Make haste slowly; you can take care of this later in Rome."

"There are a few other changes; I do not like to put them off."

"You are in a hurry for yourself, but not for me . . . still, you are the only one to decide on the urgency of your document, and I neither dare nor shall I hinder you from drawing it up now; but as I cannot wait for it, I must ask you to give it to me later or send it on so that I can affix my seal to it in testimony and confirmation . . ."

"Plotius or Lucius, or both together, will bring you the will, Augustus; be thanked."

"My time is limited, Virgil; I sense the impatience with which they await me over there . . . Vipsanius Agrippa should have come in the meantime . . . I have to leave . . ."

"You have to . . ."

Enigmatically the room had suddenly become empty; they were quite alone.

"Alas, I must go."

"My thoughts go with you, Octavian."

"Your thoughts as well as your poem."

A sign from Caesar and there, conjured out of the void, stood two slaves beside the chest, their hands gripping the handles.

"Are these going to carry it off?"

Lightly, swiftly, Augustus came to the bed, and bending over it almost imperceptibly he became Octavian once more: "It will be kept in safety, not carried off; take this as a pledge." And he laid the bit of laurel that he had held between his fingers on the bed-cover.

"Octavian . . ."

"Yes, Virgil . . ."

"Accept my thanks for so many things."

"My thanks go to you, Virgil."

The slaves had raised the chest, and now as they started to carry it off someone sobbed, not very loudly, but still violently, and with that fervor one meets when eternity breaks suddenly into human life, as when pall-bearers are shouldering the coffin to bear it from the room and the relatives feel themselves stricken for the first time by the inexorable power which has already begun to take its course. It was the same eternity-sob which is wont to be sent after a coffin, it was this eternity-cry and it came from the broad and powerful chest of Plotius Tucca, from his kind and powerful human soul, from his moved and mighty heart, sent toward the manuscript-chest which was being borne away and which actually was a casket, a shell, bearing the remains of a child, of a life.

And now again the sun had really darkened.

Reaching the door Augustus turned around once more; once more friend's glance sought friend's glance; once more their eyes met: "May your eyes rest on me always, my Virgil," said Octavian, standing between the wide-opened wings of the door, here still Octavian, only to hasten off as Caesar, svelte, proud and masterful; at his heels a tawny lion, which followed the casket with steps heavy and slow, and many of those present joined in the procession.

THE goodly moist sobbing of Plotius persisted a little while before passing over into a breathy gulping, interspersed with many an "Ah, yes!" and it only completely subsided when the sun came out again and the doves on the window-sill went on once more with their cooing.

"Let your eyes rest on me always." Those were Octavian's words, that is the way they sounded or something like that, and that is how they continued to sound, remaining in the room, floating there, imperishable by their bond with him who had vanished, imperishable by their fulness of meaning. Imperishable the bond, but Octavian was gone—, why, why had he gone away? why had Plotia gone? Alas, they had gone like so many others, vanishing into their own fates, vanishing into their activities, into their aging, into their increasing tiredness, into their graying and their senility, vanishing into a dunness from which a voice no longer issued, and despite that, those invisible bridges had remained, and likewise those invisible chains that had linked them together once and seemingly forever, the invisible laurel-bridges, the invisible silver-enchainments, and the bond had remained, indestructible, built and forged for eternity, binding with, and reaching—where? Toward an invisible nothingness? No, the invisible thing on the opposite shore, that was no nothingness, no, for all its invisibility it was true existence, it was Octavian as he had always been, Plotia as she had always been, except that they had been most curiously and completely stripped of their names and their bodily forms; oh, deep, very deep within us, not to be reached by our bodily disintegration, unharmed by the fading of our senses, immune to all change, immune in the most unthinkably far regions of our selves, of our hearts, of our souls, perception lived on, imperceptible, unevocable, unexplorable, unrecognizable to itself, and it sought the counter-perception in the other soul, in the other heart, in the invisible depths of the other, sought to call it out just there in order that it might become forever perceptible to itself, eternal the bridge, eternal the spanned chain, eternal the encounter, lasting beyond all transfigurations, because the full significance of the word, the full significance of the world, relied on the encounter alone, perception perceived in its echo; nothwithstanding that his lids were closed, immensity lay outside, visible and full of meaning, breath-golden, wine-golden, transported in the stilled, shimmering glare of the sun's noontide, washed over the brownish-red, black-striped, dirty, spongy roofs of the city, visible and invisible at once, a mirror waiting for its reflection, waiting for the floating word, the floating perception, which although not quite revealed, was already at hand within the room, a care-free state, participation in which would not be a perjury, beauty risen from true knowledge, its existence permitted again, within the law of the pledge-protecting, the unknown god; and then, yes, and then, some of the doves left the window-sill with a puffing, almost pompous, fluttering and flew up, whirring their wings in the sunlit blue, sinking upward in the fever-heat of day's prime; thus they sank upward in the circle of the glance and dropping below it they disappeared— Oh, let your eyes rest on me always.

Plotius wiped the tears from his plump cheeks: "Too stupid," he remarked, "it is too stupid to be so moved just because Virgil has finally recovered from his lunacy."

"Perhaps it was Octavian's behavior that caused your emotion."

"Not so far as I know . . ."

"I want to make my will now."

"That is no reason for being emotional . . . everybody makes wills."

"It has nothing to do with your emotion; I must draft it now and that is all there is to it."

Lucius it was who now objected: "Augustus is perfectly right, one can only agree with him that you could leave such things to the time when you will have recovered, and you have all the more time as we understood there was already a valid will."

Plotius and Lucius were present in actual visibility, and Lysanias must also have been present even though he might be hiding in some corner of the room, perhaps annoyed that because he had not been summoned earlier the slave had been left in possession of the field—, but where was the slave? even so, where was he? there was nothing to indicate he had joined the train of Augustus, on the contrary, if he were anywhere it was presumably in this room, since this in a certain sense was his natural place, and yet in spite of it, he could not be found; however, this was not entirely true; if one began to look a little more intently, if one strained one's sight just a little more, in addition to the complete visibility of the two friends, some invisible things could be seen, things unready for living or for viewing, perhaps even unready for both—the ability to differentiate being insufficient—there especially where strips of sun-dust came in, there various motes of human-like invisibility were swarming so thickly it seemed the crowd that had left the room in Caesar's wake had streamed back into it, at least in part; nothing was likelier than that the one sought for was among these images, certainly not to be summoned, having been unwilling to disclose his name.

"Lysanias . . ."—even though the slave could not be called, one could call the boy; he ought to come and give some explanation.

"Again and again you mention this Lysanias," remarked Plotius, "you speak of him, yet he never appears . . . or has he some connection with the will you are so urgent about drafting?"

It was not to be denied that neither the boy nor the slave had any direct connection with the will; however, he was still unable to explain the association to Plotius and could only take refuge in a seeming motive: "I want to bequeath to him some object or other."

"The more then is it his duty to show himself at last; otherwise I shall feel obliged to doubt him and his existence."

The boy appearing at that very moment proved the implication unjust; anyone who was willing to see him could, and the reproach redounded upon Plotius. Nevertheless it would have been better if Lysanias had not been summoned, for now, having actually arrived, he had come in the twofold guise of slave and boy, just as if both bore the same name, to which each, whether slave or boy, had to respond. On the one hand this was not very remarkable; on the other it was remarkable that this twofold advent lacked concord, that the boy, although at pains to approach the bed, was not able to get ahead of his larger and stronger companion; again and again the way was barred to him and one would have thought that the boy Lysanias had lost all his wily skill.

Plotius walked back, sighing, to the armchair where he had sat before: "Instead of taking it easy as everyone advises you, you busy yourself with codicils and with what you have in mind to bequeath to this one or that one . . . Caesar was with you for more than an hour, and one can tell by your voice that this wore you out . . . well, for my part, I shall take care not to interfere with a pighead such as you . . ."

"Yes," added Lucius with a speculative curiosity, "well over an hour . . . and did you talk of nothing but the Aeneid? . . . stop, do not answer if it tires you . . ."

Standing sturdily beside the bed, the slave appeared to have grown in a most unforeseen manner; a stilly coldness emanated from him as from one who has come into a room from the iciest winter weather, and he stood there so broad and mighty that he made it impossible for the boy to send over a single glance, although the latter had climbed up on the table in order to peer over his shoulders.

"The slave should leave . . ."

"Ah, because of the will?"—Plotius from his armchair looked around the room—, "all of them have left anyway, you may begin."

Lucius, fussing as usual with the folds of his toga, sat down cautiously on the chair near the bed and, folding his long,

402

slender legs one over the other in a worldly posture, he held his long-fingered hand palm up in a gesture of explanation: "Yes, when the Exalted One once starts talking he is inclined to let one have a fair amount of it. And yet, if we are frank, he is anything but a gifted orator, at least not captivating in comparison with the Roman eloquence of classical times, which we, as surviving witnesses, are entitled to claim . . . do you remember the senatorial speeches of the past? what a pleasure they were, all of them! However, Augustus' eloquence does for the present, since, as it is, no one discourses today, and it will have to do . . . but, Virgil, by no means must I fall into the same blunder as he, praised be his name; I do not want to tire you . . ."

Why did the slave not move? He was set up here motionless and firmly rooted, like an ice-block, like an iceberg, always threatening to grow higher; by now he covered little Lysanias completely and the cold made itself felt ever more dangerously, issuing from him as though inexorably, bringing great waves of weariness in its wake.

"You need a complete rest,"—Lucius' hand put a finishing stroke to this pronouncement—, "you need rest, and had you consulted the doctor again he would have told you so; it might be best if we left you alone now."

His need for rest could not be gainsaid, a sweet and seductive need that had come over him, coming to him on the weariness-waves of chill, dangerous in its inescapability: Oh, it had to be fought, fought immediately! and so it proved most welcome that Lucius had mentioned the doctor and that he, answering the summons, started to emerge solidly from the swarm of transparent figures and continued to emerge no less solidly, a bland smile on his lips: "You have recovered, Virgil, and I am proud to be able to tell you so, for as I may be allowed to state in all modesty, my skill has contributed not a little to this favorable outcome."

It was a gratifying though not quite unlooked-for announcement: "I have recovered . . ."

"That is a slight exaggeration though on the whole, the gods be thanked, it may be correct," Plotius was heard to say from the alcove.

"I am well . . ."

"You will be soon" . . . corrected the slave.

"Send him away," the boy's voice sounded weak and plaintive—"send him away if you wish to recover; he will kill you too."

The weariness-chill became downright physical; proceeding from the ice-block it turned into an ice-block itself, turned into a curdled wave, enclosing, enwrapping, fiery at the core, enforcing a warm repose by its freezing embrace: "I have recovered; the doctor did not lie."

"Perhaps so, at least insofar as a doctor is able to be entirely truthful, but this truth implies that you have to behave live a convalescent who does not want to have a relapse"— Lucius was standing up—"and as for us, now we are going to leave."

"Stay!"

His voice had failed; the word had not been heard.

"Oh, let them go, let all of them go," begged Plotia coaxingly, though unable to conceal her own fright, "and him as well, send off him who holds you embraced; my arms are softer than his, and he is loathsome."

Then it became clear that the glowing-icy clasp was caused by the giant's arms, lifting him up from the bed and from the earth, and that on the giant's breast, in the immensity of which there was no longer heart-beat nor breathing, the sweetly-alluring repose of immutability would have to be found.

Clay was the earth from which he had been lifted, but not less earthlike and full of earth's forces was the giant's breast on which he lay.

"He is crushing me," sighed the boy hopelessly overcome by weakness.

"His time is up," said the giant, and it was almost like a smile, "it is not I who molest him, time does that."

Mighty as earth was the giant, bearing earth, bearing rest, bearing death—, did he not bear time as well?

"I am timeless," rejoined Plotia, "I do not alter, do not let him kill me too."

Did Plotia need to be saved, did the boy? was he himself in need of salvation? was there a need for the will, or for the Aeneid? the embrace became still vaster, heavier, mightier, more and more icy, more and more glowing, the glow and the iciness already melted into a common lifestream, carrying existence toward non-existence so that it could unite with it; the quiet had already become so dense that it threatened to let no sound escape, no sound that might shatter it, and it seemed already past shattering, and not for Plotia, not for the boy, no, but for his own life's sake, a final effort must be made: "I want to live . . . oh, Mother!"

Was it a cry? It could not be ascertained whether it had pierced the borders of stillness. The breast of the giant was without heart-beat or breathing, without heart-beat or breathing the world. And it was quite a while before the giant said: "I am not freeing you because of the woman's entreaties nor those of the boy, neither because of your own fright; I am freeing you because you have a mind to accomplish your earthly service." It was almost an admonition; and withal he felt the clasp loosen as if the giant were restoring him to the clay floor of earth.

"I want to live . . . I want to live!"

Yes, now it was a cry, realized by the voice and the ears, hoarse, it is true, but still loud enough to cause the two friends to jump up in alarm; Plotius rushed over and pushing aside the helpless Lucius he reached the bed with a reproachful: "This is what comes of it!"

But the clasp was broken, the giant had vanished, the frightful seduction had subsided, and what remained was the usual fever, only the usual fever, which was still like a glowing ice-block, crushing the chest and compressing the breath to a painful rattling, however, so often experienced and so well-known that even the taste of blood rising in the mouth was no longer alarming; one was again in an ordinary sick-room, Lysanias was crouched on top of the table, he likewise was greatly exhausted and looked attentively across the room.

"This is what comes of it . . . this is what comes of it . . ."

It was not easy to decide whether the reproachful grumbling was meant for the sickness, the sick man, or Lucius, and the latter said: "The doctor . . ."

One was again in an ordinary sick-room; Lysanias was present as was proper, but these two old men, Lucius and Plotius, were out of place here, and Mother was missing. Why was Plotius sitting in grandfather's place near the window? Probably because he was as stout and ponderous as the latter. Under his weight the feet of the arm-chair had made a jagged dusty groove in the clay floor and through the window one could see the rolling meadows of the Mantuan landscape in the sunny light of noon. One must call Mother from the kitchen: "Thirsty . . ."

Before Lucius could turn around, Plotius, with clumsy agility, had discovered a beaker and had returned with it from the wall-fountain to bring moisture to the expectant lips of the sick man, whose head he supported meanwhile with his other hand. "Are you better, my Virgil?" he inquired, still short of breath and perspiring with excitement.

Speech was difficult to restore. It was possible to thank Plotius only with a nod. And besides the voice of Mother was now audible in the kitchen. "Coming," she called cheerfully, "coming . . . my child shall soon have his milk." This meant that Mother was still alive; without altering, she was timeless, and this assurance made for inmost well-being. "Am I still sick, Mother?"—"A little, but soon my child will be out of bed and able to play again." Yes, he would play again on the kitchen floor and out there in the sand of the garden, at Mother's feet. But how could Mother approve of such a play that, in forming the clay-like earth, repeated and continued doing what Father had done, and what the god still does? was not this game a crime against the earth that wished to remain unformed, a crime against its primal loam? did it not awake horror and scorn in the knowing mother-goddess? However, it was now impossible to reflect upon it, because of Plotius who was still standing beside the bed; and what he had brought was not milk but water, clear water from the springs of earth.

After a second long gulp, having sunk back into the pillows, speech was again possible; "Thank you, my Plotius, much better, you have restored me . . ."

It was a beaker of brown horn, but the figure of a cock was etched upon it. It was the good solid beaker that farmers use.

"I will bring the doctor," persisted Lucius, moving toward the door.

"Why bring the doctor?" It was curious; the doctor was already here, and the somewhat uncertain and nebulous shape in which he was cast seemed to take on solidity with every passing moment.

"We want to ask him," said Plotius, reflectively, "whether or not he will bleed you; how often have I myself had attacks like this, even worse, but after getting rid of a few ounces of blood one finds oneself again in the midst of life and is aware that the whole unpleasant procedure has been most beneficial for one's health."

The doctor, Charondas, combed his beard: "Roman school, Roman method of treatment, we will have none of it; in your case we have not to withdraw any fluids from your body but on the contrary we must add to them . . . I bid you drink as much as possible."

"Let me have another drink! . . ."

"Do you want wine again?" asked Lysanias, lifting the ivory goblet.

"Nonsense," the doctor snapped out at him, "no wine; you have nothing to say here."

Verily, the cool trickling was medicine: "I have recovered; the doctor himself said so."

"Then we want him to confirm it," said Lucius from the door, his hand on the knob.

"We have always to reckon on little relapses," said the doctor and smiled blandly, "this was nothing but a little relapse."

"Stay here, Lucius . . . we shall not make a lot of a little relapse; now I must draw up my will."

Lucius came back to the table: "Postpone it only until this evening; I promise you we shall finish it before our departure."

No, it had to be done at once; otherwise the giant might believe that the will had been used only as a subterfuge to escape him. Had not the retreat into the earthbound been altogether too cheap? Shame arose in him, a crippling and scourging shame, as crippling and scourging as the freezing heat of the fever which persisted, although there had been only a slight relapse.

Lysanias, now as before atop the table, wanted to dispel it. "The shame lies only in the chance but your path was chanceless, Virgil, and all that you did was necessary."

"He who goes backward on his path feels ashamed."

With a heavy sigh, Plotius sat down on the edge of the bed: "Now what is that supposed to mean?"

"The will is urgent, I cannot put it off."

"Nobody would understand your feeling as shame the postponement of a few hours, and you yourself cannot be in earnest."

"For Augustus' sake I renounced my wishes in regard to the Aeneid . . . now, for your sake should I renounce them in regard to my will?"

"We are only concerned with your health."

"And it is this that permits me, aye, even forces me to go forward on my path. I do not want to go backward."

"I have never led you backward," the boy defended himself, "we have always gone forward."

"And whither now?"

Lysanias was silent; he knew not what to answer.

"His guidance reached only to where I was," said Plotia, intruding, "what follows now is our common path, the path of our love."

408

"Whither? I have to find my way alone."

"You are unjust, Virgil," pouted Plotius Tucca, sitting heavily on the edge of the bed and causing the mattress to bend under him, "you are unjust; nothing warrants you in rejecting our help and our love like this . . ."

Plotius, who was usually so loudly domineering, and was wont to let nothing oppose him, sat there quite helplessly on the edge of the bed, and Lucius, otherwise so secure in his worldly wisdom, seemed quite shaken; it was plain that they had become submissive, both ready for submission to a patient whose impressionability had formerly made him bend almost constantly to their will. What had wrought this change? Were they submissive only to the sovereign power of illness, although formerly they had given little heed to its voice? or were they now beginning to be aware of the greater voice waiting behind the illness? the annunciating voice of love uniting life and death? oh, they must divine it, otherwise they would not oppose so strongly a last will which wanted to prepare for death!

And Lucius said: "I do not wish to oppose you further, but . . ."

"Do not add a but, my Lucius . . . yonder in the corner is my luggage, and in the traveling bag you will find my writing utensils and everything that pertains to them . . ."

Plotius rocked his head to and fro: "Well, one must let you have your own way as there is no holding you back . . ."

In the face of such docility it was neither appropriate nor pleasant to have to admit to these two that the physical pains were continuing; but there was the danger of an oncoming chill: "Will you just get me a second blanket . . ."

The sulky face of Plotius became worried and the sulkiness increased: "You are taxing yourself far too much."

"Just a second blanket . . . that is all."

"I will get it for you," said Lucius.

But scarcely had Lucius called for the servants and given them the order before the slave of the impenetrably stern countenance appeared, already equipped with the blanket, no giant he, but just an ordinary lackey who politely and deftly spread the second blanket over the bed, replacing upon it the laurel sprig hallowed by the touch of Augustus, and this happened so swiftly, so obviously prepared for in advance, that one was inclined to ask oneself whether the request for this blanket had been altogether necessary or justified—, had it not just been an excuse to order the slave back? or an excuse for the slave to steal in again? some explanation was needed: "Were you not here just a moment ago?"

"I have been ordered not to leave you any more."

The boy Lysanias slid down from the table and came quite close, no doubt so the slave could not push him away again: "Without being ordered I stayed with you always, and now without orders I mean to stay on."

What the boy said was of no consequence, indeed it was almost like a forgotten, now scarcely understood language, while the words of the other one, despite their curt sound, brought with them a strange kind of confidence: "Why did you not come sooner?"

"You too had to serve before I could serve you."

Plotius felt worriedly for the cold feet beneath the blanket: "They are like ice, my Virgil!"

"I feel quite well now, Plotius."

"I hope you are telling the truth," said Lucius, who meanwhile had been arranging the writing utensils and the pad of paper on the table, "and here is everything that you requested."

"Give me the paper."

Lucius was astonished: "What! do you even want to do the writing yourself?"

"I want to look at the paper . . . give it here."

"Do not be so impatient, Virgil, here it is." And Lucius, who had opened the leather portfolio, took from the clean-cut pile of paper the topmost sheets and handed them over.

Oh, it was a good quality of paper, it had that rough, cool surface that is easy on the pen, and it was good to pass over it with padded fingertips as though one were about to write.

And by holding it against the light one could see through its ivory color the brownish network of the grain. Oh, the first stroke of the pen on the clean white fold of paper, the first line drawn toward creation, the first word to enter into imperishability!

It was hard to part from it: "This is good paper, Lucius . . ."

"My body is white and smooth and tender," sighed Plotia in a whispering lament, "but you did not care to touch it."

Lucius took back the sheets, then he too stroked the surface with tentative fingers, testing it and holding it against the light: "Yes," he confirmed expertly, "it is good paper." Then he sat down to write.

Plotia had been untouchable, her fate too heavy to be borne, yet light as down, too light to be borne or to be allowed to be borne, and unknown she had vanished into the unknowable, there where no meeting exists; her ring remained, but she did not appear again.

Plotius said: "If it is only a codicil and not a modification of your former will, you can make it extremely brief."

No, Plotia did not appear, other shapes came forth, however, from the shadowy swarm, some of them strangely familiar, some of them difficult to recognize as they were immediately whisked away, all sorts of people, among them many whores with blonde wigs, many drunkards and pot-bellies, also waiters and pleasure-boys. For a moment Alexis was visible, insofar as he was recognizable from his back, for he was standing at a ship's railing and looking down into the water in which all sorts of refuse stewed about. And the boy said, admonishingly, and sadly: "We have gone down all paths together and I have led you through them all; oh, that you might remember . . ."

"I know many . . ."

"Does this belong to your dictation?" asked Lucius.

"I know many . . ." No, no one was recognizable any longer, just a single one, and this was astonishing, for the parting from Octavian had been painful and final, the parting could not be repeated, and, contrary to all mutual understanding,

Octavian was here again; he stood near the candelabrum, apart from the shadowy swarm, and though he himself was invisible, his dark eyes glanced toward the slave, giving him leave to speak.

"Speak," directed the slave, "give your permission."

Thereupon the order, which in reality was nothing of the sort, was given by Caesar: "I permit you, Virgil, to dispossess the heirs of your first will in favor of your slaves."

"So shall it be; I will provide for the slaves but along with that I must settle the question of the Aeneid and its publication."

"I shall take care of the poem."

"That is not enough for me."

"Don't you recognize me, Virgil?"

And the boy said: "Look at the rising star, the star of Aeneas, the star that is Caesar's, the one that is blessing the harvests, gladdening the fields with full grain and enpurpling the grapes in the vineyards."

"I see," said Lucius, "you want to make stipulations for the publication of the Aeneid . . . What is still lacking in this respect?"

The boy had lied: There was no star to be seen, least of all that which had been promised to shine in the future ripeness of time, the star of meeting where all cognition and recognition were surrendered, the great revealing mystery which brought the empty stream of time to a standstill by fulfilling it; brought to a new beginning the stream, which could not be stayed,— no, the boy had lied, nothing was to be seen of it, still nothing.

"Not quite here, but yet at hand!" Who had said this? the boy, or the slave? Both of them were looking toward the east, joined in a new concord by their eastward glancing; and the star would rise on the eastern firmament.

"The Julian star shines westward," spoke out of Caesar's invisibility, "and you, Virgil, will no longer see it . . . will your hatred never subside?"

"The Aeneid is lovingly dedicated to Caesar, but the new star ranks still higher."

Caesar answered no more; in silence his voice sank back into the invisible.

"The Aeneid . . ." Plotius puffed a little and ran his hands through the gray wreath of his hair—, "yes, the Aeneid, the Julian star will shine through it forever."

"If I am not mistaken, the dedication of the Aeneid to Caesar should be included in the will," said Lucius, and dipped the pen in the ink-well, his face attentive, and waiting for further instructions. He waited, however, in vain. For that was no ink-well in which he held the pen, instead it was the fish-pond in front of the house in Andes, and he was sitting at no ordinary table, since the whole country-seat at Andes was suddenly erected upon it, the estate that from now on would belong to Proculus, and behind it, like a counterfeit in minia-ture, was the mausoleum, a prison built of leaden blocks, while the waves of the Posilipo crossed, shimmering, the waves of the pond; yes, Lucius was dipping his pen in the pond, soft water-circles were lightly spreading from the place he dipped towards the pond's borders around which the geese and ducks were quacking, doves were cooing on the roosts of the dove-cotes; the table, moreover, was surrounded by innumerable people who were waiting for the will; it was understandable that Cebes who was to live on the farm was among them, but on the other hand it was scarcely permissible for Alexis to be hanging around, and to come strolling hither over the double bend of the entrance-path. This gathering for the will was unseemly, and it was with greatest unwillingness that these people let themselves be dispersed by the slave; it took some time before they had all been banished into invisibility, and for the table to stand clear in front of Lucius. "I am ready, Virgil," he announced again, "I am waiting for you . . ."

It was not so simple quickly to find one's way back again, and actually Lucius should have known this: "Presently, Lucius . . ."

"Take your time . . . we are in no hurry," said Plotius.

"Listen, my friends, before we begin . . . do you recollect the words of Augustus . . . ?"

413

"Certainly."

"Well, Caesar is familiar with my first will and I feel it is only proper that you, who are assisting me, should know about it too . . ."

"We are not alone . . ." broke in Lucius, and pointed to the slave.

"The slave? yes, I perceive him . . ."

Perceiving and perceived—, it was an encounter lasting forever, it was enchainment forever, eternal, simultaneously within and without, an enchainment to him who bore the chain.

"Did you not intend to dismiss the slave before, on account of the will?"

It was odd that Lucius dared to utter this, and it lacked reverence, but nothing came of it; the slave left the room with an unmoved countenance, remaining there at the same time as if having doubled.

Plotius folded his hands with thumbs crossed over his abdomen; "Well, now we are by ourselves."

Quite scornfully and contemptuously, he was rebuffed by Plotia: "Why do you want to be by yourselves? Love needs to be alone; but here you are speaking of money."

"Not my money, no longer my money . . ." It hurt that Plotia could speak thus, for, far away as she was, she must know that never had there been a question of money or property.

"It was your own money that you willed away, and it is your own that you are now willing," objected Plotius, "for you to say anything else is humbug."

Luckily this could be answered without exposing Plotia: "I have received my money through the grace and goodness of my friends, and it is only right and reasonable for me to return it to them . . . consequently, I still harbor some doubts as to whether I am justified in providing as liberally as I did in my first will for my brother Proculus to whom, because of his kindness and straightforwardness, I am quite partial."

"Of course that is just flim-flam."

"Time-honored custom and the prosperity of the state demand that fortunes be kept within the family, there to be cherished and husbanded," said Lucius with a grin.

"To speak seriously," said Plotius, settling the matter, "you may and you should do as you deem best in disposing of your estate; for whatever you may have won, you have finally to thank yourself and your achievements."

"My achievement bears no relation to the prosperity that has flowed to me through my friends, and that is why my first deposition is that my Roman house on the Esquiline as well as my house in Naples should fall back to Caesar, whereas my Campagna estates should be restored to Maecenas . . . Furthermore, I ask Augustus to allow Alexis, who for years now has lived in the house on the Esquiline, to stay on there, and I ask the same favor of Proculus for Cebes, for whom country life has always been beneficial and even necessary because of his poor health, and his poetry, and so I want to secure permanent hospitality for him in Andes . . . the best solution would be to let him help a little in cultivating the grounds there . . ."

"Do these two get nothing else?"

"But yes . . . It is no secret to anyone, least of all to both of you, that my assets in currency are far in excess of my needs, and I dare say have increased to several millions, much against my wish, however much in accord with that of my friends, . . . well, from this fortune Cebes and Alexis are to receive each a legacy of a hundred thousand sesterces, just as I have set forth some other small legacies that I need not enumerate here, and to these will be added a few more for my slaves . . ."

"All as it should be," agreed Plotius, "moreover, many of your decisions will be changed in the course of the next years, as, for all your alleged contempt of money, you are still a peasant, convinced like every peasant in the depths of his heart that the gods are often quite disposed to bestow their blessings by way of gold; accordingly your property is bound to grow still greater . . ."

"We shall not go on arguing this matter now, Plotius . . . but whatever may be, or will be, after the deduction of these legacies I want half of my current funds to go to Proculus, a quarter to Augustus, and the remaining quarter to be divided equally between you, Lucius and Maecenas . . . so that is the general picture."

The back of Plotius' neck, his bald-spot and his face were suffused with a dark, purply red, and Lucius threw up both his hands: "What has gotten into you, Virgil! we are your friends, not your heirs!"

"You yourselves have given me leave to dispose of my property as I deem best."

A limping man with an upraised stick came threateningly nearer to the bed: "Whoever has money gets more; and who has none, gets none!" he shouted, and had the slave not disarmed him so that, still shouting, he had to withdraw again into nothingness, without doubt he would have started a fight.

"Yes, I am forgetting that I want to add to the legacies another of twenty-thousand sesterces to feed the people of Brundisium."

"You may as well add my portion to it at once," muttered Plotius, wiping his eyes.

"What you are to receive can in no way measure up to what I have received from you."

The mobile actor's face of Lucius Varius became ironic: "Virgil, will you assert that you have ever seen much of my money . . . ?"

"And will you maintain that you did not precede me in epic poetry? that I have not learned an enormous amount from you? Well, Lucius? Can this be repaid with money at all? it is just lucky that you are never in funds and always need something, for in this way the legacy is not entirely useless . . ."

The flush had not faded from the face of Plotius; now his heavy jowls were taut with scornful resentment: "You are not indebted to me for any of your verses, and I am blessed with enough riches to be able to renounce your money . . ."

416

"Oh, Plotius, shall I let you stand back for Lucius, this giddy person?! For thirty years you have been my friends, and you have advanced me no less than he, with all his verses; I do not want to speak of what I have had from you in money's worth . . . you are my oldest friends, you have always been united, and so it must be with this inheritance, and you will accept it, you have to accept it, because I ask you to do so."

"I am your oldest friend," objected the boy.

"Incidentally, you too are a peasant, Plotius, and so it follows that everything you said about me must hold good for you as well . . ." ah, gradually speech became quite painful—, "but I wouldn't like my friends to be reminded of me only by cyphers . . . in my apartments at Rome and Naples you will find some furniture and my personal belongings . . . and my friends, that means you Plotius and you Lucius, but Horace and Propertius likewise . . . my friends are to take from them any objects, especially books, that please them and that might help to keep me in memory . . . what remains shall be given to Cebes and Alexis . . . my seal-ring . . ."

Plotius struck his lusty thigh with a clenched fist; "Now that's enough . . . what else are you going to fling at us . . . ?"

The visible world moved off further and further, and Plotius' blustering, loud though it was, came out of a haze; it would have been good to have done with everything, but there was still so much, so very much to say: ". . . from you I ask still another service in return."

"And do you not ask anything of me? are you dismissing me offhand?" asked Lysanias plaintively.

"Lysanias . . ."

"Tell us at last where that boy is hiding . . ."

Yes, where was he hidden? but Plotius himself was not much more visible or audible than Lysanias, suddenly he too was hiding within the unreachable, and that was as though behind a thick pane of glass that became more and more cloudy, as though turning into a leaden wall.

"Shall we seek him for you, perhaps?" joked Lucius. "Is that what you want of us?"

"I do not know . . ."

"I am standing in front of you, Virgil; I, Lysanias, stand in front of you and you have only to stretch out your hand, oh, that you might take mine!"

It required an endless time to lift one's hand; it did not want to obey one at all, and then it grasped into emptiness, into blindness, into utter blindness.

"Every eye, I replace every torn-out eye," said the doctor, "look in my mirror and you will again begin to see."

"I do not know it any more . . ."

Could these be words? what was it that had suddenly fallen into nothingness? was it these words or something quite different? Just a moment ago it had been intelligible, and certainly one's own speech, and all at once the words were no longer here, having glided off into nothingness, an alien mumbling, lost in the voice-thicket, imprisoned in ice and fire.

But the limping one was again on the spot, and with him an enormous train of shadow-shapes, a procession so long that one life would not have sufficed to figure out this multitude; verily, a whole city was coming along, no, rather many cities, all the cities of the world, their steps shuffled over the stony floor and a fat hag shouted: "Go home now, march on, go home!"

"Go on," ordered the limping one, "go on, you, taking yourself for a poet or something extraordinary; go on, you belong to us . . ."

"Along with him who has forgotten how to walk and has to be carried," the fat female followed up the command, to make it more effective.

A roar of laughter from the rest of the women accompanied this speech, and their outstretched fingers pointed lewdly, yet not in actual lewdness, toward the street of misery into which the procession now turned. The way led down the steps, the end of the alley was not to be sighted because it went down so far, but there, amid the band of children who, scrambling between the goats, the lions, and the horses, raced up and down the steps, there was Lysanias, gaily armed with his torch— it was an extinguished, cold, and sooty stump of a torch that he held in his hand—squabbling with the others as if nothing beyond such play existed.

"So you have brought me back anyway, Lysanias, although you have never admitted it."

And behold, Lysanias offered no reply; he gazed up as though confronted by a stranger, only to turn back immediately to his play.

The descent continued, step by step.

Plotius, however, who was also seated on the litter, his stout legs dangling, said warily: "Back? oh, indeed, we are taking you back into life."

"Come away from here," said Plotia, "it smells bad here, dreadful."

Yes, it reeked; each single door-gap yawning in the mouldy walls exhaled overpowering excremental fumes from the body of the house, and the dying gray-beards reeked in their blackened prison-cells. Augustus lay there too, whimpering.

Step by step the descent continued, haltingly, but not to be halted.

There were masses and masses of people, greedy for metaphors, greedy for victory. And there in their midst, in the midst of these pushing and crowding people, in the midst of turmoil Lucius sat writing; he sat there entirely given over to his task, writing down everything, everything that occurred inside or outside, and continuing to write he lifted his head: "What is it that we are to do for you, Virgil? What was it that you asked for?"

"Take down everything, everything . . ."

"Your will?"

"You need no will,"—Plotius' voice darted over, hard and thin like a gnat, only to waver off like a dragon-fly—, "oh, you need no will for you will live on forever, forever living with me." A little black Syrian, a broken chain hanging from his

419

neck-ring—where had his one-eyed fellow remained?—came leaping up the steps, slipping between the sundry figures, crying out the while: "The golden age has begun . . . what was on top is now at the bottom; what was below is above . . . he who has remembered must now forget; he who has forgotten may now remember . . . down with you, down with you, you overgrown piggling . . . past and future are one, forever, forever, forever!"

Meanwhile the crowd had become more and more dense. But that the litter floating above it had been forced to stop was a surprise, and beyond that, a surprising glimmer of hope, the more as hope was indubitably strengthened by the doctor's behavior; for despite his corpulence he moved lightly and fleetly through the conglomerate human mass, taking with a quick sleight-of-hand the money which the ailing held out to him, and his smiling lips with the instant quickness of a mirror, offered the recompense: "You have recovered . . . and so have you there . . . yes, you have also recovered . . . and you over yonder have gotten well again, too . . . you have recovered, all of you, all of you . . . terrible is death, but you are all well again . . ."

"Terrible is life," said the slave who, although he had not changed his shape, must evidently be standing by himself on a very elevated spot, for he was looking down upon the litter.

Now Augustus lifted himself from his ragged couch; he staggered with uncertain tread, on his neck-ring bobbed—as though he were the missing erstwhile mate of the little Syrian— the end of a chain, of silver it is true, and his speech came, uncertain and tremulous: "Come Virgil, come with me, lie there with me on my couch, for we must go back; we must keep on going back, we must reach beyond the first forefathers; we must return into the mass that sustained us, we must go back into the humus of the beginning . . ."

"Away with you . . . !" ordered the slave.

Thereupon everything was wiped out, and even Caesar, hastening to become dwarfed, shriveled to nothing; the human likenesses dwindled away to mere shadows of puppets whose wires had suddenly been cut, indeed, it was like the abrupt severance of every worldly filament, a general collapse within and without simultaneously, just beginning or reaching its peak —one didn't know which because of the speed with which it occurred—came about as one sank back once more into the pillows of the bed-boat, which had immediately resumed its placid journey: truly, one felt a sense of release, both inwardly and outwardly, like the relaxation of a clutching hand, a hand that had once been a brazen fist and that now, quietly-quieting, had turned into soft repose.

"Are you coming now?" asked Plotia, almost impatiently, giving herself in nearly the same breath the disappointed and disappointing answer: "Alas, you do not wish to come . . ."

"Out with you . . . !" ordered the slave again. "Even you are not able to bring help . . ." and thereupon—for a moment perfectly visible—Plotia floated off as though she were a fury, her ivory body crowned with hair that was streaming flame.

Who would bring help? No one had been allowed to remain, not even Plotia; all of them had been frightened away, and yet the isolation was like rest, yes, it was very quiet now with a quietness that bade fair to grow beyond itself, foretelling a ramble among flowery groves under the shade of laurels, a promise of that prenatal land into which it would blossom, to be meted out in a mild flow to the wanderer who would no longer have to pursue it in himself, absolved of the torment of searching, absolved of existence, absolved of his name, absolved of his anguish, absolved of his blood and his breath, he a wanderer in the forgotten land, and in the purity of forgetfulness!

"Forgetfulness will bring no help to you either," said the slave.

Oh, who would bring help if there was no surety even in forgetting; oh, who could comfort one for one's inability to rectify what had been done, or retrieve what had been left undone,—the done and the undone, one like the other, were forfeited and sealed—, what effort was still required for the re-

421

deeming and redeemed help to come? Once a voice had spoken, but it was only an annunciation, not yet the deed, and even the voice could no longer be heard, even the voice was forgotten, as forgotten as one's own voice, forfeited and sealed in the irrevocable.

And now the slave said: "Only he who calls out for help by name shall partake of it."

To call out for help? to call out once more? Once more to struggle for breath, once more to fight against the taste of blood on the tongue, once more, gasping with fatigue and fatigued with gasping, to have to call back one's self and one's own voice? Oh, what was the name, for the name had been forgotten! For a moment, for just a short moment came the vision of a face that could not be lost, that face of hard, brown, stiffened clay, kind and strong in its farewell smile, the never-vanishing parental countenance in its last calm—and then it faded away into the unforgettable.

"Call," urged the slave.

The mouth was full of blood thick enough to stifle one, and all that was or could be outside of oneself remained imperceptible, remained behind endless, paralyzing layers, dim, opaque and impervious to sound. If there was no telling the call's goal, there was no way to detect the name!

"Call!"

The call had to be forced out through the stifling, the paralysis, through strain; oh, voice calling out for the voice!

"Call!"

— Father!—

Had it been called?

"You called," said the slave.

Had it been called? The slave affirmed it as if he were the mediator to one who should have received the call, and who perhaps had already heard it, even though he did not choose to answer.

"Ask him for help," said the slave.

And with recaptured breath, the plea came without effort,

without premeditation, of its own accord: "Come to me . . ."

Was this the moment of judgment?—Who would pronounce it? Or had it already been pronounced? On what would it fall? Would it ring out and be audible? would it appear as a deed? When, oh, when? The judgment between good and bad, separating guilt from innocence, the judgment which calls up the name and joins it to the innocent one, the law's truth of reality, the last and only truth—, oh, the sentence had been pronounced and now one must wait until it was executed.

But nothing followed, neither a deed nor a voice, but despite that something did follow, something that one could scarcely capture; for messengers were coming from there where the call had penetrated, they were coming through the air on silent, soft-hooved horses, coming like an echo or its herald, and they were approaching slowly, ever more slowly, so that one could almost think they would never arrive. But even their non-coming was an oncoming.

Then, however, dimmed by many intervening clouded panes of glass, only barely visible, a kind round face was bending over the bed and saying in a sound-distant, sound-deadened voice: "How can one help you? Would you like another drink?"

"Plotius, who sent you hither?"

"Sent me? . . . if you want to put it like that, our friendship . . ."

Plotius was not the messenger; he was perhaps just the forerunner of the messenger, or perhaps a still further link of the chain. And besides it was not a question of this or that kind of succor, even though it would have been comforting to be allowed to drink once more; the blood-taste would not subside. But at the beginning of the chain stood he who had sent Plotius hither, stood he who sends water to the thirsting; even the non-coming was oncoming.

"Drink, if you are thirsty," said the slave. "Water wells from the earth, and the service that you are consummating is still an earthly one."

In the breast something fluttered with too great speed, and, despite this too great and disquieting speed, something was there akin to joy, because it was the heart, the heart that was still beating, yes, that could even be curbed again to a quiet and more regular beat; it was almost an awareness of an imminent, ultimate victory, the victory of complete serenity: "Curbed to duty . . . once again to earthly duty . . ."

"You have only to curb yourself for your health; beyond that no other duties exist for you at the moment."

"The Aeneid . . ."

"That will become your task once more when you will have fully recovered . . . until then the poem is well protected in Augustus' care, and you will find it again, unharmed."

It seemed scarcely credible that Augustus would be able to guard the Aeneid under the couch of rags on which he was forced to lie, aged, naked and powerless, and anyway, Plotius' speech, although intelligible, sounded most strange, stiffly-hollow, even though the glass-pane had started to clear and to melt away. Everything was incongruous. All the works of men were incongruous. The Aeneid was an incongruity.

"Let not a single word be changed . . ."

Now it was Lucius who understood immediately what he meant: "No one would ever dare to touch a manuscript of Virgil or even to suggest a correction, not to mention that Augustus would never permit such a thing!"

"Caesar will come to be powerless; he will not be answerable for anything."

"For what should he be answerable? there is nothing to be answerable for; you give yourself too many worries."

It was still an unfamiliar language that was being spoken here, the language of an alien people whose guest one was, a language that one was barely able to understand while one's own was already forgotten or still unlearned; certainly the words of Augustus, in spite of his raggedness, had been much more familiar.

Plotius brought the goblet: "Here you are, Virgil."

"Presently . . . first let me have another pillow." The heart

424

was fluttering and needed to be brought into another position in order to curb it.

In a flash the slave was at hand with the pillow, and stacking it neatly behind the back, he warned softly: "Time presses on."

The fountain drizzled. From somewhere the heavy smell of damp clay, the lighter odor of glazed pottery and earthen jars came floating by on a breath of air, easy to draw into the painful lungs, and grateful to them: somewhere a potter's wheel was buzzing, gentle its high-pitched whirring sound, which came intermittently, almost tonelessly, and finally stopped: "Time . . . indeed, time presses on . . ."

"It doesn't press on at all . . ." growled Plotius.

"Reality awaits you," said the slave.

Reality towering behind reality; here the reality of friends and their language, behind this an unquenchably lovely memory of a boy at play, further back, that of the caves of misery where Augustus was obliged to live, and beyond these the threatening, brittle and linear entanglement spread out over all existence, over world upon world, behind which was the reality of the flowering groves, oh, and behind this, oh, undiscernible, so undiscernible, the genuine reality, the reality of the never heard, though ever forgotten, ever promised word, the reality of the creation rising anew in the rays of the unbeholdable eye, the reality of the homeland—, and the goblet in the hand of Plotius was of ivory.

Timidly, perhaps confused by the presence of the slave, perhaps intimidated by his stronger will, nevertheless sure in her knowledge, Plotia made herself known, but from the inaudibility of an infinitely remote distance: "You have disdained the homeland of myself; rest now, slumber on to me."

Where was she? Close about him living walls of impenetrable green shot up suddenly as if the leaden prison had been transferred again into the shadowy grotto of leaves which once had been on the point of embracing him and Plotia,—the impenetrable thicket stretched out endlessly, it extended into the infinite distance on every side, but in the midst of its green shone a bush with golden leaves, almost within reach of the hand, although one would have had to grasp across the width of the stream, which unmoving, barely trickling, was now flowing past; the flowing mystery which could not be checked. And from over there, from out the branches of the golden bush Plotia's sibylline voice could be heard, lightly taking farewell.

Alas for the vanished one! alas for her who was already wandering beyond the stream, beyond all desiring, and beyond reach: "Without a wish . . ."

"That is right," said Plotius, "very right that you have no wishes."

"And should you need anything," added Lucius, "that is why we are here . . . a while ago you said you had something to ask from us."

Beyond the empty stream! the shoreless stream without source or outlet; impossible to discriminate the place of our emergence from that of our re-immersion, for it was the time-bearing, oblivion-bearing flood of the creaturely, returning without beginning or end—was there a ford in such a stream? certainly, with or without a ford, one was still not permitted to attempt a crossing, and the stream flowed away, disappeared, as the slave, already quite impatient, emphasized the essential: "Do what has become your duty."

Raised up on the pillows, breathing was easier, the cough was looser, and speaking once more became natural; but much remained confused: "I am still without guidance."

"You have left your work in time to guide one through the times; this was the sum of your wisdom, for yours was the divination of light."

Standing near the bed, attentive and motionless, a serving slave uttered these words—; but had he uttered them? Considering the change which suddenly came to pass, this must have been so, for even had the words been mute, they had wrought a change: restored again the first plane of reality's existence, the surrounding things were familiar, familiar the friends; one was no longer a guest in a strange land with a strange language, and even if the image of the true and promised homeland stood fixed before one's eyes, without having become discernible, even here in the midst of earthly things repose had again been granted for a time, though presumably the time was short.

And Lucius corroborated: "Your poem is guidance, and guidance it will remain."

"The Aeneid . . ."

"Yes, Virgil, the Aeneid . . ."

The stream had vanished, the leafy grotto had vanished, only the drizzling went on; but this, it is true, might be coming from the wall-fountain.

"I may not destroy the Aeneid . . ."

"Are you still thinking of that?" The angry distrust welling up in Plotius seemed on the point of breaking out anew.

The stream had vanished, but the fields still remained, lying there in the vibrant stillness of afternoon, filled with the chirping of crickets. Or was it the potter's wheel sending up its gentle, whirring song again? No, it was not that—only the drizzling persisted.

"Destroy . . . no, I no longer wish to destroy the Aeneid."

"Now you are really sound, Virgil."

"It may well be so, my Plotius . . . but . . ."

"Well?"

Something still resisted, something lodged there deeply and ineradicably, demanding sacrifices and eager to offer them; and the slave, as though aware of this resistence, said: "Let your hatred fall from you."

"I hate no one . . ."

"At least we hope that you no longer hate your work," observed Lucius.

"You hate things earthly," said the slave.

There was no contradicting this; the slave spoke the truth and one had to bow to it: "Perhaps I have loved them too much."

"Your work . . . ," said Lucius, both elbows supported

reflectively on the table, and the pen-holder pressed wistfully to his lips, "your work . . . love that as we love it."

"I will try, Lucius, . . . but first of all we must take care of publishing it."

"As soon as you shall have finished it the publishing will follow . . . before that you would hardly want to bother with it . . ."

"You two will have to see to the publishing of the Aeneid."

"Is that what you wanted to ask of us?"

"Yes, that is it."

"Nonsense . . ." Plotius now actually grew cross—"you have to look after your own affairs, although we are willing to help you with them."

"Do you want to exclude entirely the possibility that this task may fall on you two alone?"

Plotius wagged his large round head this way and that: "Nothing can be entirely excluded . . . but in this case, Virgil, consider that we two are rather old fellows; it would seem wiser to look for an executor who is somewhat younger."

"My first choice falls on you two . . . it gives me peace of mind, and I want to have everything settled."

"Very well, we have nothing to say against that," agreed Lucius quite readily.

"And you have to take over this task, all the more since I am bequeathing the manuscript to you, oh, not as payment for your pains, but because I like the thought of your having it."

The effect of this communication proved something of a surprise; after a few moments of sheer stupefaction a deep gulp was heard from Plotius, so that it seemed as if he were about to weep again, while Lucius who, although with gratitude, had accepted the legacy of money with composure—at any rate he had remained seated—now sprang up, gesticulating wildly: "Virgil's own manuscript, Virgil's own manuscript . . . really, can you estimate the greatness of your giving?"

"A gift weighed down with obligations is scarcely a gift."

"Oh, ye gods," sighed Plotius, who had pulled himself

together to the point of being able to speak again, "oh, ye gods . . . but one must consider the matter carefully, remembering that you can hardly take back the manuscript from Augustus after having surrendered it to him . . ."

"The Aeneid was written in Caesar's honor . . . therefore he must be given the first flawless copy; this is customary, and I shall designate that it be so done, and for this purpose he will deliver the original without more ado . . ."

This solution seemed plausible to Plotius, and he nodded; however, he had one more objection: "And then, Virgil, there is something else to consider . . . namely . . . I am a simple person, I am no poet . . . the main work as far as the publishing goes will fall back on Lucius, and therefore he seems entitled to the exclusive possession of the manuscript."

"That is right," said Lucius.

"It would be, if you two did not stand for a unit to me in every possible respect . . . besides you will have to bequeath the manuscript with all its burdensome obligations to each other so that the presumptive survivor may take care of it."

"Very wise," agreed Lucius.

"And what is to happen when both of us shall be dead? This too will come to pass sooner or later . . ."

"That, from now on, is something for you to worry about, but no longer for me; but you could appoint Cebes and Alexis as successors, the one as poet and the other as grammarian; both are young . . ."

Again Plotius gulped with emotion: "Oh, Virgil, you shower us with presents, and your presents give pain . . ."

"They will pain you in earnest, my Plotius, when you start with your labors, for verse after verse, word after word, yes, actually letter after letter must be carefully gone over . . . that is no work for you, and I could almost rejoice should it please the gods to exempt me from such labor and burden Lucius with it instead . . ."

"Do not blaspheme . . ."

"Yes, Lucius will be saddled with a hard task, and therefore in my will I shall request Caesar to recompense it properly."

Lucius parried: "Virgil, this is no work to be paid for; on the contrary, I could even name many persons who would be so glad to undertake it that they would be willing to pay any sum for the privilege . . . and furthermore, you know this yourself."

"No, I know nothing of the sort, because just for a poet like yourself, Lucius, for a poet who has a faculty for improving a great deal or even all of it, and who therefore is sure to find much that is incongruous and in need of improvement, it will be hard to limit himself to merely textual corrections . . ."

"I would fight shy of wanting to correct any verse by Virgil . . . not a word should be added, not a word struck out, for I see clearly that this is your wish, and that only in this way can one meet it."

"So it is, my Lucius."

"The abilities of a poet are not needed for such work, rather those of a skilled grammarian, and I may flatter myself that there are not many who are better fitted than I for this very task . . . but Virgil, what are we to do about the verses that you once called waiting-stones?"

The waiting-stones, indeed! they were still there, those parenthetical verses which were later to be replaced by perfected ones—, ah, now they would never be replaced! It was not good to think of it, and speech had again become labored: "Leave them as they are, Lucius!"

This did not seem right to Lucius; one could see that he was hurt as much on his own account as for the Aeneid, and his commission seemed somewhat spoiled for him: "Very well, Virgil, very well . . . we do not have to go into that now; sooner or later you will change the verses yourself."

"I?"

"Who else? you, of course . . ."

"Never . . ." it was rather the voice of the slave than his own which had said that.

"Never?"—Plotius flared up—"are you only trying to

430

frighten us with this kind of talk? or do you actually want to call down on yourself the indignation of the gods?!"

"The gods . . ."

"Yes, the gods, they will not suffer you to keep on blaspheming . . ." And Plotius, with arms bent like an oarsman, shook his hairy fist.

The gods did not wish him to finish the verses, did not wish him to correct the incongruity, for every human work has to arise from twilight and blindness and therefore must remain incongruous; thus have the gods decided. And yet now he knew it; not only the curse but grace as well was mirrored in this incongruity, not only man's inadequacy but also his closeness to the divine, not only the soul's incompleteness but its magnitude, not only the blindness of the blindly-born human labor —otherwise it would never have been done at all—, but also its divining strength, for in the kernel of all human labor lay the seed of something that reached beyond itself and beyond him who had created it, and in this wise the worker was transformed into a creator; for the universal incongruity of circumstance began only when men became active in the universe— for there was no incongruity in the circumstances of the animal or of the gods—and only in this incongruity was revealed the fearful glory of the human lot which reached beyond itself; standing between the muteness of the animal and that of the gods was the human word, waiting to be silenced in ecstasy, beneath the radiant glance of that eye whose blindness has come in ecstasy to seeing: ecstatic blindness, the confirmation.

"Oh, Plotius, the gods . . . I have known their grace and their displeasure, I have encountered benefits and burdens . . . I am thankful for both."

"That is as it should be . . . it is always so . . ."

"I am thankful for both . . . life has been rich . . . I am thankful also for the Aeneid and even for its incongruities . . . incongruous as it is, may it endure . . . but the will, Plotius, just for this reason it must be finished . . . for the sake of the gods . . ."

"One cannot argue with a peasant . . . so you do not intend to postpone it?"

"It must be done, Plotius . . . and you, Lucius, are you able to write it down as I have given it to you?"

"That is not difficult, my Virgil . . . of course it would be more in accord with the rules if you were to dictate your wishes; I hesitate to write down anything about taking a recompense for myself for the publishing job in prospect."

"All right, Lucius; for my part you may settle that personally with Caesar . . ."

"Then you wish to dictate?"

"To dictate . . . I shall dictate . . ." —was this task still to be achieved?—, "I shall dictate; but first give me another swallow of water so that my cough will not interfere . . . and meanwhile, Lucius, . . . you may write the date on the document . . . as of today . . ."

Plotius gave him the goblet: "Drink, Virgil . . . and save your voice, speak softly . . ."

The water ran coolly through the throat. And when the goblet had been totally drained, there was renewed breathing, and voice complied to will: "Have you put down the date, Lucius?"

"Certainly . . . at Brundisium, the ninth day before the calends of October in the seven hundredth and thirtieth year after the founding of the city of Rome . . . is that correct, Virgil?"

"Without doubt, that is the date . . ."

The drizzling continued, the drizzling of the wall-fountain, the drizzling in the leafy shadows, the drizzling of the stream, the uncheckable stream, which, it is true, had become so broad that the other shore could not be reached, aye, it could not even be seen. But it was not necessary to stretch the hand out over the stream for already here on the shore, yes, here upon the cover, within reach of the hand, was a golden shimmer: the laurel shoot! placed there by Augustus, by the gods, by fate, by Jupiter himself! and its golden leaves were shimmering.

"I am ready, Virgil . . ."

And voice complied to will:

"I, Publius Vergilius Maro, today in the fifty-first year of my life, in full possession . . . , no, do not write full, rather put possessed of sufficient physical and mental health, see fit to add to my former testamentary provisions which have been deposited in the archives of Julius Caesar Octavian Augustus, as follows . . . have you written all this, Lucius?"

"Certainly . . ."

And voice complied to will:

"As by the wish of Augustus, who has bestowed on me many a favor, I have been deplorably restrained . . . no, strike out the deplorably and if you have not written it so much the better, . . . now, as through the wish of Augustus who has bestowed on me many a favor, I have been restrained from burning my poems, I designate firstly, that the Aeneid be considered a dedication to Augustus, secondly, however, that the entire bulk of my manuscripts be passed over in joint ownership to my friends, Plotius Tucca and Lucius Varius Rufus, and that in the event of the death of either, these automatically become the exclusive property of the other. I entrust to these same friends the exacting supervision of my poetical legacy which is herewith given over into their possession; only the most meticulously examined texts shall have validity, and above all, nothing is to be struck out or added to them, and copies for the librarians are to be made from these authorized texts alone, should the librarians desire them. In any case a clean and correct copy is to be delivered immediately to Caesar Augustus. The full responsibility for all this rests on Plotius Tucca and Lucius Varius Rufus . . . have you written it, Lucius?"

"Certainly, my Virgil, and it will be carried out exactly, should it ever come so far."

And still voice was compliant to will:

"In accord with Augustus' permission, I am allowed to set my slaves free; this is to be done directly after my death, and each slave is to receive a legacy of one hundred sesterces for every year spent in my service. Furthermore, I set aside twenty thousand . . . , no, make it thirty thousand sesterces to be distributed as soon as possible toward feeding the people of Brundisium. All further money settlements are to be found in my first will, to which I have already referred; this remains in full force except for the reduction of the bulk of the estate necessitated by the aforementioned new legacies which my principal heirs, namely Caesar Augustus, as well as my brother Proculus, together with Plotius Tucca and Lucius Varius and Gaius Cilnius Maecenas, will indubitably not consider to be unfriendly . . . , that is about all . . . that will suffice, will it not?"

"Be assured, Virgil, it is sufficient . . ."

"It . . . is it? . . . yes, it is sufficient . . ."

And voice no longer complied to will. Even the last words had to be fetched out of an enormous emptiness, and now nothing remained but this emptiness, a wretched, exhausted, and boundless void, endlessly extended, unsurveyable in the large as well as in its intimate recesses, a frightful emptiness, empty of fright, a void of forgetfulness, filled with a curiously grievous, forgotten wakefulness, a void with a whistling fever straying within its shell. But besides the fever there was something else rustling about, something unsaid, something that had to be said without fail, something connected with all that had gone before, and yet not quite connected, so that it too must be found, otherwise what had previously happened would not suffice. It was of no less importance than the verses themselves, which at first were to be destroyed, and must now be preserved.

"Where . . . where is the chest?!"

Plotius looked up sadly. "Virgil . . . with Augustus, well cared for . . . make your mind easy . . ."

But now Lucius drew near with the document, which still seemed inadequate, in order to get his signature. Or was it merely the signature which had been lacking? Was it this which had to be found?

"Give me . . ."

The signature was placed, but the text was not legible; evidently because it did not yet suffice, the letters were dancing over one another. "You still have to add something, Lucius . . . add something . . . the cantos are not to be torn apart . . ."

"Yes, my Virgil."

And Lucius sat down again waiting for dictation.

"The cantos . . . are not to be torn apart and . . . I forbid a single word to be added or deleted . . ."

"We had all this before . . ."

"Write it . . . do write it down . . ." There was no help at hand, and his strength was at an end; the void would yield nothing, no sound, no memory, not even the gray trickling of the water. Only the fingers led a life of their own, they wandered over the blanket constantly interlacing and loosening only to interlace again. The cantos were not to be torn apart, nothing was to be torn apart; that had been very important, but that was not the real thing, was not yet that which concealed itself in the darkness. Oh, even the void might not be torn apart before it surrendered what it was concealing, and his fingers were aware of it, for they wandered about searching the void, pressing it together, forcing it to disgorge the hidden thing, and as they pressed against each other more and more frantically, it happened: between the fingers, deep in the void, scarcely perceptible, as if all the cloudiness of the firmament had been drawn away from it, glimmering there weakly, vanishing like the sign of a fading star, and already on his lips in a sigh of deliverance, there was that which had been sought and was now so wondrously found: "The ring belongs to Lysanias."

"Your seal-ring?"

One had yielded enough to things earthly; there was radiance now and a soundless buoyancy: "Yes, to Lysanias."

"And he doesn't exist," something murmured, and perhaps it was Plotius.

"To the child . . ."

AIR — THE HOMECOMING

Was there still something murmuring? Was it still the kind murmuring of Plotius, protecting and kind and strong? oh, Plotius, oh, that it might endure, oh, that it might endure murmuringly, quiet and quieting, welling up from the unfathomable depths within and without, now that the labor was over, now that the labor sufficed, now that nothing need follow, oh, that it might go on forever! and verily it went on, murmuring and murmuring, rolling in softly in endlessness, murmur-wave after murmur-wave, each of them tiny yet all of them radiating in a boundless cycle; it was simply there, no sort of hearkening, no effort whatsoever was needed to hold on to it, indeed this murmurousness was not to be held onto, for it strove onward, mingled with the trickling of the fountain, with the trickling of the waters, merged with them in the vast and colorless might of a rest-bearing stream, itself the thing carried, itself rest, itself a moving stream, softly lapping the keel and sides of the boat with slithering foam. The destination was unknown, unknown the harbor of departure; one was shoved off from no pier, coming out of infinity, pressing on to infinity, the journey went on of itself, nevertheless strict and true to its course, guided by a sure hand, and had it been permitted to turn around, one must have glimpsed the steersman at the helm, the helper in the unchartered, the pilot who was acquainted with the exit to the harbor. But Plotius likewise had remained no less a helper and a friend; degraded and exalted, he had taken upon himself the servile office of an oarsman, his murmuring mouth was dumb, dumb and delivered up to the universe, the gasping of his breath almost inaudible in the ease of these happenings, free of suffering and strain; thus keeping silence he rowed on with bent arms over the colorless, murmuring, silent surface of the water, not half as vigorously as might have been expected of him, but instead with oars barely lifting and sinking to cut into the moisture: forward at the prow sat Lysanias, or perhaps he was standing there, a youth who should have lent singing to the voyage, but that Plotius, faced with the injunction against turning around which applies to every earthly being, paid no attention to him, he did not turn toward him; it well may be that he wished to avoid catching sight of the journey's end which was forbidden him, and, facing backward, he kept his eyes fixed straight ahead, looking past the traveling companions toward the steersman at the helm whose directions he had to follow, beyond the steersman toward the immensity of past happenings from which they had come. The shores were left behind and it was like an easy leave-taking from the human life and human living that still persisted there, a farewell in a changed scene essentially unchangeable, a leave-taking from the diversity of familiar things, from the familiar images and faces yonder, not the least of these being the tomb fading into the gray fog, and the constant Lucius, still at his writing, who had however been pushed with his table so close to the edge of reality that a crash from its steep, rocky ledge was greatly to be feared; and it was a leave-taking from the many others wandering about there, among them Horace and Propertius who waved to them with gestures of friendship; familiar images fading back gradually and without pain though still ready to accompany them, and the waters across which the boat was gliding were populated by all sorts of craft, though by very few going in the opposite direction to come home again to the forgotten haven of departure, instead many were being sent out from there, one fleet after the other, so many that to provide them all with the space needed for traveling the immense ocean had to widen out to a second immensity, an immensity so boundless that there was no line of demarcation between the liquid and the sheerly airy, giving the impression that the ships were swimming in pure light, extending so far that the ship-covered sea and the procession of ships advancing toward the unexplorable, common goal were goals in themselves: herdlike this procession, enveloped in a mild zooming like an invisible cloud; every sort of vessel was to be seen, merchantmen and warships, among them, gold-gleaming and purple-sailed, there was also the parade ship of Augustus, numerous fishing smacks and coastal boats, but especially a host of tiny barks emerging first here, then there, as though being born from the water; these participated in the endless voyage, all of them curiously keeping the same speed, no matter whether like the little barks they were drawn by a single pair of oarsmen or whether like the Augustan galley they were propelled by a gigantic rowing-mass several stories high, they flew along as if all together they were without weight, as if they were not obliged to dip into the water at all, as if they could float above it, and their sails were taut as though pressed by imperceptible storms coming out of the airless void, for it was windstill, complete calm reigned, and the mild zooming hummed in a nowhere. The sea heaved in flat, soft, almost slab-shaped waves, soft and dusky-gray, as though of a breath-soft lead, the murmur became blurred in this smoothness, in this dusky vigor which carried the ships with breath-lightness on its mirrored surface; pearly though colorless, the shell of heaven opened above it, Plotius was rowing, and left behind were the sounds of life from the distant and disappearing shores, left behind the uncapturable song of the mountains, left behind in a realm eternally receding was its flute-tone, lost with its echo which had resounded in his own breast; the audible had sunk back into the unmanifested, and along with it the murmur of the murmuring universe, and the boy's song stayed unsung, remaining as a soft, golden shimmer in the shimmering heaven. As though the silence were too loud, a new stillness set in, a second and more intense stillness on a loftier plane, shallow-waved, gentle, slab-shaped and smooth, like a reflection of the water's mirror above which it was laid

while yet merged with it; the inaudible was transformed again
to a new interstate of audibleness, just as the waters had been
changed to something new, to a stilled liquidity in which the
speeding boats no longer drew a furrow, and which consisted
so little of drops that none clung to the drawn-back oars, none
dropped down from them; remaining in the invisibility, the inaudibility, the impalpability of a long-left and undiscoverable
immensity, the visible, the audible, and the palpable remained
intact, though fallen back into namelessness and non-existence
they were nevertheless not without name and being; all of this
was left behind while yet remaining, left behind because overtaken, staying by virtue of such overtaking, changed by it to a
transformed permanence; and because it was the universe that
had been in this wise overtaken, the universe in the full multiplicity of its material and human content, nothing was excluded
from it: ship after ship was overtaken easily, not because of the
rowing skill of Plotius who had surely done his share, but who
now with quieter breathing and idle gear was resting himself
bent forward on his bench; no, it was no contest, no race between
the boats, no, all of them, having come out in greeting and for
escort, held back of their own accord, their commission ended,
they no longer needed earthly rowing-gear and, whether they
lifted these out of the water or let them drift therein, the oars
soon vanished altogether, the dissolution starting as one vessel
after another was taken out of existence, sinking back into forgetfulness and into the receding immensity. Augustus, standing
under the purple canopy of his parade ship, with the short
scourge of the ship's overseer in his hand, let this drop when he
had to realize the futility of speeding on or even of continuing
the voyage, his power was slipping from him, slipping away with
his name, with all the names which he had previously borne, all
of which he must discard, even the name Octavian, but he was
still himself, and in the last hurried glance he was allowed to
send hither, in this last leave-taking with no prospect of return,
in the farewell of this handsome face aged by weariness there
was, at the same time, an eternal permanence, a transferred per-

manence, unlost even in the losing, so that as he sank quickly—
alas, so quickly—into the irrevocable, with his face, his earthly
form, and his name, abruptly stilled by being forgotten, yet he
won a new identity, a new aspect, in a new stillness on a loftier
plane. For the transformation which had taken place was the
transformation of outside to inside, the merging of the outer
with the inner face, always striven for, never attained, but now
fully achieved by this final exchange: suddenly, as suddenly
as his dropping into infinity, this man, who had hitherto been
called Augustus, was seen from within, seen in that completely
inner way usually reserved for the dreamer, the dream-lost, when
he forgets his earthiness and—gaining perception through the
dream—recognizes himself in the image of himself, seeing the
ultimate, inseparable, crystalline, essential source of his qualities revealed as mere form, as a glassy play of lines, aye, as an
empty cypher in its final dream-existence; this insight had now
grown beyond itself, and had comprehended the one vanishing
there, the friend—oh, unlosable is he who is seen from within in
his nakedest wholeness. Oh transformation of the end into the beginning, transformation of the symbol back into the arch-image,
oh friendship! And although few faces had been so familiar as
his whom in friendship he had been permitted to call Octavian,
the same thing happened to all the other faces sharing the
voyage on the ethereal boats, one after the other they were overtaken just as his had been, they vanished into eternity without
disappearing; and whosoever continued to share the voyage, seen
for one moment and disappearing in the next, whatever they had
been called or were still called—, who were they? was that
one there actually Tibullus, the melancholy Tibullus in his
blighted youth? was that one Lucretius, great in the relentless-
ness of his powerful mania? was that one yonder not the manly
Sallust, always at his ripe fifty from his first appearance to his
last? was this one not he, the name-giver, stripped of his own
name? and was not that shape yonder the venerableness of
Marcus Terentius Varro, bent with age and shrunken in figure,
but still strong in the mildly mocking wizard's smile of the

vanishing old man's face?—, oh, whoever they might be who had gathered for the easy farewell of friendship, face after face, bearded or beardless, young or old, male or female, however quickly or slowly they discarded their features, they had taken on the consummate transformation as, with the last remnant of their names, they sank into the irrevocable, for as they were falling into oblivion, their faces had become an unspeakable and unspeakably clear expression of their essential qualities, they were freed of all ties, deeply genuine in the boundless, nameless self, no longer in need of an earthly mediator and an earthly name-caller, because all of them, seen from within, visible from within, recognized from within, were absorbed into the glance of friendship, absorbed with that glance into an experience of a knowledge, self to self, which arose from the deepest recesses of the self, from the depths of a self that stemmed from a sphere beyond the senses, which no longer saw the material person and the material metaphor, but only the crystalline archetype, the crystalline entity formed by the essential qualities, resting so purely in the core of their essence, so free of memory and therefore so completely remembered, that all these friendly forms passed into a new interstate of memory, into a new interstate of comprehensibility, full of light-casting shadows within muted sounds. They passed into the second immensity.

Stillness within stillness—on all sides the borders were opened, but as nothing can be lost in the universal orbit, although much indeed has been left behind and remained in the undiscoverable, this was neither impoverishment nor isolation, and even betokened an enrichment, since the forgotten had been preserved. The space of non-recollection absorbed further stretches of recollection, nevertheless it remained within the domain of the latter, more and more unified with it, and both spaces united to form a second memory-space within the first one, a space in which the transparency and inclusiveness of memory were so intensified, so deeply embedded, were so much a doubling of existence to a new integration, that the soft leaden-colored stillness of the waters and the stillness spread over them as their soft, golden reflection were joined to a new unity— memory within memory—, at one with that hush which greets the singer before he has plucked the strings, and in this stillness, the lyre unstruck, the waiting without expectation, fuses the singing and hearing, the singer and the hearer, into a single harmony; for the silent power of the spheric song was now stirred to sound, born out of the muteness but also born from these two components, sounding out of the stillness but sounding in them both, the accord based on their duality, brought into unison with the stillness, the waiting, the lyre, identified with them by virtue of the song, the living world taken into the life of the spheres; the expectant one and the thing expected were no more, neither the hearer nor the thing heard, neither the breather nor the breath, neither the thirsting one nor the drink, there was no more division in the doubled new unity, the parts had closed to a difference-annulling communion, to waiting as such, to listening as such, to breathing as such, to thirsting as such, and the waiting, the listening, the breathing, the thirsting, became the endless flood about him, drawn into the unity, becoming more and more unified, more and more intense, more and more ineluctable, becoming a command, an annunciation, even for Plotius, for as if aware that all duration was abolished, that beginning and ending were one, but also as if aware of the duality to which all unity is subject and to which he too must submit, he cast off the unity of his being and became, at least for a certain time, doubled; for in one form he remained seated there on the rowing-bench, quietly resting, and yet in the duplication of that form he arose and now drew near with the rolling gait of a seaman to offer again, and apparently for the last time, the goblet so that the thirsty man—oh, was he thirsty?!— could drink from it once more: and as he did so, behold, it was not liquid which was being drunk, it was not thirst which was being quenched, no, this was participation, it was partaking in the wholeness of doubly-reflected being, it was absorption into the endless flow of the waters, it was penetration of the invisible from within, but at the same time however it was recognition, thought-freed, on the terminus of the perceptive cycle that encloses the nothing, it was the juncture, the closure, of the dual boundlessness in which the future crosses to the past and the past to the future so that—oh duplication within duplication, reflection within reflection, invisibility within invisibility—here no mediator nor implements were needed, not that of the goblet to surround the liquidity, nor that of the hand to extend the goblet, hardly that of the mouth to accept the drink, there was no longer need of them because all action, call it drinking or anything else, and beyond that all living, had been absolved by virtue of an entwinement that abolished every incongruity and therefore suffered no sort of separation; and behold, thereupon the goblet changed from ivory into one of firm, brown horn, only to evaporate again into a light brown vapor, and along with the goblet all the past vanished also, not simply as a mere shadow-play of dream but as a real vision which was allowed to last in the assurance that all was not in vain; and for this very reason Plotius too had vanished, obliged by the dwindling duplication to take the same path as the other companions, sunk with them into eternity to the last shred of his name, though still remaining, though still having substance as the one he had been, as the friend. Thus while the liquid without moistness, the drink without taste ran over the lips and down the throat, without lips, throat, tongue being moistened, the farewell from Plotius took place, came to pass by the help of his friendship; and in the rays of the universal eye, veiled by the tears of the universe, by the obliterating moisture of all existence, cleared by truth, friend's glance sought friend's glance, both granted to remain without tears, so softly lifted above sorrow, freed from sorrow, that it became easy, an easy farewell—, stillness within stillness.

Nothing held firm any longer, nothing had to be held onto, there was no more incongruity, and he who had taken the drink, he Publius Vergilius Maro, he likewise was no longer in need of the name, he might cast it off from himself, he could let it

fade to a mere knowledge, to an indistinct and actually knowledgeless knowing, to a gentle and wondrously chaste forgetting,
because lonely if not alone the journey continued through the
second immensity. No trepidant longing drew him on now,
there was no longer the need for encounter. The light too was
lonelier, purer and chaster even than before, it had turned to
dusk, to a strange and almost miraculous dusk of indefinite
duration, uncertain the hour of its beginning, inestimable its
duration, for the sun having sunk down to the immeasurable
border of the waters could not decide to dip under them, but
unmoving, as though in gentle indecision, as though spellbound
by the image of the Scorpion which it had been pursuing, hung
with a dull gleam in the cloudlessness, surrounded by the dome
a-twinkle with the whole galaxy of stars. Time was exempted
of duration, and the voyage went on and on over the empty
stillness in a peaceful, almost imperceptible gliding devoid of
all speed, its destination unknown although the direction in
which the journey continued could be ascertained by the stars.
The boy stood forward at the bow encompassed by the dusk,
yet his figure stood out clearly from the firmament, its overdistant clarity already beyond the border of clarity, and while
it could not be determined whether the gesture was that of way-
showing or of longing, he lifted his arm, his body inclining
toward its outstretched motion, wishing for the goal to appear
without being able to reach it. Could this still be called a
voyage, this drifting without aid of oar or sail? was it not rather
a standstill, a make-believe of sham motion caused by the
opposite movement of the starry cupola? Voyage or no voyage,
it constituted an interstate of knowledge, it was still that, and
the steersman back there stayed quietly at his post, his presence
not less felt now than before, all security came from him and
not from the far too fugitive, far too transient boyish figure,
no, the steersman determined the course of the voyage, he alone,
even if in reality it depended on the course of the star. Deeper
and deeper sank the sun, flaming into the dark red of its fire;
its glow became duller, notwithstanding the cloudless, fogless

view, so dull that the evening clarity became more and more nocturnal, more and more sparkling the starry spaces. Though it was nocturnal it was not yet night; the silent song of the spheres became more nocturnal, richer and richer the night, permeated by the mute cymbal-tone of the starlight, and the more fully this resounded through veil after veil of sound, the more perceptible became the boy, the more he detached himself from the darkness; for meanwhile it had become plain that this perceptibility was wrought by a silent radiation, the source of which lay in the outstretched way-showing hand of the boy, and which deepened with soft increasing intensity to the central point of its emanation: it was the ring, the very ring intended for Lysanias, and now held proudly aloft by him, which sent out this radiance, a mantle of light over his shoulders, and if in the beginning it had been only like the blinking of a star, flaring up and fading out in the gray light of morning or evening, it was now like a way-showing gleam floating on ahead, the way-showing smile of a star held aloft in the hand of a boy, held high that it might shine, wafted hither like a blessed memory from the innermost space of earthly forgetfulness, the space that had been flooded by width, height and depth, flooded by time, by the pain of fire and ice; itself flooded by memory, wafted hither by the ring's shining, brought gently hither like echo, childlike as echo, belonging like echo to the throes of a blessed receptivity. For nothing any longer bore a name, only the boy Lysanias still bore his, and the memory which now twined through the memoryless present with fugitive blessedness, this memory in the interstate of the senses yet devoid of sensuality, this afterglow of a former doubling and halving, this afterglow at the fading point, in whose echoing call the boy Lysanias was allowed to participate because of his name, this died out in the calling as it entered a higher plane in the knowledgeless knowing of the second immensity, there where every other knowledge falls away; it faded out with the radiation of the ring, preserved in the radiation, flooded into the smile of Lysanias, into his voice that would speak no longer, into his glance which would look hither no more, flooded into him as a soundless music, streaming back as an insight of the boy, as a simultaneous knowledgeless knowing of nearness and farness, involved with the lightening of the dusk and with the spread of a dawn that without nearness or farness encloses all doubleness to oneness, which, even as he beholds it, fills the beholder with light. Oh dusk, oh interrealm, streaming and subsiding in the past, the inflow and outflow of soul! However, although it was not really night, the actual dusk had been left behind, the interrealm abolished; under a myriad stars gleaming in their full brightness the ball of the sun was resting coolly in a dark, reddish pool deep down on the watery horizon, leaden and golden together; one could almost imagine that it had actually dived under and was reflected upward by an unusual refraction of light, for, as if bound to the sphere below, and in a reflection of its under-oceanic course, it began to roll slowly along the horizon, cutting across one constellation after another, making for the eastern point where it would rise again bringing the morning, sun remaining in the night, night's image or the night itself, sun in reflected movement or that of its own, in earthly imprisonment or in spheric freedom, it was hard to tell which, circle and counter-circle shrunk to a blankness, consummate and great in the majestic movement of the starry orb; as if the voyage were heading for the sun, as if this were its aim, the steersman, seemingly in response to the boy's longing gesture, followed the path of the red-glowing image, and the point of the boat in its gradual turning remained constant to the path of the sun, drawn by it in a real or sham turning, in a real or sham movement, now it was quite indistinguishable, because in the course of this most unnocturnal night the boat had indubitably lengthened to an extraordinary degree and was continuing to grow longer, plainly seen by the growing distance to the boy at the bow, plainly felt by the steersman's falling back at the rear, a lengthening of the ship both backwards and forwards, a growth that in and of itself claimed a part of the journey's speed and assimilated it, speed changed into growth, into such an irresistible, all-embracing growth that, were it to persist, must finally bring the voyage and even the night itself to a complete standstill, must bring revolving mutability to immutability; the voyage had become immeasurably slower and in equal quietude the roundness above and that below, reflected in the luster from the stars, had expanded on every side to meet this becalmed gliding, the quiet glance of the spheres reflecting itself in itself, the gray eye of the water and the darker gray of the heavenly eye above widening and merging to a day-impregnated night, to a dawn-dusk in which there was no duration or occurrence, no name, no chance, no memory, no fate. And soon lying there was no longer a lying, neither a sitting nor a standing up, rather a bodiless beholding in drifting onward, still bound, it is true, to the middle of the boat while yet being loosened from it, and so very detached that it seemed as if the last fetters were being struck off, as if this were the final fulfillment of a long-forgotten, no longer rememberable premonition, a premonition of floating in freedom; ever stronger became the wish to take part in bringing this floating premonition to reality, to float within it, to float in a state of unrecollection which was at the same time that of a surmised future, to float onward to the radiance of the ring, to float freely on to Lysanias who alone still bore a name, fate and memory; ah, that it were given one to float on to him, to him flooded in radiance, who might still be a peasant boy, but also might already be an angel moving ethereally on spreading wings of a Septemberish coolness, ah, that it were given one to float on to him so as to touch those wings and to search again that once-more familiar countenance, the unveiled depths of the countenance in the kindly light of the star-ring, filling one depth after another; ah, ever stronger became the wish, the yearning for him of the yearning gesture, the longing toward the mild stir of a former flux, toward the soft gray trickling in which the past had lingered, alas, the woebegone wish that is but anguish at taking leave of the final face, woebegone yearning that wards off the final awareness, trembling in the anguish

of farewell; for however much the soul, fore-knowing her future, thirsts to float free at last, yet it weighs heavily on her to
leave forever the interstate of the voyage, to go irrevocably
into the second immensity, and heavy the injunction not to turn
around to the immensity of yore, still heavier the command
to relinquish the many connotations of the past for the sake of
the future's single import: even though the boy pointed so
singly and so yearningly toward the future, yet the many connotations remained, the surrounding radiance was of manifold
meanings in its reflections and counter-reflections—red-glowing
the image of the sun, the constellations flickering, dull-gold the
moon's disk, the diffused radiation of the ring—so that past and
future criss-crossed into a single effulgence, the radiance of
the dark-shimmering sea and sky dispersed and ambiguous,
enmeshed with that of the pointing seraphic apparition, and
even though this in itself remained consistent, consistent in his
future-pointing gesture, it was filled with shimmering incon-
sistency, it was shot through by every sort of multiplicity and
the whole complex meaning of the past; it was inconsistent by
reason of his constantly changing shape, in his change of features which at one time assumed the likeness of Alexis and at
another that of Cebes, and occasionally, though less capturable
than all the others, even the likeness of Aeneas, yet all of them
nameless, and repeatedly covered by his own Lysanias-face,
being for all that no less an enticement to seek the past in the
future, no less a seduction in its forward pointing to turn back,
yet already ceasing to be seduction, being instead merely a new
knowledge, for the boy was floating in the realm of the intangible, surely no misleader, scarcely any longer a leader, only
a way-shower, one who points forward, one whose forward-
pointing hand were it to be kept from falling was never once
to be touched—a farewell; verily, this revelation of farewell,
this consciousness of farewell, was also embedded in the floating
in-turned smile of the boy, and the leave-taking became a knowledge shared between them, an awareness of the abolishment of
the interrealm, an awareness of the second immensity in which

451

the journey was to come to a standstill, an awareness of the
steersman at the rear, of the pilot at the helm, the protection-
giving, the help-giving, rest-giving one, who now had to become
the sole guide, the serving, the final and perfect guide, because
he alone, notwithstanding the growing distance, and over and
above it, had the power to gather the soul into his guardian
hand, to enable it while nestling into that hand, lying within
it, leaning against it and upheld by it, while embraced by the
loving command, to participate in this awareness without fear,
poised in the tension between certainty and yearning, floating
between the immensities, in readiness for knowledge, the knowl-
edge-awaiting soul, waiting without anticipation. The premoni-
tory, floating ardor began to be fulfilled, came to be floating
fulfillment. Floating like the boy forward there at the bow,
consciousness as well as the voyage tended to merge into a
floating calm, and the longer this lasted, the longer the growth
of the night and the nocturnal boat—incalculable the duration,
incalculable a measure in the shadow-saturated, shadow-sated
clarity of the night—the more evanescent became the evaporating boyish figure, more and more evanescent, naked and
nakeder, drawn into the starry brightness, embraced by the
shadows, divested of raiment and more than raiment, stripped
to complete transparency, thus hovered the night and the boy,
melting into each other, oh, transparent! Not quite here but
yet at hand. Was this the fore-court to reality? the fore-court
of a homeland above which circled all suns, all moons, all stars,
filled with glory? The boy pointed yonder but it was toward
a beaming uncertainty that he pointed, and thither the boat was
heading, although things were almost at a standstill because
the growth of the boat had apparently reached the borderline
of immensity; it was cognizance, the knowledge of night, not
yet of day, merely the apprehension of a knowledge to come,
and yet a fully valid knowledge; it was an invading flood of
knowledge, greater and milder than any streaming of air and
water, though just as immutable as these and arched over by
the self-same heaven, it was stillness about to turn into a new

stillness on a loftier plane, stillness prepared for a new stillness, knowledge ready to be organized into a new knowledge, indeed prepared for this, and the gliding thing, carried as it were on stillness and knowledge, and borne as though aloft and disburdened of its weight, was now scarcely a boat, it had almost ceased to touch the water, it was an endlessly floating phantom of night on the point of dissolving into immensity, immense in itself and prepared for rest in the unimaginable uncertainty of increasing infinity, floating toward the rainbow of night, which afloat itself, the floating portal of time at rest, was spanned in seven colors from east to west, reflected in the liquid element without touching it. Retarded like the voyage, slowed down to a standstill, as slowly as the irresolute sun delaying at every stage of approach its course toward the point of its re-arising, delaying it more and more till it came to a standstill, most slowly, really unnoticeably, the boat was dissolving, becoming invisible, became invisible, and forward in the darkening distance the figure of Lysanias had detached itself and was flying ahead of the boat, flying radiantly out into the night, in the guise of a leader, as a guiding hand, as radiant guidance; thereupon, as though the night wanted to unfold once again to its full earthly magnificence before its inevitable vanishing, the stars increased in brilliance, the stars assembled as if in final greeting and attendance, fuller in number than ever before, assembled to a final earthly show of beauty, crossed over in their complete arch by the Milky Way, all of them simultaneously visible to the eye, although no permission had been given to turn round or to look back, all of the stars beheld and known, inexpressibly known, star-face after star-face, name after name, in spite of having long since passed with their names into the region of oblivion, transcendent in beauty beyond any beauty, a second memory-space of stars within the first one, wheeling about the frigid pole of the sky guarded by the sign of the dragon, and so complete in number and sign that even the vanished ones emerged mirror-like out of the flood: to the north was the crooked, flickering body of the Scorpion pursued by

the pointing Archer, but to the east the outstretched serpent
reared her sparkling head, and deep in the west, readier for
leave-taking than all the others, lingered the Pegasic horse of
the well-tapping hoof, lingering at the edge of the cupola, at
the edge of the glittering multiplicity; transparent unto the last
depths of the cupola, the multiplicity was only crystalline
essence, curiously familiar, curiously unfamiliar, now also seen
from within, far-near near-far also, changed into a waiting
awareness—the waiting reproduced in the starry profusion of
the celestial spaces, the universe seen from within, unlosable
in its perception now perceived, the untouchable, unbeholdable,
unevocable, inaudible face of the star—and in the transparent
radiance of the heavens this became the fleeing figure of the
boy, naked in its transparency although still that of Lysanias,
wondrously changed, this figure heading onward yet arrested,
the seraphic apparition, the image of a star, a symbol, was
transmuted into the intrinsic substance itself, the intrinsic substance of the spark-showering universe into whose opened arch
it was flying, entering the seven-colored portal of the rainbow
and passing beyond it. And as this was happening, yes, even
before it happened, the serpent blazed up in a glow of red, the
whole eastern horizon blazing, the seven-colored thing disappeared into the glow of red, paling to a quickly vanishing strip
of ivory, for the sun had detached itself from its quiet course,
had mounted so slowly as to be almost imperceptibly, but in
keeping with a complete stripping of weight, in a weightless
upward floating, lifted up by the ceaseless turning of the starry
orb, lifted up by the guiding gesture of the fleeting apparition
of the seraph, lifted up by the common occurrence in which one
thing is activated by the other, movement by counter-movement,
quiescence by counter-quiescence, interknit, implicated, reflected
one to another from the natural source of all substance; this
was in a simultaneous state of change and repose, was in its
constant repose so changeable, in its constant changing so repose-
ful, but in both so vibrant, such a reposefully-changing vibrancy
that it came to be the unity achieved by the mute song of the

454

spheres, sounding as a mild cymbal-stroke emanating from the
rising of the day-star, sounding as an ivory-colored lyre-tone
emanating from the gesture of the seraphic image toward the
flaming disk, and the star-throng, enveloped by the mute sound,
was drawn toward the rising sun and its conscious ascending,
the universe looking and listening. Not a star vanished, in spite
of the increasing brightness of the advancing day by which
their brightness was overtaken, they remained in their full
number, starry-crystal in their dome, an enduring starry-
countenance of an unspeakably clear expression, and flying on
through the crystalline arch, flying to the sun, the seraphic
apparition had finally freed itself, had finally separated from
the dissolving, floating form that had once been a boat; and,
wrapped in the gleaming mantle of its own radiance, becoming
more and more luminous in a final transformation, in a final
gladdening, becoming more and more compelling, more and
more lovable, the same face though with a new name, the nameless, transported boyish face became that of Plotia Hieria, the
boy inseparable from her, she inseparable from the boy, identical in the blurred and fading gesture she had taken over from
him, pointing, the ring on her finger, to the east. The serpent
glistening coil on coil had glided up a further stretch of the
red-glowing firmament to receive her, the new guide, the serpent
enflamed by the sun and commanding the east, while westward,
yielding to the day, the winged horse sank down palely along
with the steersman whom he took with him and who, now that
his strict service was accomplished and the chains broken, gave
way to the sun whither he had been leading the voyage. Oh,
final transformation! The apparition of a seraph sent hither
as a comforting memory from the first immensity, gone over
into the second one for the sake of hope—, must she not also
vanish, now that the day had dawned? must she not likewise
turn homeward into the unknown, into and in deference to a
higher consciousness on a loftier plane? She flew ahead, her
body of shimmering ivory shimmered off into the incorporeal,
her star-streaming hair a cool-soft flame; the distance to her

kept growing, the pointing ring-hand already touched upon the
unattainable, already touched the peak of heaven, but there was
no vanishing, instead a tarrying, a spellbound abiding, spun
into the light which was now day, as if this transformation of
shape and that which had previously been experienced by the
vanishing boy were one and the same, the one conditioned by
the other, born from the other, blossomed from the other: the
day had blossomed, a blossom in itself, and it unfolded to a
gracious enchantment, resting in its own light, remaining in
itself, since the fire of the beginning from which it had risen
had been expunged, and the visible world along with the day
had become bound in a spell of graciously changed permanence;
the soft, golden light had changed, transfixed within the heavenly blue, and bore, together with this splendor, the crystalline
dome of day, the lovely, pristine crystal of infinity, dissolving
the crystal countenance to something like a gentle un-radiance,
so that the abundance of stars, out-shimmered by the azure
clarity in which they hung, gave forth no more light, and the
radiance—silvery opal the stars, milkily silver the moon's soft
disk, insubstantial as ivory vapor, like a memory of the night's
splendor which had spread like a hoop over the heavens—the
radiance which emanated from the hoop on Plotia's hand was
dissolved into a no-gleam, to a still softer ivory vapor that enveloped her as she floated onward, shrouding her charm as in
a cloud, yet, breath streaming into breath, lifted her to her
transparent consummation, an opaline shimmer in the pearly
blue. Had the journey ended? had one really come so far?
there was no further need of a vessel; he floated, he stepped
over the waters, and surrounding him was the stillness of morning, a spring morning of no season, surrounding him was the
breath of quiet and the day of rest, breathed up to heaven by
the liquid mirror, breathed back by heaven to the gilded waters,
above and below inhaling each other, the stillness of sun and
stars and sea in one, in a single breath of never-ending spring-
time; and there a landscape came into being, a landscape that
was spring, as beneath the sunny arch, drawn upward by it,

the existence of one dependent on the other, the shore emerged from the waters, growing out of the floods, and established itself as a reality entirely stripped of metaphor or symbol, the reality awaited without anticipation, the veritable journey's end. Thereupon what ensued was a wafting, a floating that became easier and changed effortlessly to a transference thither. There, washed round by the morning light, stood Plotia, descended from her former floating guidance; there she stood, she who had flown ahead to await him who had floated after; and about their heads, belonging to her and to heaven, gleamed a star of opaline softness, the star washed in the morning light. Had it not been for the starry luster, the mild splendor of this one star diffused over the entire cupola, persisting poignantly despite all its mildness even in the reawakened golden clarity, it could almost have been an earthly spring morning, a quiet re-awakening to life in limpid serenity; Plotia's figure was almost an earthly one, no gleaming mantle enveloped her, furthermore her hand was ringless, rayless, for all that she held to her pointing gesture, and this aimed heavenward as if she had left the ring in the star which shimmered upon her, as if the ring's gleaming had been drawn back into that of the star, transformed and united with the starry gaze to a soft eternal vigilance.

Trees framed the moorage at the shore, its shadow-flecked and leafy pathways rising gently toward the interior of the land invited one to come nearer, and the water, notwithstanding the ever-enduring placidity of its mirror, washed on the shore with a swift, soft, white-bordered overflow, leaving behind a little foam that seemed like sound in the silent inaudibility, friendly in its murmuring onflow, friendly in its trickling ebb. The liquid element lay behind him, the solid one in front of him, both of them limitless while merging limitlessly into each other, a landing but still not the end of the journey, because there was neither a before nor an after, and though he felt the firm ground under his feet, this was neither a standing, nor a going, but rather a state of half-movement, a detention in drifting onwards, held fast in a limitation without limits, held fast within the limitless

457

center of existence which drew everything unto itself and retained everything for the integration of that which was within
and without. The silence of the middle—, was it the middle
of being which had thus been reached? And towering aloft,
here was a tree, rather like an elm or an ash, but bearing an
unfamiliar golden fruit; and now as the star shimmered through
the frail branches, it too basking in Plotia's responsive upturned
glance, her glance-echo, her welcome and her greeting, the tacit
concurrence between above and below became a memory-freed
recognition more poignant than any greeting, became a flowing
unanimity between inertia and activity, indistinguishable from
within as from without, indistinguishable whence the occurrence
arose, whether it was the woods which were being carried hither
or whether he was being drifted on to the woods, the borderline
between abiding and pressing onward was being dissolved: he
had been landed, but even the landing was no ending, and in
this almost motionless gliding across terrain which seemed too
imponderable for any foot to touch while being too ponderable
for Plotia's buoyancy, in this gliding into something gliding
to meet them, he and Plotia were taken along, both of them by
compulsion, both of them spontaneously, her step carefully
halted to accord with his own; she was naked in a charming
natural nakedness, clothed in naturalness, as naked as the
seraphic boy from whom she had emanated, and the pure sweetness of her nudeless nudity received the song of the spheres in
order to be received by that song, subsumed in its ethereal
ringing, in its continuous vibration, mute and forever. Nakedness? He too was naked; he noticed this without remarking on
it, so little was he abashed, and Plotia's nakedness was likewise unremarkable, for without this detracting from her bodily
charm, he was scarcely able to see her any more as a woman,
he saw her as it were from within, and beheld from the core
of her individual essence, she was scarcely any longer a body but
rather a transparent intrinsic substance, no longer a woman, no
longer a virgin, but rather a smile, the smile which gives meaning to everything human, the human countenance opening in a

smile, freed of shame, and exalted through a forlorn preparation incapable of consummation, sublimated to a transported-transporting love; strangely touching, strangely wintry, was this smiling, loving gesture toward the star swimming there in cool, virginal light, and strangely cool, aye, almost childish in its virginal, sex-stripped lucidity was this yearning gesture sent up to the utter clarity of the remotest spheres. And yet this yearning, upward gesture was already fulfillment. For the transparent cloudy dome which is stretched between above and below, impenetrable for those on earth, prevents the song of earthly longing from entering the sphere of the infinite, so that it reverberates, an echo of the soul, an incomplete outer-echo of the mute inner face, and a still more incomplete one of the yearned-for song of the spheres, this separating echo-wall dissolves and disappears when the miracle of the unearthly comes to pass, when the outside and inside pass into each other, merging the self with the universe; and just as no earthly song is then needed, no song of yearning, no song of love, perhaps not even an upward gesture, because the yearning is fulfilled and the song of the spheres resounds inside and outside at once, so now Plotia's innermost essence was transmuted to a quality of the universe, to that all-embracing, universal validity which annuls but transports the earthly chance from which it has sprung, assuming the shamefulness of chance and the chance embodiment, revealing the chance-delivered, the shame-freed, the sweet and terrible dignity of a transported and primal innocence. It was the innocence of final concurrence through which they were striding, or rather floating, the innocence of final immanence which connotes simultaneous permanence in every transformation of shape, which connotes the truth in every transformation of essence, in all transformations of error, they moved through an innocence which uses no measure and which had not yet learned to do so, sweet and terrible in its inordinacy, sweet and terrible in the passivity of its concurrence—and sweet and terrible was the morning's serene quietude in its verity, in its immeasurable echo of the star-face, the human-face, the animal-face, the plant-face, all without measure: here in this prodigal and prodigious garden with its terrorizing sweetness and sweet terror they made their way, blessed with innocent nakedness, acquitted of naked guilt; the forest stretched out shadily and flowers grew there beyond the height of trees, the forest gave on to flowery meadows where, without overtopping them, dwarfish shrubs were standing among the flowers, for no matter whether it was oak or beech, whether poppy or cassia or narcissus, whether nightstock or lily or grass or bush, there was not a single plant that could not have taken on any size whatsoever, and in tranquil simultaneity boundlessness was joined to boundlessness, the grass-blade rose up high as a tower, rigid and entwined with ivy, nearby to some spring-soaked moss opening out into shrubbery, each of these a living essence and yet resembling one another in the shadowed and serene tranquillity. For in all this restful green, surrounding the wanderers with a stone-cool drizzling breath, there hovered the darkness of its inmost rooty-soil, the darkness of the rooty-abyss that had pushed up this plant-life and saturated it to its last fiber, a hint of the last countenance in which star-face, human-face, animal-face, plant-face were again reflected hither from the earth, bound up with the unity of their earthly lives as the reflections of that most profound face, the face of the earth in its shadowed maternal calm. Thereupon the wandering, the striding, the floating turned into a resting, welcomed into a laurel-scented hopefulness by the universe opened for repose, and by its smile. Round about, the animals rested also in a vegetative earthly way, boundless their rest, boundless their aspect, immeasurable their stature, whether great or small, immersed in darkness and mostly asleep. And when they awoke their eyes followed the wanderers: the large eyes of the cattle which had ranged themselves fearlessly near the lion had a wondering look, the eyes of the lion, drowsily commanding, were watchful but not threatening, giant long-necked lizards peered with yellow dragon's eyes from the leafy caverns of the beech trees, toadlike creatures in the form of wolves blinked between the water-roses and the acanthus, and

an eagle-headed dwarfish bird glanced sharply in amazement
as it swung upon a branch of the white flowering privet, while
an insect with scaly body and tubular legs a yard in length
stared back at them with unmoving lidless eyes. Yes, many of
the animals made ready to accompany the wanderers. The
serpent alone glided off, green-spotted its outstretched coils,
gliding off into the gold-shimmering green of grass and leaf.
Rosy grapes hung down from the wild thorn-bush, honey-dew
oozed like resin from the bark of the hardest oaks, gray-green
quinces, chestnuts, wax-yellow plums and golden apples hung
in profusion throughout the woodland, but there was no need
to touch the fruit in order to be sated, no need to bend over
the water to sip of it, appeasement and refreshment came floating along invisibly on a smile sent hither from shame-freed innocence, sent hither from the expansive smiling of the garden,
from its immeasurable, boundless depth, sent hither without
need of name or speech, the faceless smile at rest in itself.
The scent of flowers drenched with sunny rain arose and spread
arching over the rivers, wafted from grove to grove, and wherever they wandered, along the river or through tawny-tossing
meadows or over the unseen bridges, wherever they went there
gleamed at their heads the tranquil star of the morning, the
herald of the beneficent eastern sun, the mild bearer of light
that, without light of its own, lets there be intimations of unending light, the tender iridescent reflection of the seven colors,
their last echo in the universal dome. As boundless as the spring
and just as peaceful, the mountains reared up in smiling severity, and in the stripped smiling peacefulness of their crags, the
grayish white sides of the ravines rose skyward, the hard bones
of creation, scarcely touched with green; yet high above the
stony barrenness the meads on the summit were greening in a
light gold under an expanse of opalescent be-starred transparent
blue, and there eagles, vultures and falcons were wheeling in
calm flight without darting down toward the grazing lambs and
the speckled kids nibbling quietly at the laurels which grew
there at the forest's edge below, there where the black-shadowed

461

slope turns into a pasturing vale; and here where brooks were flowing, drizzling between the fragrant willows, drizzling between shores verdant with trembling reeds, their pools holding the reflected constellations of the sky, there rested, immobile in the soft welling, the round-eyed fish-folk; deep in the remotest basins of pellucidness the shadows of their bodies played about while the herons, streaking across the upper air, they also did not dart downwards. There was sun and there was shadow, but nowhere just sun or just shadow, for the opal-shadowed light-circle of the cupola above was more than heaven, and the star-strewn shadowed darkness of the garden country below was more than earth, cupola like garden was boundless though not unbounded, rather it was enclosed in the real, the second immensity, in the immensity of the veritable light, in the immensity of true inglowing discrimination, which no longer created shapes from light and shadow but from their essence, making them in this way perceptible, so that darkness and light melted into each other and, above as below, nothing was to be found which would not have been at the same time both star and shadow; even the human spirit having become a star no longer cast the shadow that is language. The spirit was resting. And star and shadow likewise were these two who wandered here; their souls walked hand in hand, their communion, liberated from language, came to be chastely at rest, and the animals which followed after them participated in this communion. Restfully they wandered and afterwards they rested from their rest, resting within rest as evening came on. Ranged round by the animals they rested and gazed up to the westward-turning orb, gazing up to the motionless star, divining in it the invisible presence of the second immensity behind the cupola, gazing up until the sun-ball had sunk down to the edge of dusk, and that on which they gazed had the appearance of beauty—yet it was beyond the realm of the beautiful, for with all its loveliness, its buoyancy, its profundity, its harmony, that which came to them so blithely was in no sense the obtuseness of beauty but was, on the contrary, an awareness which streamed out from

the innermost and outermost borders of existence, not only
as a symbol, not only as a symbol of the border, nay, but as
the very essence of existence in which they participated so easily
that nothing appeared as strange but everything as familiar,
every spot saturated with distance, every distance brought into
closest proximity, distance and nearness charged with the illumination of an immediacy that was theirs in common, establishing
the inner communion of their souls. However, when the dusk
became deeper, it too reposing on into the night, and when he
was so completely at rest under the star, its opal shimmer having
come into its own light, that soon he beheld nothing other than
this gleaming star, neither the companion resting near him nor
the animals resting around him, then his bondage to the star
turned more than ever into an insight of wholeness, his own
wholeness as much as that of the happenings near him, it became more than ever an alliance, as much an alliance with himself as with heaven, star, shadow, animal and plant, a twofold
alliance with Plotia in the perception and self-perception of a
doubled insight: and as soul, animal, and plant were being
reflected into each other, reflected as substance in elemental
substance, as the whole reflected in the whole, and he too was
reflected in the elemental darkness of Plotia, he recognized
mother and child in her, he saw himself as having taken refuge
in the mother-smile, he perceived the father and the unborn
son and Lysanias in Plotia, and Lysanias was himself; he perceived the slave in Lysanias, and the slave was himself; he
perceived the great descendant and the great ancestor in the
inclusiveness of the ring which had strayed from Plotia's hand
to the heaven, wandered there as the source of light, and he
saw therein the universal fusion beyond fate, saw the beaming
fusion of elemental substances, layer by layer, limb by limb,
he perceived the living oneness of the elemental substance which
was his own soul and, for all that, so very much that of Plotia's
that she was bound to have reached him in spite of having
sprouted from other roots, of having been delivered from another tree, of having risen from another level of animality, and

she had reached him, having passed through many mirror-surfaces, through mirrors and more mirrors, she had come as the reflection of his soul and in order to be reflected in it, the great disclosure of balance in the whole creation. Overcast by mirror after mirror, mirrored in himself, he fell asleep. However, continuing his perception even in sleep, he felt the unquenchable persistence of the fusion and reflexive insinuation of Plotia into himself, into the constituent parts which made up this self, insinuation into the sensible and insensible, wholeness gliding into wholeness, earth-dark and soft, stone-cool and hard, insinuation into wholeness of his life, into the rocky bones of his skeleton and into his earthbound roots and marrow, into what was vegetative and plantlike in him, into what was the animality of his flesh and skin, he felt Plotia becoming a part of himself, of his innermost seeing soul, and he felt her glance resting in him, seeing, as had his glance in her, from within. His sleep was the ancestral chain and likewise the chain of descendants; the line of substances through which he had passed and the seed of those he carried in himself had united in his sleep, contracted to his sleeping self, absorbed into him nameless along with Plotia to whom a name no longer clung—a spaceless reflection of all that had been built into the recesses of sleep so that it might unfold again as a reflection in space, there where sleep would turn into waking. It unfolded to a bright day into which he awoke, surrounded by images of all these substances, the sun playing about him, the stars above, although the universal equalization was simplified, for Plotia was missing. She had vanished without loss, left behind in the second space of memory, infinitely forgotten, infinitely unforgotten; nothing had changed since nothing had been lost, since nothing could be lost, and without changing him she had become a part of himself, without remaining she still stayed on. The mute song of the spheres continued to resound. Only the smile had left the garden through which he now had to wander alone, only the smile had vanished, for only serenity can smile, serenity and nothing else. And it was certainly unrest or, at least, a lack of serenity which kept him constantly roving. Or could this unrest appertain to the animals? Could he have taken it over from them? In increasing numbers they joined themselves to him in order to accompany him on his path, they came on from every side, soundless the tread of their paws, their hooves, their soles, their claws, an inaudible trampling, nevertheless an even tread, or rather a tread enthralled to a ghostly restless evenness, to a common buoyant alertness that joined with his own and forced even his own gait to turn into an inaudible even tread like that of the animal; the longer this continued the more like an animal's his walk became, the more compelling the animal trends that rose up from below, from the ground up, from his moving feet, the animality invading his striding body, making him into an upright animal, since he felt himself a beast from top to toe, from toe to top, a gaping jaw, even though he did not snap, a claw-bearer even though he rent no game, a feathered thing with a hooked bill, even though he swooped on no prey; and bearing the beast in himself, seeing the beast from within, he heard the dumb language of the beast, heard with them, heard in their speech, heard in himself the mute melody of the spheric song continuing to sound, carried by an echo of profoundest earthly darkness, in unison with the unincarnated, uncreated elements slumbering uneasily at the dark source of all animalhood and vibrating through all its dumb speech; whereas before it had been a perception of qualities, a recognition of wolfish, foxish, cattish, parrottish, horseish, sharkish attributes, he was now becoming fully aware of the beastly lack of qualities in quality as yet unborn, inexistent, still-unformed; and seen from within the animal, the yawning gulf beneath and behind the animal proclaimed itself to the perceiver, recognized as the roothold of every creaturely qualification. Whatever was round about, striving with tongue too light or too heavy toward speech, grinning with frustration, struggling to be created, all this was the animal in its manifold forms, nevertheless the animal as such, scattered like rain-drops, yet gathered like them to a plenum, just as raindrops are gathered in a rain-cloud, falling

moisture rising again in fullness from the unity of the interwoven roots, and this animal totality in its invisible transparency
was the goal of his conscious knowledge, he knew himself to
be one of them in the animality of his transparently striding
body. The light was transparent, but more transparent still the
recognizing beam at the rear of the heavenly cupola, that of
the steady star, symbolizing the light on high and sending it
below as a transparent, floating alertness so that even the
animals seemed to be seized by it. The aimless and restless
roving in the boundless fields lasted the whole day, and with
the sinking sun the restlessness mounted even higher; in its
entire expanse over mountain and valley the garden began to
be filled by a disquieting restlessness, and as the sun-ball retired to the low horizon the onset of night came to be a prodigious occurrence: all of a sudden the wandering of the animals
came to have a common goal, became unified, yes, all-embracing
this wandering, they came on from every slope, from every
forest, from all directions, and they wandered along the rivers
toward the great water, even the fishes heading down-stream
in a wandering without fear or haste, yet one under a forceful
command, for the banks closed together immediately behind
the animal train, the earth was pushed forward by the irresistible growth of the plant roots, all plant-life shooting up to a
most immeasurable height, every shoot branching out to a most
impenetrable jungle, the earth steaming in the mass of primal
growth, so that only salamanders and reptiles could live in it,
the thicket being too dense even for the birds and they just able
to nest in the uppermost tree-tops; not a beast was lost from
the many herds during the wandering, none died, they only
disappeared into the nocturnal oceans, into the nocturnal ether,
taking their places among the scaly ones and the feathered ones
inhabiting the day-and-night ocean, the night-and-day air. And
he who wandered with them, he the animal set upright, he
having become lidless, sleepless, fish-eyed, fishy-hearted, he
stood on the swampy shore tall-ly erect, covered with sea-weed,
scaly, reptilian, tangled in the plants, like a plant, save that

the singing of the spheres did not cease for him, he kept on hearing it, it continued to sing because he had remained human; unlost, the great human sense of wandering beat on in him, nothing had been lost for him and the star of the east was still sparkling at his head. Thus he waited for the morning, he an upright monster and yet a man, awaiting the morning. It came again and sun lay over the damp mists; these ascended in reeking fumes from the boundless plain of green which, like a single heaving plant-being grown mountain high, was spreading over the erstwhile garden, while overhead the cloudlessness became iridescent in the pearly gray light, a quivering mirror of the green plain below, heaving as it did, more and more overcast by the ever denser mist which shifted only to settle down as clouds, and the opal gleam of the star glimmered into gray. He saw this and anticipated rain. But it did not rain although birds were flying low, clouds of bird-beasts and other bird-like creatures which, soundlessly screaming, swarmed about his unmoved head and often alighted on his shoulders. His feet among the teeming fishes he waded through the brackish water, he waded along the shore, seeking something, he knew not what, certainly not Plotia, more likely the place on the shore where she had met him, but nothing was to be found, nothing could be recognized again, no tree overtopped another in the uniform covering of green, and in the midst of his wandering, the duration of which could not be measured in time, he stopped again not far from the shore, it may be because the place where he found himself held him enchained in a most inexplicable way, it may be because an inexplicable almost plant-like weariness had overcome him, and, even though his arms were like wings with which he could have flown over the green summits, he did not stir. It was like a presentiment of an immobility yet to come. Unspeakable things flew overhead, unspeakable things swam below, immense dragonish things flew with the birds, swam with the fishes, innumerably multiplied, inconceivable in their monstrous shapes, and above melted with below, since fresh swarms of fishes were constantly diving into the water, one like the other transformed into dragon-shapes, caught in a constant interchange, exchanging fins for wings. The difference between the flying and swimming animal was fading out more and more, the living stuff of both having slid from the egg, and it seemed as if they were pressing backwards into the amorphousness of their herdhood so that voluntarily they might come to an indiscriminate uniformity like that of the plants, its gigantic spread of green conceding nothing more to the single growth; although they were still flying, although they were still swimming or clinging like plants to the bed of the sea, although each of them was in its own particular form, whether covered in feathers, scales, shell, or skin, whether with feet or claws, whether finned or beaked, there lurked reptilian-fashion in their eyes or non-eyes the glance of the serpent, and this serpentine look, to which they all tended and to which they came home, was like a last creaturely essence which they had shared in common, plant-like, beast-like, primordial, yes, even stemming from pre-creation, the last origin of quality from which beings were created into life, the only one that guaranteed their remaining in life and in creation. More and more the flying and swimming animals were amassing to an impenetrably dense heap, increasingly commingled by monsters, the mass becoming increasingly monstrous, more and more threatened by uncreated and precreated elements, more and more both sky and sea were filled with them unto their most transparent depths, for it became apparent that just here everything was streaming together in great masses, that just the spot at which he had stopped was acting as a mighty crux of a creaturely occurrence by attracting it from every side. And now the well-spring of the waters also became visible, their deepest root-abyss, the fountain within the fountain, and there in the uttermost depths of the fountain lay the serpent itself, rainbow-colored yet transparent as ice, closed to a time-cycle, coiled around the nothingness of the middle. It was that which transmutes by reason of its own immutability. The fountain was enlarging like a crater as if the serpent-ring were to be-

468

come all-embracing, and whatever came near to it stiffened to immobility, all flow and flight stilled, made rigid by the green staring sent out from the nothingness, the serpent's glance sending nothing out. Were these things here still beasts at all? Were they not about to lose their final substantiality in this last transformation, having become inescapably appropriated by the serpent's glance? The sky was also rigid, and rigid the cloud-blanket of uniform gray which could let down no rain and behind which the sun, a shapeless, stolid and dead light-spot, was tracing its rigid course. And he, the man, having remained human notwithstanding his concourse with the un-created, involved in the community of beasts slid from the egg, of plants sprouted from seed, in a class with both, feather, fin and leaf transparent, a weed to himself and in himself, he was included in this benumbing occurrence, he, too, immobile in his unexpectant waiting, he, too, a stolid evanescent creature, yet his human eye had forfeited none of its discrimination and he had knowledge of the starry countenance behind the cloud. Now the sunspot, dimmed by night to a grayish red, reached the lower edge of day, and the glimmering stars, glowing up to nocturnal intensity, were able to break through the fog-blanket with their uncertain gleam, haltingly at first and then with in-creasing clarity, slowly they came to be full in number and splendor, not only above but below as well, turning here to a second starry heaven, to that of a mirrored image which shone up equally from the black watery depths and from the blackly-moist spread of plant-life and transformed them into a single black mirror-shield, to a single cupola set with stars; now noth-ing separated the flood of plant-life from the flood of the waters, the seas had overflowed all their shores, streaming into the plant-life which streamed into the life of the seas in turn, and, between the stars above and those below, the beasts of the air and the beasts of the water floated rigidly. The lower cupola was but an echo of the stars—but was not the upper one already an echo of the plants? unity above as below, one like the other upheld by the doubled heaven, upheld by the doubled seas, united to

469

a single entity grown over by plants and stars, so very inclusive and self-contained that in its space no sort of isolation was any longer possible, none was permissible because everything was being resolved; whether eagle or heron or dragon-bird, whether shark or whale or a water-lizard, they were now but a totality, a single blanket of beastiness, a single space-filling essence which became more and more transparent, an animal-fog losing itself in ultimate invisibility, absolved into starriness, absorbed into plantliness; the animal totality was swallowed by the night, the animal breathing of the world was spent, no heart was beating any more, and the icy serpent had burst asunder, the icy serpent of time. Abruptly, unhampered by time, the night went over into full day, abruptly and time-exempted, the sun stood at the peak of day surrounded by an opalescent starry throng from which no star was missing and neither the whitish moon, and likewise, increasing in splendor, there glittered the abiding eastern star. So it came to pass above, while no less suddenly in the lower mirror there began a last enormous growing of the plants, partly as a struggle against their root-and-stem enchainment to earth, partly as an attempt to attain to something beyond themselves, to burst through the plantliness in order to win to an outright animal differentiation and motility, for, warmed by the sudden light, and beyond doubt driven on by all the animality it had absorbed into itself, the verdure on its side was growing with unbridled and irresistible subanimality out from its former immeasurable rooty-network, growing aloft, growing far beyond itself, the very humus of existence growing instinctually in this incessant change, in this constant self-renewing, sprouting and pushing, propped by tail-stems, constrained by snake-stems but long past being a tree, a blade, a flower, having shot up beyond reach, gnarled or pliant, spiralling or rampant, in a terrible unpredictable wildness—and he, who even while in its midst might watch it, could watch it, must watch it, moved on by the animally-invaded plant-life, became like a plant himself, inside and outside, throbbing with the flow of earth-sap, rooty, basty, tubular, woody, barky, leafy, though still remain-

470

ing human, with the unalterable human eye: for even though quality after quality be lost, though substance after substance be overtaken and abandoned by the creation, the eye remains human as long as it looks forward, and that which has been created remains unforgotten to it through all transmutations, unforgotten even in the forgetting, left back in the second immensity, the on-impelling and ever-impelling, the unlosable star. He was a seeing plant although he was not struggling back to anything, neither into beastiness. Hours elapsed without being hours, the day had no end, endless, just endless, neither fast nor slow was the circling of stars in their courses, endless the progress of the sun, and without end the growth surrounding him, the all-grappling, aeonic plant-growth in which he participated in a plant-like way, aeonic and endless in such a way that inertia and movement, interchanged and time-exempted, united to an indistinguishable flowing rest, so changed by the aeons from one into the other that—just as abruptly as the daybreak—suddenly the night broke out from the course of the stars, from their endless, moving stability, broke out as the primal darkness which had held itself hidden behind the furthermost starry orb and now, independent of the arching path of lights, indeed, without putting out a single one of them, it filled the dome of existence with impenetrable darkness: the essential world-darkness burst forth, that uncreated darkness which is infinitely more than mere loss of light, mere lack of light, or the absence of light, for it can never be lightened at all by any force of the sun, even at full noon, to say nothing of being completely dissipated by light; so, with its mid-day radiance undimmed, the sun also was standing unchanged and, it seemed, unchangeable, still in the zenith, cast about by the stars in their full abundance but framed, along with them, in the profoundest stuff of night, a nocturnal figure sunk into the night-shield and, together with the starry abundance, the sun was reflected from the blackness above to the blackness below, becoming there a twin image of itself, a lower sun, a lower zenith, caught by the well-shaft of the middle, in the flowing depths of which its brightness swam, to be lifted up once more on the waters of creation, an echo flooded in darkness, dying out as it was flooded up. Starry countenance above, starry countenance below, and, in the doubled darkness of the duplicated night-dome, the green of the plant-billows faded to a pale reptilian shimmer, to the innate light of plants, so that these attained to an almost transparent perceptibility even unto the furthest ramifications of their stormily-wild growth of filaments and interlacings. Not less gleaming, not less perceptible became the roots under the earth and under the waters, and soon these, together with the stems and branches and all their stormy sprouting, wove themselves into a palely-wild single network, stretching out to every corner of the night-dome, creeping in all directions, shooting up in all directions, anchoring in all directions, being in the diversity of its directions almost as chartless as infinite space itself, an ether thicket hanging in itself, but despite this always striving upward, its direction indicated by the light above, by the invisible linear-play of the stars in which the gleaming countenance of the heavens was invisibly engraved as the archetype, and to which every single echo was carried; now the fountain of the middle was growing and extending itself upward and downward, welling with liquid elements, having become transparent in conjunction with its own incipient light, stretching upward and downward, coming into planthood, scarcely a shaft now, far rather a transparent tree branching out with the sun-echo in its rooty depths, caught into a gleaming inscrutability of plant-and-star growth, and at this point it was sheerly unperceivable whether there was still a borderline between plant and star, whether star and plant were not already touching in the archetype, star-echo and plant-echo enmeshed and intergrown in each other, merged together into that mirrored depth where the firmament above and that below touched and dissolved the boundaries of the other and flowed together to form the orb of the world. Visible yet invisible was this occurrence of the skies, visible yet not recognizable—, he, however, he the beholder, caught into this universal growth, he the

472

plant-involved, the beast-involved, he also stretched himself from firmament to firmament, stretched himself through the starry tides of the universe, and standing in the earthly realm with his animal-roots, his animal-stems, his animal-leaves, he stood at the same time in the furthermost sphere of the stars, so that at his feet lay the sign of the serpent which, root-entangled and seven-starred, had sunk deep into the west while, transferred to his heart, sparkling in a twofold triad, shone the sign of the lyre, and high, oh, high over all, his crown reared aloft, reaching to the uppermost height of the cupola, reaching toward the eastern star though not quite attaining it, reaching for the star of promise whose infinite beaming had companioned him on his way, the star coming into more immediate proximity, coming nearer and nearer. No longer as an earthly face but just as a beholding tree-top, he gazed upward to the stars, into the face of heaven which had gathered into itself the lineaments of all creatures and had transfigured them, the human and animal face having become one, and bore them now enfolded in itself; he gazed toward the sun-bearing transparent gleaming sunward-turned shaft of the middle that held captive in its branches the rounded universe with its oceanic flooding and heaving as though for a future uniting, and caught likewise in this oceanic trembling, swept into this oceanic surge, his heart was beating and surging in unison with it, his heart that long since had ceased from being a heart, only a lyre, ah yes, now a lyre, as if at last the promise were to ring out among its starry strings, not the song itself but the annunciation of it, the hour of song, the hour of birth and rebirth, the hour of twofold leading awaited without expectation, the singing hour at the closing point of the circle, crying out the unity of the world on the last breath of the universe: it was preparation, a mighty preparation, mighty in its tension, but the lyre did not ring out, could not ring out, might not ring out, for the unity achieved here by the flow of the universe in its oceanic heaving from one firmament to the other was that of plant-life in its power of growth, was the unity of the inviolable muteness of plants, the universal silence pulsing under the unbroken reticence of the stars, inviolably mute even the enormous power with which this unification was accomplished, as, in a final spurt of growth, the sprouting roused itself to the limits of its range, palely glistening its earthy might, palely shuddering from the exertion by which it had thrust its transparent tips into the furthest and topmost border of the dome of darkness, so irresistible, so all-compelling, star-compelling, heaven-compelling, that the heaven, as if to ward off this onslaught of plant-growth, had become enhanced in a final burst of flame, in a final flaming transport of its sun-bidden, sun-related midnight face from whose creatureliness beamed out the human aspect, purer than of yore, purer, greater, milder, devouter, more transfigured, more transparent than ever before, but still destined to extinction, still able to be vanquished, vanquished forevermore, vanquished by the onslaught of plant-growth, sucked in by the sucking strength of the darkly-pale submerged roots; and the heavenly countenance vanished, overgrown by the ether-thicket, star after star vanished, one after the other vanished into its own mirrored image coming up to it, vanished to the complete disappearance of both in their common marriage; yet inextinguishable in its extinguishing, no star's light was lost, each remained in safe-keeping, unlosably passing into the conquering innate radiance of the plants, light after light dropping into its counter-light and impregnating it with an ever increasing strength, becoming more dense within it, growing and growing until at last the sun itself crashed into its own reflection, received into the transparently flaming tree branches of the world-shaft, the sun also fading into its own reflection, the reflection fading too and vanishing as the sun vanished, vanishing with it into the sparkling, upturned elm branches of the middle which, for this moment, for this one short moment of the crash, had unfolded to the full splendor of its whole arch hung with sun-golden fruit, only to evaporate in a mute, heaving sigh that was like a breath, only to vanish with star and reflected star, with sun and sun-echo, fading in the pale universal glimmer of the star-sated, sky-soaked universe of plants. The boundary of plant-life had been reached, the amplitude of growth covered space after space, covered sky after sky, enveloping the starry abundance; the welling, glowing, life-giving fountain of the middle was dried up and dissolved into cool light; the climax was past. And this universe of plants, as if exhausted from the enormous effort of its attack, breathless after its final flare-up, breathed itself out in a sighing silence; it hung in the darkness like a pale gleaming underbrush, visible within it if not lighting it, but it had given up its growing, and not only its growing but its light as well, its brightness given over bit by bit to the darkness, endlessly vanishing into its second immensity just as the world-shaft and the world-branching had done, and, weary of a fading perceptibility, it had filtered into the darkness, fading into its depths. Primal darkness now ruled over whatever still existed, existence, being no longer divided by any star-light or plant-light, was abandoned to darkness, given over to it alone, dominated by primal darkness, dominated by its dumbness, even the plant-breathing stilled, outside as inside the breath was being held, it passed into an immobility in the breathless blackness of which the scales of time balanced quietly, breathless in their equilibrium. Shadowed in immensity, though not yet into the final consummation, the primal night glided on—, nevertheless it was not yet consummate: for this darkness, like everything graspable by the senses, was all too perceptible not to be harboring its own counterpart, and, even though the tides of heaven, the tides of the heart may have ebbed forever, a translucent beam seeped once more from the darkness, almost as though it had preserved within itself the pale light of stars and plants while making them essentially one—star and plant having their common essence in the primordial stone, pregnant with darkness—, then darkness gave way, surrendering space to an indistinct brightness reminiscent of day without being day and yet being more than day, a brightness spreading over all existence and lacking the breathing of star or plant or animal, a breath-stripped universal day. Night-black under the shadowless universal light extended the motionless floods in which no sunlight was reflected, night-pale under the shadowless light the mountainous root-forests, which had not won back their green, spread immeasurably over the boundless fields of earth, and they faded away. He, however, divested of his animal-likeness, his plant-likeness, was now a being of clay and earth and stone, mountain high, an unwieldy shapeless tower, a spar of clay, destitute of all limbs, a shapelessly-powerful, shapelessly-towering stone giant, certainly of no size in comparison to this immeasurable earth-shield curving itself before him under the sky-shield, shield and counter-shield bonelike and horny in color, certainly of no size in comparison to this measureless plain over which he stalked, no, over which he was being moved, no, over which he was being carried, he the stony-faceless one, divining the light behind the shield of the curving sky, the light which he saw because the morning star, grazed by his head, had sunk into his rocky forehead as a third eye above the other two which sat stone-blind in stone, a third eye above them as a seeing eye, divine and discriminating, and for all that a human eye. Sparser and sparser became the pale gigantic forests, looser and looser the mat of their reptilian branches, limp and limper their withering trunks, drooping back into the earth from which they had germinated so impetuously, now already dead in their withering; and when in this wise the transparent plant-life had drifted back into the earth to its last shred, so that nothing remained but naked stone extending the width of the world, the very roots stone-absorbed to their last transparent filaments, then darkness came again into the universe, turning again into night, into a breathless breath-stripped, breath-robbed universal night that was no longer nocturnal and yet more than nocturnal, awful even though not awe-inspiring, immeasurable in the might of its growing dark amplitude. All this happened apart from continuity or time, fixed but not final, as something seen and sensed, and in the course of this un-nightly boundless nocturnality he felt everything which had been firm and able to be retained dissolving, felt the ground slipping beneath his feet, dropping into forget-fulness and its infinity, into the memory-less remembering of its immense flood, which coupled the true image and the arch-image to oneness, and flowingly transformed the earth-darkness back into fluidity—the mirror of sky and the mirror of sea merging to a single essence, earth changing to light. That which had sunk down was changed to liquid light, brought after an im-ponderable span of eternity back from immensity into the dome of the sky which was again becoming light; however this re-trieving was not recollection, stone and earth remained forgotten, and forgotten was that over which he had trod and from which he had been formed, and the shapelessness of his gigantic form was just as intangible in its transparency as the light, just as intangible as the fluid dome of the world surrounding him, an ultra-transparent shadow; he came to consist merely of his eye, the eye on his brow. Thus he floated between fluid mirrors, floating in the space between the liquid light-fog above and the liquid swells below, and the eternal light hidden behind the fog played in the waters, establishing wholeness, sustaining it. Mild was the gentleness of the fog, mild the gentleness of the flowing waters, both of them merged in the softness of the light; and it seemed to him as if a very large hand like a cloud were carrying him through this mild occurrence, through the mild-ness of this twofold dusk, motherly in its gentleness, fatherly in its calm, embracing him and carrying him on, further and further and forevermore. And then, as if to fuse together the gentle unity above and that below, as if to wash away the last separating wall between the liquefaction above and below, the rain began to fall. At first it was a lazy trickling, gradually becoming denser and denser, finally turning into a single stream of water falling through space, almost languid in its enveloping softness, an enveloping, streaming, infinitely-great gentle dark-ness, so all-permeating that it prevented one from knowing whether the stream was pouring upward or downward; con-summate now the darkness, consummate the unity in which there was neither direction nor beginning nor end. Unity!—

never-ending unity, a unity which did not end even when the final darkness was achieved and began to emit light again, as it now did: at the center of the darkness, as though with a soft stroke, with a gentle sigh, the cover of the sky-cupola was drawn back: wondrously gleaming it opened up suddenly, becoming like a single star, large in the skyey round, becoming a single eye in which his own was reflected, being at the same time above and below. Heaven, simultaneously within and without, heaven itself the inner and outer border, including the crystal of unity in the transparency of which all moisture had gathered. And held within its radiation, so that the heavenly whole as well as the earthly, infinitely unlosable in unending refractions and reflections, should be taken up by the crystal's light forevermore, there was the starry face with its crystal rapture, the first light of being's wholeness to shine forth and give light to the beginning, to the ending, and to each fresh attempt of creation. Where, however, was his own face in this universe?—Had the crystal receptacle of the spheres already received him, or was he in a void, excluded from all inner and outer realms of being?—was he, who was no longer even floating, no longer held by any hand, actually here at all?—Oh, he must be, because he was looking, he must be, because he was waiting, but his enraptured looking, caught into the sparkling rays, was, at the same time, the crystal itself, and his waiting, this prolonged yearning for the holding hand to grasp among the strings of the boundless transparency and make the heart of the universe, the heart of the waiting and of the waiting one resound, this unexpectant waiting was at the same time that of the crystal itself, was its consciousness of growth, a consciousness intent on developing to a still more embracing unity, to a purer equilibrium, to a more complete breath-stillness, so much the crystalline will, so much a fore-echo of the still unsung song of the spheres, so much a fore-echo of the ether that, in a last, flaring up of the universe, in a last flaring up of the creation, the light again crashed into the darkness as the darkness opened to receive the light, both of them—in plunge and counter-plunge—committed to a unity which was no longer a crystal one, but just the darkest radiation, having no quality, not even that of the crystal, but which was the essence of no quality, the borderless, universal abyss, the birthplace of all essential qualities; the middle of the star had opened, the middle of the ring: the birth-giving nothingness, opened to the glance of the glanceless one—the seeing blindness.

THEREUPON HE WAS PERMITTED TO TURN AROUND; THEREUPON CAME THE COMMAND TO TURN AROUND; AND THEREUPON HE WAS TURNED AROUND.

And there, before his once more perceiving eyes, the nothing was infinitely transformed once more, turning into the present and into the past, widening out to the aeonic cycle once more so that this, having become infinite, might close once more; infinite the round of heaven, infinite the heavenly dome arching once more, infinite the endless shield of the world, surrounded by the seven-colored bow in endless recollection. Again there was light and darkness, again day and night, again nights and days, and again immensity was regulated according to height, breadth and depth, and the plan of the sky was defined, opening out to its four directions, again there was above and below, cloud and sea; and in the middle of the sea the land rose up once more, the green isle of the world bedecked with plants, with forests and with pastures, the mutation within immutability. And up came the sun in the east on its course over the round, and the stars followed at night, conforming to the northern pole with its star-free center, where righteousness maintaining the equilibrium was enthroned, beamed upon by the rays of the Northern Cross. Yet again in the morning light eagles and sea-gulls streaked through the upper air, hovering about the island, and dolphins emerged to hearken to the mute song of the spheres. From the west came a trail of animals, coming to meet the sun and stars, the beasts of the wilderness and those of the field mingling in a harmony innocent of conflict, lion and bull and lamb, and the goat with its bulging udder, streaming eastward all of them, seeking the eastern shepherd, striving toward the human face. And this face could be beheld in the middle of the world-shield, in its infinite depth, beheld there amidst infinite human life and human living, beheld for the last and yet as for the first time: peace without conflict, the harmonious human countenance innocent of conflict, beheld as the image of the boy in the arms of the mother, united to her in a sorrowful smiling love. Thus he saw it, seeing thus the boy and the mother, and they were so familiar that he was almost able to name them without being able to recall their names; yet, still more familiar than the face and the missing name was the smile that bound mother and child, and it seemed as if prescient in this smile the whole *significance* of the interminable occurrence were comprehended, as if the law of truth were proclaimed in this smile—the mild yet terrible glory of the human fate, begot from the word and, already in the begetting, coming to be the word's substance, the word's comfort, the word's blessing, the word's advocacy, the word's redemptive strength, the law-founding force of the word, the word's renewal, once more expressed and expressible in the insufficient but still sole sufficing representations of human actions and wanderings, made known and preserved and repeated in them forevermore. In loving perception the word received the yearning of the heart and that of the mind for their great communion, the word becoming the confirmation by force of innate necessity, assuming the yearning of the lodger who longed to become the son, his task fulfilled. Thus drawn hither by the summons of the word, the brooks and streams began to trickle, the surf with a soft booming struck the shore, the seas swelled steel-blue and light, ruffled by the nethermost fires of the south, and everything could be seen and heard in simultaneous depth because, turned round toward the immensity which he had once left behind him, he saw through it into the immensity of the here and now, looking backward and forward at once, listening simultaneously to what was behind and what was ahead, and the rustling of the past, sunken into the forgotten invisibility, was rising up again to the present moment and became the simultaneous stream of creation in which the eternal rests, the first image, the vision of visions. Thereupon he shuddered and it was a mighty shuddering, almost beneficent in its finality, for the ring of time had closed and the end was the beginning. The images sank down but, preserving them unseen, the rumbling continued.

The welling fountain of the middle, gleaming invisibly in the infinite anguish of knowing: the no thing filled the emptiness and it became the universe.

The rumbling continued and it was emitted from the mingling of the light with the darkness, both of them roused by the incipient tone which now actually began to sound, and that which sounded was more than song, more than the striking of the lyre, more than any tone, more than any voice, since it was all of these together and at once, bursting out of the nothing as well as out of the universe, breaking forth as a communication beyond every understanding, breaking forth as a significance above every comprehension, breaking forth as the pure word which it was, exalted above all understanding and significance whatsoever, consummating and initiating, mighty and commanding, fear-inspiring and protecting, gracious and thundering, the word of discrimination, the word of the pledge, the pure word; so it roared thither, roaring over and past him, swelling on and becoming stronger and stronger, becoming so overpowering that nothing could withstand it, the universe disappearing before the word, dissolved and acquitted in the word while still being contained and preserved in it, destroyed and recreated forever, because nothing had been lost, nothing could be lost, because end was joined to beginning, being born and giving birth again and again; the word hovered over the universe, over the nothing, floating beyond the expressible as well as the inexpressible, and he, caught under and amidst the roaring, he floated on with the word, although the more he was enveloped by it, the more he penetrated into the flooding sound and was penetrated by it, the more unattainable, the greater, the graver and more elusive became the word, a floating sea, a floating fire, sea-heavy, sea-light, notwithstanding it was still the word: he could not hold fast to it and he might not hold fast to it; incomprehensible and unutterable for him: it was the word beyond speech.

Translation begun November, 1940,
finished October, 1944.
J. S. U.

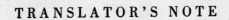

TRANSLATOR'S NOTE

The real significance of "The Death of Virgil" was borne upon the translator more than a year before she undertook the English version, through her reading and translation of the five elegies on fate. These elegies stand at the intellectual as well as actual center of the work, crystallizing both its meaning and method.

It is conceded that no poem is entirely translatable, and "The Death of Virgil" is a poem, although neither in the sense of a single lyrical outburst nor a sequence of poems on a single theme, yet one that sustains its tension through nearly five hundred pages. The form of this poem, whose subject relates it to the antique epics, is consequent upon two inherent characteristics: Most salient, of course, is its poetical unity in which the fullness of expression lies not alone in the words themselves but quite as much in the spaces between. For in a poem the words are less integers than points in a configuration: indeed, one might well describe the structure of the lyric (and the nature of this work is unquestionably lyrical) as the expression of the interval. The second aspect is the musical composition of the work as a whole: the four main parts of the book stand in the same relation to each other as the movements of a symphony or quartette, and somewhat in the manner of theme and variations the successive part becomes a lyrical self-commentary on the parts that have preceded it.

The style of this book is the inevitable outcome of its structure, since style itself is only the outer and inseparable manifestation of method. But it is with the concretization of method that the translator must directly deal. It may be of interest briefly to summarize a few problems that arose from the style.

Broch's syntax, which is an essential element of his work, had faithfully to be preserved, despite far-reaching and radical differences in German and English modes of expression. This syntax emerged from the functioning of two main ideas which are indissolubly connected, deriving on the one hand from the musical structure of the work, on the other from the inner monologue. The narrative proceeds in the third person, but it is soon discerned that for all its comprehension of multiple levels of

485

experience, both internal and external, it is from first to last an inner monologue, into which even the book's conversational scenes are drawn. Although these conversations are reproductions of outer events and actual dialogues, their inclusion into the inner monologue gains for them an abstract quality, in a measure reminiscent of Plato, and certainly far removed from the effort at naturalistic representation. From such a monologue, however, arise its own stylistic demands, but Broch's syntax fully meets these when—retaining the musical analogy—the four symphonic parts of the book press on through the various tempi, from the Andante of the beginning to the Maestoso of the end. The more headlong the tempo, the shorter the sentence, the slower the tempo becomes, the more complicated the sentence structure; the sentences in the Adagio of the second part are probably among the longest in the world's literature; undoubtedly they put a strain upon the translation. Broch's syntax, which he considers purely functional, and which may be summed into the principle: "one thought—one moment—one sentence," permits him to gather within a fleeting moment of consciousness all the thought-groups of the inner monologue, whose emotional and philosophical contents are often of a highly disparate nature. Yet the force of this principle pervades the book, sustaining its poetic and musical unity. While complicated, the sentences are never confused: mirroring the feverish yet lucid thoughts of the dying poet, in their great rocking rhythms they reproduce the sensation of the floating journey on which he is being carried by the bark of death.

It was not easy to capture this rhythm and these long sentences in the English language, whose genius more often finds expression in a shorter line. Nor was this the only difficulty. The greatest challenge sprang from intrinsic differences in the two languages. With its mass of composite words, and especially with the emphasis which Broch gives to the substantive, German achieves a concentration of meaning which, both in its associations and grammatically, permits of a many-dimensional expression; a German sentence may have at the same time a concrete and a metaphysical meaning. While no language, rightly understood, can be called one-dimensional, and above all the English language with its rich inheritance of poetry,

486

nevertheless a clear and unequivocal expression has always been held a virtue of English writing. If the long sentence with many subordinate clauses has been used with great power by eminent English writers of the 18th Century, and with extraordinary subtlety by Henry James, it is not characteristic. As a rule, richness has been achieved by the exfoliation of the subject in a successive and natural development, rather than by trying to sound multiple levels of meaning at one stroke. Certain modern poets, it is true, have sought subtlety and complexity through a wealth of allusion, sometimes so abstruse and esoteric that communication is largely imperilled. Joyce, who like Broch, was searching for a language of many dimensions, often ignored the tradition and, dismissing syntax and grammar, formed new words in combinations hitherto untried.

Such experimentation is admirable in the daring innovator, who, of course, assumes sole responsibility for his work; it is impermissible and impossible for the translator. To have substituted rhythms different from those of the author would have been to misrepresent him; to have taken greater liberties with the English language would have been a double betrayal. The translation has adhered as much as possible to the shape of the original German sentences, to the general rhythmic pattern, and to the maintenance of as many levels of meaning as the language would allow. Instead of representing the ever-recurring ideas by constant repetition of the key-words, in the manner of the leit-motif, an accretion of nuances was sought through the use of synonyms in order to approximate the multi-meanings of the German composita. Broch uses the symbol of the rainbow throughout the work. This iridescence, this glowing and fading and merging of color, tone and meaning, gives the book a kind of natural magic, spanning symbolically the new world that seems always to be arising out of the elements to which the existent one is being constantly reduced. The translator has endeavored with all her resources, following the author scrupulously, to carry the spell unbroken from one language to the other; the method was identical with that used in the translation of a lyric.

One radical departure was made, in deference to the psychological and grammatical differences of the two languages. Virgil enunciates his philosophical insights and revelations in the present tense; the truths of life seem to burst upon him fully only in the hour of death; his illumination assumes the accent of prophecy. In German the present tense, which Broch consistently employs in these passages, is not only natural but often mandatory. Yet, if prophecy is akin to memory, as this book hints, both may be considered as phenomena of the stream of consciousness. English usually represents that stream in the past tense, treating it grammatically as a form of indirect discourse. Therefore, in recording the data of consciousness, the simple past tense was in most cases substituted: to have done otherwise would have imparted an unbearably didactic character improper to the poem. And seeing that a thought which has found its form in words must already have occurred in time, even though its truth may have an immediate as well as a timeless cogency, the translator deems herself to have been faithful to the author's spirit.

Translation is always a hazardous enterprise; translating poetry even quixotic. But poets must have more of courage than of common sense, and in so far as she is a poet the translator dares to hope that her labor has not been vain; that her admiration for this work and her identification with it these past years have, for its sake, afforded "to every power a double power."

At various times help has been given the translator in reading the more difficult passages, and it is her pleasure to thank for their services the following: Mrs. Josephine Kahler, Dr. Viktor Polzer, Dr. Wieland Herzfelde, and for more continuous help, Mrs. Marianne Schlesinger. She also desires to express her gratitude to Roger Sessions and Paul Rosenfeld for their sympathetic reading of the first English drafts; most of all she acknowledges her deep indebtedness to Jule Brousseau, who read the complete English manuscript and gave generously of her gifts as writer and friend.

J. S. U.

SOURCES

Historical source material concerning Virgil's life and work is far from voluminous. It goes without saying that this material was consulted in "The Death of Virgil." For the most part reference was sought in standard works so generally known that a bibliography seems superfluous.

However, it may prove of interest to present here one example of the legends which grew up about the figure of Virgil during the Middle Ages:

"PUBLIUS VERGILIUS MARO sprang from humble parents, especially on his father's side, of whom a few averred that he was a potter, the majority, however, relating that he began by being the paid servant of a certain traveler, by name Magus, but that soon, as a result of his industry, he became the latter's son-in-law. When his father-in-law turned over to him the overseership of the planting and harvesting of his fields and the care of his flocks, he increased his holdings through the purchase of woodlands and the pursuit of bee-culture.

He (Virgil) was born on the Ides of October in the village of Andes not far from Mantua.

The pregnant mother, Maja, dreamed she had climbed on to a limb of a laurel, which, when it had touched the earth, she saw take root and grow to a full-blown tree full of flowers and fruit. The next morning, accompanied by her husband, she was wandering in the immediate neighborhood when she had to leave the path to give birth. It was said that as the child was being born he did not whimper and was of such a mild countenance that even then there was no doubt that his future would be favored. And other portents followed. A poplar shoot which was planted in the same village, following the local custom at the birth of a child, took root so quickly that it soon reached the growth of poplars which had been planted much earlier. Thereafter it became known as the tree of Virgil, and was dedicated as a shrine most sacred to pregnant mothers, who went there to make their pledges and returned to fulfill them.

Virgil passed his earliest childhood until his seventh year in Cremona. In his seventeenth year he donned the toga of manhood. By a coincidence the poet Lucretius died on that very day.

Virgil, however, went from Cremona to Milan and thence soon departed to Naples. There, after eagerly delving into Greek and Latin lore, he turned with utmost earnestness and application to the study of medicine and mathematics.

When he had surpassed all others there in knowledge and skill, he betook himself to Rome and, after having won the friendship of Augustus's Master of the Horse, soon healed various illnesses which befell these animals. After a few days Augustus permitted Virgil to be given bread in payment, as if he were one of the equerries.

Meanwhile a young Crotonian horse of extraordinary beauty had been sent as a gift to Caesar. This horse seemed to give promise of real soundness and unusual speed. When Virgil saw him he said to the Master of the Horse that the stallion had been born of a sick dam and would be neither strong nor fleet. And this proved to be true. When the Master of the Horse related this to Augustus, he ordered Virgil's pay to be doubled.

Later, when Augustus was presented with some Iberian dogs, Virgil predicted their courage and fleetness. Augustus, being apprized of this, again ordered Virgil's pay to be doubled.

Augustus was uncertain whether he was the son of Octavius or of another, and be believed Virgil could divine this for him, inasmuch as he had known the qualifications of the dogs and horses, as well as their pedigrees. He summoned Virgil into a remote quarter of his residence and asked him privily if he knew who he was, and whether or not he possessed qualities which would confer happiness upon mankind.

"I know," said Maro, "that you, Caesar Augustus, possess almost the same power to confer happiness as do the immortal gods, if such be your wish."

"I intend to make you very happy," replied Augustus, "if you can give me the true answer to my question."

"Oh," exclaimed Maro, "that I may be able to answer you truly!"

Whereupon Augustus: "Everyone believes me to be the son of another man."

Maro said, smiling: "It will be easy to tell you this if you order me to speak as I think, without fear of punishment."

Caesar vowed he would take nothing amiss, and furthermore that Virgil would not be permitted to leave until he had so spoken.

Thereupon said Maro, looking the Augustus straight in the eyes: "It is comparatively easy to discern the characteristics and lineage of the other creatures by means of mathematics and philosophy; in the case of man it is impossible. But in your case I have a close surmise of the truth, so that I am able to know who your father was."

Augustus waited attentively for what Virgil was about to say.

However, the latter: "In so far as I am able to judge," he said, "you are the son of a miller."

Caesar was astonished, and pondered how this could have come about.

Virgil interrupted him and said: "Listen, this is how I came to my conclusion. When I pronounced and foretold what could be known by none but the most experienced and learned men, you, Lord of the World, ordered time and time again that bread be given me as payment. That was the conduct of a miller and his sons."

This retort pleased Caesar. "At last," he said, "you will receive gifts not from a miller but from a generous monarch."

He held Virgil in high esteem.

Virgil was of stately carriage, dark coloring, rustic appearance and uncertain health, for he suffered constantly with pains in his head and throat; he spat blood frequently; he partook sparingly of food and wine.

It was said of him that he had a passionate leaning toward young boys. But kindly people thought he loved the youths as Socrates had loved Alcibiades, as Plato his young followers. But most of all he loved Cebes and Alexander. In the Bucolic Eclogues he calls the latter Alexis. Both youths were presented to him by Asinius Pollio, and he discharged neither of them until they were educated; Alexander as a grammarian, Cebes as a poet.

It was known that he loved Plotia Hieria. But Ascanius maintained that later he took care to tell the youths that while it was true he had been invited by Varius to live intimately with the woman, he had resisted most stubbornly.

As for the rest, it is certain that in his life, his way of thinking, his appearance, he was so upright that in Naples he was commonly called "Parthenias." And when he appeared publicly in Rome, where he came but seldom, he took care to flee into a neighboring house from those who followed after him.

When Augustus offered him the estates of an exile, he remained firm in refusing them. He possessed almost a hundred sesterces through the generosity of his friends, and had a house in Rome on the Esquiline near the Maecenas-Gardens. Yet, for the most part, he enjoyed the seclusion of the Campagna and of Sicily. Whatever he asked of Augustus was never refused him.

Of all his studies, as mentioned above, he continued to give his greatest devotion to medicine, and above all to mathematics."

This legend apparently derives from the Middle Ages, as may be inferred from the monastical character of the Latin text, and was found by the author in a seventeenth century translation of the Aeneid.

"The Death of Virgil" contains almost a hundred passages from the Virgilian writings; for the most part they have been incorporated as part of the narrative, many, however, are inserted as distinct quotations. A list of the most important of these follows, with indication of the page numbers in this book:

137   Easy the pathway that leads down to Hades, and the gateway of Pluto stands ever open . . .   *Aeneid* VI, 126/52

156   But the Ciconean women, whom he had offended out of love for her who was dead, had torn the man into pieces . . .
        Georgics IV, 520/27

169   Now are the waves of the sea set to foaming, churned by the oar-strokes . . .   *Aeneid* VIII, 689/90

192/97   Charmed is Aeneas, and letting his eyes rove in quick admiration . . .   *Aeneid* VIII, 310/69

238   Lying down on the dry sea sand, wearily we care for the body . . .   *Aeneid* III, 510/11

252   Nevermore shall I sing songs, and no longer am I your guardian . . .   *Eclogue* I

258   Now there arises a new line, one of a loftier order . . .
        Eclogue IV

262   Twofold the portals of sleep, and twofold 'tis said in their nature . . .   *Aeneid* VI, 893/901

273   Thou shalt not escape me today; whither thou callest, there shall I appear! . . .   *Eclogue* III

283   All that Apollo once sang and Eurotas heard enraptured, all of this was sung by that one . . .   *Eclogue* VI

296   Henceforth let it be the wolf who flees the sheep, let the rugged oaks bear golden apples . . .   *Eclogue* VIII

305   Actium's strand shall be honored by contests at Ilium . . .
        Aeneid III, 280

307   There on the shield was the bronze-armored fleet in the Attic encounter . . .   *Aeneid* VIII, 675/88

313   Others, I doubt not, will hammer the flexible bronze to soft features . . .   *Aeneid* VI, 847/53

336   The glory of the ages . . .   *Eclogue* IV

358   Oh, it was Lucifer rising, and washed by the waves of the ocean . . .   *Aeneid* VIII, 589/91

359   Even the moon's shining orb, even the sun's very fire . . .   *Aeneid* VI, 725/27

380   To thee, thou new star, as thou joinest slow months in their passing, where Erigone leads on the Scorpion . . .   *Georgics* I, 32/35

381   In heaven the thunderer, Zeus, is reigning, but on earth you are the visible god, oh Augustus . . .   *Quoted from Horace* **Carmina, Book** III, 5

394   Behold Caesar there and his issue, all of the Julian line that is destined to mount to the heavens . . .   *Aeneid* IV, 789/800

412   Look at the rising star, the star of Aeneas, the star that is Caesar's . . .   *Eclogue* IX

Confronted with the Latin verses, the translator looked for an English version of the Virgilian writings in dactylic hexameter from which to draw quotations. None that was available suited her purpose, and after consulting with several classical scholars she took the advice of Dr. Werner Jaeger, distinguished professor at Yale University, and made her own versification, relying heavily on Fairclough's prose translation. When incorporated in the narrative, the meter was sometimes ignored, but in most of the larger quotations the translator essayed a contrived hexameter, although fully aware how seldom this meter has found felicitous expression in English poetry, and of its inadequacy when compared to its classic original.